MW01099132

See My Soul ~ End My Search

A Romantic Thriller
By Staci Reyes

See My Soul ~ End My Search

Copyright 2012© Staci Reyes

Cover Photo Copyright 2012© Staci Reyes

All Rights Reserved. This book and chapters
contained within may not be used or reproduced in
any manner or form without written permission by the
author.

This story is entirely fiction. Any similarities to real
persons or events is not the intention of the author.

CreateSpace

Fiction / Romance / Thriller

First Edition (July 2012)

ISBN – 13: 978-1478125280

ISBN – 10: 1478125284

To my husband and children.

To my readers: Kim, Laurel, and Stormy.

You made me an author.

Table of Contents

A SHOT OF JOE

The floor in *Shot of Joe* is already sticky from the shoulder bumps of the morning rush. Newspapers tossed haphazardly by the last patron in a makeshift pile for others hang halfway off the tables. The shouting of drink orders between cashier and barista periodically echo in a spontaneous excitement.

"Mocha!" the cashier says.

"One shot?" the barista says.

The Cashier throws his arms into the air. "Two Shots!"

"Coffee!" everyone in the café says – including me.

We all respond on cue as one hum of radical existence. Then in that same one-mind sync, the callout of *coffee* dissipates into the drone of small talk and dismal dread of the workday. Forced together in close proximity as we wait desperately for our first fix of caffeine are bodies of various shapes and sizes. I stand among them hoping for a change in my normal routine. Waiting to play my role of being obnoxious with the rest at *Shot of Joe*, I yell coffee at the top of my lungs and it feels good. I don't want to exchange this normal for a new routine.

The original *Shot of Joe* started in my home state of Oregon when I was in High School but it was introduced to New Yorkers about four years ago. I am a New York City transplant from Oregon. I could say *Shot of Joe* is the exception of east to west trend setting, but most of the crowd remains pseudo New Yorkers from the west coast. Identified by the fashion of the west and our willingness to be senselessly nutty in the confines of high society, we shout, every morning to the scowls of purebred New Yorkers. It brings me a sense of western pride - a small homecoming to start my day.

I like the shout out of orders. I participate most of the time when I am having a good day. On mornings with a hangover, my girly time of month, or just being tired - it is painful. Today I'm good. In fact I am being open – to anything, come what may … I am ready.

I force my thoughts toward being open as I stand in line. Making every effort to convince myself I'm over the last relationship and open to a new one – three months should be easy to let go. Whom am I kidding? It is much easier to let the hum drum of my life engulf me, robotically moving in and out of routine. Consciously forgetting, or repairing by building walls, is hard. My boutique provides the perfect opportunity to disappear into the wave of human forward movement without direction. It is the easy way to forget the heartache.

The stomach cramps from my misery tighten.

I should be happy, I say to myself.

I own a boutique sandwiched between two large buildings only a couple blocks from *Shot of Joe* in Central Park South. The bottom floor of the 1900s brownstone is floor to ceiling windows where I display a four-poster bed of eras past. It's the only display item in the windows and adorns the latest fashion in high-class bedding. Linens, Lace, candles, and bath salts are my inventory in its entirety.

A rod iron staircase at the back wall leads to a loft scarcely decorated in classic elegance - reflective of my cheap budget. As sole proprietor, I would have to say *The Boutique* is not bad for a woman of twenty-five years.

I started my business when I was twenty-three with a large sum of money I inherited from the passing of my great aunt. Her death gave me the money to live my dream. The sacrifice was the loss of my confidant – we were close. Every dime went into *The Boutique* making me now solely dependent on my yearly profit. Thankfully, it is doing well.

I take a step forward with the line, returning to reality from my thoughts. It is uncomfortable. The three-month relationship planted multiple feelings of infatuation. Again, I thought I was within reach of love. I have to be open to the signs - I must have missed one. Before my unconscious replays the three months in detail, I push my thoughts back to my business and avoid turning into a tearful public mess.

I run through opening my boutique for the day. A high pitch laugh draws my attention over to a couple and I am reminded of my single status. My soul begs to start searching. I am not mentally ready to look for a new relationship but I should try to stay open – for my soul.

This is life, right? Trying on relationships until the right one comes along. I think to myself.

No matter how many times I tell myself this after being dumped, I still struggle to believe it. I have a knack for getting into and being thrown out of wonderful relationships.

My best friend Lana has been increasingly finding

humor in my bad luck with relationships. Last night over our too often Italian take-out and red wine dinner in my loft, she offers to buy me a life-size boyfriend cutout online.

"He'd never dump you," Lana says. She tries to hold back a smirk, and attempts to look concerned for me. I push her off the couch and she misses our half-filled bottle of wine.

"Maybe I should join an internet dating service," I say. "My screen name can be *imdumped*. The best one-nighters are in rebound dating."

We both laugh and pour ourselves another glass.

"Latte!" the cashier says.

"One shot?" the barista says.

"One Shot!"

The mob comes alive instantly shouting, "Coffee!" and then returns to the hum.

I get in on the tail end of the 'coffee' shout and my voice trails all the others - not the best way to be pulled out of your thoughts. I focus on a crack in the floor to hide the burn of my cheeks. Now second in line I feel safe if my thoughts wander again. Even if I miss the next call entirely, I don't need to think. I am a regular. Sixteen-ounce green tea, whole milk, latte with a shot of vanilla. The cashier is also a transplant from Oregon. We were both Oregon Ducks – the unspoken affinity of alumni.

I scan the coffee shop as I wait to place my order. It is the usual crowd for the most part. I half smile when my eyes make contact with some of them. We don't know each other, maybe a few by first name, but even those are soon forgotten.

Our morning routines are all intertwined - giving the familiarity towards each other.

The middle-aged man in a business suit probably from an interview ten years ago, is just leaving with two coffees in hand. Then comes in Sweet Sue, as I call her, never says hello to anyone, speaks softly to the cashier, but has a permanent smile pasted to her cocked head. The thoughts floating between her ears must be interesting. Then there's the player - he must be running late - I don't see him. A different day means a different girl. His rainbow wardrobe of suits also adds to the mystery of his attempt at high fashion. The girls on his arm cling to him under the weight of their make-up as they periodically shift a hip side to side in the shuffle of line advancement. Silently I hope he will come before I leave. My daily trip to *Shot of Joe* is not the same without a glimpse of him.

Out of the corner of my eye, there is a new face. My involuntary breath of air sticks in my throat from the silhouette walking through the door.

He is dressed in washed jeans and a rust thermal crew neck. In this humdrum of routine, he jolts it to a halt. The door closing behind him makes a loud thud in the momentary second of silence. His black leather jacket hangs straight and fitted around his torso. However, his physic, perfectly enunciated through his clothing beckons a strong desire to hold my attention before looking at his face. I want to remain in this moment but there is more of him, I have to force my eyes away from his chest. Fighting my own resistance to leave his pecks, my gaze travels up his neck. His face is olive in color and his green eyes become visible underneath his dark eyebrows, as he moves closer to the coffee line. Jet-black waves flow off his forehead, a few strands dangle next to his ears. I look up and down his body twice before I pull my attention away, realizing he is walking straight toward me. My observations take less than a few seconds but they are enough to make the hair on my arms stand up. My stomach gurgles with excitement.

I am last in line and feel him walk up and take the respected coffee line stance, leaving the socially acceptable distance between us. His cologne engulfs the air around me. Musk, with a hint of woods ... and something I can't describe but makes my head light and wistful. I tune out the noises in the coffee shop and concentrate on the presence behind me. My checks flush as I strain to listen to his breathing, knowing my own effort to be secretive. His breath is steady until he shifts his weight. His clothes rustle, drowning out the soft sound of his breathing, and pushes his smell over my shoulders. I am able to get another fresh whiff of him. I inhale deeply, then consciously let out the breath slow and toward the floor. He shifts again. I can't stand it anymore - I have to look at him. I slowly shift my weight and turn as though I might be looking for someone to come through the door.

I stare at the front door, as I quickly count to three in my head. Then I scan the room toward his direction. My lungs push out all the air contained within and leave no chance to inhale discretely when his face comes into view. He catches my gaze and smiles.

His teeth are so white against his olive skin.

I quickly turn back to face the front of the line, almost

losing my balance.

Okay, I am open to anything, but this one – not possible.

I hear my name and look up. The barista greets me and asks if I want my usual.

"Ah yeah," I say.

"You okay?" he says. "Should I make it a double?"

I blush, hoping the guy behind me didn't catch his question. "No, I'm just tired, the usual will do it."

"Latte!" he says.

I unconsciously jump. The barista raises one eyebrow. I give a short laugh at the same moment he shouts, "One shot?"

"One Shot!" the cashier bellows it out more forcefully, returning my smile.

"Coffee!" everyone says behind me.

I don't yell and I don't miss the silence behind me. He did not join in.

I pull out my wallet, pay, and walk to a table. Normally I would order, take my drink when called, and then walk out the door back to my boutique without a second glance. Today I am compelled to sit – it is a sign. I look around for something to read. Something to make it look like I planned to stay and drink my latte.

"Coffee!"

I miss his order call and look up to find him smiling back at the cashier as he moves to the side. I wonder what he drinks. He looks like a straight up coffee guy.

After only a minute or two of sitting, the barista calls my name. I walk up to the counter. The guy is standing off to the side waiting for his order so I take the chance to inhale and catch another breath of his cologne as I pass.

One foot in front of the other, Clarissa.

Sitting down again, I rack my brain for some way to stall, I have to wait for him to get his coffee and see if he will stay or leave. Not one of the piles of newspapers are within reach. Walking again would bring on embarrassment – I have no trust in my balance right now. I rummage through my purse.

Yes! My phone. Just text a bit, that's normal for coffee shop etiquette.

I scroll through and push a few buttons, erase the message, then hold it close to me as if I was waiting for a response. I keep an eye on the front door. When enough time has passed, I pull the phone into view and make a frustrated face, letting out an exasperated sigh. I scan the coffee shop, starting with the barista counter. He isn't there anymore. My heart rate kicks into overdrive.

He must have left when I looked down at my phone. I roll my eyes. *Reality, Clarissa. Keep a hold on it.*

I shove my phone into my purse almost pushing it to the floor between my legs. I lean forward to get up and hear a voice in the most seductive Spanish accent speaks from behind me.

"Is this seat taken?"

I look up. It's him, walking around to stand in front of me. He lays his hand on the empty seat.

I force the words to my lips too hard, making them escape with my gasp of surprise. "No!" I say.

He raises an eyebrow then forms his lips into a slight

smile.

"Did I startle you?" he says.

"Ah, no."

His smile opens, showing his beautiful white teeth and his eyes seem to light up. I know I am caught.

"Well maybe a little, you can have the chair," I say.

"Thank you," he says.

He pulls out the chair with his free hand and sits down. There is no way I will be able to speak. I tighten my grasp on my purse

He continues to smile at me as though he notices the effect it causes. I take a sip of my latte and he does the same. His mouth is only slightly hidden behind his cup. His cheeks give way to an increased smile as I take an extra long sip of my latte, causing my skin to flush with embarrassment from the burning of the inside of my mouth. I pull the cup away too quickly and feel hot coffee dribble down my chin. A quick laugh escapes his lips and I sheepishly wipe off the drip with the pad of my thumb.

We sit drinking our coffee, sometimes mimicking each other in the rising and falling of our cups. He seems to stay focused on me but I have to take breaks and scan the coffee shop to maintain some kind of composure. It seems forever before either of us says anything.

"Do you live in New York?" he asks.

"Yes," I manage to get out without a gasp. I quickly put my latte to my lips and take a sip. I want so much to keep the conversation going without scaring him off. "I own a small boutique two blocks from here."

A small polite smile spreads across his face and he

nods twice. Silence again. I take another sip.

"How 'bout you? I haven't seen you here before," I say.

"No," he says "I am here visiting my sister. I am from Spain. My name is Paulo."

He seems to force the words out slowly and deliberately as though he wants me to clearly understand him despite his strong accent.

"I'm Clarissa. Welcome to New York."

He nods again. He puts his cup on the table and leans a little forward. A strand of the hair around his face falls and he pushes it back with his hand, entangling it with the rest of the waves on his head. This doesn't help as more waves fall. He jerks his head and raises his chin, then looks straight into my eyes as he places his arm on the table.

"I will be in New York for some time … in fact I am looking to move here." He pauses, cocking his head to one side as if he is trying to remember something. "Relocate? You call it?"

I nod.

"I have a job offer I am considering," he continues. "Maybe you can show me some of New York to help me make my decision."

Shock riddles through my body electrifying every nerve - this is too easy. My defenses quickly snap into place but they cannot guard against the gleam in his eyes and slight tilt of his head as he waits for an answer. Nothing about his body language gives off an alarm. He is a polite stranger in a big city only asking for help from a boutique owner.

"Sure," I say.

A woman crosses the floor behind Paulo. With graceful command of step, she walks to our table and stops towering directly over him. She touches his shoulder; he turns casually without any hint of being surprised, and then introduces "Selina" to me in name only. He stands and gives her a kiss on each cheek and asks if she is ready to go. She utters a soft sound and raises her eyebrows.

"It was nice meeting you Clarissa, thank you for sharing your table," Paulo says, giving a slight bow.

Selina gives him an inquisitive look, but he does not acknowledge it. As they both turn to leave, Paulo puts his hand gently on her back and walks with her out the front door.

I sigh then I look up at the ceiling in my head and give a sarcastic thanks to God. The day will be normal after all.

"Coffee!" The café rumbles again as I watch Paulo and Selina walk across the street. I leave just after they are out of sight.

I return to my boutique. Scolding myself internally for hoping the impossible, I climb the stairs to close the sliding panels of my loft apartment, then return to the floor and light the candles to cover the home smell. Lavender and vanilla quickly began to fill the small storefront floor. Sighing loudly at my misfortune, I grab a clipboard from under the register and half-mindedly start to inventory. It is my go-to task when I need a diversion from my own thoughts.

After the passing of a few mundane hours, the antique gold bell that hangs over my front door announces the entrance of a customer. I turn, launching into my usual perky greeting without looking up from my clipboard.

"Hello, may I help you fi-"

My voice disappears causing the words to trail in silence as my eyes fall upon the customer standing only a few feet from me. The tendons in my jaw seem to give way in my surprise and I feel it drop open. Paulo smiles with a slight laugh.

"Hello," he says in his deep Spanish accent. He takes a couple steps toward me, leaving the comfortable distance for interested strangers.

"I am sorry about the way I left. My sister tends to be a bit impatient. Will you still be my tour guide?"

I can't seem to get the words into my mouth to speak. Paulo doesn't let the pause linger.

"I have to give an answer to the company by the end of the month. I have a lot to consider before then."

His accent melts any control I have over my facial expression. It takes every amount of strength I have mentally to nod in response; attempting to speak at this moment would be futile. Paulo's approach is fast, but not alarming. He is smooth. Every bone in my body warns me to be aware, but there is such a comfort about him that I can't - won't listen to the warnings.

"Where do you want to start?" I ask.

"Here?"

He rolls the word right off his tongue. I tilt my head. He could mean a number of things.

Pointing to the four-poster bed in the front window he asks "Do you sell beds? You only have one left."

I smile. A bit relieved. "No, I sell bedding."

He raises one eyebrow and pulls up a corner of his mouth. I blush. I open my mouth to explain but at the exact moment the bell from the storage room door rings.

"Saved by the bell," I say. "I'll be right back."

The awkwardness of the moment causes me to walk slow toward the back door, making periodic glances behind me to confirm Paulo is real.

Opening the door, expecting to see a delivery man, I am caught off guard with the brick wall of the other building staring back at me. Taking a small step out into the alley, scanning for any signs of who rang the bell, my eyes fall upon the most beautiful, intricate, wooden armoire standing against the back wall of my boutique.

The dark wood appears old world, worn with age, and dented on the edges from possible moves – maybe this one. Around the outer edges are roses carved into the wood including two dollar-coin sized ones for handles. Vines are carved throughout, following the pattern of the natural grain. The armoire stands about six feet tall and the wood appears to be maple. The whole thing towers over my own five foot five inch frame, giving it a sense of awe as I crane my neck to look at a single wooden rose at the top - centered between scalloped carvings of wood.

I am so taken with the beauty of the armoire that I do not hear Paulo step out into the alley.

"Are not those intended to be on the inside of dwellings? Not much privacy out here for dressing."

A smug expression begging to be smacked from his face taunts my restraint. I did not miss the forced humor in his tone. I stare at him, my brows crease toward my nose

"Need help?" he says.

"Yes. This is much too beautiful to be left in the alley." I emphasize the word beautiful to give him a hint of boundaries.

The veins bulge slightly in his neck as he lifts his end of the armoire. His cologne intoxicates me as I try to hide the excruciating pain in my fingers and arms by breathing only through my nose. The armoire feels full. My head, dizzy from the minimal oxygen I am allowing myself, warns of only seconds before I pass out.

We heave the massive armoire inside the storage room. I allow a deep breath through my lips when Paulo takes over and pushes the armoire against the wall. I wipe my forehead. Paulo still looks fresh, the only sign of exertion is a single bead of sweat on his left temple.

"There is a note," Paulo says pointing to one of the doors.

I had missed the worn looking beige paper taped to the right door. Paulo pulls it off and hands it to me. The short note is written in perfect script.

My gift for your beautiful boutique. Your storefront has been such a wonderful part of my many lives. This small gift is but nothing to what your boutique has given me. This armoire is returned to you for display only. Moments of time for your patrons to enjoy. Please NEVER sell the armoire or its contents. Please never remove its contents. The consequences would be grave.

The note is not signed. Paulo makes a low guttural snort under his breath. He whispers from behind, "I say we open the doors and get dressed!"

I half laugh at him and put the note in my pocket.

"Well now that you've seen the store, when should I pick you up," I say.

I am taking the lead, and a bold one at that. The note feels private - tempting. Paulo's teasing is ruining the mood, but he still holds my interest curiously strong.

He raises one eyebrow in response to my question then smirks. "What time do you close your boutique?"

"Six."

"Done," he says. "I'll be back before you lock the door."

He saunters out of the storage room. I follow him. Before he leaves, he turns around and seems to force a smile but catches it before it takes form. His eyebrows come together and I think he might say something. He relaxes his eyebrows, then slightly shaking his head he turns quickly on his heels and leaves. I keep him in sight pass the windows. The hairs on the back of my neck rise.

Consciously I block the thoughts of warning in my head. I will not listen to the caution that will squelch my joy.

A Chance – that's what I have to give it. I'm being open.

The day becomes busy and leaves no time to get back to the storage room to look more at the armoire. The note remains in my pocket.

One hour before closing, the lull of customers finally comes. I'm bagging the last customer's purchase and the street does not appear to be bringing anyone else through the door. My thoughts have a brief moment to catch up and reflect on my introduction to Paulo this morning as I attend the last customer.

It is in this brief moment of recollection that I realize I did not leave any time to change or even freshen up when I had agreed to Paulo's arrival.

Quickly, before anyone else can come into the boutique, I turn the sign to *closed* after opening the door for the remaining customer to leave.

Glancing at the clock I calculate exactly twenty minutes to get the smell and sweat of the day out of my hair and change clothes. I run upstairs to my loft. Keeping on the jeans I am already wearing, I choose a loose purple blouse with a black camisole underneath to dress it up a bit. My feet refuse to be pushed into my heels from the accumulated sweat my socks left, but I manage with only a minimal amount of pain to force them. Quickly and hastily I wash my face dampening the strands of hair on the sides. I don't have time to wash it so I spray my brush with perfume and combed it through. Once clear of all snarls, I loosely spin my hair around my fingers and clip it to the base of my neck, leaving the wet strands hanging against my face.

With only five minutes to spare before closing, I hide my rushed attempt to clean up by turning the sign back to *open*. I take a deep breath and begin circling the storeroom floor, blowing out the candles and straightening shelves. My breath brushes over the last flame, leaving a streak of smoke floating toward my lips, as the bell of the front door chimes.

Paulo is on time. I turn to look at him, a smile

spreading across my face of it's own free will. He flashes a quick smile back and walks toward me. His legs appear to move the floor beneath them with the strength his thigh muscles suggest with each stride. He grabs my shoulders easily and kisses each cheek. When he draws back he slightly laughs at my rigid stance and hanging jaw.

"It is a customary greeting in Spain," he says.

"Oh," I say forcing back my smile.

Paulo just laughs louder then offers me his elbow, turning toward the door. "Shall we dine?" he says.

I place my hand into his elbow, not taking my eyes away from his. "Sure."

As we pass the counter, I slip away and grab my purse from under the register. I turn the sign to *close* on our way out.

A HOT CUP OF MINT TEA

My identity as a transplant New Yorker from Oregon showed painstakingly through with my choice of restaurant. The body odor of the waiter added an unwanted flavor to our meal. Our sporadic gagging is still unknown in origin – a toss up between undercooked chicken and the waiter's aroma. My attempt at being savvy when I should have stuck to what I know, crashed with any hope to pull off a native New Yorker image.

Walking back to *The Boutique* I apologize for my extremely poor taste in restaurants. Between our laughter about the waiter I squeeze in one excuse after another until I finally admit out loud my inept ability to judge restaurants.

"I promise I'll look online at the reviews next time," I say. "Especially if I'm the tour guide."

Paulo throws his arm around my shoulders, bringing me close as his laugh fades into a low 'hm.'

"How about the tourist tries his hand at a restaurant," he says.

"Couldn't do much worse," I say.

We reach the storefront door and I turn to thank him for the dinner - he had paid and tipped. Despite a strong internal attempt at being open, I force myself not to expect him to come inside with me. He steps in close and asks if he can kiss me goodnight.

Using everything I mentally can for control I answer "Yes."

With the side of his index finger, Paulo lifts my chin. When my eyes meet his, he thanks me for an interesting evening, then he gently presses his lips against mine increasing the pressure until he slowly pulls away. I feel my breath pass over my lips as if his retreat steals from me the exhale and my soul within. I hesitate before opening my eyes. When I do, his chin is raised and he looks down at me, causing his eyes to narrow, as his lips pull into a tight smile.

He whispers through a corner of his mouth, "Thank you."

Composing myself discreetly, I turn just enough to put the key in the door, but not enough to have my back to him. I am intent on leaving an opening just in case he wants to kiss me again … not expecting one … being open.

Once I turn the key he reaches pass me and opens the door. I look up at him.

"Thank you," I say.

His lips curve up. "See you tomorrow," he says.

I mirror his satisfied expression and walk inside. I notice the sharp turn on his heels like a solider before he walks up the street and watch from the store window until he is out of view - he never looks back.

Excitement of a new romance contradicts my idea of sleep – ecstatic with the anticipation of future dates. I wallow in this euphoria, ignoring the necessity to begin the usual bedtime routine. The depressive fact of having to go to bed alone sets in as the memory of Paulo's departure forces through my haze of happiness. Frozen now at the door, looking wistfully up the street, there exists absolutely no desire to walk upstairs to my loft.

My thoughts drift through past relationships and how each of them had said good-bye. Paulo's departure is so confusing, contradicting entirely the intent to have another date. Consciously fed up with my own analyzing of the situation I define his exit as a miscommunication due to cultural differences. It satisfies me enough to free my mind and walk away from the door.

Placing a hand in my jean pocket, my finger touches the folded paper. I stand across from the storage room door and contemplate looking inside the armoire. I am not tired. I do not want to force the usual feeling of loneliness upon myself, which is imminent once I start my bedtime routine. Anticipation grows slowly in me. That same little bit of excitement that I feel every time I sign onto my email tickles my stomach.

I place my purse on the counter by the register then walk to the back of the storage room. My head is empty of thoughts as I make my way to the back wall. I do not feel in full control of my own actions, as though I am a small magnet drawn to the armoire. I do not think I can resist this building curiosity in it even if I try – there is no turning back now. I can feel it.

The armoire stands where Paulo and I had dragged it into the storage room. I admire the wood and intricate carvings. I pull the note from my pocket, open it, and read it again … taking in every word. The note is comforting, confusing, and ever more intriguing. It warns not to take any of the contents out – display only.

Contents? What's inside?

Shoving the note back into my jean pocket, I open the doors. The contents are nothing but dresses. Four dresses. Nothing seems extraordinary about them but I can't take my attention away or my hands off the wooden roses that are knobs. I stand, staring at them hanging inside. They all appear to be costumes of different eras of the past. One is green, the second a cream color, another is a soft blue, and finally a deep black dress of a material that I cannot recognize by sight alone. My hand juts forward for the black dress, too fast to be a conscious effort.

Every girl needs a little black dress. I think to myself.

I take it and hold it up above my head. It's not little by any means. It hangs floor length.

Adding touch and smell to my inspection, I feel my thoughts searching for an explanation as to the occasion for such a dress.

What became of the owner? She could possibly have been a woman, in her mothering years, who wore it to a funeral or some great ball.

The dress implies eras past, when structure and restraint was commonplace in society. I think of a loving mother who was also a wife and perished after giving birth.

This might be the dress worn by a dear sister. The dress then put away ... neglected in the armoire after the one use ... descended many generations ... never touched, until I found it.

The contents are sentimental to someone and belong inside. The armoire must have some connection to the clothing and to part them would almost be an act of throwing them away. To disconnect someone from their history, their memories, would surely lead to a grave consequence.

Focusing again on the dress, I look more intently at the design. The sleeves are short, extending just below the bodice line. A black silk ribbon is sewn and tied in a delicate bow at the middle of the back and trails down the dress to just an inch from the hem. I am confident gloves would have been required with such a dress and open the two drawers at the bottom of the armoire. A pair of black long silk gloves lay neatly in the drawer on the right.

As I reach for the gloves, the dress seems to draw my attention back. I run my hand over it, making it wrap around my wrist. Tracing the gathering of material near the bodice with my fingers, I brush the silk ribbon, holding it gently between my pointer and middle finger. They glide down the back of the dress until my arms stretch as far as they can - the end of the ribbon is barely within reach.

As one arm is holding the dress off the floor and my other is reaching in vain for the edge of the ribbon, an odd feeling of remorse simmers inside me. I hang the dress on the inside of the door and grab the material between my fists, letting the excess softly drape over my arm. Grief begins to seize any thought of command from my nerves to my limbs. I stand rigid with the dress draped over my forearms.

The hanger comes loose from the doorframe suddenly and without cause; I scoop it up with a gasp, catching it within inches of the stone floor. The desire to put on the dress shoots through my body riddling my muscles with commands to undress.

I try to ignore it; the emotion whirling inside me is

too strong to be trusted. Yet something about the dress calls to me, refusing to relinquish the intensity of my feelings.

Feelings of longing, passion, and desire flood over the last remnants of remorse that had frozen me. I put the dress back on the hanger, returning it to the inside of the armoire door. My various emotions command every movement as curiosity paves the way for me to relinquish control. I am no match for this foreign power of emotion and quickly unbutton my jeans. I do not think twice about undressing in the storage room. Not one sane thought is strong enough to take back the conscious use of my extremities. I pull the buttons of my blouse open, unconsciously thrusting my chest out with a sudden inhaling of air. In one fluid motion, I reach my arms up into the dress. The hanger falls to the ground with a crack and the dress seductively slides down my body.

A perfect fit.

I close my eyes and feel the softness of the fabric clinging to my skin. The dress sways a bit as if I am standing on a hillside in a gentle breeze. The smell of grass penetrates the air around me. The dusty smell of the storage room is gone and I inhale deeply to fill my lungs with this realistic sense of fresh air.

"Are you alright, Clarissa?"

I freeze and now consciously hold my breath. I listen for other sounds but only feel the presence of someone behind me. The warm breath on my neck as the voice waits for an answer pushes away the coolness of the breeze I was enjoying. I make myself slowly release the air and open my eyes. The surrounding change of scenery jolts me off balance and I feel someone grab me by my elbow, steadying me on my feet.

"Should I take you home," the voice says again.

I blink and manage to whisper, "I'm fine."

I turn my head slowly to my right and meet with a concerning gaze from a man about a foot taller than myself, his image slowly coming into focus. As the multiple outlines of his body combine into one, I notice his eyes are a deep blue against olive skin and his hair jet black. He does not remove his hand from my elbow but also does not make any other contact with me. He straightens his body and looks over my head. His face takes on a solemn composure. I follow his gaze, turning my head forward.

The fresh air and smell of grass is in fact those things. I am standing with other people all dressed in similar costume on a hillside in front of a grave. The casket is still above ground and the minister is saying prayers at the head. Looking down at my hands, I notice the black gloves I found in the bottom drawer of the armoire, are on. I am holding three long stem Cali lilies. I blink several times but the scenery remains the same. My heart starts racing.

Click your heals together, Clarissa.

I release a small laugh at this vivid imagery. I can feel the stone floor of my storage room against the bottom of my feet but when I look down I notice I am standing on grass, my feet inside a pair of slippers. The black soft satin of the slippers hugs my feet in delicate appearance but I cannot feel it on my skin. I wiggle my toes slowly and as if by this single effort, the material responds and I can now feel the roof of the slipper. I close my lips to a single note laugh that almost escapes.

The hand on my elbow squeezes a bit with the sudden restraint of my voice and I feel the warm breath against my neck again. The man behind me, however, says nothing.

Many emotions inside me rise. The tear ducts of my eyes begin to fill without any knowledge of the reason. The hairs on the back of my neck are tingling, but not from the man's breath or the slight breeze in the sky. There is a sense of familiarity, specifically with the man behind me, a desire to turn and bury my head into his chest. I hesitate and rapidly taking in any small detail I can without moving.

The voice of the minister is hollow, not yet clear like the whisper from the man behind me. The man behind me is making contact in a protective and caring way, but not enough to suggest an intimate relationship. Around the casket - three pairs and two children stand in one posture or another that suggests the body in the casket is possibly a relation.

To my left, one more person comes into focus out of the corner of my eye. I discretely turn and see a man that looks much like the one behind me but smaller in stature and maybe a few years younger. He meets my gaze and immediately closes his eyes as he bends his head toward the ground. I look out over the people across from me and take in the greater picture of where I am.

The minister's voice, now clear, recites prose and praise of leaving earth and returning to God. It is background noise in my confusion. I feel physically present, the grass soft beneath my feet and the satin smooth against my skin, but there still lingers a sense of my storage room.

The grassy hillside is scattered with plain white headstones. It reminds me of my trip to Arlington Cemetery

– sadness for the unknown death of another. The sun is shining but the breeze blowing up the hillside to where we stand has a nip to it. There are no trees to gage the season, but everything else gives me a sense that it is sometime in the early fall.

The minister concludes his prayers and the group of people across from me begin to move forward. I feel a push on my elbow and the deep whisper from the man behind me.

"Do you want me to assist you," he asks.

I shake my head and then slowly step to the casket. I swallow hard in an attempt to wet the back of my throat. I relinquish myself to instinctive movements and thoughts as I place my flowers upon the casket. Without thought to initiate such movement, my body works without conscious effort on my part.

As I pull my hand from the stem of the flowers, my fingertips are extra sensitive and visually they appear to move in slow motion, the control of my actions returning to me as the images of those around me come into focus. A feeling of deep sadness brings the tears to the edges of my eyes and down my cheeks. The man that was standing behind me is suddenly at my side, wrapping my arm into his, and leading me back to where we were standing.

"You will be well cared for, Clarissa," he whispers. "I will assure your standing in society, and we will have an adequate place for you to stay until the wedding."

Wedding? Mine?

I look up suddenly into the man's blue eyes and he quickly places his hand on top of mine.

"I am sorry, how ignorant of my manners to discuss

that topic here," he says. "If you want to reconsider our engagement I will surely understand with these new circumstances you face. Please -" He bends closer to my ear and lowers his voice. "Please consider, however, my love for you is strong, and I will do anything in my power to ensure you have a home that is suitable to you."

I adjust my expression and smile slightly to him in an attempt to mask the multitude of emotions inside me. The man straightens up and looks forward toward the oncoming patrons approaching me. I let a sigh of relieve compress my lungs silently as I stand next to this man, my arm still intertwined through his.

The small group of people who had stood across from me now line up, one after another, placing their flowers on the casket. Slowly they walk to the head in procession stopping briefly one at a time to give their regrets. Most of the sympathy are statements about my now changed status and circumstances.

A woman with light skin beneath a bonnet of red hair leads the line. The man next to her gently pushes her toward me from the small of her back. As she comes to a stop in front of me, she raises her chin high, adjusts her shoulders back, and takes in a deep breath. One tear falls down her cheek. Her eyes swollen with the evidence of her sadness, makes me wonder if my eyes are red as well. She places a hand on top of mine and lowers her chin. Her head falls slowly to the side.

"I will assist you, Clarissa," she says. Her voice cracks slightly. "I will not leave you alone now ... I promise ... we ... Antonio .. will provide the opportunity for your happiness." She looks to the man standing next to me; the same one she nodded to when she said 'Antonio.'

"You have my word, Katherine," says Antonio. "She is most fortunate to have an older sister such as you."

I glance at the man behind Katherine. He bows his head, disengaging his eye contact. Katherine steps to the side without a word and the man looks up to Antonio.

"Robert requests you stay at the house after we return," the man says. "Can you spare some time to discuss your affairs?" The man's eyes flash to me then back to Antonio.

"I can," Antonio says.

The man links Katherine's arm through his and takes a step away. I turn to Antonio. He is looking over my head toward the next person in line.

"He confirmed our meeting," the next man in line says. Antonio bends his head in a slow and controlled nod.

He looks to the short woman who has her arm laced within his. She does not try to hide the tears like Katherine. Instead, she appears to have allowed them to flow continuously down her cheeks onto her dress. The black material clings to her collarbone.

"Rosemary will attend to you," the man says to me. "I have our father's affairs to consider as you know … and the family's reputation -" his voice trails off but his attention remains focused on Antonio for a second then continues off to the side.

Antonio follows his gaze as it falls on the man standing a few paces down the hill. "My brother will be of no consequence to you, Robert," Antonio says.

"I do not doubt your intentions, Antonio. It is his ability to respect the boundaries you will direct upon him that has me troubled."

Antonio says nothing but the final glance between the men before Robert walks away with Rosemary causes a cold sensation beneath my skin. The man on the side of the hill stands in similar stature to Paulo whom I had just watched walk up the street minutes ago. I beg silently for him to turn around. My brow furrows in my analyzing. Antonio squeezes my hand gently.

"Let us take you home, Clarissa," he says. "Your brother and I have some things to discuss and then we will have information that may ease your mood."

As we walk toward a line of carriages, I gather more of a sense that I am physically part of this time. Far away, the storage room still seems to exist but I am lost in thought. If someone were to walk in the storage room and touch me, I believe everything around me would fade into a blurred image and disappear. Without an interruption, this memory continues to hold hostage my mind until an end … if an end exists.

Antonio helps me into the carriage and then Katherine enters. Jonathon climbs in after, followed by Antonio who sits next to me and again takes my hand, placing it through his arm. I bend my head to my lap but look up underneath my brow. I take a deep breath to ease my frustration of the silent carriage. Antonio places his other hand on top of mine. His lips curve slightly up as he readjusts my arm to fit tighter underneath his.

After what seems thirty minutes or more, the carriage

stops at a modest estate of the era our clothing suggests. The double wing, stone building has two floors. Five windows are symmetrically spaced across each wing on either side of what looks like the main entrance. A member of the house staff approaches the carriage and opening the door greets Jonathon as Master Bentley. He then steps aside for Antonio to exit, referring to him as Lord Bellesara.

A flicker of excitement stirs inside me but I keep it from causing any exterior expression. I am to marry a Lord?

Katherine exits the carriage first with the assistance of Jonathon. I reach out to the waiting hand of Antonio, and as I put my foot onto the flimsy carriage step, the house staff greets me as Miss Lanton. I smile. My name has a good ring to it - Clarissa Lanton. The man does not immediately disengage eye contact.

Antonio looks at me then to the house staff, his tall gangly frame still bended in a slight bow. "Thank you, Dillard. You must excuse Miss Lanton, as you know she is saddened from her loss."

Antonio laces my arm back into his and follows Dillard into the house. Dillard's long gate is infectious and I find myself paying close attention to my own. The simultaneous movement of his shoulders and feet up and down tempts me to copy him in a childish mimic.

Just before we reach the doorway, I see Rosemary exit a carriage parked behind ours. She catches up and pulls me delicately by the elbow into the parlor. Antonio nods to her as he follows Dillard and the rest of the men into a room directly across the entrance hall. Katherine enters the parlor and orders tea from one of the female house staff as she leads me to a mustard-yellow upholstered bench.

Once the house staff leaves, Katherine sits us both on the bench. She takes my hand into hers and speaks softly to me. I have to lean in to hear her.

"Clarissa, Antonio will work out a nice arrangement," she says. "You will not be left unattended or forced into living away from your dear Antonio."

I glance up quickly. "Leave? Can't I stay? It makes perfect sense."

Katherine's face bursts into a look of shock, but she quickly subdues her expression and pats my hand. "You are greatly distressed," she says. "I understand ... but you cannot be proposing that we allow you to move in with Antonio before the nuptials or remain in this home without supervision?"

I shake my head as I watch my fingers rub the fabric of my dress between them. The societal constraints are suddenly clear. The grave consequence of putting on this dress blatantly sits before me. Sibling relationships I covet in Lana ... the engagement I desperately seek in the present but both are given to me with a price of societal rules and restraint.

I look at Katherine, pushing sadness and longing to the brink of my eyes. I will be a part of this memory ... accept this sacrifice. Maybe I can learn something that will lead to the reward of marriage in the present. As though the acceptance of my internal commitment causes it, the lingering sense of the storage room disappears from my thoughts and I become fully trapped in this memory. My current circumstances now my reality. Small beads of sweat form on my hands at the thought of the condition of my body in front of the armoire and the time passing without me in my boutique. I cling desperately in my head to the only thing I believe will keep me sane in this overwhelming ambiguity – Antonio.

"I can't be apart from Antonio," I say. "He's my strength."

Rosemary puts her hand over her mouth. Her attention darts toward the large window opposite her. She has been sitting on one of the couches silently to this point. Her tears periodically wiped with a handkerchief before they soil her dress anymore.

Katherine scowls at Rosemary's reaction and pats my hand as she pulls in her lips. "That is why the gentlemen are discussing your situation," she says. "Pray tell I do not believe Antonio can live long without seeing you daily, but I do not believe he would risk your reputation for his own desires."

My lips spread upward automatically.

The tea arrives and Rosemary quickly offers me a cup in what appears a feeble attempt to gain her composure. I accept the tea with a slight nod, which causes more tears to fall from her eyes. She quickly begins to prepare another. I raise the china teacup, intricately decorated in painted pink roses, to my lips. It is hot and the sweetest flavor of mint warms my throat. It is far from the awakening of my normal morning latte. A sense of calm flows over my skin and raises the small hairs on my arms to their tips. I close my eyes and inhale through my nose.

Katherine breaks my serene moment gently with her

motherly tone.

"I believe the gentlemen are discussing Robert's intent to delay the sale of father's estate," she says. Her eyes meet mine over the rim of her teacup.

"Delay?" Rosemary asks. "Is not this estate to provide the dowry for Clarissa to marry Antonio?"

"Indeed," says Katherine.

She places her teacup upon the saucer in her hand. Combing a few loose strands of hair back with her fingers, she sits up straighter, one side of her lip curves up. "Robert, has been persuaded by my letters to inquire about all possibilities for Clarissa ... including one that might have her stay here in our father's estate," she says. "I know Antonio to be of a character that he does not align with Clarissa for the sake of her fortune alone."

Katherine pauses for a sip of her tea again peering over the rim at me. She lowers the cup to her lap.

"Robert, as you know Rosemary, is in no need to maintain our father's estate and would rather be rid of the burden, being that his home is in France," she says. "The government has provided you both well with living accommodations. If he parts from his post he has quite the finances to obtain a home to suit your desires."

"I am well aware of my husband's finances." Rosemary says through tight lips. "And his desire to be rid of this home ... no offense to you Clarissa." She shakes her head as if trying to rid herself of a thought. "It is a lovely home but much more than I can manage if it were to remain with Robert."

"Precisely!" says Katherine. Her teacup wobbles in

REYES

the saucer with her quick adjustment on the bench. "That is why I have written to Robert with the request that you be allowed to remain here. In return, I have offered to assist in the management of the family home while he begins the process of selling it. Having me within a two days ride and you here, Clarissa will not be apart from Antonio. He will have the luxury of calling on her daily."

"Robert has mentioned this as an option," Rosemary says. "But why does it require such secret discussion?"

Katherine places her teacup on a small wooden table next to her. "Antonio deserves the respect to be approached with the plan as an option. He is a Lord after all," she says. "Antonio must agree to enter into an alignment with Clarissa, absent a dowry."

Katherine lowers her voice, Rosemary leans forward and I tilt my head closer to Katherine.

"He already endures family disgrace from his brother's conduct," Katherine says. "To add an alignment without receiving a dowry must be Antonio's doing. He must propose such an idea to Robert and convince him to accept this arrangement." Katherine straightens up and a wide mischievous smile forms on her face.

"You are quite the strategist, my dear sister-in-law," Rosemary says then turns to me. Her wide dark brown eyes appear to shrink as she raises her thick eyebrows. I smile hesitantly back.

"But what of Jonathon?" Rosemary says. "You have not mentioned his position in all of this."

"Jonathon? Why he was the first to whom I approached my idea," Katherine says. "He has assisted me in the understandings of how best I write to my brother. We have already, and secretly, begun preparations for me to manage two homes until this one is released." Katherine softens her expression. "This is my offer for you, Rosemary. I will assist you in the managing of the house and will return for the holiday season."

"You are blessed, Clarissa, to have an older sister with such wit and influence over Robert ... and in the absence of your father none the less. I thank you, Katherine, for providing an alternative to managing such a home alone."

"You are both welcome," Katherine says. She throws her shoulders back and shuffles in her seat appearing to try and heighten her already long torso. "If I can give anything to you Clarissa, it would be time with the man you love," she says. "You are so fortunate, as the youngest and with a small dowry, to have found someone of such importance to align with in marriage. The marriage, if I have any control of the matter, will not be delayed." She sighs and looks over my head toward the window. Her chin raises with the delicate close of her eyes.

Robert enters the room. Katherine shifts quickly to recover the teetering cup in her hands from the sudden opening of the door. Following close behind is Jonathon and Antonio. Each of the men has a guarded look on their face, but I catch a quick upturn of a lip from Antonio before he corrects his expression. His long even stride ends with his leg barely touching mine before he flips his coattails up and turns to sit down next to me.

He extends a leg out to balance his weight on the edge of the seat. He takes my hand into his and whispers in my ear, "I think you will be satisfied with the arrangements we have made, I am most thankful for your brother's kindness to us."

Robert clears his throat and we all give our attention to him. He does not take a seat as Antonio and Jonathon did, and he begins by looking directly at me.

"As you know, I am unable to return here to England, as my duties in France cannot be neglected for long periods of time," he says. He shifts his weight and lifts his chin as he scans the small group. "I will be selling our parent's home to provide a considerable dowry for my younger sister. We have discussed this matter to length, and Antonio and Jonathon have provided great insight into our options." Robert shifts his weight again and puts both his hands behind him. "I have decided, if pleasing to my dear wife, to maintain this estate until the nuptials."

Katherine and Rosemary both give quick glances toward me. I am able to catch a glint of excitement in their eyes.

Robert continues. "I will leave for your care my wife, Clarissa, who can help you through the grieving of our father."

Rosemary smiles gently toward me then nods agreement toward her husband.

"Antonio has agreed to receive a delayed dowry that will be his after the selling of this estate when you settle with him at Kenwood."

I smile, the feeling of excitement tingles in my stomach.

"And I will not be more than a two days ride. You

may come and visit me, or if I may be so bold as to invite myself to spend the holidays with you," Katherine says to me.

Jonathon adds, "We would love to come back to this home for the holiday season." Turning then to Robert he says, "I can offer my services to you for any business that would need to be concluded if you cannot return from France."

"Thank you for your kindness," says Robert, "I will be sure to make time so that I may spend the Holidays here."

Rosemary smiles and her cheeks quickly flush a bright red. I feel compelled to thank the group but refrain from doing so. The societal rules are rigid and I opt to be cautious when I am in Antonio's presence.

The conversation dissipates after what seems like an hour or so of reminiscing about the man in the casket – my father. Antonio takes my hand and leads me to the far wall of the room. We sit down on a small couch and look out the window to a garden. He breathes deeply and when I look up he smiles wide.

"Robert is very generous to allow you to stay here with Rosemary," Antonio says. "We must be sure to maintain our behavior so that he does not regret his decision." His lip turns up on one side and I feel my cheeks warm. I turn my attention to the cracked paint along the edge of the windowsill.

"My brother …" Antonio takes in a deep breath. His shoulders rise in tension but he pulls them down. "And your sister Rosemary will make adequate chaperones should the weather permit a walk." He raises his eyebrows.

I look at him and play along. "I do so enjoy walking during this season. The trees are changing and the colors are so beautiful." My voice rises a bit high in my attempt to talk with societal grace. It is a failed attempt. I am not one to carry off the poise of a woman this era requires. Lana is much better suited for this type of situation. I sigh wishing she were here with me now.

Antonio squeezes my hand pulling me back from my other thoughts. "I shall make a concerted effort not to burden my brother with too many tasks of business so that he is readily available for chaperone duties."

I take this opportunity of being apart from the group.

"Tell me about the first time you noticed me," I say.

He smirks and shakes his head as a laugh escapes his lips. "You are not bored of this story? I believe I have told it to you more than five times in the last month."

I look at him with the softest expression I can manage. "You tell it so well and I like listening to your voice."

I dread the ending of this private moment with him. The feeling of desire that grows inside me every second longer I am in his presence is more real than anything I have felt in past relationships. There is something more here – old and more deeply rooted in me than I can reason with simple definition of circumstance.

Antonio's expression takes on a soft look of concern. "In that case I will not deny you, if only for the sake of providing ease during your grieving. How far back shall I go this time," he says.

"Start with the time you first noticed me."

He runs his hands through his hair. "I do not believe the night is long enough to start our story from there. I was a man of fourteen and you were my best friend's sister." Antonio laughs. "You were an honoree younger sister at that. You possessed such a fire within that I must say I admire how you have managed to tame it." He leans in and whispers in my ear "I hope it is not fully gone. I do miss it."

I laugh out of embarrassment. His opinion of me is so close to how he could describe me as the child I remember being in my current life. The rest of our small group stops mid-sentence and looks in our direction. We cease our laughing.

"It is not gone," I say. "I can still hold my own."

"I have no doubt in that," he says. "Unfortunately your back side suffered from your inability to hold your tongue."

"I could not have been that unruly as a child," I say.

Antonio laughs loud and the others' conversation silences. He turns toward them still laughing. "Robert, my dear friend, were we not witness to Clarissa's backside being subject to punishment for her frequent disregard of her behavior."

Katherine and Rosemary both gasp but I see a smile spread across Robert's face for the first time.

"It was a painful thing to see as it was a frequent occurrence," Robert says. "She had to learn and as we are all witness to her manners now, the punishment was successful."

Antonio nods his head as he rubs his hand on his thigh and turns back to face the window. "Now you can see why I began to court you from the moment you came out to society. I am yours, Clarissa. No other woman can be capable of holding my interest the way you do."

Antonio looks at me, his eyes searching mine for several seconds. I inhale deeply and his scent mixed within the air, causes me to want him more. This connection takes hold of both of us as his breath moistens my lips. The blue in his eyes seems to lighten the longer I stare into them. Eventually they become blurry and the rest of his body fades slowly away until I am staring at the wooden armoire in my storage room.

A shiver runs through me. I have no gloves on my hands or shoes on my feet. The cement floor is cold.

I take in a deep breath to clear the fuzziness in my head. The dusty smell of the storage room fills my lungs and I cough it back out. I run my fingers through the fabric of the black dress still hanging in a perfect fit on my body. Slowly I pull it off my shoulders and let it slip to the floor. It lays in a circle around my feet, as I stand frozen in the replaying of the recent images. I try hard to bring back the memory, pulling at the lingering shade of Antonio's blue eyes, but I stay.

A bit dazed and confused I search for my jeans and shirt. They lay in the exact place where I had dropped them. I step out of the black dress. Effortlessly I pull on my clothes, staring intently at the inside of the armoire. It is now empty – none of the other dresses are there.

For display only.

The note had warned me. I gather the dress and carefully lay it over the hanger inside the armoire. The air in the storage room feels stale – suffocating. I closed the door, pull the note from my jean pocket, and read it again.

One specific phrase holds me captive. The note dampens underneath a small amount of nervous sweat secreting from my fingertips.

"*… the consequences would be grave.*"

I begin to mentally dissect every moment with Antonio. Rapidly the memory flashes repeatedly in my thoughts, each time giving me a vision of something I had not noticed. I see the making of his fist on his knee when Robert was talking to our small group and wonder if I had caused this tension. I question his choice to return with the men and stay away from me all day. I crave to know why he did not try to steal a kiss or take me to another room, away from the others. I refuse to accept the societal rules of the era for my answer and groan aloud.

I shake my head as I slip into my shoes. Whatever the grave consequence will be, it cannot be anything more than the torment suffered in my failed relationships.

Six months is my record. If I can find someone to marry me within six months - maybe, that is what this memory tried to show me. I laugh, releasing my anxiety. I could look into arranged marriages – say 'I do' first, then fall in love.

I walk out to the storefront wondering how much time has passed. The clock on the wall behind the register shows eleven o'clock, but it's no help because I can't remember what time I put on the dress.

I run through in my head the evening with Paulo. I see the clock on the wall as it was then - about ten thirty. Only a half hour has passed but I still wonder how long I was actually with Antonio.

Craving the taste of mint tea to wash the dryness of my throat, I walk upstairs and put some water on the stove. I flop down on the couch where I stare up at the ceiling. The image of Antonio calms me. It feels as though he is next to me in his long blue coat, tight pants, and high riding boots. The memory is so vivid I can smell him now.

Water bubbles over to the burner, sizzling as it touches the grate. I get up and pour it into a cup. Staring down at the steam, I shake my head. Not one tea bag exists in my kitchen. I take the cup back to the couch with me. The warmth of the water penetrating the ceramic in my palms takes me back to the depressing reality of being alone and single.

I lean back, balancing the cup on my thigh and close my eyes. I wonder to myself what memory I may have if I put the dress on again … but nothing penetrates Antonio's image. A fixed picture in my mind now, he has found his way into my thoughts and the connection is something beyond plain interest. It is deeper.

TORTILLA ESPAÑOLA AT PATATAS BRAVAS

The morning sun wakes me to wet jeans. I roll my eyes remembering the cup of hot water. I pick it up from the floor and place it in the sink on the way to my bedroom. I undress and get into a hot shower.

Mechanically I pull on my clothes and check the clock before heading downstairs to the storefront. I have enough time to walk up the street for coffee before I open my boutique.

The air is muggy and the smell of rain floats off the pavement. My thoughts wander to Antonio and play the only memories I have of him. Yet each time it plays over, the connection feels stronger. It grows every time I see his eyes.

When I reach the coffee shop, the man with the rainbow wardrobe is walking out. Today his suit is a bright yellow and the new girl clings to his side as he holds the door open for me. I smile at him and he raises his paper cup in reply. The café ends a shout of 'coffee' as I walk up to place my order. Today there is no line. I ask for my usual and wait. Before I step to the side, I remember the tea and ask the cashier if they sell any. He graciously and with vivid animation tells me about their display of loose tea, bags, and of course their own special brand. The barista puts my cup on the thin shelf above her station and nods in my direction. I mouth a thank you to prevent interruption of the cashier who is still going on about the tea. The barista rolls her eyes and turns away from her station with several stainless steel pitchers in hand. I raise my cup to the cashier and say thank you at least twice before he stops the sales pitch. I walk toward the display.

There's an overwhelming amount of options for tea. I pick the mint medley with a hint of rosemary, seeing the image of Rosemary's tearful eyes over the rim of her teacup. As I reach for the tea, I hear a strong Spanish voice behind me.

"Changing an ingrained routine before finishing the first cup of coffee can have grave affects."

Startled I turn around and see Paulo smiling at me.

"The damage may have already been done," I say. "Meeting you yesterday was very much outside my normal routine."

Paulo raises an eyebrow and his lip turns up on one side. "Already I have damaged you and I barely know you. I am sorry. Maybe if I sit with you again today, my company can be considered routine and the damage can be reversed."

I smile. Paulo's accent and request to sit with me again this morning eases the loneliness of being apart from Antonio. I accept his offer and Paulo leaves to order his drink.

I choose a table by the window. The time it takes for Paulo to return allows my thoughts to snap back to reality and catch up to the moment. I replay the events of yesterday in my head remembering the woman that had interrupted us the morning before. Then the sense of time creeps into my thoughts and I realize I only have another fifteen minutes before opening the boutique.

When Paulo sits down with his drink, he starts to take off his coat but I reach across the table and excuse myself. He gently smiles and asks if he can walk back with me. I say yes.

"I never really got a chance to browse your boutique yesterday," he says. "If I decide to remain in New York, I will need some bedding." He emphasizes the last word.

On the walk back, my mind wanders again to Antonio, leaving me a poor companion for conversation. Paulo has to repeat many of his questions and a couple times, he asks if I am okay. I blame the absentmindedness on a lack of sleep, which is partially true. The couch kept me from passing beyond REM sleep into the necessary deep sleep.

I apologize to him several times for not being a part of the conversation, but only out of respect. I like his company as it keeps me from feeling single but I would rather be with Antonio.

Once in my boutique Paulo takes off his coat and places it on the counter near the register - I had rather hoped he would leave. Having him here will help me remain in the present for my customers, but I'm not sure it can keep my thoughts from Antonio entirely.

I put my coffee and purse on the shelf under the counter and hang his coat on a hook by the door. Again, the haze of my thoughts taunts me. I grab the lighter and start my normal morning routine setting off the scent of lavender and vanilla. Paulo walks towards me and reaches out. Placing his hand on mine, he makes my heart race involuntarily and the sweat pushes out of the pours in my skin. A feeling of guilt strangely rises inside me at his touch; I like Paulo being real, but I want Antonio.

"Your lack of sleep has made it difficult to hold a conversation with you," Paulo says. "I can always have a second chance at that." He takes the lighter from my fingers and holds it up. "But if I let you use this, neither of us may be able to escape a fire for that second chance."

He smiles with one corner of his mouth higher than the other. I force a smile back and inhale. It is filled with the smell of his cologne causing the image of Antonio to slip away. My heart picks up a rapid pace. Both of us walk quietly around the store and I point out all the candles.

After lighting the last candle, Paulo places the lighter on the counter then turns and leans against it. He does not take his coat and leave as I thought he might. I lean up against the counter next to him, warming to his presence and happy he did not go. The heat from his body and the racing of my heart from the closeness of our proximity, seems to heighten the smell of the lavender and vanilla candles. My boutique has not smelled this good to me before.

The day is overcast but warm and it gives the candles more opportunity to light the storefront. An image of snuggling with Paulo on my couch fills my thoughts. My eyelids grow heavy and I want to lay my head on his shoulder, allow his scent to hold me to what is real, his arms wrap around me, and his steady breathing lull me to sleep.

"What's next?" Paulo says.

I jump. He laughs and folds him arms at his chest as he looks down at me.

I raise an eyebrow. He straightens up, turns toward me with one hand on the counter and the other on my shoulder.

"You have been unable to carry on a conversation with me," he says. "You have said you are tired, but you still open your boutique. I am intrigued by you so I will make more attempts for your attention, but I do not know if your customers will do the same. What do you want me to do? I am your employee for the day."

I half laugh, training a new employee in my state is more work. If he only knew where my mind was, he would probably not make any more attempts for my attention, but he does have a point with the customers.

"I can't pay you," I say. "I have a strict rule about dating employees."

Paulo tilts his head, his brow creases. "Dating? Well that does promote a problem."

Crap! I just defined prematurely the status of the relationship. The good-bye apparent in his creased brow - I brace myself for his sprint out the door. He does glance toward it but he does not run.

"How about I offer my services as your apprentice," he says. "I know nothing about bedding so you can teach me." He raises his chin in thought. His face takes on a smug but professional tone, and his air of confidence in this negotiation feels a bit unnerving to me.

"We will agree our dinner last night was a business meeting and acceptance of my apprenticeship," he says. "At the end of the day, you may fire me for inappropriate behavior toward my employer as I will be asking you to dine with me tonight. It will be our first date."

I blush. *He's too good – in bargaining and romance.*
"I accept." I say.

Paulo leans down and kisses my forehead.

His kiss brings a sense of comfort. I play along. "I hope you mind your professional manners so I can have your assistance all day … a measly five minutes won't do me any good. That kiss can get you fired before the training begins."

He laughs and takes two steps back from me. He stands at attention and raises his hand to his forehead in a salute. "Yes ma'am! What shall be my first duty?"

My body becomes suddenly rigid as chills electrify it with alert. Consciously, I have to make my muscles relax. His salute has a terrifying sense of familiarity. I refuse to let it build tension between us and I walk it off while showing him the layout of the storefront. In the back of my mind, the terror lingers quietly as a warning. The confusion of my reaction grows as it seems to demand reason but I force myself to remain open to Paulo.

He helps me with the inventory and I remain in a state of good humor. I am amazed with his genuine efforts to understand the difference between one cotton sheet and another. For a guy he does well. I imagine myself in a tire store for comparison to his interest. I don't believe I would be as willing to understand the difference between one tire and another.

The day passes quickly with his help and the sense of reality grabs a more permanent hold on me. The memories of Antonio stay away with the common events of the day. I am even able to resist a temptation of opening the armoire when my duties take me to the back corner of the storage room. Not completely withdrawn from the intrigue of what might be inside, I do glance at it.

At the end of the day, Paulo helps close up the shop. He decides on the restaurant during one of our spurts of mundane conversation throughout the day, which included types of food I've tried or prefer. We leave out the front door and walk through the park hand-in-hand.

After crossing the street on the other side of the park, we walk to a restaurant called *Patatas Bravas*. The threat of rain in the dark clouds above leaves the patio-seating empty. Paulo steps in front of me then meanders with my hand in his through the patio seating to the front door. Inside, the dining room is bustling with the low hum of conversation. Paulo speaks to the hostess in Spanish and I find myself straining to single out his low soft request. The hostess gives a smile as she looks over him to me and we follow her to a table tucked in the corner next to the kitchen door.

I frown at the location of the table. We are almost a casualty of the rush when a waiter side steps quickly as he pushes open the swing door and finds us standing in his path. Paulo ignores the narrow escape and nods away the host.

"We're right in the middle of traffic aren't we," I say.

"It's all in your perspective," he says, and then leans forward. "The next time the kitchen door swings open take a look inside. Make sure you inhale deep before the door closes.

Intrigued I ignore my menu and keep my eyes on the swing door. Paulo watches me over his menu. Through the small glass window near the top of the door, I see a large tray filled with plates. I let out a breath in preparation to inhale deep. When the door opens, I squint to see inside and take a large breath in. The back of my throat burns pleasantly with the smell of sautéed chili peppers, onions, and something spicy. The commotion in the kitchen is reflective of celebration, far from my expectation of stressed chaos.

"Mm." I sigh and close my eyes until I hear the swinging door stop.

Paulo laughs and I open my eyes to a smug expression on his face. "As I said ... it's all in the perspective," he says.

I watch the trays as they are carried out of the kitchen and point to what looks like an omelet.

"That is Tortilla Espanola," Paulo says. "It has sautéed onions, bell peppers, the best chorizo you will ever taste, and potatoes. At this restaurant, before serving the Espanola, the waiter drizzles pure olive oil from Spain over the top."

My mouth waters. "What're you having?"

"Patatas Bravas!" He says and pounds a fist on the table.

I laugh. "What's that?"

"It is dangerous." He leans in on the table. "It is not for the weak."

I raise an eyebrow taunting him to divulge the ingredients.

"It is fried potatoes smothered in olive oil, and a paste of chilies, garlic, cumin, and paprika," he says. "It is very hot."

He raises an eyebrow and sits back folding his arms

against his chest.

I mimic his facial expression and silently hope they offer after dinner mints. Paulo informs the waiter of our choices and orders a beer for both of us.

Dinner conversation becomes a class by Paulo about the food served to us and other authentic Spanish delicacies. His accent pulls me in with each breath and I find myself hypnotized by his voice listening attentively to his stories. If I had any ability to cook, this would be a great conversation, but as I have no interest to learn, or desire to pick up any culinary hobbies, I just allow myself to melt in his voice.

After dinner, we walk back through the park and making small talk about our own superficial interests. Paulo holds me with his arm around my lower back. His close proximity mixed with the excitement of his company, causes the small beads of sweat to soil my blouse. I'm thankful I am wearing a coat.

We arrive at my boutique and Paulo does not give any hint of leaving. He stands behind me as I unlock the door then follows me inside without prompt. I take advantage of the moment.

"Coffee," I call back toward Paulo as I head for the stairs to my loft.

"One Shot!" he shouts back.

I stop on the third step and rest my weight on the lower leg. I smile. "Straight up coffee, I'm out of espresso." I push my lips down in a pout.

"Coffee!" Paulo shouts, throwing both hands in the air.

I laugh. "Wait here."

Paulo follows me toward the stairs.

I turn sharply and place a palm on his chest. I am struck with a strong urge to grab his shirt in my fist and wrench him toward me. Instead, I breathe in his smell slow and blink twice to focus.

"Please. My loft is a bit of a mess." My voice comes out in an unintentional whisper.

Paulo shrugs his shoulders and gives a pouted look then takes his earlier stance against the counter with his arms folded across his chest.

"You know," he calls up to me after a few moments of silence. "I used to work as an apprentice in a store like this. Did you know that cotton sheets can be very different from one another?"

I laugh. "Is that right?" I shout downstairs to him. "What happened to that apprenticeship?"

Without missing a beat he says, "I asked the owner out on a date and she said yes … but then she fired me."

"Oh what a shame. Sounds like she killed your hopes of a career in the cotton industry. I don't doubt you would've been successful."

Paulo meets me half way down the stairs and takes his cup of coffee from me. He does not move out of my way and even though I am a full step up the stairs from him, we are eye to eye. He looks down at his coffee with a forced pout.

"That date was definitely the demise of my career in the cotton industry," he says. "But it did not cause me any great sadness … my heart felt no pain." He sighs and looks up at me from beneath his brow. "My employer was a kind woman, and she eased what she believed to be my broken heart from losing the apprenticeship with a passionate kiss."

Paulo does not move his eyes from mine. He looks into them and I notice the intense shade of his green eyes that I first saw at *Shot of Joe*. His face is still playing some of the bantering with his raised eyebrows. My hands are clutching to my cup for fear of dropping it and a loss of words. Consumed by his eyes and the sound of his breathing, his exhale pushes his scent toward me, I am incapable of any independent thought.

He is good! I attempt to focus. *Even if this is planned and rehearsed, it's coming off so smooth!*

"Do not mistake the type of woman my employer was," he whispers caressing my cheek.

I blush at his warmth.

"She was not a forward or presumptuous woman, she was very classy and a bit reserved." His soft voice draws me closer. "I had stolen the kiss and she merely accepted my thievery, giving into her own desires."

Paulo leans in and presses his lips gently to mine at first, but when I do not resist or pull away, he increases the force. Pushing hard against my lips, he moves his hand to my back. Bringing me into him, we hold our cups to the side and I find myself following his prediction. I give in to my own desires and return the passion. His tongue in my mouth and his teeth against my lips sparks the passion between us.

Paulo pulls away sooner than I want him too. His smile and eyes appear to be glowing from the intense passion.

"So as you see," he says. "My heart never felt any

pain."

I smile back at him and let out a small sheepish laugh, feeling my cheeks burn with blush.

He takes my hand and leads me to the counter. We both place our coffee cups down. He lifts me by the waist onto the counter, making us somewhat eye level again. We stay here in this position and talk into the early morning hours of the night. There is no more kissing, but oddly, I do not mind it.

Paulo finishes an account of one of his trips to San Francisco, comparing it with unbelievable detail to New York then pulls me back onto the floor. He does not take his hands from my waist when he looks into my eyes.

"Seeing as you no longer have an apprentice to assist you in your boutique," he says. "I must leave you to ensure you receive a full nights rest."

I nod and put my arms around his neck. I don't want to be alone but I thank him for the dinner and conversation. He leans down and kisses my forehead, then each cheek, ending with a small gentle kiss on my lips. I walk him to the door and watch as he saunters up the street. He does not look back.

I sigh. I am alone again. I grab the coffee cups and walk upstairs. Briefly, I think about the armoire, it is still in the back of my mind, but thanks to my date with Paulo, I do not have too strong of a desire to open it. I change into sweats and a ratted t-shirt and walk into the bathroom. After washing my face, I collapse onto my bed alone, but tired, and hoping sleep will come quick tonight.

A DEAR JOHN LETTER AND A BOTTLE OF PORT

Dinners with Paulo become a frequent activity over the next several days along with his surprise visits at lunch. His secrecy about where he lives while or weighing his options, as he calls it, only slightly dampens our time together. We have silently agreed to avoid this topic of conversation. I know at the end of the month he may return to Spain permanently but I hope he will end this secrecy with some news of renting or buying a place.

I am closing the register just as Paulo sneaks in through the front door. He creeps around the display cases as I pretend not to notice. Positioning myself for his routine surprise, I stand at the counter with my back to the rest of the store. He comes up from behind me, wraps his arms around my waist, and buries his mouth into the base of my neck. Despite the many times it has happened, I can't resist his breath on my skin, and I release my legs from the weight of my body. He is strong and lets out a playful groan as he holds me up against the counter.

"Hello," he says into my neck.

"Mm," I sigh.

"Ready to go?"

"I will go anywhere with you," I say.

He picks my feet up off the floor, which is my signal

that I will be put down and have to carry my own weight. I turn quickly before he can step back and kiss him.

He pulls away laughing. "Later. I want to take you somewhere. Are you done closing up?"

"Yeah. I'll grab a sweater."

Paulo steps back and I walk upstairs to grab my purse and a sweater. Just before I head back, I change my mind and grab a coat. The nights have been getting colder and I don't know when Paulo will stop lending his for the walk home.

While in my bedroom, my cell phone goes off in my purse. I know the ring and ignore Lana's call intentionally. I have neglected her a bit since meeting Paulo because I know she will not approve of my sudden jump back into a relationship. Since my ex-boyfriend is a co-worker of hers, my avoidance probably gives the impression I'm mad, which is far from the case. The truth of my hesitancy in talking to her for any length of time is the armoire. My experience from it may come up in conversation. I don't want to tell her about Antonio because I'm not ready for her to minimize my feelings for him with reason. I know he is not real and I also know she will not take my cheap excuses much longer.

Paulo is at the door holding it open. My phone stops ringing by the time I reach him.

"An ex-boyfriend?" Paulo asks. He motions to my purse with a jerk of his head.

"No. Best friend," I say.

He tightens his lips into a closed mouth smile and bobs his head. "I'm more important than a best friend?" He says.

He closes the door and we start walking up the

sidewalk toward *Shot of Joe's*.

"I found a great place to dine." Paulo says. "Do you like a good American hamburger?"

"Yes."

Paulo runs across the street through a small opening of traffic dragging me behind him.

We walk along the park on the other side for about five blocks. It takes me a full block to catch my breath.

"Right there," he says.

I follow the imaginary line from Paulo's finger to a large sign that says *Simon's* in black letters against a white background. Four lamps hanging from the top edge illuminate the sign. When the light turns green, Paulo takes my hand and leads me through the crosswalk.

The restaurant staff greets Paulo with pats on the back and jovial salutations the moment we enter. I step to the side to let one of the waiters near him but he tightens his hold on my hand and pulls me into his hip. He puts his arm around my lower back and introduces me to the owner who has just come over to the small gathering of people around us.

"This is Clarissa," Paulo says. He extends his hand toward the owner and then he looks at me. "This is Simon," he says.

Simon throws his hands out to his sides leaning back, his mouth drops into an exaggerated gasp, and then he claps his hands together in front of him. "Oh Paulo you are forgiven! I thought you had forgotten me, but now I see you have been very busy." He takes my hand into his long fingers and brings it to his lips. "Ah she is sweet."

Simon releases my hand and I nonchalantly wipe it

against the back of my thigh - failing to be discrete. Paulo laughs and squeezes me around the waist having caught my rudeness. Simon frowns but quickly changes it into a forced laugh then waves it away with his hand. He turns on his toes and walks through the dining room with a swivel to his cadence. Paulo and I follow closely behind as the rest of the people who had gathered around us return to their work.

The dining area is loud with the voices bouncing off the wooden floor and walls. Heard, but muffled by the voices of the patrons and jazz music, the tables and chairs grind across the floor as people pull them in and out. The walls, painted in a forest green, darkens the room but allows the candles on each table to set a romantic tone in this energetic atmosphere.

Simon leads us to the far corner of the dining room. The table's position is at an angle that does not remove us from the energy of *Simon's,* but gives a sense of privacy from the majority of the patrons. Simon steals a kiss to the back of my hand, then skips away before either of us sits down. Paulo is laughing beneath his breath.

"You've been here before," I say.

"He's a business associate," Paulo says. The smile disappears from his face into the reserved warning of the taboo topic.

I pick up my menu and scan the choices. When the waiter comes to our table, I order a bacon cheeseburger medium well. Paulo orders the steak burger for him and a beer for each of us.

"I have been enjoying my tour of New York," Paulo says.

I smile, holding in the desperation to ask him when and if he is leaving. "Me too," I say.

"I have been enjoying the company of my tour guide," he says.

He stares at me. I shift uncomfortably in my seat and he reaches out, takes my hand into his and pulls it toward him with a firm grip. My chest against the table edge prevents me from moving any closer.

"I want to ask you something," he says.

I take in a large breath to hide my anticipation for his question.

"Do you believe in your soul?" he asks.

My mouth drops open and I quickly close it but I can't control my face from contorting with confusion. I didn't take him for being religious.

"Um. What do you mean?" I say.

He lets go of my hand and leans back into his chair. His lips curve down as he pulls them inward. "It is really simple, Clarissa. Do you believe you have a soul?"

"I guess," I say.

"You guess." He shakes his head. "So how was your day?" he says.

"Paulo, I don't mean to brush off your question. I'm just a little confused about the direction - "

"There is no direction, Clarissa. I am curious about your belief in your soul, but since you don't seem to have one there is no reason to push the issue."

"Issue? My opinion about my soul is an issue? Religion isn't just a topic you spring on someone out of the blue."

He smiles wide and puts up his hands with his palms facing me. "No need to be offended." He puts his hands flat on the table and leans forward. "I don't believe I was talking about religion. I asked about your soul."

I look away from him to avoid our conversation progressing to an argument. I am not sure if what I'm feeling is offense because to me it seems more like confusion. I had attended catholic school as a child so the topic of souls and religion is not foreign to me. My confusion seems to be manifesting in my realization that I do not have an opinion about my own soul … or my own belief in religion. I grew up with an understanding of souls in general, not in relation to my own.

I turn back to Paulo. He is watching me. His face is absent of any strong emotion. I look into his eyes and feel an invitation to reveal my thoughts.

"I know about souls in general but never explored an understanding of my own." I say.

Paulo takes my hand into his again. His grasp is more gentle and he rubs his thumb over my knuckle.

"You should," he says. "You need to remember."

"Remember what?"

"The identity of your soul … your other half," he says and as quickly as he brought the subject up, he lets go of my hand and adjust in his chair.

I know this sudden change in body language to mean the topic is closed. His reaction is the same every time I breach the secrecy of his decision about the job offer.

Our food arrives and we eat in silence through the first half of it. Paulo breaks it with a question as to the taste of my burger and we fall into the light conversation of miscellaneous topics.

We leave the restaurant in much the same fashion as we came, amidst several pleas to return and kisses on the back of my palm by Simon. Paulo's retreat from my boutique falls into routine also as he walks up the street without looking back. It has only been little more than a week of dating but the passion has heightened on many occasions to give him an opening for more. Every time I kiss him, I want to wrap my legs around him or pull off his shirt and press my palms against his chest. I want something more than this kissing and hand-holding.

The dinners with Paulo go on for several more days. Adding to the mix are picnics, sightseeing, walks in the park, and other mindless activities as reasons for us to be together.

During this time, I continue to neglect Lana, aside from phone conversations. I use excuses that suggest I am busy with the changing of inventory and then pitifully beg for her forgiveness. It is time to change out the fall look and bring in the winter whites but I am neglecting those duties as well. I'm still not ready to tell Lana about Paulo until he tells me the final decision about his job offer.

Despite the happiness I feel when I am with Paulo, it does not keep my thoughts entirely from the image of Antonio that lingers in my head. As Paulo's silhouette shrinks with the growing distance from my boutique window, the image of Antonio becomes stronger.

Having just left after an early morning surprise of coffee and pastries, I watch him, hoping he will turn around for one last look. I watch him until the crowd of people on the sidewalk engulfs him without even a glance in my direction. The latte begins to burn my palm, drawing me away from the window to the immense duty of exchanging out the inventory. I walk to the back corners of the storage room to pull the winter stock.

The armoire stands against the back wall unchanged except for a slight layer of dust. It has been several weeks since I opened the armoire. I have thought about it occasionally, when Paulo's company does not keep me away from the image of Antonio, but it has not been often. I turn away from the armoire to the winter merchandise on the shelves.

Reaching up with one hand, I over-extend and lose my balance. Unable to catch myself in time, I fall back, hitting my head on the door of the armoire - causing it to open. I stand up, rubbing my head, and reach out to close the door muttering obscenities over the large puddle of coffee at my feet.

Only one door is open but it is enough to notice that this side of armoire is empty. The pent up curiosity gets the better of me with a rush of desire to see Antonio that I cannot resist. I open the other door. A single dress is hanging, but it's not the black dress. This is a green dress – one of the original four, but it's hanging alone. The choice of the original dress selection no longer seems to be mine.

I look at the dress and move it toward the center of the pole. It reflects the same era of the black one but appears better suited for spring. I immediately think of the wedding to Antonio. I stare at it for a while, and then shut the door. Enjoying my current relationship, I am apprehensive to complicate it with an infatuation for a man only accessible in my head.

I walk out of the storage room and reach for my cell phone. I want to hear Paulo's voice, needing to stay connected to reality so the power of the armoire does not increase the force of temptation. I dial his number. His voicemail comes on, I listen, and then I hang up. I am stronger for the moment but instead of seeing Paulo's green eyes on his face when I think of him, the image of Antonio's deep blue comes into focus. I shake the thought away and begin pulling the sheets off the four-poster bed.

It is not enough, the thoughts and curiosity of Antonio grow to a nagging desire. Trying to keep my mind in the present, I mindlessly remake the bed – three times. Aside from the thread count of the sheets, I have not changed the look at all. It is still modern white. I don't have any sheets that can make the bed reflect Antonio's era.

I remember Tuscany Textiles, a supplier I had signed on with when I first opened. It is a small business based out of Italy and never really interested me until now. I pull the catalogue from under the counter and flip through the pages. In the center is a fold out of classic lace sheets and other linens. I circle several styles and leave it open to complete the order after closing.

The sheets from the bed lay in front of the door. I bend down and heave the pile over and onto the counter. Taking two corners of a sheet, I begin the mundane task of folding.

The desire to see Antonio again is getting stronger, becoming almost irresistible.

REYES

I don't know Antonio well. I think to myself.

I consciously replace the memories of Antonio with those I have made with Paulo. The intrigue of my connection with Antonio does not relent becoming almost physically painful now. I want to be with him again.

My gaze falls to watching the day go by outside as I fold sheets. My thoughts seem to cover my vision because I do not notice anyone passing by or the sound of the cars and city noises. It is not until I fold the last sheet that I take notice of outside. For a New York City street it is very quiet but my mind quickly dismisses it for an accident up the street that has traffic stopped. I begin the task of pulling off the fall merchandise from the shelves.

The quiet continues and sends a chill of danger through the storefront. It feels like earthquake weather. I remember the deafening of normal sounds and eerie calm that goes unnoticed before an earthquake. I turn around and walk to the door to get a good look outside.

There is no traffic – cars or people. I walk outside and look up and down the street. It is not deserted but no one is walking down the section of the street where my boutique stands. I look across to the park. Aside from the horse and carriage that usually takes tourists around Central Park, there seems to be no real movement of people.

Concentrating on the carriage - the only thing that seems ordinary - I notice the driver is ready to give the signal for the horses to trot off on his command. There is also someone sitting in it, but the sidewalls block my view. By squinting, I am able to make out that it looks more like a man.

I walk about two doors up the street but I cannot see the front of the driver. The man in the back is dressed in a tuxedo – motionless, no longer ordinary, nowhere on the street is there anyone else that appears to be with him.

Desperate to define this silence I scan the street. There are a few people gathered by the stone wall in front of the park. Somehow, I didn't notice them before. They don't seem to be dressed for a formal affair unlike the man in the carriage. Conceding to the explanation that it is my own apprehensions interfering with my vision, making something out of the ordinary, I turn back to my boutique

In turning, my eyes remain on the man in the carriage out of pure curiosity. He looks directly at me, and my heart stops. The last beat almost bursts through my lungs at the sight of him.

Antonio?

This clash of what is real and my memory of Antonio hits me hard. I turn quickly toward my boutique, half running back inside. I close the door hard enough for the bell to break from the door jam and barely miss my head on the way down. It falls into a perfect indentation previously made on the old wood floor.

Antonio. No possible way. I'm losing my mind.

I straighten up and concentrate on slowing my breath as I walk over to the counter, grab the sheets, and take them to the storage room. I throw them on the shelf almost undoing the several minutes it took to fold them.

The armoire is visible through the shelf. Blatantly within my eyesight it calls to me, dares me, to put on the green dress.

"No!" I shout to the armoire. "You're already messing with my head!"

The sound of the door to the storefront gently closing stops me from running toward the armoire in frustration. I don't know what I would have done to it – if I were strong enough physically to do anything. I walk out, quickly composing myself as I pass through the threshold of the storage room.

"I brought some lunch," Paulo says standing just inside the door holding up a white bag.

The smell fills the room. I recognize the aroma of melted Swiss cheese and caramelized onions. I am suddenly hungry.

"Louie's Subs?"

"And soda," Paulo says. He holds up a tray of two drinks.

I nod and take the bag from him leading the way upstairs. He knows my rules about food downstairs. I make all attempts to keep the storeroom floor with the smell of a boutique not a home. I try to avoid his eye contact because I'm not fully composed yet to hide my surprise. He knows me enough now that he probably already senses something is off, but he's polite enough not to mention it.

We sit at the table. He compliments my outfit, my hair, and looks off toward the storeroom floor. He seems a bit off with his complimentary small talk as we eat and it makes me suspicious. His unannounced visit is not out of the ordinary, but we are far beyond complimentary small talk. Our attraction is reciprocal and includes an intensity of passion that can push it to the next level, but he won't take the next step. He seems to ignore my hints.

As he slowly eats his sandwich, watching me cautiously, my own instincts bring clarity to his body language. I almost choke on my food. It has been just over three weeks of dating with no sex, great conversations, and we spend all of our free time together. Every thought in my head leads me to where he is going with all this. It is now a few days shy of a month, he has kept a safe distance from me in regards to intimacy

Don't let it show, Clarissa.

My jaw tightens. Avoiding the end, I force an interested look on my face. "Tell me about your day," I say.

"It is going absolutely wonderful right now," he says a seductive smile appears on his face. It does not faze me. I am preparing for the *it's been nice knowing you speech.* Maybe he will tell me he wants to be friends, blame the job offer, or return for a family catastrophe in Spain.

One thing is for sure, I know he is leaving me. I rack my brain to find a way to lead the conversation toward the real reason he showed up with lunch. I want to get it over with and go on with life. I am ready to call Lana, close the shop, and drown my sorrows in cheap wine and Italian take-out.

I don't notice that I am looking down until Paulo reaches under my chin and lifts my face to look at him. His face shows curiosity with a hint of smugness. He must know I have caught on to what is coming. I refuse to lighten my own expression.

"How is your day, Clarissa?" he says. He raises one brow and takes a large bite of his sandwich – his lips part as he chews.

"I have a gut feeling it is going to become a really bad day in a few minutes." I say looking him in the eyes. He swallows hard and makes a guttural sound.

"You are most perceptive, Clarissa. If your day gets worse due to the lack of my company, I must confess it will not be good once I leave."

I knew it! I think to myself. "Where are you going?" I say. I pick at a crumb on the table then flick it back onto my sandwich wrapper.

Paulo again lifts my chin to look at him. "I have to return to Spain. I must attend to some last minute business that cannot be done from here." He hesitates and appears to study my reaction. His accent lingers in my ears. He takes his hand from my chin and leans back in the chair crossing his arms against his chest. "I have taken the job offer."

My jaw drops and he laughs making my anger bubble more.

"Did you think I was leaving you?" he says.

I feel the tears of all my emotions well up into my eyes. He gets up from his chair and abruptly pulls me up into a tight embrace. I lean my head on his chest feeling the rumble from his laughing.

"You really have been mistreated by men," he says.

Mistreated?

I wouldn't necessarily explain my failed relationships on the bad behavior of men, but instead on my inability to control how quickly I get attached. How easily I fall into love.

Paulo grabs me gently by my upper arms as he

extends his, pushing me away from him. He looks intently into my tearful eyes. "I very much adore you Clarissa. I will be back, and would like to continue seeing you."

"I would like that too," I say.

I push against his extended arms and lean my face back into his chest. After a few seconds, I straighten up and look at him. He smiles affectionately down at me. His eyes show nothing of secrecy or inhibition in what he is saying to me, they are a clear crystal green.

"When are you leaving?" I ask.

Paulo releases his embrace around me and sits back down in his chair - leaving me standing. He extends his arms, palms up.

"Tonight … on the red eye," he says.

I sit down with the immediate buckling of my knees. "When did you plan on leaving?"

He frowns and tilts his head in confusion.

"When did you buy your ticket?" I say.

"Last week, but I did not believe at the time I would have to use it."

"What does that mean?" I say.

"Don't worry about it, Clarissa. Just know that I will be back and I want to see you when I do."

"When are you coming back?"

He takes a deep breath in. "I don't know how long it will take to finish up my business in Spain," he says.

"What did you tell your job?"

"They are being very flexible with the offer. I possess a special talent they have been unable to find in anyone else and therefore I have the upper hand in the deal."

"Oh," I say.

The red flags I have been ignoring heighten with his words. Every nerve in my body sends the electrical surge to my brain telling me to break off this relationship entirely. I can't do it. He has had no reason to lie to me; maybe he really means what he says.

"Can I drive you to the airport?" I ask.

"No, no. I would not ask that of you. It will be late and I do not want to fly out knowing you are driving back through the city alone. I will take a cab. Stay home where it is safe. I will think of you drinking wine with your friend. What is her name? Leena?"

"Lana," I say.

Paulo is already up and walking toward the stairs before Lana's name has left my mouth. He pulls me up from the chair when he passes and gives me a kiss on the forehead.

"I will be back before you miss me," he says.

"Then don't go because I already miss you." I say.

He laughs and walks down the stairs. I watch from the top step. He saunters out the front door of my boutique and does not look back.

Paulo's lunch, half eaten, was only an excuse to open the topic of his leaving for Spain. He never intended to have lunch with me. The small talk was just to test the waters of my mood and how to approach it without making himself look bad. The tears well up in my eyes. I have been so blind these past three weeks by my own desperate need for a boyfriend. It is a good chance I may never see Paulo again.

"Good-bye, Paulo." I whisper.

I must keep hope. He is real and said he wants to see

me again.

The arrival of the holiday season gives me the perfect excuse to shove the loss of Paulo deep into the back of my thoughts. I dive into the daily routines of my boutique and allow the holiday cheer and frustration to engulf me. I welcome the happiness and bitterness of others. At times, it is quite entertaining. As long as it keeps my thoughts from Paulo or Antonio I can remain strong.

I return to spending my free time with Lana, keeping both Paulo and Antonio a secret. The constant battle in my head now that neither of them are around is hard enough to maintain without talking about it aloud. I know Lana will either not believe that Paulo exists or severely reprimand me for ignoring my gut instincts about his departure. She will most certainly laugh me into the psych ward if I tell her about Antonio.

She stops by for our usual Italian take-out and wine having forgiven me from the neglect of our friendship the past month. She tells me about the planning for her office Christmas parties. To be politically correct, and for an excuse to drink and be merry - her office decided to have a Christmas, Kwanza, and Hanukkah party.

"That way," Lana says during one of our evenings discussing life, over bottles of wine. "We can make everyone happy and have more reasons to get off work early on a Friday."

Lana, of course, invites me to all three parties. She even offers to set me up with a co-worker who is new and cute, as she describes him. I quickly remind her of the first guy she set me up with from her office; this is not something new. I try to use that as an excuse to get out of the parties but she does not let it go since that break up was about five months ago. I dread attending any holiday party without a date.

"Well it took three bottles of wine and a good month before I was open to any other dating again so that should at least give me three years to use it as an excuse."

"Not a chance," she says. "You can get out of one party, but you are going to the other two with me, date or no date."

I frown at her and stifle my protest with another drink of wine. My look doesn't faze her and she proceeds to tell me all about the parties, as she is head of the planning committee.

The night ends earlier than usual because she has an important conference call the next morning but we make plans for tomorrow night. I am to meet her at her office so we can go pick out a few new holiday dresses. Lana is not one for formal black and white balls so she made sure her holiday parties were formal enough for the *stiffs* at work, but not too formal to allow her to wear a dress with color.

"Preferably bright," she says over the phone the next day when she confirms our shopping plans. I have a good feeling that she will try to force me into a bright dress as well for her parties.

A full two weeks have passed since Paulo left. I have not heard from him even in response to the messages I've left on his cell phone. I do not know much about how cell phones work internationally, but I've little hope that his phone is the reason for him not calling me back.

I close up the shop at seven o'clock, the normal hour extra for the holiday season, and hail a cab outside my boutique. Lana's office is in the business district across town so I have a twenty-minute cab ride, with holiday traffic, to prepare myself. I need to stand strong and fight against the loud and obnoxious dress she is bound to pick.

Christmas lights are shining on all the buildings, even though Thanksgiving is next week. The melding together of Thanksgiving and Christmas to make the Holiday season begin early and last through the end of January is very helpful to a boutique owner like me. However, I do miss the clear distinction it had when I was a child. It was always exciting to go shopping the day after Thanksgiving and see the lights or mall decorations. Now they're all up long before November and so the day after is just another shopping day. That is aside from the massive crowds jacked up on coffee and lack of sleep. The cab arrives at Lana's office and she's waiting outside for me.

"Crappy day," she says.

She wraps me into a quick hug then turns me around by the shoulders and starts walking quickly up the street. "Let's eat first," she says. "I need a glass of wine, and then I can concentrate on having fun looking for a dress."

"That will only give us an hour to shop," I say. I am breathless half walking, half running, to keep up with her.

These are the times when her five foot eight inch frame have greater advantage and leave me in the dust. Usually her beautiful, natural wavy, blond hair that falls effortlessly down to her middle back carves at my jealousy.

Today it is for the mere fact that she can cover twice my distance in one stride.

To me she seems to have it all. A high corporate job that offers generous traveling abroad, a cool boss that allows her to make her own hours - workaholic or not - and above all, she has no problem getting dates. Ironically, unlike me, she has absolutely no desire to settle down. She likes the short relationships – the shorter the better. Yet regardless of all this, she is sharp. I don't really know what her job entails and probably would not understand it even if she explained it slowly, but I do know with it she has power, finesse, and luxury. She always tries to hide the luxury part from me, coming to hang out at my place instead of her high-class apartment but I'm savvy enough to catch this.

"I'll eat quickly," Lana says. "Worse case we'll get to go shopping again."

I groan.

"Oh come on. You know you like shopping."

Lana slows to my pace. I give her a sarcastic look.

"Shopping for clothes I would wear, yes." I say. "Loud dresses to make me the center of attention for all the wrong reasons? Big fat No!"

Lana laughs. The rest of our walk to *Antipasti*, is dominated with specific reasons as to why her day was so bad. I try to look interested but all her high corporate lingo loses me. I make sure to nod and gawk in the right places, playing off her own expressions.

She does eat fast and we have a good two hours left for shopping because of the extended hours during the holiday season.

As I had predicted, Lana pulls out one bright dress after another and demands that I try them on. I am not successful in keeping her away from the bright colors, but somewhat triumphant in staying away from the dresses that seems to accent my lack of a model figure.

Lana drags me into a quaint dress shop that sells only designer brands. She is determined to get a one of a kind dress. I'm absently browsing the clearance rack and shake my head at the tags. Not one dress is under a thousand dollars, which to me is not much of a clearance.

They are the left over summer gowns and evening dresses. I push aside an electric blue chiffon bridesmaid dress when my attention falls upon the next, taking with it my breath.

Hanging on the rack is a soft green dress reflecting the era of Antonio's world with a modern twist. The color looks identical to the last dress I had seen in the armoire but refused to put on. Again, I remember the upcoming wedding.

"Oh! You should try it on," Lana says from behind me. Her sudden remark startles me into breathing again.

"No!" I say.

I push the dress to the side and turn to walk out the store. Lana pulls it off the rack and holds it up. She manages to grab my shoulder with her other hand causing her shopping bag to hit me in the back. I turn back and my gaze locks on the dress. The way Lana holds it, high enough that it does not touch the floor, makes it look identical to the dress I had seen in the armoire.

"I admit it's overly classic but the Victorian era is coming back," Lana says. "You gotta admit it's not loud."

I cannot take my eyes from the dress. My face feels numb and my legs seem locked.

"You want to try it on," Lana says. Her voice sounds distant. "I can see it all over your face. That's how you look when you find new sheets and must have them. Come on. I won't take no for an answer."

Lana pulls me to the back of the store and shoves me into the dressing closet. She shuts the door then throws over the dress, hanging it on the inside.

"I want to see it on," she demands.

I stare at the mirror; the dress hangs behind me. It matches perfectly to my memory.

Thoughts of Antonio flash too quickly for me to comprehend. My anxiety begins to make my heart rate speed up, escaping though the sweat glands in the pores of my hands.

What if I fall back into a memory once the dress is on? I think amidst the rushing thoughts of Antonio. *What am I going to say to Lana?* I close my eyes. *Get a grip. I'm not in front of the armoire and this dress is in a store.*

I slowly undress, forcing myself to pull off my shirt and step out of my jeans. Turning with only my bra and underwear on I take the dress from the hanger, the material feels so comfortable. The color is so soft but it can easily blend into the flow of dresses at a holiday party, due to the shimmer the material gives off. Even under the florescent lighting of the dressing room, it sparkles. The color, closer to a soft emerald than a spring or summer green, appears to lighten and darken depending on the angle of the light reflecting off it. I pull the dress over my head and let it drop to my feet. With eyes closed I prepare for everything around me to change, I listen but hear nothing. I am afraid to open my eyes but take in a deep breath to smell anything new.

"Come on, Clarissa. The store is closing in about ten minutes."

She's still waiting. Relief flushes through me and I open my eyes. My head is clear and the images of Antonio have slowed to only the ones I consciously command. I am still standing in front of the mirror. Focusing on me, I see the shape of the dress gently cling to my body. The fit feels perfect, as if made for someone with my shape but more specifically for me alone. I gasp at my own beauty in the mirror. I've never found a dress to flatter my figure like this. The excitement to show it off makes my fingers tingle.

"Hello, Clarissa. Are you coming out or do I have to come in." Lana says.

"In," I whisper.

The door opens and her mouth drops as she looks at my image in the mirror.

"Oh my god! Clarissa, you've got to get that dress! You're like a Greek Goddess! It's almost as if your body was made for that era. Come out here. You gotta see yourself in the three-way mirror."

Lana pulls me out. I nearly trip and grab the door of the dressing closet to catch myself. In regards to fashion, I agree with Lana for the first time on something she picked out for me. I do look good and the dress feels so comfortable and elegant. The three-way mirror shows the back of the dress as it dips to just below my shoulder blades. The material that gathers at the lower waist creates its own design as it elegantly falls to my heels. The front hangs in a low scoop and clear beading accents the gathering of the material under the bodice. I direct the light to different creases of the dress as it drapes to my toes.

My hand slides to the tag hanging within the folds underneath the beading. I look at the numbers. "I can't afford it, Lana."

"You don't have to. I'm buying it." She says, but before I can protest she adds, "You will pay me back by wearing it to all three parties."

I quickly turn to look at her, ready to take off the dress and leave. She is standing behind me with her hands on her hips.

"You know you'll never find another dress like this. This is your dress Clarissa. It was made for you ... as if it is your one dress ..." she smiles slightly, her eyes glaze over, "As if it were made to be your wedding dress. I've never found a dress like this for me." Lana blinks away her glaze with a shake of her head and a laugh. "But then again, I have no intention of getting married ... unlike you."

As much as I feel guilty for letting her buy a thousand dollar dress for me, I am eager to compare it to the one in the armoire.

"Okay." I say. "Three parties and I pay you five hundred dollars."

"Deal," Lana says, smiling triumphantly. Now get out of the dress and I will go pay while you get your clothes back on."

We end up back at my loft apartment and complete at least two bottles of wine before Lana calls a cab to leave.

"I'll be calling in sick tomorrow," Lana says walking out the door. "Maybe you can bring me some chicken soup on your lunch break."

I smile and wave to her from the door of the boutique. "Sure. Or … when you feel better tomorrow night you can come over for girl's night Friday."

She gives thumbs up from the window of the cab as it pulls away.

It's past midnight but that doesn't stop the curiosity of comparing the two green dresses from rising excruciatingly inside me. I run up the stairs, grab the shopping bag and a spare hanger then head into the storage room. I pull out the dress Lana bought me and slide the hanger through. Taking a deep breath, I hold the dress in one hand and pull open a door of the armoire with my other hand.

The armoire is empty. I pull open the left door. Nothing! Anger quickly fills me and I slam both doors shut. I let the dress drop to the floor. This is becoming increasingly frustrating. First four dresses, then one, and now nothing. I didn't even wear the green dress.

I take both knobs in my hands, look intently at the armoire as if to will the dress to be there and pull it open. Empty.

I groan, pick up the dress form the floor, and throw it into the armoire slamming it shut. I lock the storage room on my way out in an emphasized attempt to clear my mind and go to bed.

It takes about two more hours to calm myself down, and then an additional hour because my thoughts keep taking me back to analyzing Paulo's absence. He still has not called and I'm unable to stop myself from milling over the reasons why so I don't fall asleep until about four o'clock.

The sound of my alarm comes too quick in the morning.

At *Shot of Joe* I take the cashier's suggestion for a double shot. After being up until four in the morning and feeling hopelessly betrayed by love, I need anything I can just to make it through the day.

"Latte!" the cashier says.

"One Shot?" the barista says.

"Two Shots Today!" The cashier leans over the register to me. I can smell the stale coffee on his breath. "Do we have a new usual?" he says.

"No. I just need an extra jump start today."

"We'll see," he says and hands me my change.

The wind is starting to pick up during my walk back and the air feels cold enough to snow. There are a few clouds in the sky but nothing to threaten a large snowfall, maybe just some flurries. I open my boutique as usual and brace myself for the hustle and bustle of a Friday shopping day during the holiday season. I shake my head as the cold in the air guarantees an increase in customers now that it feels more like the holidays.

I should have ordered three shots.

The wind picks up more throughout the day and keeps some customers off the streets. Despite the slower pace and my constant struggle to stay awake, the day still passes quickly but it would be better with an apprentice. My thoughts stray to the day Paulo helped me only making my refusal to count the time since his departure harder.

The early afternoon brings the mail and I quickly notice the light paper of airmail tucked between catalogues and slip it out to glance at the return address. It's from Paulo and a stamp shows it left Spain three days earlier. My hands tremble. I wonder why he sent a letter instead of calling. I have three customers in the store so I place the letter on the shelf under the register and try to keep my thoughts busy. The nagging desire to open it tempts me every time I walk to the register. He would have called if he were coming back, I think to myself. The steady pace of the day dissipates with the arrival of his letter; minutes seem to pass with my occasional glances at the clock.

I am able to chase the last customer out at six o'clock. She was only browsing, I tell myself, justifying my haphazard way of answering her questions. I turn the sign to *closed* after shutting the door behind her.

I have two hours until Lana stops by if she takes me up on my offer to come over tonight – she always does. This is plenty of time to read and reread the letter. I take the letter and walk upstairs; purposefully prolonging the inevitable break-up, I believe he wrote on the paper. I sit on the couch and stare at the letter for a good five minutes until the hope I am wrong compels me to open it.

Clarissa,

I have been very busy dealing with the business that caused me to return home. I miss our dates. I will be returning to New York in about two weeks. That is the week

after your Thanksgiving Holiday. I want to see you. I have
something very important I need to share with you. Please
take this letter as asking you on another date. I want to take
you to dinner when I return. I will call you.

Paulo

The letter is typed and has no enduring salutation like
"Love" or "Yours Truly" leaving a very distant feel to it.
What does he mean by 'something important to share with
you?' Is he going to profess his love or breakup with me?

My mind goes crazy analyzing all the possibilities. I
need a second opinion. One that is not in any way tied to
Paulo nor will tell me what I want to hear.

I have to tell Lana about Paulo. I need her
straightforward opinion on the letter.

Lana shows up at eight o'clock sharp with a bag of
Italian take-out and two bottles of red wine from *Antipasti*.

"I'm feeling better so I got chicken picatta instead of
chicken soup," Lana says. She holds up the bag handing me
the bottle of wine.

"Sounds good." I take the wine and we head upstairs
to the loft.

After we eat dinner and she has a good three glasses
of wine down, I spill out the story of Paulo from my first
sight of him at *Shot of Joe*. Despite her ranting about me
holding back and not introducing her to this "Spanish Prince"
as she nicknamed him, she forgives me. I hand her the letter
and she reads it over twice. She flips it over and back, and
then looks up at me.

"I'm sorry, Clarissa. This is a Dear John letter, but much more cruel. He wants to do it in person. Be prepared for a break up if he does come back."

"Really! No. There has to be some hope that he wants to move forward."

"Come on, Clarissa. You've been through this enough. Let yourself recognize the signs. The damn letter is typed and ... it's a letter! What happened to a phone call?"

"I have been leaving messages but I don't think the phone has international reception. Maybe a letter is all he had," I say.

Lana gives me her pathetic puppy look. "Do I really need to point out all the red flags you just said yourself?"

I fall back into the couch and put my hands over my face. "No. I knew it all along."

I sit up and look at her. My eyes are burning with the beginning signs of crying. "But he was so gorgeous. His accent kidnapped me, holding me to his every word. He came when I wasn't looking, doesn't that count for anything?"

Lana smiles and pulls me into a hug. "They usually are gorgeous, and Clarissa, no matter what you tell yourself, you are always looking for love. You are a hopeless romantic."

Lana is right. I am always looking for the romance and sweep-me-off-my-feet kind of guy. Paulo had done just that and I had ignored all my gut instincts.

"This calls for the port!" Lana pushes me off her. "You didn't drink it already did you?"

"No." I laugh and get up to grab it from a box on the floor next to the refrigerator - my secret reserve of wine.

I come back with two new glasses and the bottle of Port we agreed to save for emotional emergencies, already open. Lana takes hers and we clink our glasses together. The night ends as many of our Fridays. Two single working women, drowning their love and misery in wine.

"Next Friday we go to the bars," Lana says.

"Next Friday is Black Friday," I say.

"All the more reason. Lots of guys will be shopping for their girlfriends. We can be their reason to dump them before Christmas."

She pours us each another glass of port. Our conversation continues into the early morning hours of the night until Lana passes out on my couch and me on my bed.

MY GREEN DRESS GOES MISSING

I am invited to Lana's home for Thanksgiving. Being the second to oldest in a big family that, amazingly to me, gets along, she does not allow me to be alone. I try to tell her I am going to fly out to Oregon to spend the holiday with my family but she sees right through me.

"Give me more credit, Clarissa." Lana says to me. "You can't stand your brother and his fourth wife … or is it his fifth?"

Lana's family is very kind and festive. Her mother always welcomes me as one of the children and Lana's nieces and nephews all call me auntie. We eat enough to be full all winter and drink enough to fill a decent size Irish Pub.

As Christmas draws near, Lana's office party planning occupies most of her free time. I don't have to make any excuses while I wait for Paulo's call. Despite Lana's harsh interpretation of his letter a week ago, I silently hope she is wrong.

I am miserably wallowing in my thoughts as I close my boutique the Wednesday after Thanksgiving. The week is almost over and my hopes of seeing Paulo again are diminishing by the day. I turn the sign to *close* and walk to the storage room.

I have not opened the armoire since Lana and I returned from shopping. I only threw my new green dress into it out of frustration when I found it empty. Now I need it in a couple weeks for Lana's office parties. I open the door nonchalantly; there is no strong desire pulling me toward it.

The dress is there. Without much thought, I take it out of the armoire and close it. When I am almost to the storage room door, I notice I am holding the dress on a hanger. I stop and walk back to the armoire, open the door, and look at the bottom where I remembered throwing the dress. It is entirely empty. The dress in my hand is the one Lana bought for me; the price tag is still hanging within the folds beneath the beading. I glance one last time into the armoire before closing it then walk upstairs. A feeling of curiosity stirs images of Antonio in my head.

The material brushes my arm with my cadence forming a sense of passion. Goose bumps rise on the surface of my skin. Unconsciously I smile and see Antonio's deep blue eyes gaze upon me from the slits above his raised cheeks.

When I reach my bedroom, I hang the dress from my closet door, slip out of my clothes, and soap up my face without losing the hazy image of Antonio's eyes. By the time the soap is washed off - so is the image of Antonio.

Once Saturday arrives, I will give up on Paulo. I think to myself.

I walk out of the bathroom, naked, and accidently brush against the dress. It falls over my shoulder and the hanger drops onto the floor. The material caresses against my lower back and when I bend over to grab the hanger, it sends chills up my spine. I ignore the hanger and pull the dress in front of me, holding it close to my body I sigh as the material brushes against my breasts.

Resistance to the material is impossible, the apathy toward the dress I had earlier is far from what I feel now. I want it to touch my whole body, indulge myself with the feelings I began to have with Antonio. I slip on the dress, closing my eyes and take in the softness of the material brushing against my face as it falls. It is how I believe it would feel if Antonio were to brush his hand on my cheek.

With my arms still in the air, I turn in a circle, seeing the image of myself in the three-way mirror when I first put it on. A smile spreads across my face. Happiness fills me with the excitement of walking through a room full of people at a Christmas party – I have never felt this confident.

"Oh Miss Lanton, it is magnificent!"

An excited throaty voice fills the air around me. There is a sound of hands clapping together then a rustling of material. My arms drop to my sides. Slowly, I open my eyes and find myself in a room with a four-poster bed decorated in antique linens. It's the exact look I hope to achieve with the order from Tuscany Textiles. A frumpy middle-aged woman, not matching the voice at all with her small round eyes and tiny pursed mouth, is standing in my peripheral vision. As I concentrate on her from the corner of my eye, the rest of the room comes into focus slowly. I am aware that I'm remembering as I did with the black dress and I look at my feet now adorned with a matching pair of slippers. They feel soft against my skin. My surroundings feel more real this time, but I can still hear a low hum of traffic in the back of my mind. I turn to face the middle-aged woman. She smiles when my eyes meet hers and the sound of traffic fades completely. She takes two steps toward me.

"Now ye must turn for me to finish yer dressing," the woman says.

I crease my brows.

"You can't be expecting to show Lord Bellesara yer backside, nor anyone else fer that matter." The woman walks around and begins to pull in at the back of my dress. "There you are Miss Lanton," says the woman. She steps back and folds her hands in front of her.

My anxiety begins to increase my heart rate and I feel my throat closing. "Do you think I will present well -" I glance out the window – dusk. "Tonight?"

"Oh yes ma'am. Lord Bellesara will be most delighted to take all yer dance sets tonight. Yer brother may not have the chance to take his turn about the floor with ye." The woman's eyes widen with her bobbing head.

"Thank you," I say.

I turn and take a seat in the chair by a desk, unaware of what I should do. I wait for this memory to slowly fade or take me onto the dance floor.

"Are you in need of more time, Miss Lanton?" the woman says. "When should I tell Mr. Lanton you will be down?"

"No," I say. "I was just so taken with the feel of this dress that I forgot someone was waiting. I am ready."

The woman steps aside so that I can walk out of the room. When I reach the door, she calls me back and hands me a pair of long white gloves. I pull them on and proceed down the hall, hoping I am going in the right direction. I come to the top of the stairs in the same estate I had seen in the memory from the black dress.

At the bottom of the stairs Robert, Rosemary, Katherine, and Jonathon are all adorned in elaborate dresses and suits. My anxiety is quickly diffused and an odd sense of excitement rushes over me with the sight of them. I feel an intense affinity toward Lana's stories of her yearly return home as I scan my ulterior family. From the holiday colors of our attire, as well as the snow upon the ground outside, I settle on an assumption of this being Katherine's return to the estate for the holidays.

Anticipation flows evenly through me knowing I may be seeing Antonio in a short while. I will have missed many walks and conversations since I last saw him if this memory is related to the last. Again, I have very little knowledge about the events and am unable to act with control upon any feelings I might have. There will be a delicate balance to maintain tonight. The lack of knowledge about my past visits with Antonio, or what Rosemary and I had done since the funeral, is frightening. I am mentally blind in this memory.

We all enter a carriage waiting outside. I listen carefully to the discussion in the attempt to gather information about our destination. Robert rides on horseback alongside since there is only room for four.

"Your dress is simply amazing, Clarissa," Katherine says. "Doesn't she just look divine, Rosemary. Lord Bellesara will for certain not allow you out of his sight."

Rosemary, sitting beside me, turns her head slightly to show her agreement with a smile. I feel the blush rise to my cheeks. I remembered looking at myself in the mirror, I see Lana's face at her first glimpse in my thoughts, causing my cheeks to burn a deep red.

"Rosemary, do tell me, is there any word of young Miss Hensford since her coming out in the Fall?" Katherine asks. "I have not been to see her yet and I feel somewhat afraid of her reaction."

Rosemary looks at me with an expression that seems to suggest I must answer.

My mouth goes dry as the sweat pushes toward the rim of my pores. I try to make light of my facial expressions and the loss of blood in my face that must be causing it to be a pale white. I am happy for the darkness of the night.

Rosemary takes in a breath. "Clarissa and I have called upon her when the weather allowed it. Miss Hensford is quite the proficient young lady and very musically inclined. She will be a lovely alliance to any man. Her inheritance is comfortable and her brother is very protective." She hesitates and looks to Jonathon then at the floor of the carriage. My eyes follow hers. When she speaks, her tone fills with quiet contempt. "Miss Hensford has developed somewhat of a reputation in this short time, to be incapable of recognizing certain boundaries."

"Boundaries?" Katherine says.

"Yes."

Katherine gasps. "Has Miss Hensford flirted with Antonio?" she asks.

"There were attempts," Rosemary says.

"Do explain," Katherine says.

"Once at a dinner in the home of Lord Bellesara-"

"She was at his home!" Katherine says.

"It was a small dinner party. She attempted to touch his foot beneath the table but she stepped on mine instead. I shrieked aloud-"

Jonathon covers a smirk with his gloved hand. Rosemary cuts her eyes toward him.

"Lord Bellesara promptly and publicly admonished her for the neglect in the whereabouts of her feet."

Rosemary looks out to the window and slightly smiles at Robert on the horse. He raises his hand to the brim of his hat in response, the darkness makes it hard to see any facial expression.

"Dear Clarissa, what disgust this must have caused you," Katherine says. "But all the more, I am happy to hear your Antonio did not succumb to simple flirtations of a younger woman."

Katherine leans back into the seat and laces her arm through Jonathon's, causing him to momentarily glance at her. He quickly turns back to gazing out the window when Katherine begins talking.

"This news will make watching all the unattached ladies tonight quite entertaining." Katherine says. "I will especially be entertained in trying to catch a glimpse of Miss. Hensford's flirting."

"I believe that in the presence of her brother and her father, Miss Hensford's behavior will be more controlled." Rosemary says.

Katherine scowls. "Rosemary, have you been married too long to remember the liberties we took at our balls."

Jonathon looks quickly at Katherine with a creased brow. I stifle a laugh. She ignores him and he returns to looking absently out the window.

The atmosphere in the carriage grows with

Katherine's anticipation to catch a glimpse of Miss Hensford with her newfound information about her. As we round a corner of trees the countryside opens to a gravel path where I can see an estate illuminated by candles along the pathway. The yellow hue behind the window glass gives a warm winter touch to the light snowfall on the ground. My stomach flutters with nervous energy in my excitement to see Antonio.

We arrive in succession to many other carriages and proceed through the line of the Hensford family reception. Sir Hensford is a stout man of wide girth that exhibits his ability to enjoy his wealth. His wife has either maintained her figure or keeps herself otherwise occupied from a constant day of eating. My gaze darts to the young Miss Hensford who curtseys as I step in front of her. I mirror her greeting and bite the inside of my cheek as I notice her eyes scanning the room beneath her bowed head. She is not unaware of the gentlemen watching her from a far wall but her brother seems to also notice the gawking and he looks over my head during his bow to me. His jaw tightens as he nods to me but glares out the corner of his eye to the young Miss Hensford.

When I rise from my curtsey to her brother, I turn into Antonio's line of site. He is standing off to the side smiling at me and he closes the distance in three long strides. He takes my hand, placing it into his arm.

"Good evening, my dear Clarissa. You are so beautiful tonight," he says

"Thank you," I say. The breath of my surprise escapes with the rising emotion he stirs in me at his sight alone. I can only guess the time away from him has made me want him more. Now that he stands next to me, engulfing me with his height, I can do little to keep from leaning into him. I want him to be my prince, take me away, and never let me be pulled out of this memory.

He smiles at my flustered response. I remember him being gorgeous but seeing him in front of me again takes my breath away, literally. I inhale deeply and smell a light musk to his natural odor. The stench of his wool suit enhances the masculine scent of his cologne. I lean toward his shoulder a bit and take in another breath. I can smell vanilla and another delicious aroma like a campfire but not so strong. He notices my lean and meets my gaze with a smile and a squeeze of the hand.

"Clarissa, I request all sets of dances tonight aside from those Robert and Jonathon insist upon," he says.

"You may have all the dances you desire," I say. "But should the host desire a turn about the room would it not be my obligation to oblige? And what about your dear brother?"

"Yes. I dare say I would be obligated to part from you should the host desire a turn about the room. So my task tonight is to keep you away from the host."

"And what about your brother? Should he want a dance?"

I tilt my head and flutter my eyelashes a bit. He laughs.

"My brother has come here with his own preconceptions and although your beauty is more than any other female here I do not believe he will be bothering me for permission to dance with you."

"What if it is I who would like to dance with your

brother?"

Antonio's brow creases sharp into the bridge of his nose and he stops walking. I raise one eyebrow. He relaxes his expression, pulling up a corner of his mouth.

"I do not believe your character involves the ability to intentionally cause two brothers to fight for a lady who is already promised," he whispers. "My heart is yours, Clarissa ... but know this; Now that you have pledged your heart to me I will fight to keep it safe from harm or hurt. Not even my brother will come between us. That you may be sure."

I am confused and a bit fearful of his remark. There must have been many lost memories since the last time I was with Antonio. I concede to abide by the customs of this era and hold my tongue.

"I have willingly given you my heart Antonio," I say. "It belongs only to you. Nothing has the strength to separate us."

Antonio appears frozen but his eyes seem free to search my face as though he sees right through me.

"Is it ...?" he says but stops mid-sentence then leans into me with his eyes closing.

He frowns pulling his lips inward and slowly shakes his head. I know he wants to kiss me. My heart beats faster with my own desire to kiss him. The room begins to blend into a drone of voices and music muffled by our own circle of passion.

I am unable to control my desire to the social constraints I know this era dictates. Antonio straightens up slowly and I am relieved for the air that rushes between us but disappointed he could not throw societal dictation aside for one moment. If it were not for his own restraint, we would have shocked everyone with a very passionate kiss. His lips turn up with a seductive glance from the corner of his eye and then he leads me to the dance floor.

It is now my turn to freeze. I have no idea how to dance in this era!

I feel light-headed and my mouth goes dry. I am on the brink of a full-fledged panic attack. There is no way I am going to pull this off. No excuse comes to mind. Antonio looks at me with a confused expression.

"Clarissa? Are you alright?" he asks.

"Ah yes … yes. Just taken aback with the beauty of the room," I say, barely making the words loud enough to hear.

He smiles and again leads me farther into the ballroom. I pray silently to myself for anything that might help. I make myself relax and as I take position for the dance with Antonio across from me, the light-headed feeling turns to dizziness. I scold myself, committing every muscle in my body to relax.

Listen to the music. How much harder can it be than a loud club in New York? Let the music and other dancers guide you.

I inhale and look around me at the other couples. Antonio catches my eyes. The hard lines of his face that caused fear in me moments earlier have disappeared and are now replaced with the softness of the blue shinning in his eyes.

The music begins and out of the corner of my eye, I see the lady next to me take a step forward. I follow and am able to keep up thanks to many years of my childhood spent in a dance studio. I find that the more I relax, my body takes over and for some strange reason I actually do know the steps - as if I had danced these numbers several times before.

I am able to complete a set of two dances without tripping or bumping into anyone else. My small mistakes can easily be explained away with my distraction of the ball itself and excitement if needed. Candles are lit all over the ballroom and the adjoining rooms for sitting. Candelabras are abundant with the wax slowly dripping down the sides as the night wears on. The walls and ceiling are draped with green pine garland that fills the room with its scent. It is strong and masks the unwanted stench of increasing body odor.

I have no opportunity to make excuses for my dancing mistakes and it seems no one has noticed. If any glances are thrown in Antonio's or my direction it appears more for idle gossip and amazement than criticism of my dancing.

Antonio offers to get me some punch as he leads me over to the wall by the open double doors. The fresh air is inviting. Were it not for the obvious pairing of couples in the outside courtyard I would venture out on my own.

I study the dances while waiting for Antonio. The guests seem to glide over the floor, intimacy pouring out of their eyes and emanating slightly from their body language. It makes me ache even more for Antonio's touch.

"Has my dear brother left the most beautiful bride-to-be alone in this room full of men searching for such a woman?" A husky voice rises just above the music behind me.

Startled I turn quickly and face a man in British military uniform bowing slightly. Quickly, I respond with a courtesy, remembering my social duty. I rise and make eye contact with the man immediately stifling the sound of my surprise. Standing in front of me is Paulo. The anger immediately rises inside me and I bite my lip to keep in the reprimand I want to scream at him.

I continue to stare, holding my breath to prevent the gasp stuck in my throat. My stomach feels like it turns over backward and inside out. I want to hit him, ask him why he didn't call. The anger mixes with fierce growing confusion. The one question - only question - I need him to answer is why he is here in my memory. I bite my bottom lip and raise my eyebrows; an expression that would have invited an explanation if we were in my boutique.

Paulo laughs shaking his head side to side. His thumb caresses his pointer finger in a motion that appears he is asking for money.

"I do not mean to offend you Miss Lanton. I only mean to point out that my brother has managed to steal the most beautiful woman at this ball and I regret not being able to have her for myself." he says. He slides one foot back and bends in an exaggerated bow, then lifts his head. He straightens and leans in toward me. "Where are my manners? I have shared with you before this observation and received a good slap on my cheek for correction purposes."

My jaw falls open and I clap my hand to my mouth to hide it.

"Do not worry," he says. He rubs his cheek with a look of pouting and then pulls his lips into a thin line; his jaw becomes tight. I can smell the alcohol on his breath. "I did not tell my brother of your correction," he whispers. "I found it all too amusing and private between the two of us."

Antonio suddenly pulls Paulo upright by one shoulder.

"My dear brother," Antonio says. "I hope you are minding your manners this evening. I demand you provide my fiancé the respected distance that a lady deserves."

Paulo nods with an exaggerated expression of compliance on his face and stumbles to the side. Antonio, with his hand still on Paulo's shoulder, places his body between Paulo and me. With his other hand, Antonio grabs mine and pushes me almost completely behind him.

"I believe your comrades are waiting for your company in the other room." Antonio says. I notice the sharp lines of his face return. "I suggest you take this opportunity to join them."

Paulo makes an exaggerated salute, turns on his heels, almost losing his balance, and saunters away. Antonio, keeping my hand in his, leads me to the courtyard.

"Do you mind some fresh air?" he says.

We exit the ballroom through the double doors.

"That would be nice," I say.

I study his face. It is still hard and determined but this time it makes me feel safe, not fearful. We walk to an empty bench that looks out onto a vast garden of shrubs and a large reflecting pool. The moonlight darts off the pool onto the droplets of mist upon the maze of shrubs. I sit next to Antonio in silence.

"I am sorry for my brother's behavior," he says. "I am

so grateful that despite his reputation you have agreed to marry me. I do not deserve your love and feel the risk to your reputation will be grave."

I am caught off guard. The language of this era is thoroughly confusing me but my gut tells me I am being dumped.

"Antonio. Please," I say.

Antonio holds up his hand and unconsciously I fall immediately silent. He takes in a shallow breath.

"I know we have discussed this before," he says. "I know your feelings toward me are strong and will not change. It was much easier when my brother left after your father's funeral but now he is back. I do not know how long he intends to stay. I am his only provider, Clarissa. I have told him I will no longer support his lifestyle and because of this, he is angry with me." He shifts his body so his knee is barely touching mine and he grabs both my hands into his. "Clarissa, I fear he will unleash that anger in ways to ruin us or ... you."

I take in a deep breath to subdue a growing anger at his absurdity for my reputation.

"Antonio, I won't have this discussion with you," I say. "My reputation may survive without you at my side, but I will not."

"I would never ask you to be so tormented," he says. "I could not live knowing you are bound to another man -"

"I won't marry anyone else."

He squints and groans deep without moving his lips. "This is the fire I love so much but if I let you go Robert will find you another suitor."

I yank my hands out of his. "Don't leave me – plain and simple."

"You are strong and determined, keeping my heart alive with your breath. I am foolish to think it would be better for you if we were apart," he says.

I smile triumphantly. Antonio lifts my hand in both of his and gently kisses it. He leaves his lips on my fingers closing his eyes and takes in a deep breath. Looking up he exhales and smiles back.

"We should return to the dancing," he says. "I do not know if I can maintain my manners with how you look in the moonlight. For the sake of both our reputations I ask you for another pair of dances."

I laugh. If he only knew how much restraint I am using at this very second. "Yes. Dancing would be to our benefit," I say.

We return to the ballroom and wait for the current melody to stop. Taking our positions for the next dances, we keep our eyes upon each other. It is as though we are the only two people dancing - the music playing only for us. When we pass closely by each other, as a dance step allows, I hear his deep inhale. The tension and desire building between us holds our eyes captive. We maintain perfect composure of our face but our eyes speak loudly the desire to feel the heat of our bodies in closer proximity.

The two dances end and Antonio takes my hand. "May I have the next pair of dances?" he whispers into my ear.

"Yes," I say. "I don't want to stop."

Antonio smiles and bows to me, which I return with a

courtesy. We again take our positions and flow with the rest of the dancers on the floor.

Aside from only two breaks, Antonio and I remain on the dance floor. I do not see Paulo for the remainder of the night but the questions of his presence, and why he is in this memory of mine, still lingers in the back of my thoughts. I wonder if it is because he helped me carry in the armoire and his touch somehow connected him as well.

Antonio walks with me to the carriage. It is the early hours of the morning and the sun lights the sky in a pink hue. We say good-bye to the host on the way out and receive congratulations on our engagement. Antonio assists me into the carriage where I find Katherine and Rosemary smiling. We are then joined by Jonathon after Antonio steps aside.

"Do not worry, Clarissa." Katherine says. I watch Antonio looking at our carriage as the horse trots away jerking the carriage into movement. "He will be joining us for Christmas breakfast tomorrow," she says.

"I do hope his brother will not be attending," Rosemary says.

Jonathon flashes a glance toward me with a click of his tongue, "You can be assured my dear sister, that Paulo will not be welcomed in the home … regardless of his relations," he says.

I am unable to control my face or regain my breath, my lungs strain at the lack of oxygen. My mind is tight with the collision of this memory and Paulo in reality. Closing my eyes, I command myself to inhale. I succeed and my almost panic attack goes unnoticed.

Katherine and Rosemary talk about the ball with

animated expressions. They ask me multiple questions and comment on how they watched me dance with Antonio all night. I smile and answer the questions when I can get a word in before their next one.

When we reach our estate, I excuse myself and walk to the room where I first appeared in this memory. The middle-aged woman is waiting for me. I am unsure how or when the atmosphere around me will fade and I am again standing in my own room with the green dress at my feet, but I know I am not ready to leave now. I want to relish in the silence of Antonio's world, inhale the musty smell of the room and study the linens on the four-poster bed. If I cannot control my return or which dress I choose, then I can at least replicate the look of this bed – bring back with me the memory of Antonio's world.

I dismiss the woman and she pleads for me to ring when I am ready to undress. I nod and waive her gently away with my hand as I sit at the writing desk. My thoughts weave in and out of my head replaying the ball and Paulo's face in front of mine. He did not seem to know me - as he does in reality. There must be a way to control how long I stay in Antonio's world if Paulo is here.

I imagine Lana finding me unconscious in my boutique as my mind feeds me the strain of events in Antonio's world. She would rush me to a hospital and I would lay there in a coma while I live the rest of my life here with Antonio. I halfheartedly smile at my morbid idea and promise to tell Lana that if I am ever found in a coma, not to pull the plug.

A quill lies on the writing desk in front of me next to

a piece of paper. I dip it into the ink jar and place it onto the paper. I do not know what or why I am writing, it just feels right to have it in my hand. The ink bleeds into the paper as I hold the quill in one place. Tears well in my eyes and the fatigue of the night take over. I know at some point I will be pulled away from this world.

The quill begins to move in circles across the page, not one circle forming into a letter. I see Antonio's face; his blue eyes are bright with passion as he looks to me on the dance floor.

I love you. I say to him in my thoughts.

I repeat it out loud then let the quill drop and relinquish myself to this memory of the dress. Scanning the room I wait for everything to lose focus and the sound of the traffic to increase in volume from the back of my mind. Nothing changes.

I put the quill back in the bottle, stand up with my eyes closed, raise my hands over my head, and bring them to the base of my neck where I unfasten the first button. I take several steps forward, still with my eyes closed, and stop when I feel the bed against my thighs. I slide my hands to the back and fumble with the rest of the buttons until the dress falls to the floor. Keeping my eyes closed I collapse onto the bed and allow sleep to take over me. I will deal with the disappointment of my real life in the morning.

The morning sun hits my eyelids with great force. I moan turning over and pulling the pillow onto my head. The memory of Antonio's world has jumbled my grip on the present so I quickly play over the week following

Thanksgiving to get my bearings.

"Thursday morning," I groan.

I turn back over with the pillow covering my face. I have to face reality - open my boutique. I take a deep breath and pull the pillow onto my stomach, making an exasperated sigh then open my eyes.

Sitting straight up, fast enough to induce a head rush, I throw my hands over my mouth to muffle my scream. I am in my bed … in Antonio's world!

I lean over the side of the bed and see the dress lying on the floor. I immediately start to analyze how I stayed but the excitement growing inside reminds me Antonio will be here for breakfast. I look around the room for a good twenty seconds before I slap my forehead - there is no such thing as a digital clock in this era. The sunlight seeping through the window suggests early morning. I would probably be on my way back from the coffee shop and therefore estimate it to be around seven.

Somewhat aware of the time, my stomach growls in demand. The feeling of being helpless in a memory unknown to me but somehow mine sends a rush of panic through my thoughts. It does not seem logical that I am still in this memory while the dress lies on the floor. I wonder what more I am to be shown, why my mind feels the need to keep living in this past era and if it is truly my memory or just one that belongs to the owner of the dress.

I need serious help … and food.

I walk over to a narrow door that is slightly ajar. Opening it, I find it full of dresses and under garments. I have no idea where to begin. I think of the middle-aged woman and pull on a cord next to the bed. Within seconds she appears, scolds me for leaving the green dress on the floor, and not ringing for her to undress me last night. When she pauses to compose herself from the personal exchange between us, she apologizes repeatedly for her lack of manners. I wave it away with my hands.

"Lord Bellesara will be joining us for breakfast," I say. I pause anticipating the woman to confirm this for me. When she does not I continue. "I do not know what would be the best attire for me to wear. I do not want to look too comfortable or too formal. What would you suggest?"

The woman's eyes seem to light up with my request. She waddles over to the bed and places the dress from the ball onto it. She then enters the closet.

"I have just the thing Miss," she says. She pulls out a simple light red dress with a green sash. It looks a bit formal to me but then I remind myself it is Christmas morning. This is when I realize presents may be given and I have no idea if I had purchased, or made, any. Taking the dress from the woman and watching her return to the closet, I play into a façade of wanting to make a good appearance. It would not be hard to play this as the anticipation to see Antonio makes my want of food hurt my stomach more than the excitement alone.

"Do you know what time Lord Bellesara is to arrive?" I say.

The woman surfaces from the closet beneath a pile of folded white cotton that I take to be the undergarments. "He is downstairs with Master Bentley at this moment," she says. "Miss Katherine was going to wake you but Lord Bellesara insisted she let you sleep."

The woman roughly tosses the pile onto the bed and pulls out a girdle, wrapping it around my waist. It takes only one pull after she laces it for me to grab the bedpost so I don't end up falling into her.

"Have I missed breakfast?" I say. The final pull of the corset strings pushes the air from my lungs and I grip the bedpost harder.

"Oh no. They are waiting for you," she says. "It has not been long. Miss Rosemary only woke but fifteen minutes ago."

"Oh." I say and bend under and up into the dress. "I seem to have misplaced the gifts I want to give everyone," I say. "My head has been so preoccupied with the ball I do not remember where I put them."

I catch the woman's surprise at my question before she hides behind me.

"You gave them to me yesterday and asked that I place them on the breakfast table this morning with the others," she says.

"Oh yes. Thank you." I breathe now a little more at ease knowing I have presents to give.

Dressed and made presentable in all the proper fashion for this era, I cautiously descend the stairs, unaware of what or whom I may find. The thought of Antonio being here causes my palms to sweat.

Robert, Jonathon, and Antonio emerge from the library just as I reach the bottom step; the burning flush quickly heats my cheeks before I can acknowledge their presence and bow my head as I courtesy.

Antonio catches site of me on the stairs, and he quickly turns toward me in a low bow. It was quick even with my minimal understanding of proper Victorian manners to notice. This helps me relax more, seeing that he too is excited to see me. I return his bow with another courtesy, afraid this bobbing may continue due to my lack of understanding as to how I might be able to stop it. Robert and Jonathon bow just as Antonio is rising from his – making Antonio's quick reaction even more noticeable by others. Antonio offers me his arm and releases me from having to bend again.

"Merry Christmas my dear Clarissa," he says. He leans lower toward my ear. "I missed you after you left the ball."

The burning returns in force to my cheeks. "Merry Christmas. I missed you also," I say.

Despite pure exhaustion and the intense fear that I would wake up in my loft I had thought of Antonio. Antonio looks at me with such softness and desire that I feel he might be sharing in my angst to be alone with him. He must sense the passion for him pushing from inside me to be in his company every waking moment. I know this feeling from the many times when I thought I was in love but with Antonio, it is different. Aside from being all together fictional in probability, the feeling, emotions that our connection stirs within are true. It is so vividly real that if given the choice I might choose to spend the rest of my life here.

The breakfast is joyous in its entire Victorian postcard flare. The allowance of the family's disregard for high attention to manners surprises me – several faux pas are ignored or go unnoticed. It is so different from the impeccable and rigid manners I thought the focus of this era. Many allowances are in regards to the young Miss Hensford. Even Antonio jabs at her lack of character in one slight way. He says that during a conversation with her father, he noticed her attempting to show him her ankle from the crack in the doorway. Antonio then says he had seen better-looking legs on a horse and if there was any attraction possible before it was undone at that moment.

Yet not without notice, one topic, or name, that is never mentioned is Paulo; even when the most distant relatives seem to be mentioned. I can only conclude from Paulo's absence and lack of mention that he is a man of character disgraceful enough to be disowned by Antonio or very near to it. The interaction at the ball the previous night must have been purely out of chance.

Breakfast concludes and we exchange gifts over morning coffee in the parlor. My gift to Antonio is a new chain for his watch. To Robert I give a ledger for his bookkeeping, and to both Rosemary and Katherine I give sheet music for the pianoforte.

Katherine and Rosemary both tell me that we will all exchange and share our music. I too seem to have received some from them and I am silently hoping today will not require me to play. Although I played as a child, the black dots and lines that are blurred throughout the pages in my gift are quite intimidating.

I receive a beautiful string of pearls from Antonio, which he takes from me and places it around my neck almost before I finished opening the box. His motions are slow in clasping the necklace. His fingertips linger on the back of my neck long enough to send the tingling sensation down my spine and cause my cheeks to blush a bright red. I hear him sigh ever so slightly before he lets the necklace drop on my neck from his grip, immediately cooling the skin where his fingertips have brushed. In turning to thank him, our faces are close enough for me to feel the immediate cease of his breath. Antonio is quicker to compose himself than me, quickly rising to his feet and sitting in the chair next to Robert, saying loudly how the necklace does not compare at all to my beauty. As embarrassing as his compliment feels, it makes a great diversion for my burning cheeks.

The remaining gifts to me are a new wrap with a fur-lined hood from Robert and gloves to match from Jonathon.

The sun is shining without a cloud in the sky when we finish opening our gifts. Rosemary suggests we walk about the property across the freshly fallen snow. We all put on long coats and wraps – my wrap feels especially warm.

The air is crisp and immediately chills my face as I step out into it. Antonio puts my hand into his arm and brings my body close to his. He then pulls the hood of my wrap over my head pausing to look into my eyes. He traces the fur lining of the hood and allows his fingers to brush my cheek toward the corner of my mouth. He smiles and then places his hand on top of mine and squeezes it gently. The others walk ahead and Antonio gently tugs at me to slow our pace, creating some distance between the others and ourselves.

He looks down at me; the warmth of his breath pushes away the cold air that bites at my face.

"Tell me my dear Clarissa, of how you missed me

after the ball," he says.

I feel my face heat up and he smiles at my reaction. I look away. If only I had the freedom to divulge everything inside my head. I doubt I can convey my feelings at this moment and wonder if he knows about the passion he stirs in me - the desire to be in his full embrace not just linked in arms. I have not wanted a man more than I want Antonio now - to hold him tight and never be released from this memory.

"My apologies," Antonio says. "I am prying into the private thoughts of a lady." His voice pulls me out of my anguish momentarily.

I look up at him and the fine lines of his face make me feel safe. "Private thoughts that you will soon know, I hope, but nonetheless private at this time," I say.

His lips turn up in a large smile and I think I catch him blushing as well. He looks away quickly. A dead silence falls upon us. Charged with an understanding too strong for either of us to acknowledge or explain I change the subject immediately to save us both.

"Rosemary missed Robert when he was away," I say. "I wish that she could remain with me, but I can't ask her to be apart from him again. I will have to return to France with them or stay with Katherine if she will have me."

Antonio looks at me with his brow high and eyes wide. "Has your brother not told you about Jonathon's plan to return to your father's home after a fortnight at theirs?" he says.

"When was this decided?" I say.

"Your brother had told me upon my arrival this

morning but our discussion alluded that you both had knowledge of these arrangements prior to this morning."

I look down at the small footprints made by Rosemary. I try to step perfectly into one but demolish it underneath my own foot.

"Robert did share the plan but I was fearful that they were only ideas." I lie. "I can't ask my sisters to be apart from their husbands nor expect their husbands to be far from their business responsibilities."

Antonio wraps his hand around my upper arm and turns me to him.

"I believe your sisters have been instrumental," he says. "Their encouragement toward their husbands to make arrangements that allow me to continue to call upon you has been successful. I do recall Robert saying that Rosemary had insisted you be within a distance that I may call daily if I so choose."

"And do you so choose, Antonio … to call upon me daily until our wedding?"

He releases my arm, putting both my hands between his. The warmth penetrating my gloves makes my heart beat faster; the gentle strength of his grip speeds up my breath, making me consciously slow it to keep from fainting. The desire in me to reach around his neck and pull his lips to mine grows fierce; I clench my hands together inside his grip. It is all I can do to keep control of myself; the effect he has with his mere touch is something I will never feel with anyone else.

Antonio bends down and looks into my eyes. His eyes are a deep shade of blue against the cool of his skin. His face is so close to mine now that his breath warms my nose as he exhales. I clutch my fingers together harder, the pain of my own grip keeping me on my feet.

Antonio whispers. "I choose to call upon you daily. If only to catch a glimpse of you. I must confess my desire to call upon you extends beyond what my character allows me to express, but as you recently informed me when I inquired of your thoughts, you will know those desires all too well after our wedding."

My breath stops, his lips inches from mine, he does not move his gaze, and I am lost in the reflection of the sunlight in his eyes.

Slowly, the corners of his mouth turn upward in a smile, it hints at things to come, recognition that we both struggle against our desires to break free from the confines of manners. It is at this moment that I know I had found my romance, the kind I have been long searching for – that I will never find in my present life. Here in my past I found love. I wonder if this is the reason I keep searching for it, the explanation for my premature attachments in all those failed relationships from which Lana has resurrected me.

Antonio unlocks his gaze from me and straightens up, placing my hand back on his arm. I am able to breath now but cannot take my eyes off his face. Somehow he has regained his composure, the control of manners being deeper ingrained. My knees feel weak and if it weren't for him holding me I probably will collapse. I flex my fingers to release the tingling from the pressure of holding them together within his grasp.

"We are blessed to have such fair weather on this

Christmas day," he says without looking at me.

I stare ahead of us toward the cloudless sky. I can think of nothing to say. He turns and steps into my line of sight, the corners of his lips turn up slow and even.

"Do you not agree that it is a beautiful day my dear Clarissa?" he says. I quickly disengage my eyes from his for fear of totally losing my balance.

"Yes. We are truly blessed, with the day ... and the company," I say.

"Indeed," he says.

We continue in silence until we catch up to the others.

The day ends with a grand dinner and piano playing. The piano playing, to my luck, is dominated by Rosemary and Katherine. Discussion also includes my living arrangements to come. I am to travel to Katherine's home and spend a week or two. While I am at their home, Antonio will be attending to business of his own, which Rosemary informs me, has to do with ensuring his brother will not return. Paulo is to be settled in London. Rosemary has told me that Antonio is not in a position to disown him and is greatly concerned about his character. He does not want Paulo allowed on the premises after our wedding and is making all attempts to settle him in London to be under a watchful eye.

Antonio holds the reigns of his horse as he talks to Robert and Jonathon. I stand in the doorway with Katherine and Rosemary waiting for him to look up so I may catch his eyes one more time before he leaves.

"He is expected to return tomorrow afternoon,

Clarissa." Katherine says. "He has some unfinished tasks to complete in regards to his brother ... for your sake."

I nod, not wanting to take my attention away from Antonio. He hands the reigns to Jonathon then walks toward me. Katherine and Rosemary step back with a giggle into the entrance hall. He takes both my hands into his and leans to my ear.

He whispers. "I will be back tomorrow. Please keep your afternoon open, I have a surprise."

My cheeks spread with a smile at his warm breath on the base of my ear then as he slowly straightens from his bend, he lets his lips brush along my cheek. He squeezes both hands hard very quickly before turning sharply back toward his horse. He walks determinedly to it and mounts. Just as he turns away, he looks back at me. I close my mouth and try to smile but it doesn't even change the circle of my lips before he is again facing away from me, riding down the path. I feel Katherine's hand on my elbow and turn to see her smiling at me with a hint of teasing.

I walk up slowly to my bedroom. I have no idea if I will fade. I have fallen in love and I want so much to stay. I stand in the center of my room ignoring my duty to ring for the middle-aged woman, and quietly closed the door. I reach behind me and take the first button in my hands, inhale deeply, silently praying to stay here in Antonio's world. My eyes close for fear of what I might see. The first button is unfastened. I pause to listen. Everything is silent. My ears sharp to any new sound, listening harder for the noise of traffic that is usually outside the boutique - nothing. I reach farther over my head, down the dress - my eyes still closed. I unfasten the second button. Holding my breath I listen again - still nothing. I drop my arms and reach behind for the last five buttons, pausing after each one.

The dress now hangs wide open in the back and I hunch my shoulders forward allowing the weight of the material to cause the dress to drop to my elbows. I catch the material in my hands and take a deep breath.

Slowly opening my eyes a rush of tears quickly well up then fall over my lids and down my cheeks. In front of me is the four-poster bed of Antonio's world. My tears of joy dampen the pillow as my face kisses the sheets. I stayed.

FIGHT ON THE BANK OF A FROZEN POND

I wake up the next morning in Antonio's world a little dazed from the confusion of not returning to the present time. Memories of my own life seem distant but I do not mind. The social constraints are bearable if it is part of being with Antonio. I stretch as far across the bed as I can reach. The sun is shining into the room, lighting up dust particles floating in front of the desk.

I wipe the remaining sleep from my eyes as I slide out from beneath the sheets. I walk over to the window and look out onto a garden covered in old snow, the pathway barely visible weaving amongst the sticks that will burst shades of green in the spring.

Antonio will not be around until the afternoon so I make the decision to ask one of my sisters to walk the garden with me. I want to take the opportunity to explore any part of this world before it fades away. The growing familiarity of my surroundings lends an odd comfort to who I am. Like looking through a photo album and remembering events that I had long forgotten with the passing of time. Antonio's world feels a part of me, as though I lived this life long ago.

Again, I ignore my duty to ring for the middle-age woman and dress myself in an outfit I put together from the closet. It reminds me of the soft blue dress from the armoire.

The long sleeves and heavy material appear capable of keeping me warm without an excessive amount of undergarments. Content with my own dressing I walk downstairs in search of breakfast.

Robert and Rosemary are already eating when I enter the room but Robert pauses to stand up for my entrance. Jonathon enters shortly after me; Rosemary and I almost simultaneously ask for Katherine. I let Rosemary finish the question and take a seat at the table.

"She is not feeling well," Jonathon says. "She will join us later."

"Should I call a doctor?" Robert asks.

"No. I do not believe a doctor is needed. Although our governess may need some assistance near the end of the summer months."

Rosemary congratulates Jonathon immediately as Robert gives him a pat on the back. I also join in, mimicking slightly Rosemary's remarks.

After we all eat with elated conversation about Katherine's pregnancy, Rosemary and I walk to the parlor while the men go into the library to discuss the final preparations of my supervision until the wedding. Since Katherine is still resting, I ask Rosemary if she would like to walk around the property with me. She agrees, and to my surprise says it would be good to have a moment to ourselves because she has something to share.

We put on our wraps and step outside. The air is cold but bearable with the sun shining on our backs. Rosemary looks at the ground as she begins.

"Clarissa, Robert is extremely concerned about your

reputation," she says.

I tilt my head to the side. My cheek raises with my creased brow. "My reputation?" I say. "Have I disgraced his good character?"

"Oh no!" she says. "It is nothing to do with you." She pulls at a fingertip of her glove. "It is Paulo," she says.

I breathe deep and stare at the road ahead.

"Surely you know the disgrace Paulo has brought to your dear Antonio," she says. "Robert has shared many discussions he has had with Antonio about Paulo's gambling and other activities."

I let a short soft laugh escape - barely audible. "Other activities?" I say.

Rosemary takes in a deep breath. "Oh Clarissa, you must know - you are very sharp."

I raise my eyebrows and jut my head slightly toward her. Rosemary sighs and turns her face away from me. She slows her pace then stops and rubs her palms down her thighs a couple times then laces her fingers together. She turns to me with her mouth slightly open then abruptly turns back and begins walking. I follow.

"It is rumored that Paulo is having relations with a woman whom he is not engaged," she says. "Further it is said she is not his first. Antonio will be addressing this business while you are staying with Katherine. He hopes to pay off Paulo to ensure he never returns to the family home, but he is worried Paulo will gamble away the money and return to take revenge upon you both."

Antonio's remarks at the ball now made sense and although the information portrayed Paulo only as a real jerk if he were doing the same activities in my present life, in this world his actions have a much greater consequence - consequences that could be grave. I am reminded of the note that was attached to the armoire, but intentionally dismiss it.

"Thank you," I say. "You've done so much for me. I will watch out for Paulo."

Rosemary breathes a soft sigh and rubs her hands together. "It is cold. We should return," she says.

"Would it be too bold if I continue walking?" I ask.

She tilts her head gazing up to the sky as though a passing bird in flight grabbed her attention. She smiles with her lips closed and looks at me. "I do not see a problem should you remain on the property," she says.

"I will take that path for a few moments before turning back," I say pointing to a path off to my right.

"Oh Clarissa, do be careful of the pond. Do not go near it. I believe I heard Robert say there is some ice around the banks."

"I will just go far enough to catch a glimpse," I say.

Rosemary places a hand on my arm with a nod then hurries forward toward the house. I turn down the path.

I only walk a couple yards before I see a large pond through some trees. I venture closer, holding onto the trunks as the path begins to slope. The pond looks more like a small lake to me but I am able to make out the bank on the other side. The natural vegetation around the pond is bare to the branches because of the winter season giving it a picturesque look. The sun hits the thin layer of ice on the water throwing glittering reflections off the frozen branches. The multiple shades of browns, blues, and whites combine in such a way that it captivates my attention.

"A lady must be very careful when walking near a barely frozen pond."

Startled, I grab the tree trunk ungracefully. I turn, gasping at the sight of Paulo standing a few feet from me on the upward slope of the path. He is in uniform and his hand is lazily resting on the butt of his sword, as it hangs in the holster down the side of his left leg. His eyes are bloodshot and his stance suggests he is drunk. I straighten, my body tensing to control my anger.

He stands before me in the clothing and manners of this Victorian era but in his face and eyes, he is Paulo from my present life – only drunk. Consciously, I have to hold my tongue or I will blurt out and demand an explanation for his failure to call or the absurd typed letter he sent me.

"Paulo. What are you doing out here?" I say. With my jaw clenched, I straighten up and attempt to get a bearing on my footing.

"I might ask you the same," he says. He takes a few steps forward closing the distance between us. His breath confirms my suspicions about his drunken state, as does his slight stumble.

"I never got a turn about the room with you at the ball," he slurs. "We were so rudely interrupted by my dear brother." He wrinkles his nose then steps forward with his hands out for balance. I side step slightly to widen my stance and push hard against the ground with my feet.

"But here we are," he says. "In nature's ballroom, and the only dancers, no wonder I feel the desire to dance ... and since you are the only lady available and I am the only man, then we must be destined to dance together."

He raises an eyebrow and closes the distance between us considerably fast for his apparent state. His eyes are watery from intoxication and his breath is fowl. He throws his arm around me pushing his hand hard against my lower back in an attempt to steady himself. He grabs my left hand, reaching out to the side above my shoulder. All his movements are too quick and unexpected for me to react - I only get my right hand on his chest in haste to push away from him.

I want to shove him away but internally I struggle with all the new knowledge I have learned about Paulo in this era, and the feelings I still hold for him in my present – a tiny part of me is glad to be in his arms again.

I notice, however, that it does not ignite the passion within me that I feel with Antonio's touch. It is a grave consequence that I should find love in the memory of a past life and continue to struggle in the present.

Each time Paulo exhales, the smell of alcohol is forced into my lungs. I hold my breath and push harder against him. Regardless of my current thoughts or feelings I'm juggling, I'm sure the way he acts now is not what I want.

Paulo leans in, eyes closed, lips puckered, and then sways back, opening his eyes with a raised brow. He stumbles. I anchor my footing, catching both of us from falling. He smiles at the sudden thrust of our bodies together.

"A small kiss to begin the dance, miss," he says. "I assure my lips will not disappoint your desires."

I perform one of my basic self-defense moves and

free my hand from his grip, but he responds by grabbing me harder around my lower back with both hands, pulling me forcefully against him. My freed hand is now trapped against my side in his grip. Again, he smiles as my arching back from pushing him away at the chest forces our lower bodies to come together under the pressure of his hold.

"Bravo my dear. Our desires are the same," he slurs.

"Paulo. Stop." My words come out like a whine more than the shout I had intended because of the force that I am exerting to keep him away. The closeness of our lower bodies, and the massive amount of material around my legs from my dress, makes it impossible to knee him in the groin. The repulsiveness of his breath and his forceful actions wipe any attraction to him from my thoughts. This situation feels real and fear rises inside me

I wish that I were wearing my jeans and t-shirt, allowing for more mobility. His grip around my waist prevents any turning or dropping to free myself. I inhale a deep breath despite the stench and he seems to immediately understand my intent to scream. Quickly, with a hard clapping sound, he cuffs my mouth with his hand, firms his grip around my waist with the other, and pulls me to his side. I feel his sword against my thigh.

"Shh. We mustn't allow anyone else to ruin our moment," he says.

He kisses his hand over my mouth and begins to slowly move it from under his lips. I pull my lips into my mouth bracing for the moment when ours will touch. Hoping at that moment, I can get a free hand to punch him. With enough strength behind it, I can shock him enough to escape.

I am counting on his drunkenness to make him stumble when I take off, giving me time to hike up the dress and make a break for the house - screaming.

Only his fingertips separate the warmth of his alcohol-saturated lips from mine.

Lean into the kiss - return it. He'll loosen his grip; I'll free my hand and punch him in the face then push him in the chest and run as fast as I can to the house.

Giving all my senses over to the release of his hand on my wrist and the exact second his lips touch mine, I ready myself to put my plan into action.

"PAULO!" A shout sounds from the banks of the pond below and Paulo jumps back at the call of his name, dropping me on the ground. The sudden release throws me hard; the momentum of the fall works against me with the slope of the path. I roll sideways, knock against a tree and slam my upper shoulders and head against it.

The sound of hooves running toward me, grow loud and quick. I look up through blurred vision to see the flash of a brown and white horse pass within inches of me, coming to an abrupt halt in front of Paulo.

Desperately focusing my eyes on the outline of the horses, it trots off leaving the image of Paulo lying face down on the ground and Antonio standing in front of him. Antonio turns quickly and pulls me off the ground with one arm around my waist. I catch the look on his face and for the first time I am scared to be in his presence, his eyes are such a deep blue - his face hard with rigid lines. He pushes me behind him and holds strong to my forearm.

"Get up!" Antonio shouts at Paulo.

Paulo moans, pushing himself up with his hands, but only turns onto his side, then flops over onto his back. Antonio pulls me to his side and turns to face me keeping an eye on Paulo and his body between us.

Creasing his brow and shaking his head forcefully, Antonio seems to attempt to soften his rage, for me. His attempts, though gallant, are unsuccessful.

"Get on the horse and ride back to the house! Can you do that?" Antonio says.

I open my mouth to protest. I don't want to leave him here alone with Paulo. I am afraid for Antonio ... and for Paulo with the rage I see in Antonio. What Paulo might do to him in his drunken state, or what Antonio might do to Paulo to save my reputation in this era. I am angry with Paulo for his actions but not so much I want an all-out fight over me.

Antonio shakes his head and closes his eyes, creasing intensely his forehead. He opens them and seems to again, make all attempts to soften the look - the rage only slightly resting in his eyes.

"Can you mount the horse yourself," he says. "I am not concerned with social graces right now. Just get on my horse and get away from here. Go to your brothers. Tell them where I am."

Antonio is already nudging me toward the horse before I can answer but I nod, fighting back the tears. I agree with him to get Robert and Jonathon. If I can make it to the house and tell them where Antonio is they might be able to prevent any harm coming to either of them.

Antonio pushes me away from him toward his horse that now stands only a few feet from the bank of the pond. I slip and catch myself on the reigns causing the horse to whinny and jerk his head up. I fumble through all the material of my dress and curse in my head at not being able to get my foot free to put it in the stirrup. I am about to give up on the horse and run back to the house when I feel myself being roughly hoisted into the saddle by Antonio.

"My dear brother!" Paulo is now standing up. "Did you come to cut in? I do not think I can give you permission."

Paulo's hand reaches across his body toward his sword.

Antonio pulls the reigns of the horse turning it toward the house. "YAH!" He slaps the back of the horse, which sends it running through the trees with me bent low to its neck, hanging on for my life.

The wind is cold against my cheeks. The horse either seems to know where it's going or is as scared as I am, because it does not slow its pace at any time. I grab the mane tighter between my fingers. The horse clears the trees in a matter of seconds and I see the house not more than a city block away.

I try to pull back on the reigns when I reach the house but the horse protests by jerking his head and trotting around in a circle. Robert is suddenly by my side pulling me off and Jonathon is grabbing the reigns to calm the horse. I see over Robert's shoulders Katherine and Rosemary standing on the steps with their hands over their mouths. Dillard is running out with three other men and quickly helps Jonathon control the horse.

"Antonio - Paulo - By the pond - Sword!" I say.

"Rosemary! Take her inside," Robert says; half pushing me to meet her as she runs out to me. She grabs me close and pulls me to the door where Katherine quickly takes my other side. I manage to look back over my shoulder before we pass the doorway and see Robert, Jonathon, Dillard, and three other men running into the trees toward the pond.

"Order tea," Katherine says to Rosemary.

They both shuffle me quickly into the parlor. I feel my body collapsing and my breathing quicken as I begin to realize the extent of the situation. A combination of my adrenaline pumping and the familiarity of Paulo, does not allow my mind to understand that I was very close to being assaulted by him. The men's reactions and the concerned looks of my sisters put it all in place. The tears begin flowing down my cheeks. Fear boils in the depths of my stomach rising up through my throat. I feel nauseous. Part of me wants to run back to where I left Antonio. The other part feels trapped having to wait for news of the outcome.

The tea comes and Rosemary pours it into the cups. She hands me one and I take it only out of desire to have something to do with my hands other than turning them over and around each other. Rosemary doesn't let go of the saucer and helps me steady the cup so I can take a sip.

"Clarissa, are you okay?" Katherine whispers into my ear. "Are you hurt? Did he do anything to you?"

All I can do is shake my head. I notice Katherine and Rosemary glancing back and forth at each other. They have concerned looks on their faces. Katherine occasionally glances behind her out the window. I find my voice only after a full cup of tea.

"After you left me, I walked down the path toward the pond."

Katherine gasps and covers her mouth with her fingertips.

"I didn't go to the bank, only to where the path begins to slope. Paulo came upon me from behind. He had been drinking."

Katherine and Rosemary each put an arm around my back. Rosemary pulls hers away.

"He asked me to dance then he took my hand and leaned in as if he was - he was losing his balance. Antonio shouted his name and he stumbled and fell to the ground. Antonio put me on the horse and told me to ride back to the house and tell Robert where he was. I saw Paulo draw his sword."

Katherine pulls me into her. Rosemary cups her hands burying her face inside them.

"He will be alright," Katherine says as she pats my head and strokes my hair. "Our husbands will be sure of that."

I feel the rush of tears but do nothing to stop them. "He is not armed," I say.

"Antonio knows the capabilities of his brother," Rosemary says. She places a hand on my upper arm and squeezes it gently. "You said Paulo was drunk. He will not be able to hold his sword strong enough to cause harm to any of the men."

I sit up from Katherine's embrace, pull my arm from Rosemary, and press my palms against my eyes to dry the tears. Rosemary jumps up from the couch and rushes to the window.

"The men have returned," she says.

I dart to the window and see Robert and Jonathon holding up Antonio between them. Antonio has his hand gripping his upper right arm. Blood is all over his shirt; dripping through his fingers.

"He's hurt!" I say and run to the door of the sitting room.

Katherine and Rosemary are close behind. I reach the entry hall just as the men walk in.

"To the library," Robert says turning Antonio away from me toward a door on the opposite end of the hall. I follow them into the library. They do not attempt to stop me. I hear Katherine behind me call for someone named Sheldon. I close the distance between Antonio and myself where they have seated him on the couch and fall to my knees in front of him. I look up into his eyes from underneath his jet-black hair that is full of sweat. It hangs over his face as he leans his head into his hand. I swiftly place my hand on top of his bloody fingers – he jerks away.

"How bad?" I say. "Antonio, how bad are you hurt?"

He looks up without moving his head and I see sadness in his eyes. Sadness, so close to death it overcomes me and sends a current of shivers throughout my body.

"My wound is nothing to the pain I am feeling in my heart," he says.

I open my mouth to ask him what that means but Jonathon pulls me up, and the middle-aged woman who answers the ring from my bedroom comes in. Katherine addresses her as Sheldon. She moves to Antonio and begins attending to his wound. I look anxiously around the room. No one attempts to tell me what has happened. No one will look at me.

I grit my teeth. "Please. Tell me what happened – where's Paulo?"

"Don't speak his name!" Antonio says.

I look at Robert who only shakes his head and puts up his hand.

"It has been dealt with Clarissa, you are safe now. Antonio must attend to his business sooner than expected. You will leave tomorrow."

He walks over to Rosemary and takes her hand. "You will need to go with them. I will come for you after I have helped Antonio with his affairs. Go pack your things. You all will leave at daybreak."

Jonathon bows his head toward me. Katherine and Rosemary begin to walk out of the room. I hesitate.

"Antonio … Please," I whisper. He hangs his head lower and turns away.

I walk toward the door. Before leaving the room, I turn back for one last glance. I catch him looking toward me before he drops his head back to the floor, his face is absent the rage I had seen earlier but it is replaced with sadness. I tilt my head to the side as the tears reach the cusps of my lids. I feel like the inside of my body is being torn to pieces, the pain so wrenching it must becoming physical. Antonio's sadness softens as his face begins to fade.

"No," I whisper.

The distant low hum of traffic rings in the back of my

thoughts.

"No." I try to take a step forward toward Antonio but the rest of the room begins to disintegrate with him and the image of my bed comes into focus. I drop the hand I reached toward Antonio by my side. Limp with an unknown feeling of loss so intense I cannot move. I don't want to move. I begin to shake my head side to side slowly, and then shake it faster.

"No! No, No, No," I say louder and louder standing next to my bed in my loft. "Antonio!" I cannot believe it. No. *This cannot be happening. This is not fair.*

I grab my pillow off the bed and throw it across the room, through the doorway. It lands on the kitchen table. It does nothing for the intense rage filling inside me. I grab my other pillow and throw it toward the couch. It knocks over a half bottle of wine turning the pillow purple. I yank the sheets off the bed, tugging, screaming, and dragging them to the top of the stairs. Then I throw them as hard as I can. As the sheets separate in flight, my frustration dissipates, falling onto several steps with the billowing sheets in slow motion.

"Reality sucks," I say. "Maybe I'm drinking too much."

I walk into my bathroom, shut the door, and turn on the shower. Stepping out of the heavy clothing of the Victorian era, I let the tears wash my face.

The shower does me a bit of good. I slip into my jeans thankful at least to have less material hanging on me, and then pull my favorite green sweater over my head. I am a bit more in touch with the present as I look over the half wall of my loft to the storefront floor. I cannot remember what day it is or time when I was last lost in the memory of my life with Antonio. I grimace at the thought and my heart feels like it is being carved in half.

I quickly walk downstairs and pull the *closed for inventory repairs* sign from under the register and hang it under the *closed* sign. The darkness of the night confuses me as the memory was of early morning. I tilt my head as I stare toward the streetlights along the wall of Central Park.

What day is it? I think.

I look over to the clock behind the register and according to it I have only been lost in thought for about half an hour if it is still the Wednesday after Thanksgiving. I force my mind to get back into the groove and remember where I had put my purse. After several minutes of looking for it I give up and gather up the sheets I had thrown. I put them in the washing machine and make my bed with a fresh pair of white sheets all the while wondering if time had passed simultaneously with the memory from the dress.

Stepping out to the kitchen it looks neglected and the bottle of wine that had fallen onto my pillow smells more like vinegar. I go to work cleaning up my loft, hoping it will keep my mind off Antonio and force myself closer to reality.

With my loft done, I walk downstairs with the pile of clothing I had picked out of the closet this morning in Antonio's world, cleaner, and gloves. I drop the pile on the bottom step and rub my eyes of unfelt sleep. Physically I am exhausted but my mind continues to play the last image of Antonio in my head. I dust every shelf, glass figurine, soap dish, picture tile, and every other trinket I sell in the store. I refold and stack the wall of sheets, color coordinating them with the highest thread count at the top of the rack to the lowest at the bottom. I remake the storeroom four-poster bed with fresh sheets and add several other pillows. I work on it well into midnight until I admit to myself that I am trying to make it look like my bed in Antonio's world - an impossible task without the order from Tuscany Textiles at least.

The cleaning done; I turn toward the stairs to put away the cleaner and gloves. Standing at the bottom of the first step, I stare at the clothing lying on the third step.

My body feels numb. A lump develops in my throat and the tears well up in my eyes. The cleaner and gloves fall to the floor when my knees give away underneath me.

"Why am I being so tormented?" I say.

My hands lay limp on the floor and my head falls back then I bring it forward until my chin is almost touching my chest.

"Antonio," I whisper. "I love you."

My thoughts answer back with my name in his voice. I sit there allowing my body to be open to the feelings rushing through it. When the anger rises to boiling point, I stand up and grab the pile of clothing off the step. Dragging it behind me, I walk into the storage room, open the armoire and throw it all inside.

"Here's your grave consequence," I say.

I slam the door with intentional force and walk out, not bothering to look back to see if the door had stayed shut, or reopened from the force I used in closing it.

I channel my angry energy to search for my phone and nearly rearrange the entire loft doing so. I finally find it in my purse under the register and check the date. It is now

Thursday after Thanksgiving. I put the phone back in my purse and lean over the counter staring out onto the storeroom floor, my thoughts again taking me to Antonio's world against my conscious will to block them out. Regardless of the effectiveness of sleep, I know I have to try. Reluctantly, I saunter up the stairs to my bed and collapse.

Unaware of how long it took me to sleep I awake to a knock on the door. Ignoring it I roll over and cover my head with a pillow. The knock continues. Groaning I roll out of bed and walk to the top of the stairs figuring it must be Lana. No one else would knock on a door with a closed sign. I bend low to see through the window above the door. The person's face is hidden by the sign. I start to walk back to my bedroom when the knock sounds again. Exasperated I stomp down the stairs. When I am two feet from the door, I see Paulo standing outside. He waves.

My stomach tightens and I feel the blood rush from my extremities to my heart in attempt to keep me from going into shock. I don't want to open the door but I know I must. Paulo is back.

The memory of his letter, my talks with Lana, and the shopping for the green dress all come forward in my thoughts suddenly. Paulo is standing with his arms outstretched, an exaggerated pout on his face.

I open the door and step aside for him to come in. He shakes fresh snowflakes off his shoulders as he saunters right pass me, slips off his coat and lays it on the counter. He does not attempt to even say hello or show any kind of attention. After locking the door behind him and turning around we are face-to-face. I become suddenly rigid but he does not seem to notice. He picks me up and spins me around.

Putting me down after several turns that leave me slightly dizzy, he kisses my forehead, both cheeks, and then goes to kiss my lips but I quickly pull away. The memory of my anger from his absence in calling, writing, or attempt to contact me in any way while he was gone is clear, pumping strong throughout my veins. He gives a confused look but keeps his arms around my waist. All too quickly, clarity seems to spread across his face and he smiles.

"You are angry with me," he says.

"Yes."

"But I am here now and I missed you Clarissa. Let us not waste our time being angry."

His accent is thicker than I remembered and I am barely able to understand his English. This is proof he was in Spain, speaking only Spanish for the last three weeks, but still doubt lingers. I'm not readily able to be so easily debunked.

I just smile and pull his arms away from my waist.

"How was your trip?" I say. "Is all your business taken care of in Spain? When will you begin working at your new job?"

Paulo follows me to the counter where we both lean against it side by side. I fold my arms and he adjusts his weight turning to face me, leaving one hand on the counter, his other hand in his pocket.

"Did you get my letter?" he asks.

"Yes."

"Then you know I have something I want to share with you."

"Yes."

"Will you join me for an early dinner?"

"What time is it?" I say standing in my pajamas.

Paulo laughs as he scans my clothing beginning at my feet then up to my neck. "New York time is a little after one o'clock. I am not sure what Clarissa time is." He raises an eyebrow.

"It's not dinner time," I say.

"You can call it breakfast if you want. I just flew in so it is the middle of the night for me. We still need to eat, no?" He forces his accent that I barely understand his words but the meaning is received without confusion.

"Sure," I say. You can wait upstairs or come back but I'm going to take a shower."

Paulo puts an arm around me. "I will wait as long as you want," he says and then nudges me to the stairs.

After my quick shower, we leave out the front door and begin to automatically walk to our favorite restaurant, *Patatas Bravas.* We fall back into sync with our cadence in small talk except for my unnerving feeling I have cheated on him. Over the continued superficial conversation while eating my mind recognizes his prolonging of the important news he wants to tell me. There is no mention of the letter since he asked if I got it. I try several times to steer him down the path of breaking it off, the inevitable direction a letter like that must go, but he will not follow.

When our dinner is cleared, I put my elbows on the table and lean my chin on my hands. I look him straight in the eyes, which makes him look down.

"Paulo," I say.

He looks up, "Clarissa."

"What is the news you want to share with me?" I say.

He sighs and glances over to the couple seated at the table closest to us.

"Clarissa, I have enjoyed your company. Our dates were wonderful -"

"But," I say.

"You do not know the true identity of your soul, even in my company."

The soul thing again, I think.

I can assume a little more, now that I met Antonio, that if Paulo means the connection between two people as in a soulmate, he doesn't feel like mine. Antonio is my match, the connection so strong that his image is constantly in my head but he is not real - doesn't exist. Paulo is the closest thing to it, I don't want to give up on something real - there may be potential.

Paulo looks down. I refuse to answer wanting him to explain where he wants this soul thing to go.

"I cannot love someone who does not return the passion," he says. "You cannot see your soul."

My eyebrows crease. This is definitely a new way of breaking off a relationship. "What?" I say.

Paulo takes a breath and puts his hand on the table palm up. I place mine in his.

"Do you feel anything ... in your soul when you touch my hand?" he says.

I tilt my head. Paulo looks at the edge of the table then back at me. "You are not searching. Whether it is dreams or a vice, you have not found a way to search and may be lost. I cannot misguide you in that."

"Misguide me? In my search for what?" I say.

"The other half ... of your soul."

Almost immediately, as Paulo says those words the image of Antonio stealing a kiss on my cheek as he whispers good-bye on Christmas day in his era defines my other half. I shake my head trying to regain the present – hold on to what is real.

"You are a beautiful and intriguing woman," he says. "You deserve to find your other half. If I take up your time I may take away your chance at finding your other half or recognizing a desire to search for it."

This break off is so romantic that it actually makes me desire him more. Emotions that I feel for him came back to me in my desperation to have a love that exists in physical form.

"You don't love me?" I say.

"I do but I cannot continue because my love may cloud your search," he says.

"You love me but don't think I love you ... so you are breaking it off with me so I can search ... for my other half ... to find love?"

Paulo laughs slightly, tilts his head to one side then slowly shakes it. "Yes. That is about right. You will find love, Clarissa."

"And this is the way it has to be?"

Paulo nods. I take my hand from his and fold mine together under the table.

"You wouldn't want to keep seeing me until I find love?"

"I will not take your time that way. You must begin your search," he says.

"What if I said I was in love with you?"

Paulo scrunches his napkin in his fist tight on the table and stares at it. "I did not want that. I cannot love you Clarissa, not before you have begun your search."

I lean down and grab my purse from the floor. "I think we should go," I say.

The snow turns to rain when we leave the restaurant. I opt to walk, forcing Paulo to abandon the warmth of a cab and walk with me. I am more surprised than hurt from all my preparation, not to mention his attempt to assault me in Antonio's world also festers a bit of hatred toward him. The walk is only a couple blocks and through Central Park but we are both drenched with rain by the time we reach the other side of the park.

When we arrive at my boutique I am wet and cold. I notice how unnaturally quiet the street is, making it seem as though the world is asleep and we are all that is awake.

"Must it be this way?" I ask.

He looks down at me. The rain falling from his hair looks like tears in the city lights.

"You cannot see my soul ... or yours," he says. "I know that now and I cannot hurt you."

I close my eyes to catch the tears welling up to the edges.

He sighs and sways his head off to the side then back. He wipes the rain off his face with his hands. I watch the drops bounce off my shoe. One of my own tears falls between two raindrops.

"You are getting wet," he says. "Give me your keys and let me take you inside."

"I'd rather not," I say. "I want to see you walk away. It will be better for me … to start forgetting you."

He grabs the back of his neck and rubs it. "I do not ask you to forget me. If you understood your soul -" He squints and pulls his lips together. "If it must be this way … the least I can do is to obey your last request."

He kisses my rain-drenched forehead and turns quick on his heels. He walks toward *Shot of Joe* where we had met. He doesn't look back - he never does.

I turn and place the key in the knob, open the door, then lock it behind me. Once inside I pull off my coat letting it drop to the floor. Slowly walking toward the stairs, I glance over at the storeroom entrance. I pause - the clothing is in there. I can put it on and it might take away all my pain. I can remember again a time when I was in love with someone who loved me also. Maybe a new dress will be hanging like the last time and Antonio is healed. I can press my cheek against his shoulder as he holds my arm in his or put my head against his chest and feel his heartbeat.

I sigh and it ripples out of my nose with the hiccups of holding back my tears. I have to resist the urge; it is the past - maybe the memory of my soul. Paulo wanted me to remember the identity of my soul - how is it more than who I am today?

I resist the urge and continue up the stairs to my loft apartment. Flopping onto my bed without changing out of my clothes or brushing my teeth, I listen to the rain on the roof; until the drowsiness overcomes me and I am just another

REYES

person asleep in the night.

FRIENDSHIP

The morning sun of springtime flows through my small bedroom window. It warms my cheeks, waking me softly. The smell of its heat burning the steel garbage bins in the alleyway seeps through the rip in my screen – I'm thankful tomorrow it will be picked up. My dreams last night were uneventful and bringing no gratification to my morning stretch. It was another night I needed them to take me to some happier place. The season of bridal registry brings with it vivid memories of Antonio. Before the armoire was left in my alley, the thought of marrying someone I hardly knew was out of the question. Now, I will sprint down the aisle and rush through the presumptuous verbiage just to lay my lips against Antonio's. I miss him.

Springtime seems to burst out everywhere and through everything. The trees across the street at the entrance of the park are in full bloom. Women are walking in and out of shops; flaunting the newest sundresses and heals, while men in shorts and t-shirts flip their shades to wink at them.

With spring come weddings. The side effect to them brings out into public eye the recently wedded couples and the birth of new relationships. Kissing under the trees, picnics in the park, and bridal registry at my shop – nauseating. Unfortunately I found my love in a memory of an old armoire and so I am forced to endure couples daily, by the handful, coming in to pick out sheets and accessories from my boutique. The sexual innuendos fly about the storeroom and the guys, so in love, they spend an hour in my store just to be with their fiancé – laughing at the innuendos. I am tormented daily about being single, forced to witness first hand successes in love.

I admit to myself with each passing hour of the day that I need to be busy. Bridal registry season fulfills this need enough to keep some of my thoughts occupied with something other than Antonio's image.

I have resisted the armoire's temptation successfully since Paulo left me. To endure another breakup - I don't want to know if Antonio came to find me. His eyes were fierce the last time I saw them and he had made up his mind to choose my reputation instead of the rest of his life with me.

I was unintentionally successful in dodging Lana's work parties - my dress was lost in Antonio's world. I tried excuse after excuse and was finally officially of the hook when she settled on her own conclusion that I had returned the dress. Sadly, I also lost Lana in my attempt to conceal the truth. Following my last memory of the armoire I lost in the short time of a few hours, a fiancé, a boyfriend, and the most real person of my current messed up illogical existence; my best friend, Lana. My record of failed relationships in any period of time was officially broken, and since then I have been mentally numb.

It has been three months since Lana and I had a girl's night – I could really use one this time of year. For all I know, Lana might be one of these springtime lovers. I try to call … many times … but Lana never picks up … never returns my messages. I have hurt her - the guilt has sat in the pit of my stomach since December.

My numbness, although useful and keeps me from new relationships, is not thick enough to forget Antonio entirely. The recent intrusions into my thoughts of his deep blue eyes underneath his black sweaty strands of hair only increase with time. Some nights it is so intense I drink a full bottle of wine just to relax enough to sleep.

Over time I do, internally and silently, admit to myself that what I feel for Antonio is real, even if he is only an image of a past memory ... possibly of my soul. There is no other explanation. My soul, however minimally religious that I am, is begging to connect with his.

The armoire does not cease in its power to call to me. Every time I enter the back storage area I feel compelled to open it, put on the dress, and run to Antonio. I cannot bring myself to do it because I fear rejection, and the pain of the possibility that Antonio did not come for me.

My days are spent tending to customers, looking from time to time through the storefront window. I long for Antonio to walk by so much that it now causes physical stomach cramps. Some days I think I see him watching me from across the street. His image quickly vanishes of course, with the passing of a car or question from a customer. I am convinced I will never find that passion again, unless I relinquish to the draw of the armoire.

Another night passes with sleepless dreams. I lay in bed thinking about the armoire - my mind keeping me from sleep. I sigh and roll over to drag myself out of bed. There is no reason to fight the memories or the emotional desire. Numbness is not working. Of all the available men in New

York, it can't be my destiny to fall in love with a man only accessible in the memories triggered by old clothing.

Half walking, half dragging myself downstairs to the storefront, I pull the *Closed for new inventory stocking* sign from under the counter and clip it to the *Closed* sign. I could lose one day of business. Monday is not an especially busy day for my boutique.

I glance across the street looking for Antonio, I squint to focus in hope of making out an object or figure in the morning sunlight that might resemble him. Nothing. My stomach tightens with a cramp. I walk to the back of the store and peek into the storage room. I can open it today.

I shake off the memory forming in my thoughts and half run upstairs. Coffee will do me good ... a shower will do me good. I groan loudly. Getting out of New York will do me good! I fumble through my morning routine, hoping for it to somehow make me forget.

The air is fresh and warm as I step out onto the sidewalk. I keep my head down weaving in and out of couples holding hands. The last thing I need is to make eye contact with one of them and be subjected to the love. I roll my eyes and groan.

Shot of Joe is harder to maintain my solitary walk. It is loud, bustling, and ... cheerful. The man with the rainbow wardrobe has two girls today. A brunette on one arm and an unnatural blond with dark roots on the other.

"Iced Latte!" the cashier says.

"One shot?" the barista says.

"One Shot!"

"Coffee!" The café bursts into an uproar of laughter

after the simultaneous shout.

The high-pitched voices and cheerful music blends well with the sun outside, pushing at my miserable outlook on life. I force a happier expression to my face, just to fit in, and order my usual.

I don't linger or make any attempt to let the mood of the coffee shop change mine. I am somewhat comfortable in my self-pity. I feel as though I need a day of 'poor me' to make up for one of the days I was numb or distracted by work. It would be more fun with Lana and a bottle of wine. It is time I go to her apartment and beg forgiveness.

Bring a sleeping bag. I say to myself. She is a very determined woman and I may be camping out at her doorstep for a few days before she lets me in.

The barista calls my name; I take my coffee, and walk, head down, back to my boutique. The day passes slowly. I watch sitcom reruns and soap operas. Eventually evening comes and the streets fill with more couples.

I sit at my kitchen table looking over the half wall of my loft. The tears flow down my cheeks but I do not attempt to wipe them away.

"I need this," I say.

I must let the pain fill me and numb me again. Then I can move on. After three hours of staring into space on the couch, I go to bed.

In the middle of the night, I wake up to my mind racing and physically restless. I want to open the armoire.

Happiness Clarissa. I deserve happiness.

I get out of bed and throw on my jeans, a shirt, and grab a sweater from the closet at the top of the stairs. I also grab the sleeping bag just in case. Lana's friendship not only makes me happy but she keeps me sane.

Outside my boutique, I hail a cab and give him the address to Lana's apartment. I sit back and rehearse my speech. It will have to be quick so I can get as much out as I can before she slams the door on me. Aside from a puppy dog pout, my mind is drawing blanks in way of a pathetic speech. There is nothing that can explain what happened to the dress she bought me and if the conversation goes in that direction, Lana will be lost forever.

The cab ride seems a lot shorter than I remember and I settle on the puppy dog pout and "I'm sorry. I miss you," for my speech.

I pay the cab driver with a small tip and he speeds off, nearly catching my sleeping bag in the door as he pulls away from the curb.

Lana's corporate job allows her to live in a high society building on the other end of Central Park from my boutique. I get a look from the doorman as I enter with my sleeping bag tucked under my arm.

I press the button on the elevator and wait for it to come down from the 21st floor. I feel on the back of my neck the security guy watching me from his desk. He clears his throat with a small cough and I respectfully turn in response. He is no stranger to me, being that he is the same security guard that has been on duty most of the nights we return from the bars

"She'll be glad to see you," he says. "I'll be thankful when she doesn't yell at me just for saying have a nice day." The security guard goes back to his book.

The elevator door opens and I walk in with more hope but moist hands. I rub my hand against my jeans then press the button for the 9th floor. My breath is unsteady and I prepare myself for a door slam.

Being the middle of the night on a weekday might sabotage this whole plan. I reach out to press the 8th floor button, get out, and take the stairs back down but the number 9 lights up on the panel above the door. I get out. The doors shut behind me.

I peer down the hall to the right.

First door on the left. My breathing becomes short and shallow.

The familiarity of the hallway calms me, as it seems so recent I was last here. I knock. Silence. I knock again a little harder. Again silence. I knock four times at once as hard as I can without hurting my knuckles. Still there is silence on the other side of the door.

She must be passed out. I am about to pound on the door with the side of my fist, when I hear movement behind it. The sound of bolt locks being turned causes my heart to race.

All or nothing and right now I have nothing so here it goes. The door opens slowly. When I see Lana's eyes I push my face into a puppy dog pout.

"I'm sorry. I miss you. I will camp out until you forgive me," I say.

Lana looks down at my sleeping bag then closes the door but doesn't slam it. I stand here waiting. The door opens again and she pulls me inside locking me into a big hug.

"Don't ever make me ignore you like that again!" She

says. She tightens her grip until I can barely breathe with my head in her chest.

She is taller and the embrace is getting considerably uncomfortable since she is only wearing a disheveled camisole with one strap half off her shoulder. I push away and regain my breath.

"I said I missed you, not that I'm in love with you. That was a little close to bare chest," I say.

Lana laughs, grabbing me by the wrist and yanking me over to the couch.

"You came on the perfect night. I'm ditching work tomorrow … bad day," she says. She wipes some of the sleep from her eyes.

I listen to her pour out the bad day, as it becomes a release of anything we would have vented over our take-out and wine from *Antipasti*. It includes everything, even the Christmas parties I missed but the whereabouts of the dress never comes up.

I smile or nod at the right times, almost falling asleep. Now that I am forgiven and have my best friend back, half of my anxiety is dumped and the buried exhaustion is now surfacing. When she finishes her story it is almost three in the morning. She looks at me; her face is serious.

"What did ever happen to that dress? You looked great in it," she asks.

I am shocked out of my sleepiness with the exact subject I want to prevent. I take in a deep breath and grab at the obvious, hoping that time has healed her first reactions to any reason.

"Nothing happened to it," I say. "I just didn't want to

go to the Christmas parties without a date. Remember, I was going through that thing with Paulo?"

Lana nods with her lips pulled inward.

"I didn't want to ruin your parties with my moodiness," I say. I bend my head low and look up at her from underneath my brow.

"So you still have the dress?" she says.

I nod my head but blink to avoid her immediate stare. She knows me too well.

"Do I need to see it to prove you aren't lying to me?" she says.

"Does my explanation sound like me?" I say. I turn toward her and cross my legs tight to prevent any emotion coming out on my face and stare back at her, my eyes focusing on the tip of her nose.

Lana smiles. "Yes. Very much like you. Sorry I forced the parties on you. This year you come only if you have a date."

I smile back and uncross my legs. "Deal," I say. I take her mug to the kitchen and pour us both a second cup of the coffee she brewed during her venting tirade, about an hour ago. "You really are more like a sister to me," I say.

"Taller sister, but technically younger," she says and follows me into the kitchen.

"So as a sister ..." I say. "I need to tell you something."

Lana tilts her head and leans against the counter. It comes only to her hip whereas it cuts me at the waist. I lean both arms on it with my cup between my hands. "In the worst case scenario, you will be the first person by my side, right?"

I say.

She pounds her fist down. "Damn straight I'd be," she says.

"So … it would be best for you to know that if I am ever on life support I want you to pull the plug." I look her straight in the eyes.

Lana's mouth drops open. She takes a full ten seconds or so to close her mouth and regain her voice.

"Can you tell me where this is coming from?" she says.

I can't tell her about the memories of the armoire but if my body was ever in a comatose state, I would be forever trapped and unable to remember Antonio again. I believe now the memories were from a past life of my soul and an escape from this life might bring me back to him. Lana isn't religious and right now isn't a good time to tell her I found love in a guy that exists only in my head, so I lie.

"I saw a really bad accident about a month ago," I say, making the story up as I go. "I don't think the people made it. It got me thinking about worse case scenarios and since my family is all on the west coast …" I focus on a spec of her granite counter. "I thought of you being the first and maybe last person to see me alive. I thought you should know what I want." I raise my head up to see her.

Lana blinks her eyes and I can see the tears welling up. She takes a breath.

"Okay. No life support. Pull plug on Clarissa. Got it." She nods her head as she blinks away the tears. "No more discussion on this topic, okay?" she says then puts out her hand for me to shake.

"Okay." I shake her hand.

We spend the rest of the day together in her apartment talking. When the sun starts setting I get up to leave saying she should get ready to go back to work tomorrow. She walks with me to the elevator and commits me to Friday night girl's night.

"You bring the take out. I'll have the wine," I say.

I see Lana waving as the elevator door closes.

CONTE VINEYARDS

I am exhausted from staying up all night and talking all day. I wash my face and change into my shorts and tank top pajamas, flop face down onto the bed and expect sleep to take over immediately. I am wrong. The minute my head hits the pillow the image of Antonio on Christmas day comes into the forefront of my thoughts.

I remember the feel of the heat from his breath on my nose and his hands wrapped around mine. I stare into the deep blue of his eyes, his jet-black hair is brushed back and his lips are turning up in a smile. Then suddenly his eyes turn a fierce deathly shade of blue and His hair is sweaty and hanging over his face. His breath is ice. I push myself up by the arms hitting the bed with my fists. The torment of my own mind causes me to feel trapped and the curiosity of what happens next in the last memory won't let me rest.

I walk downstairs, turn toward the storeroom and stop. I know what I expect and close my eyes to avoid the temptation. *I really should go back to bed.*

With eyes still closed, I think about the ball and dancing with Antonio. My heart physically hurts and I feel a shortness of breath. I clutch at the pain rising in my stomach as my mind changes the image to the blood on Antonio's arm. I take a deep breath, walk back out to the storeroom and lean over the counter for support in calming myself. I lay my head down and let the tears flow in silence, they drip, making a small puddle on the counter. The seconds seem to slow and the air around me feels dense.

The distant sound of a piano playing breaks through the thickness in the air. It is a classical piece I have not heard before. I open my eyes and look around the store. There is no one and the radio is not on but I can still hear the music. For nothing but the sweetness of the song and how it makes me feel I don't try to shake it out of my head. Instead, I walk around the counter to the floor and put out my hand as if Antonio has just asked me to dance. I walk a few steps then curtsey and again reach out my hand. Dancing now, alone in my boutique, my invisible partner, who I imagine is Antonio, comes close to me in a step and I am reminded of his smell.

It is comforting, familiar, and grows in strength - I stop. The music has ceased, and it is exactly then I feel the breath on my neck and his voice in my ear.

"Put the dress on," he says.

I whip my body around, only to see the storefront window and the city nightlife passing outside. I am still alone.

I run to the back of the storage area, every breath telling me I will find Antonio waiting to finish the dance once the dress is on. The passion I will again be able to feel ignites the excitement to hold him again and pushes me faster in my step.

I come to an abrupt, breathless, standstill at the armoire, my fingers barley touching the carved wooden rose knob. I am frozen by the collision of every emotion I have felt about Antonio in my head but my fingers tingle with excruciating curiosity.

Open the door.

My knees buckle and I drop to the floor, head in hands, tears bursting from the lower folds of my eyes, but suddenly free from my numbness. I curl into a ball on the floor and sob, uncontrollably.

"That world does not exist!" I say.

Sitting up on my knees, the anger consumes me, these emotions have gone on too long and I have to stop thinking about Antonio, leave the memories behind.

I can do this, I have Lana now, and I will be okay.

I shout again, even louder out of my determination to make his image stay out of my thoughts. "That world does not exist! You are only a memory of the past!" I cry, shout again through my tears, and then I sleep, on the storage room floor of my boutique.

When I open my eyes in the early morning, I pass off the events of the night before as exhaustion and a broken heart. I justify those emotions by telling myself I am coming down with the flu.

I pick myself up; walk out to the storefront, and up to my loft to get dressed. Mechanically completing my morning routine step-by-step, my thoughts stray to Antonio unconsciously.

Coffee will divert my attention. The shouting at *Shot of Joe* will keep me from fading too far into my thoughts. Purposefully I half run across the storeroom floor in a rush to immerse myself in reality but the morning sun shining through the window nearly slows me down. The effect of the light on the four-poster bed in the front window begs me to rest and lose myself in thoughts of Antonio. I ignore it and close the door harder than intended with my conscious resistance to the memory of him.

Shot of Joe is crowded as usual, vibrant and loud, owing to the weekday offering a more rushed pace to the call of drinks.

"Coffee, Latte, and Latte!" the cashier says.

"One Shot?" the barista says.

"Straight up, one shot, three shots!"

"Coffee!" The café shout drowns in the chaos.

A strong odor of used coffee beans sitting out on a back counter breaks through the steam from the espresso machine in various intervals of breezes. Looking around the room, the hurried pace of customers and drone of voices pull me far from the memories of Antonio. I let myself flow from one absent thought to another as I wait in line and listen in on the conversations or bickering about work around me. My reluctant submission to the real world allows my thoughts to stray to events I have ignored since the holidays.

I remember the time I had met Paulo and his accent. The table where he sat with me is now occupied by three women that look to be of college age. Their mannerisms and smiles lure me gently away from the thought of Paulo and satisfy a desire to drift until it is my turn to order.

"Good Morning." The cashier smiles but his brow is creased. "The usual today? Any extra shots?" He begins to punch something into the register before I answer.

"Your choice," I say.

"Latte!" he says.

"One shot?" the barista says without lifting his head.

"Two!" The cashier's mouth forms into a smirk as he

glances up at me.

"Coffee!" everyone says but I frown at the cashier.

Passive aggressive vengefulness. I think to myself.

I hand him a twenty. He's having a bad morning and our Oregon Duck commonality does not seem to count. The cashier hands me the change, the smile still on his face, and I move to the side to await my latte, eavesdropping again on conversations. When the barista shouts out my name, I take the coffee off the counter and walk out – no reason for me to stay. On my way back to my boutique, I self-debate about opening for the day. Business is always good in the spring, closing another day will not hurt, but I am probably losing some good registry lists.

I pause at the traffic light and somewhat forcefully, the woman behind me nudges me to cross. I move to the side and she passes with a sideways glance and a throw of her head. Today, it doesn't bother me - anything to keep me in reality. I hold my latte close to my lips with both hands and proceed across the street. Arriving at my boutique, I pause before putting the key in the keyhole and sense that someone is watching me from across the street. I think of how I heard Antonio's voice in my head last night. I look into the glass of the boutique door at a bad reflection of the street behind me. A gust of wind comes up and I hear Antonio's voice again, "put on the dress."

"No." I say, startling myself, and turn around to make sure no one heard me.

I open the door quickly and lock it behind me, shutting off the sound of the street outside. Without putting down my purse or latte, I walk to the back of the store, grabbing a folding chair on my way. The armoire stands as if with a personality, the old wood smirking down upon me. I unfold my chair, let my purse fall of my shoulder, and sit down right in front of the armoire, my knees together and my feet apart. I press the latte to my lips with both hands. Slowly sipping the latte, I stare at the armoire.

The dress is in there. That is fact. I take a sip. *I put on the dress and no longer can anything be proven by fact. Maybe it is not fact, but faith ... I must believe.* I drink my latte slow and deliberate until I reach the last sip. *Determination. That's what I need.*

I sigh holding the empty paper cup on my thigh. "And a little sanity."

I put down the cup and the cardboard sleeve slips to the cement floor.

I stand up and firmly place my hands on the wooden rose knobs then pull. I look straight into the armoire. A dress is hanging. Pressed and hanging on a satin hanger. It is not the pile of clothing I had thrown in from my last memory, nor the green dress, but instead one of the original four dresses.

I take it in my hand and carry it out to the storeroom. The cloth is the smoothest cotton I had ever felt between my fingers. The color, or the absence of color, make the dress elegant. It is cream, like that of an antique wedding dress. I hold it up to me and look in the standing mirror next to the four-poster bed. I cannot help feeling compelled to put it on and dance as I had the night before.

With little consideration to anyone who may be passing by, I step behind the floor mirror and slip into the dress. It fits to my body like visible air. Caressing every curve and smoothing any blemish. When I move, the dress follows like leaves in a wind current on their way down to the ground. I feel elegant, confident, and even more beautiful than I ever did in the green dress. My attention entangles with the sway of the dress, the style is not that of the Victorian era, but more modern. It signifies an era of independence amongst women, hanging to just below my knees; the sewn-in sash around my upper thighs. The sleeves are short but loose, draping over my shoulders to an inch or two down my arm, the neckline is low, but not so low that it is indecent. A sash of material is tied loosely in a bow at the point of the neckline.

Enough time has passed while observing the dress to notice nothing has happened. Nothing has gone out of focus and there has been no change to my boutique.

I walk slowly over to the four-poster bed and sit down. I feel deflated as I wait sitting on the corner. I lean my head against one of the post and watch the people passing by.

I am there for the duration of the morning and long into the afternoon, only shifting slightly to ease the tingle of my legs or arms from falling asleep, but I never get up. Memories of my time with Antonio flow in and out of my thoughts along with meaningless observations of the people passing by. The return to vintage style is more prominent than I remember.

The haze of dusk now falling to the pavement casts a surreal look upon the people outside. Focusing closer on each individual as they pass I am amazed how not one takes notice of me in the window – as though I am invisible.

The women appear to be arm in arm with a man in a suit, nonetheless. The suits reflect the early to mid-nineteen twenties, the women who do walk by alone, step with determination and wear similar twenties fashion. Little change, if any, is visible in my boutique, but outside, everything is different – from the past.

My growling stomach pushes at my thoughts and I hear a modern semi-truck horn in the far distance.

There it is. Proof Antonio was a product of my imagination.

I have been accused of vivid imagery as a child, often daydreaming at inappropriate times according to my teachers. Yet this revelation does not change the world outside. Despite the sound of the modern horn, the era of the twenties moves about outside my boutique window.

With a growing frustration to understand the armoire and determination to debunk what I see outside, I walk to the storefront door, open it, and step out.

I'm almost knocked over by a young man who grabs my arm just before I hit the ground.

"Oh gosh! My apologies," he says. "Can you ever forgive me for being late? Your coat, where is it, I will get it for you."

I am unable to speak. His green eyes look into mine - they are so familiar. He is so close that I can smell fresh mint on his breath. He appears to know me somewhat intimately, but I cannot follow why or who this might be. Biding for time I look toward the storeroom, "Um, inside. The hook behind the register." I say.

Looking over to the register as I speak, something

green dangles off the same hook I usually hang my coat.

"Good," he says. "I will fetch it for you. Come inside before you catch cold."

As he moves quickly around the register, he calls back to me, "You were not going to go alone were you? Independent you are but I do not believe you have it in you to show alone ..."

He returns with a green velvet coat and wraps it around my shoulders.

"Or were you looking forward to publicly declaring my absence to Antonio. This is the only coat hanging is it the one you wanted? We are a bit late," he says.

"Ah ... yes ... Antonio will be there?" I say.

The guy laughs. He starts nudging me toward the door. "Of course! Oh ... cold feet, I understand now. No worries, my sisters will be there."

I am thoroughly confused. I can only conclude that this is another lifetime where I have found Antonio but the phrase 'cold feet' from this guy and 'dinner' give two contradictory messages. I turn to the guy just before leaving the store.

"Will I present well?" I say.

The guy steals a prolonged glance from my feet to my head and then pulls up a corner of his mouth. He takes a deep breath in through his nose and the one corner becomes a full smile.

"Come on, we are late," he says.

I push down at the material around my thighs as the guy walks out first through the door. I check to make sure the door is secured before he grabs my wrist and pulls me behind him to a waiting car a few feet from the store front door. I did not remember hearing the car pull up previously. He helps me into the passenger seat then walks around and gets in to sit beside me. The car is cream in color with red leather seats and the top is down. My knowledge of cars in the modern world is horrid and aside from this one looking like something out of a silent movie, the make and model are unknown to me.

The guy talks incessantly and excitedly. I try to keep up, grasping at words for any clue to explain my attire. We seem to be so close, but not in a romantic way.

The car leaves the city and is soon teetering at a fast rate on a dirt road. I recognize where I am supposed to be but no homes, suburbs, or buildings of familiarity confirm my hunch. The drive continues for what feels like half an hour and all I can think about is the desire to be in a car with a more comfortable seat. The swaying causes me to bump the shoulders of the gentleman, which he does not appear to mind at all. At times it causes him to smile or laugh.

"Ah here we are," the guy says.

I look out past him and see over a valley of vineyards, a villa with three separate red tile rooftops.

"Smile, it makes you look ravishing," he says.

The car comes to a steady but abrupt stop at the front gate of the villa. We exit separately. In front of the gate I roughly count four people, standing in a not-so-formal line of welcome, which I assume is for my arrival. I desperately look for Antonio as I stand on the wide running board of the car. With a sigh I look to the ground, stepping off disappointed, but when I raise my head Antonio is standing in front of me.

He is looking down, making eye contact, and I notice his shade of blue is brighter than my memory had recalled.

"I am sorry for having to send my brother," he says. "You are a beautiful site. Come ... let me introduce you to my family."

I do not lunge at him as my body begs me to do but instead I quietly follow his lead and walk with him toward the people standing at the front gate.

He keeps his arm firmly around my waist. His smile pushes his cheeks upward as he guides me down the line of people.

"My dear mother, Rosario," he says and gently pushes me into her embrace.

Rosario hugs me tight then pulls out of the embrace leaving both her hands on my shoulders.

"It is good my Antonio finally brings me home a beautiful lady." She looks at Antonio with a frown. "There have been many other women I promptly tell him to throw back into the ocean."

I widen my eyes for Antonio to see. He shrugs his shoulders then pulls me back to his side.

"She means well," he says.

Antonio turns back to his mother who quickly throws her hands out as if to pull me into another embrace

"Oh yes, yes, you look delightful," she says. "I am just an old woman who has been deprived of seeing this creature that has made my Antonio so happy."

Antonio laughs as he guides me to the next person.

"My father, Señior Roberto Conte," he says. His body stiffens with a raise of his chin and he narrows his stance.

I crease my eyebrows slightly at the last name. It is different from our last time together. The era has also changed, obvious in the fashion and the closeness to which Antonio holds me. This gives me hope.

Antonio's father is similar in height to him, maybe only an inch shorter. His black hair is streaked with grey and his face is weathered dark olive, giving an appearance of much time spent in the sun. It is his father's eyes that hold my gaze. They are Antonio's eyes but Roberto has the intensity of wisdom. Antonio's eyes have the excitement of youth. His father appears in all his physical stature to be stern but fair. He takes the pipe from his mouth with one hand and stretches out the other.

"Miss Clarissa Debough," he says. I take his hand and give my firmest handshake.

My new last name gives me the flare of a debutant and I automatically stand up straighter when Antonio's father says it. The first touch of Roberto's hand confirms my first impression of hard work in the sun. It is rough and dry. He looks me in the eye and does not quickly release his grip.

"Welcome to our vineyard," he says.

"It is nice to meet you," I say.

Rosario release my hand with a nod.

Antonio continues to lead me down the line and I am introduced to his two sisters, Sofia and Maria. Their faces show a difference in age with Maria being the younger, but not by much. They look close to my own age of twenty-five years. Both sisters have the deep blue eyes of Antonio and Roberto.

Antonio turns sharply around and points to my driver.

"And you know my brother Paulo of course," he says.

I nod with a very slight smile but inside I tighten at the awkward presence and my breath stops immediately. This guy does not look like Paulo at all, aside from having his green eyes but I wonder if it is him from a life past - the reason he keeps showing up in these memories. I also wonder if his questions about the identity of my soul has to do with him remembering these same images.

Paulo laughs at my slight smile attempting to hide my grimace at my own thoughts. He lunges forward yanking me away from Antonio and spinning me around.

"I just wish I had found you first, Clarissa," he says. He almost drops me to the ground.

Antonio steadies me and forces a laugh.

I scowl. *You did find me,* I think to myself.

"You can call her a sister, Paulo. I expect you to give her the respect of a sister. That includes your manners," Antonio says.

Paulo laughs again and passes by Antonio. He grabs each of his sisters, pulling them into his sides in an embrace and heads away from the gate toward the villa.

"The fact that you question my manners is appalling, Antonio. I am but the best brother in this family to my sisters!"

His sisters laugh as they playfully fight his embrace. They both, eventually, are freed when Paulo lets go and they run ahead into the house. Maria turns toward Paulo and sticks out her tongue before disappearing into the archway of the villa entry.

The gate at which we stand is on a hillside. It extends

to the left and right, enclosing the Spanish style villa that is a few yards from the gate down the hillside. The vineyards are visible under the glow of the moonlight from where we stand and it appears to roll over two other hillsides.

Antonio leads me toward the main house. It is a brown stucco two-story home with an entryway made of large wooden arch doors. The handles are black iron and appear quite heavy. Two double glass doors are open onto a balcony and I can just barely make out a four-poster bed with white sheets, under the dim candle light in the room.

Antonio and I follow his sisters and brother into the main house. His father and mother follow behind. I glance over my shoulder and see his parents walking side by side. Roberto has his arm around Rosario, his other hand holding the pipe to the corner of his mouth. He is leaning into her and she is smiling back at him. Just before I turn back, Rosario lets out a small laugh and quickly covers her mouth, hiding her smile.

Once in the house, Antonio releases his embrace around my lower back, takes my hand and guides me toward another set of double glass doors on the other side of the room.

"Come on. I want to show you the courtyard," he says.

We walk through the doors into a courtyard covered in pea gravel with burnt orange slab stone pathways. The patio glows from large iron cast oil lanterns. In the center of the courtyard is a large rectangular wooden table that looks like it could easily seat twenty people and sturdy enough to hold an elephant. The chairs around the table are mismatched but create a comfortable old world look. The one at the end where we now stand is the only armchair. I figure that one to be his father's chair.

The main house encloses the courtyard behind us and to each side is an identical smaller house. They seem to be miniature replicas of the main house on the outside. Straight across the courtyard is a stucco wall with a door in the middle. Above the wooden door the stucco wall makes an arch leaving about two feet of space at the top. The courtyard also contains a raised brick grill that shows signs of regular outdoor cooking.

Grape vines climb the pillars that hold up the balconies of each house along the edge of the courtyard. The candles decorating the table are melted halfway from previous use with black strips of smoke rising from the tips of their flames. A hint of burning oil floats on the slight breeze that sporadically rustles the leaves of the vines. Antonio watches me as I look around the courtyard taking it all in.

"Do you like it?" he says.

"It's beautiful," I say. "Where does the door lead?"

"I'll show you," Antonio says and takes my hand into his.

The pea gravel crunches beneath my feet as we walk through it, the sound alone beckons to slow my step and take in every detail.

Once we reach the gate, Antonio places his palm against it. He looks down into my eyes, leans in, and smiles secretly.

"Close your eyes," he whispers.

I obey. The wooden door creaks slowly as he opens it then ceases as Antonio takes both my hands in his.

"Okay, do not open them yet," he says.

I sense Antonio move around and walk behind me, putting both his hands on my shoulders.

"Mira," he says. I understand the Spanish word for 'look.'

I open my eyes, and in front of me are grape vines as far as I can see, spreading down the hillside aglow under the moonlight in the sky above. The ground beneath my feet covered in grass, sparkles bright green, begging to be touched.

Between the rows of vineyards, the ground is compressed dirt, showing signs of foot traffic. To each side of me within view are two other hillsides full of vineyards swaying gently with the breeze under the moonlight, giving the grape leaves a magical glow.

"I want a picture of you in your wedding dress from this angle when the day comes," Antonio says. He leans in and I can feel his breath behind my ear.

I smile to myself as excitement rises inside me. He is here now, his breath hot on the back of my ear. I turn quickly around to face him.

Antonio smiles widely when our eyes meet. He takes me into his arms wrapping them around my back. I bury my face into his chest and deeply breathe in his scent. The tightness of his embrace gives the hint that I am free to unleash my passion for him so I throw my arms around his neck, lacing my fingers together. I look deep into his eyes.

"A picture of us both on that day," I say.

He bends down and our lips touch for the first time. The softness of his melts into mine, the heat of his breath in my mouth speeds the beating of my heart faster than I ever felt before. I can no longer restrain myself. I pull him down into me by hanging all my weight from my hands around his neck. He tightens his hold around my back and lifts me off the ground. Our bodies are as close as they can be. I feel his heart racing in his chest pressed against mine. Slowly, my body slides along his until my feet touch the ground. Our breathing is quick and unsteady. He creases his forehead and seems to search my eyes for something.

"You have never kissed me like that before," he says. His breathing slows down and he seems to consciously take deep breaths.

I am afraid that I may have crossed a line and pull slightly away from him. He does not let me, tightening his hold around my waist, his lips turn up in a slight smile but I see some curiosity or is it concern.

I do not know what to say. I struggle to find words but all I can think about is kissing him again. I stand up on my toes and bring my lips toward him. He grabs my upper arms. I am determined to get another kiss before I disintegrate out of this memory.

He stares into my eyes with one of his cheeks turned up and his brows furrow then slowly moves his face into a mischievous smile. He looks behind him through the open door. Taking my hand he gently, but hurriedly, pulls me with him along the stucco wall. When the wall curves slightly and the door is out of sight he yanks me in front of him. With both hands on my waist, he pushes me back into the wall, then places his right hand against the wall next to my head, lifts my chin with the other and looks into my eyes. He slowly eases his body against mine, the pressure of it increasing with his weight causing me to take short shallow breaths. I gasp as he lets go of his restraint and his body falls into mine. He smiles widely. Pinned against the wall, I look into his eyes. They are mischievous and wild but not at all in a fearful way. I place my hands around his lower waist.

"Are we breaking any rules?" I ask.

"We are breaking all the rules," he whispers and touches his lips to mine.

We explore each other's mouth, barley opening, for several minutes. When he pulls his lips away, he keeps his body against mine, my face forming a pout at the parting of our lips. I try to bring his face back to mine, weaving my fingers through his hair. He quietly laughs.

"I am almost afraid to ask what brought out your passion," he says. His voice is unsteady but soft, and full of a Spanish accent.

I smile at him then look down. I want so much to tell him the truth about knowing each other in a past life - another era. My heart aches with the thought of the last time the memory faded, unknown to me if we were ever together again.

"I'm learning to let go of my inhibitions," I say. "You'll be my husband and deserve the full extent of my passion."

Antonio smiles, leans in as if to kiss me again but stops. My eyes close automatically.

"I love you Clarissa Debough. You have made me the

REYES

happiest man alive," he says, and then he kisses me.

A HANDFUL OF BUTTONS

We have a celebratory dinner in the courtyard with all candles lit under the night sky, in honor of my engagement to Antonio. The conversation is lively and humorous, despite the soft romantic atmosphere given off by the lanterns. Antonio informs the family that I approve of the courtyard and thus the wedding will be here at the family vineyard.

"As your best man, Antonio, I get to kiss the bride at least once before she is married and unavailable," Paulo says. He looks at me with a seductive grin and fierce eyes.

Antonio tenses his hand interlaced with mine and I notice him straighten his back rigidly in his chair. He glances to his father then looks at Paulo. He relaxes his face a bit but I can still see a glimmer of anger in the line of his jaw.

"I would not ask my fiancé to kiss a hyena, and I will certainly not ask my fiancé to kiss you," Antonio says through gritted teeth.

Maria and Sofia laugh but are suddenly quiet when Paulo's fist pounds hard on the table. Roberto drops his utensils and his eyes dart between Paulo and Antonio.

Antonio and Paulo stare at each other. Antonio has both his palms down on the table with his right hand almost directly in front of me. I lean back and he raises himself a little off his chair in response, shielding me more. The sudden change leaves everyone in silent tension.

"No need to spoil our meal my dear brother," Paulo

says. "I do believe however that your Clarissa is of an independent mind to make the decision herself. I do not recall asking or seeking permission from you."

Paulo looks at me with a crooked smile; chills raise the hairs on the back of my neck. The words are too familiar to those he said during the last threatening exchange between the brothers. It only makes me believe more that this Paulo is the same soul of the Victorian era. I sink further back into my chair accepting Antonio's shield willingly – but this time I will not be cast aside but instead a part of the fight.

Paulo raises an eyebrow. "Your fiancé is quite possessive, my dear. I hope you will be able to keep your independence after he makes you sell your boutique."

It is my last connection to my great aunt and now home to the armoire. I panic with the thought of where I will end up if I decide to sell it in this memory before it fades.

"Clarissa's independence is not in question, but your cleanliness most definitely is," Antonio says.

Paulo tilts his head slightly but the evil smile does not leave his lips.

Antonio leans forward. "Your lack of regard for women and constant abuse of their virtue permits me to protect Clarissa from being harmed by men such as you."

Roberto slaps his hands on the arms of his chair and stands up. "I will not have the virtues of women be discussed at our family table," he says. "I will not allow either of you boys to disgrace this family. This conversation is done." He turns to Paulo. "You will leave now."

Paulo sarcastically bows to me and Antonio then gives a salute to his father. I grab my dress at my stomach in a fist with the flashback of Paulo by the side of the pond. He glares around Antonio at me. I feel the chills come to an abrupt halt at the base of my neck and the hairs rise.

"I will have another chance to request my kiss, Clarissa, as I have in the past," he says. He backs away from the table maintaining his intense stare.

"Paulo!" Roberto says.

Paulo turns on his heels and leaves the courtyard through the gate.

Antonio leans down to me and whispers into my ear. "I am very sorry for my brother's behavior. I know now I can never trust him with you. Please do not allow yourself to be alone in his presence. I believe you would not be safe."

"Eat!" Roberto demands. He sits down slow, picks up his fork, and stabs it into his food.

After several moments of silent eating the dinner returns to conversation about the wedding. When it slows, signifying the end to dinner, Antonio excuses us from the table and leads me out toward the front gate. I follow him around the house and down a narrow path. We walk several paces in silence. Our hands are intertwined and the warm air cloaks us under the full moon that lights our way.

We walk along the dirt path for about three minutes until we reach a large barn. There are eight stables on the side where we approach. Antonio walks straight to a brown and white palomino horse. I take in a quick breath, vividly remembering Antonio's horse from the Victorian era. Seeing it now is more than I can reason. My guess of souls being able to live multiple lifetimes seems constantly suggested in this new memory. The dresses take on a curious sense of belonging to me instead of some other person, and with it a stronger feeling of ownership for the armoire. My breathing quickens with my random thoughts and suggested clarification of my past lives.

Antonio stops suddenly. He turns to me, looks deep into my eyes, and I notice how the moonlight throws rays of light off his black hair. His eyes are soft but I can still see a bit of tension in his face.

"You are not riding alone. Give me a minute," he says.

Antonio guides me over to a bench under a large oak tree and pushes gently on my shoulders. He leans down and kisses my forehead.

"I am going to saddle my horse," he says. "I want to take you for a ride."

I watch Antonio as he reaches into his pocket. He fumbles with something hanging on the inside of the stable and then light floods the stall and washes out to the tips of my feet. He hangs the lantern on an outer hook. I continue to watch him as he saddles his horse. He periodically glances at me smiling each time.

When the saddle is on, he walks the horse out and stops a few feet in front of me.

"This is Zapatos," he says. "Zapatos, meet Clarissa."

I cup my hand over my mouth to hide a laugh. "Isn't zapatos the Spanish word for shoes?" I say.

"Do not call him shoes. He doesn't like that," Antonio whispers. He shrugs his shoulders to Zapatos keeping hold of the reins loosely in his hands. Zapatos whinnies and rears his head; Antonio tightens his grip on the reins.

"Hello Zapatos," I say.

I reach out a hand to his nose but he jerks his head away. Antonio clicks his mouth and pulls down on the reins. He then tosses them around the horn of the saddle and reaches out to me. I get up from the bench slow and walk over to stand beside him. Following the nod of his head toward the horse, I put my foot in the stirrup. Antonio grabs me around the waist lifting me up high enough for me to throw my leg over. My dress is considerably shorter than the one from the Victorian era and I blush when it hikes up to my thighs.

"Maybe I should side saddle," I say.

"Not necessary. I will be behind you and my eyes will be on the path in front of us."

His smile gives him away entirely and I swing my leg over with my back facing him.

"It will only tease you," I say. "I will not give you such a temptation."

He walks around and looks up at me. I grab at the end of my dress and pull it unsuccessfully toward my knees. He reaches up, takes me around the waist and pulls me down from the horse. He does not release me but instead he bends close enough that I feel his warm breath on my lips. The horse shifts its weight behind me and pushes me into Antonio. He laughs stepping slightly back and turns toward Zapatos.

"Thank you Zapatos, but I had it under control," he says turning back toward me. "If you insist on riding side saddle then I have to mount first." He raises his eyebrows and hides his hand behind him with the other one on the horn of the saddle.

I step aside. "Please," I say, gesturing toward the horse.

Antonio's look changes into a mischievous grin with one cheek rising with his eyebrows. "My dear Clarissa," he says with an exaggerated bow. The hand behind him cuts through the air in front of me turning in circles at his wrist until he stops it with a palm up.

He laughs then easily mounts the horse and reaches down a hand for me. Hesitantly I place my hand in his and once it touches, he closes his grip firm, leans down, and spins me around as if we are dancing, then grabs me around the waist and pulls me into his lap. He takes the reigns, his arms on either side of me, and makes a clicking sound at the horse. This all happens so fast I am unable to catch up to my shocked look and as the horse trots off into the vineyards, Antonio roars with laughter.

"No temptation here my dear, Clarissa, absolutely none at all," he says.

I attempt to cross my legs to maintain some dignity. "Can we make the horse walk?" I say.

Antonio slows the horse to a walk by pulling back on the reigns. His hand almost touches my chest but he brings me in close to him with the other hand across my front.

"Do not be embarrassed, Clarissa. I wish you could see yourself through my eyes right now, the love would overwhelm even the strongest of hearts which you alone seem to possess."

His voice soothes my embarrassment and I sway with

the motion of the horse. We ride in silence. Zapatos' hooves makes gentle thudding sounds on the path.

"Where are we going?" I say.

"The willow trees."

I watch the path ahead, weaving in and out of a mixture of cherry blossoms and Maple trees, the branches hang just out of reach above. The path veers and begins to descend along the hillside. Antonio tightens his grip on me as the horse leans forward. Ahead of us the vineyard lines stretch for miles across the hills and at the bottom I can see the moon reflecting off a body of water.

"Is that a lake down there?"

"A large pond," he says.

We reach the bottom of the hill and Antonio slides one leg from under me to jump off the horse. He then reaches up and pulls me down. Taking one of my hands in his and the reigns in his other hand, he leads me over to the willow trees. The rest of the grassy bank surrounds us providing a bright green cushion beneath our feet. The air suggests the grass was freshly cut but only small patches of clippings can be seen. It appears the possible doing of a natural mower such as ducks or other animals - we may be guilty now of disturbing their nightly meal. Antonio lets the reigns fall to the ground and Zapatos bends his head and starts eating.

Antonio walks two steps forward then reaches out his hand and parts some of the branches on the closest willow tree. He gently nudges me through the opening he has made in the branches. I duck into the canopy and pause at the seclusion; It is a perfect shelter and the grass beneath is soft under my step.

He guides me over to the trunk of one of the willow trees and sits down at the base. He tugs my hand gently and I sit in front of him so that I am between his legs, resting my back and head against his chest. He places one arm around my shoulders grasping gently my forearm, holding me close to his chest.

The canopy of the willow tree above touches the ground all around us except where the second willow tree's canopy interlocks branches. Either due to the lack of sunlight or purposefully groomed, the linking of branches between the two canopies ends three feet off the ground - just enough to see the large pond in front of us.

The moonlight illuminates the water. It is a perfect sheet of glass - not a single ripple disturbs the calmness under the moonlight. All time seems to stop as we sit under the willow trees.

"It's beautiful, Antonio."

He kisses the top of my head and I turn around. Our lips meet and his breath is warm against them. He kisses me gently for several seconds then looks back out to the pond. I follow his gaze. Antonio sighs. It blows a few strands of hair apart on the back of my neck.

"What is it?" I say. I shift my body to face him.

He adjusts his weight and pulls me to sit next to him; wrapping his arm around me. I look at his face - he seems far away. He glances at me then back out to the pond.

"I feel very close to you here," he says. "I have always had a feeling deep within me that I will come so close to having you ... and then lose you. Here, that feeling is gone and a strong sense of peace replaces it." He runs a hand through his hair. "I am not making sense," he says.

"Try again," I say.

He sighs then rests his lips on my forehead. He peels them away slow then runs his tongue between them. They recede before returning to their original shape.

"It is like a déjà vu," he says. "But this déjà vu never ends, and I never know what will happen next. I feel my soul has finally found its other half, after many years of searching."

He looks into my eyes. Again, even in the moonlight, I see the passion.

"Do you believe that this search could go on for many centuries?" I ask.

"Centuries? I do not know, but I can assure you, Clarissa, the internal exhaustion and peace I feel now definitely suggest my soul has been searching for yours throughout many centuries."

Antonio leans in touching his lips to mine. His force intensifies gently as I lean back onto the grass with the natural push of his passion. He lays his body alongside mine and places his hand on my cheek pulling it gently toward him so that we do not break the kiss. I reach my hand around the back of his head and intertwine my fingers into his hair, grabbing his head toward me. He groans pleasantly and pushes his arm under my back scooping me up and on top of him. He takes my face into both of his hands and peels my lips from his. He smiles at me, the light of the full moon dancing off his black waves.

"You feel it too?" he says.

"Yes."

"We have met before," he says.

"Yes."

"But I lost you."

"Yes."

"How?" he says.

I want to answer him with the truth. I have no idea when this memory will fade. Part of me wants to risk sounding insane. I take a breath and close my eyes, a lump forms in my throat. "I don't know," I say. "Like you, I am just sure that you lost me, and I couldn't prevent it."

I turn away from him, the dread of my single status reality reminds me that this memory will end and I will again fade out of his world.

I roll off him and sit up, pulling my knees up. My heart now physically hurts and I automatically grab at my chest as I mentally beg the anxiety attack to stay away. Antonio sits up and wraps his arms on my shoulders. He puts one hand gently under my chin and pulls my head to look at his.

"You left me physically maybe," he says. "But my heart never forgot you. My soul always searched for you. I will not lose you again." His lips barely touch mine with his last word.

I have to change the subject. I think to myself.

It is getting too hard to keep my identity from him. The whole story about the dresses in the armoire bites at the tip of my tongue to get out.

"What day are we getting married?" I ask.

Antonio brushes a strand of hair off my face. I narrow my mouth into a hard line and push back my shoulders. He takes the hem of my dress between his fingers and slides them across my thigh. "You agree to sell your boutique?" he says.

Paulo's remark about selling my boutique did have validity to it. My instinctive reaction returns and the fear of having to let go of my boutique in exchange for Antonio speeds up my heart rate. This consequence would be grave if it is the sacrifice to have him.

Antonio leans a little back from me, creasing his brow. "Are you intending to manage it from Spain? I know you are perfectly capable, but two boutiques are hard to manage in one country let alone two. I do not know if I can part from you as often as you would need to travel back to New York."

"We are going to live in Spain?" I say. I straighten out the hem of my dress.

"That's what we agreed, Clarissa. You know my family is interested in the region outside of Madrid for a second vineyard."

"Oh."

Antonio inhales a breath between his teeth. "Clarissa, I cannot stay here, I am the oldest-"

"What about Paulo?" I say.

Antonio takes his hands away from me and sits up rigid beside me. "My father and I cannot trust him. I cannot trust him to refrain from taking liberties with you when I am not around."

"Liberties!"

Antonio's eyes widen and he takes me abruptly into his arms. "Clarissa I do trust you, but everything I have,

Paulo covets. Every woman I have had feelings toward he has seduced in one way or another." He takes my head into his hands. "I confess part of taking you to Spain is to keep you as mine. My fear of how Paulo may try to seduce you or what he will do if you refuse ..." He kisses me midsentence, letting his feelings come out in the intensity. I push him away.

"Okay," I say. "For your peace of mind I will keep my agreement to live in Spain. We will go immediately, but I will not sell my boutique entirely. I will pick up a partner."

Antonio sighs, shaking his head as he looks down to his knees. "Clarissa -" he says.

I pull his face up with both of my hands. He resists at first but then gives in. "My boutique is part of me. Are you asking me to give up what defines who I am?"

He slightly smiles and strokes the side of my face with his hand. "No," he says.

"Can we marry on Saturday?" I say.

He laughs with a confused expression spreading across his face. "That's in three days!"

"We have the vineyard, your family is here. I can buy a dress in the city and be back by Friday. Just me, and you ... and your family."

He smiles softly and brushes the side of my face with his fingers.

"My dear Clarissa, I am yours. If a wedding is what you want then I will give it to you. In my soul there is nothing more that could marry us than your agreement. I have that now ... here ... under the moonlight and blessings of God that surrounds us."

Antonio pulls me into a tight embrace with a kiss. He gently caresses my back as our lips explore delicately with passion. His hand traces my spine from my lower back to the base of my neck pulling slightly my dress to my upper thighs. I intertwine my hands into his hair and grab a chunk in each hand. He groans and rolls me over.

The wind seems to pick up, a gust blows against my back, I feel as though I'm falling and keep my eyes closed to give way to his sense of touch. It is when something hard slams against my back, thrusting the breath from my lungs in a gasp, that my eyes burst open.

Everything is out of focus and I grabble around me looking for Antonio, I call his name, closing my eyes tight in an attempt to focus them; but when my eyes clear, the clarity shoots through my veins with the feeling of physical pain on its tail. My entire body aches more than the blow to my back.

I look up, staring at the ceiling of my boutique, as I lay next to the four-poster bed on the storeroom floor. I hadn't even stayed but a few hours in his world.

The sadness slows my breathing almost to an end, tears come flooding down my cheeks, and the lump in my throat blocks the sound of my crying. Slowly, I roll over and reach behind to my back. The buttons of my dress are missing and it is open wide. I push up onto my hands and knees and see four buttons between my fingers.

My head hits the floor just as I find my voice and the air for my lungs to release the sound of my compulsive crying.

The beginning of another end. Is the single thought in my head.

I cry myself to sleep next to the four-poster bed unwilling to move – my insolence toward returning to my present.

The cold hard wood beneath my body wakes me out of a restless sleep. Still lying face down, my cheek is pressed hard against the floor, sticky with tears. I feel the pain in my muscles from the hours of lying here. The agony of my soul separated from its other half rises from deep within hearing the logic of my present life and shouting out my stupidity from the darkest corners of my brain. My inhibitions being given up too quick to any guy who says he loves me. This time is worse. He only exists in a memory of a dress. I cry myself to sleep again.

I wake up on the hard floor periodically but cry myself back to sleep as my mind races through the last moments with Antonio; time seems to pass with no end. I have no desire to move ... or dress - nothing has any importance for me. I have lost him and I don't have the strength to get up and put on another dress just for a few more seconds with him.

The sunrise starts to creep across the floor near the counter. Images of my present life push at my thoughts, as they demand to be heard. Soon people will be passing on the sidewalk as they mechanically follow another day of their routine. I should be one of them.

I push myself up onto my hands and knees, grab the four buttons, gripping them in one hand, and attempt to get up. I collapse under my own weight. The shoulders of the dress fall to my forearms as I lean onto my hands, pushing my knees from the floor, at another attempt – again I fall.

The pain in my muscles from lying all night on the floor is unbearable, the emotions rushing through my veins, pushing at my mind, is excruciating. I sit back on the balls of my feet - the buttons in my hand. I promise myself I can spend the day in bed if I just get off the floor. I reach out to the edge of the bed and forcefully hoist myself up.

I pull the black shades reserved for major renovations and reveals down over all the storefront windows. Printed on the shades is 'closed for inventory restructuring.'

I shuffle to the back of the storage room. The armoire stands just where it has always been. I let the dress fall to the floor and step out of it. Bending down, I reach for it with my free hand, the buttons clenched in my other underneath white knuckles. I reach out to a knob of the armoire with my left hand, eyes closed. I don't want to know if there is another dress. I can't start all over again with Antonio or succumb to the vivid images of these memories. My grave consequence might be the loss of my sanity or soul. I feel the lump in my throat rising and I quickly pull open the door, throw in the dress and close it. I don't open my eyes again until my back is to the armoire.

I walk out of the storage room, naked, dazed, and sore; straight into the shower upstairs.

Whether it is because of shock or an ability to make myself physically numb when met with extreme emotional angst, the shower water does not seem to get hot enough to stop me from shivering. The steam building in the bathroom makes it even harder to breath, and my legs barely hold me up as I let the water fall against my back.

The shower does nothing for me but still I have to

force myself to get out. My body is free from the sweat and dirt of the storeroom floor on the outside, but pain continues to riddle against my insides. When the water turns cold, I get out and put on the first pair of sweats and t-shirt I find on the floor then shuffle to the couch.

My tears flow over the banks of my lids again. There is little strength left in me to make a sound. Willingly I give in to the flood of emotion dripping down my cheeks.

It will stop. My shirt becomes soiled with tears. *My emotions will dry up or my body will die – but this will stop.*

Strength slowly returns with the release of more tears. The intervals of crying are eventually broken with my shouting to the air of how cruel the armoire is to me. I scream Antonio's name forcefully trying to command his sudden appearance. I receive no answers to any of my ranting.

After one such outburst, I collapse to the floor, face down, and cry convulsively long enough to cause my eyes to burn and my chest to ache. I roll over onto my back, breathing deeply. Enough sanity has finally been able to build in me to give me the strength to breathe normally. I stare at the ceiling for the rest of the day, not moving, not willing to put forth the effort to live my life.

My only definition of time is a voicemail left from Lana.

"Hey girl! It's eight o'clock. I came by your store today and saw the black shades are down. What happened to the warning? Isn't it a little early? I mean this is the wedding season! Call me. You owe me at least a time frame." (click)

Eight o'clock at night. What day is it?

I sit up and rest my weight on my hands, my feet

straight out in front of me.

I should call Lana. I'll have to tell her everything. She'll know that something major has happened. She'll continue to pressure me. Curiosity will get the better of her and she'll open the armoire. She'll find Antonio and her soul will fuse with his.

The feeling of jealousy rises with my anxiety as I play through the imaginary events inside my head. Things always click quickly for her. That's why she works in the corporate world, she's quick to understand and make the right decision without thinking.

I see the image of her in my place on the bank of the pond with Paulo. A sense of protection for her rises in me. Lana is smart, but Paulo is strong and evil. I can't allow her to have those memories. I have to protect her from Paulo - get rid of the armoire. The intensity of my emotions push me back down to the floor, the tears flooding over my lids again but this time I cry for Lana. My grave consequence is her.

I lay awake on the floor of my loft apartment for the rest of the night - left with only sorrow and the compulsive images of how to destroy the armoire.

Keep it. I take my first deep steady breath. *Keep it ... and keep it close ... so I can watch it and never let anyone near it. I will call some unknown movers and have them move it into my bedroom.*

My breathing eases a little. In some sick way I feel close to Antonio, knowing the armoire will be in my bedroom and I can fall asleep gazing at it.

Enough time passes that I grow tired of my self-pity and I am able to get myself off the floor to make a cup of coffee. After not eating for a full day, my stomach does not take well to coffee alone. I put some bread in the toaster but leave it sitting there after it pops because I cannot get up from the table - I am physically exhausted from my emotional tirade. The black shades are still drawn on the storefront windows and I made up my mind about what is to be done with the armoire. There are no immediate responsibilities to make me return to actively living my life.

I spend my day on the couch and the floor, despite my one hour at the kitchen table with my coffee. Lana calls three times today. I screen the calls but never answer. She is worried. Her last call hints to a suspicion that I have been murdered or abducted. I know I have only tomorrow if any days at all to relish in my exhaustion from self-pity. It will all end when she finds me. She knows me too well and there will be no lie to explain my current state of being.

Lana leaves a fourth message at seven o'clock in the evening, according to my answering machine, stating she is coming over. She must have called from her cell phone in the cab because not five minutes after her message I hear the sound of a key in the door of my boutique.

She has a set of spare keys for emergency purposes. In her mind, ignoring calls for a full day without any precipitating argument to suggest otherwise is an emergency. I can't blame her; I would do the same.

"Clarissa?" The door shuts behind her. "Clarissa, where are you? You better answer before I head back out and call the police."

"Up here." I get the words out in barely a whisper, my voice hoarse from shouting and crying.

I hear her footsteps bang against the iron then her stumbling over the last step. She nearly runs into the table as she turns toward the couch where I am sitting. I turn my gaze to the carpet beneath me feet. Not even her probable face plant into the table, which would have cursed me with hysterical laughter, nudges my lips into a smile. I am still numb and frozen.

"Clarissa! What the hell is going on with you? Oh yuck! It smells like crap in here."

Lana walks around from the back of the couch and looks down at me.

"You look like crap!" she blurts out. Her tone is half filled with anger and the rest in surprise.

I raise my head up and look at her. She is my best friend and I cannot hold in the tears.

"Oh shit!" she says.

Lana plops down onto the couch next to me and wraps her arms around me tightly. All I can do is cry into her shoulder.

"I'm here, Clarissa. No questions asked."

Lana lets me cry on her shoulder until I am ready to pull away. She doesn't ask any questions. She doesn't make any comments. She is just there for me – here. Her presence alone gives me a desire to let reality take me back.

I sit up and dry my tears with the back of my hand. I take a deep breath and look at Lana. Her face shows concern but I can also tell she is scared to death.

"I was not raped or assaulted. Physically I am fine." I say.

Lana takes in a breath and I see some of her fear

disappear from her eyes.

"Then tell me Clarissa, why are you white as a ghost and, well, don't take this in a bad way ... but stink to kingdom come? Are you sick?"

"No."

Lana keeps her eyes on my face but she doesn't ask any more questions.

"I've never seen you like this before," she says, "The closest thing to it would be a breakup, but even that is worlds away from how you look now. You're scaring me to death."

"I know," I say. I take a deep breath. "I'm not going insane ... well maybe a little ... but not enough to be committed. I am not sick. You could say I am going through a major breakup but it is so hard to explain."

"I can follow."

Lana repositions herself on the couch, giving me space to turn toward her. Her face seems to soften with the hope of clarity in my state. I know she is genuinely worried.

"No questions," I say.

She holds up her hand, palm facing me, and crosses her heart with her finger. "No questions," she says.

My brain fumbles for a way to explain what has been happening to me for the last year. Nothing comes forward that will lead in a direction of sanity. I am going to have to blurt it out and go with my gut but I have to be careful.

"I've been having a very vivid, reoccurring, dream for about the past year," I say. "Actually since the day I met Paulo. I don't have it every night but enough that when I wake up from it I have a hard time pulling myself back into reality."

Lana runs her hand through her hair, stopping at the base of her neck. I realize with her raised brow that I am leaning in the direction of craziness and voices instead of vivid dreaming.

"My dream was, of course, about a man," I say. "Each time I dreamt of this man I was in a different era. I was with him long enough to fall in love. I never had sex with him."

She drops her jaw and I raise my hand to stop her from saying anything.

"In two of the dreams we weren't even able to kiss because we weren't married."

"That sucks," she says.

I smile slightly and cross my legs underneath me. "It's okay because I was always his fiancé. Just being with him was enough."

Lana raises her eyebrows then sighs as she extends her hand out along the back of the couch. "That sounds like a really good dream, Clarissa, especially for a hopeless romantic like you."

Her company is making me feel better and finally being able to tell her about Antonio relieves a bit of my anguish.

"You would think so," I say. "But every time I wake up from one of the dreams I feel a loss - like I will never see him again."

Lana tries to give me a hug but I wave her away with my hand.

"The dream is so vivid," I say. "I am able to smell him on my clothes when I wake up. They stir emotions in me that I am very good at protecting in reality, and in the dreams I let go of all my inhibitions and allow myself to get close to him."

"Clarissa, you let every guy get close to you. That's why the breakups are so hard on you," she says. She takes my hand into hers. I pull it out.

"You don't get it, Lana. My last dream was two nights ago. He noticed my release of inhibitions. He told me he loved me, Lana. Every nerve in my body felt it was true. That it was real. I told him I wanted to marry Saturday."

Lana's mouth drops open. "That's the day after tomorrow. Were you going to tell me? Was I in the dream?"

I tilt my head with my eyebrows bent toward the bridge of my nose.

"Oh sorry … no questions … just trying to cheer you up," she says. She puts her hand over her mouth.

I smile. Her attempt at cheering me up is working.

"Lana, I gave him my full trust and love in the dream, and then I woke up. I don't think I can ever fall in love again."

Lana yanks me into another hug as my tears flood down my cheeks. I push away and wipe them with the palm of my hand.

"Only you, Clarissa. Only you would have such a romantic, vivid, dream of true love, with the stipulation of having no control of keeping it. You are truly cursed in the area of romance."

I half laugh and seeing my slight change in mood, she laughs too, jumps up, and runs downstairs.

"How many bottles of wine should they bring?" she

calls up to me. "This definitely sounds more serious than our normal two."

"Ask for three bottles of red," I say. "You can ask them for as many as you want to drink."

Lana's laugh echoes around the bottom floor then up into my loft.

"Bring a case of your house red. We need to drown some serious sorrows," she says.

The beep of her phone sounds behind me on her way back up. She pulls me off the couch and shoves me into my bathroom. She turns on the shower and directs me to get in and spend as long as I need.

"I'll wait downstairs for the take out," she says. "You might need at least an hour in there. You do stink. I won't pop open the first bottle of wine until you're done."

She leaves my bedroom shutting the door behind her. I take a deep breath, letting it out slowly. It feels so good I close my eyes and do it two more times.

"Thank you," I whisper with my head back then I step underneath the water. I take her suggestion but almost after an hour, the water runs cold.

With my hair up in a loose bun at the nape of my neck, I pull on my jeans and a clean t-shirt. Lana has the entire loft straightened up and several take-out containers scattered around on the coffee table. The case of wine is on the kitchen counter with one bottle missing. A big smile spreads across her face when she sees me. In her hand are the missing bottle and a bottle opener.

"Ready," she says and she pops the cork.

I nod and walk over to the couch. I sit down slowly.

The few days without moving seem to have seized my muscles.

"Good, let's drown some sorrows and get you back to reality," she says.

Lana pours us a glass. She gives me one and holds up hers for our ritual first glass of the first bottle toast.

"My offer still stands," she says, "imdumped is not a bad sign-on for a dating service." Then she throws back her head and drinks half the glass in one gulp.

Laughing, the wine nearly splatters back into my glass. I have to take a large gulp to keep from spitting it out of my mouth.

"Let's eat," she says. "I got three different meals and lots of bread. Here's your fork. Dig in and then we'll switch."

The warmth of the food feels good on my sore throat and chest from all my crying. Lana and I drink and eat while talking about everything except my recent emotional outburst. Her job is getting worse and so my night to drown sorrows becomes hers but I welcome the diversion openly. It helps me forget about Antonio for a while and store up strength to deal with the loneliness when she leaves.

She delves into a colorful description of a new co-worker. According to her, he is slimy and inappropriate and she does not restrain herself in using profanity to paint a very clear picture of him for me.

"I would not set you up with this one, Clarissa. In fact if you ever find a guy like this … well … hopefully you will be able to see through his shit."

Lana shakes her head and sticks out her tongue. She drawls on in her description until it becomes rhetorical ideas of how to expose his true nature to her boss.

I am slowly lost in the sound of her voice. Although my reality will never be what it was before I found the armoire in my back alley, I am accepting the change. Her voice gradually brings me back to this newly defined reality despite my belief that it will never have the possibility of true love.

IT SHOULD BE IN A MUSEUM

A full two months pass before I am able to call some movers for the armoire. New York is full of them so it is not a matter of scheduling. It is a matter of me being able to look at it without tears welling in my eyes and a lump forming in my throat. After these two months of purposefully ignoring the armoire, although difficult at times, I have not opened it. I can now say I have no desire to look inside - yet. I know the day will come - maybe after another breakup if I allow myself to date again. Right now, I only have slight feelings of anger and betrayal when I stare at it before falling asleep. Even those feelings are fading away ... like the memory of our last kiss.

Thanks to Lana's rescue of me, I did not succumb to a depressive blob and my boutique only suffered a few days closure. I have become successful at squashing the thoughts and feelings of Antonio from the time I wake up to the time I close my boutique. I have also mastered my composure in front of Lana so that she thinks I have moved on.

She is curious about the armoire when she first sees it in my bedroom. I tell her it is from a great aunt and contains her century old clothing. Lana is intrigued by the beauty of it; as I was. It takes all my strength and nearly biting her head off to pull her away.

"It should be in a museum," I say. "My family entrusted it with me thinking it would look good on the storeroom floor but I am scared it might get damaged down there."

I cannot have anyone else touch it. It is possessively personal to me, and there is a sense that it can be dangerous if owned by the wrong person.

My nights alone are now welcomed and somewhat anticipated. It is when I allow myself to cry out the tension of pretending to be happy all day. With the armoire now in my bedroom, these lonely nights begin and end with physical exhaustion releasing through emotional tears. I cannot remember the last night I did not cry myself to sleep.

The balmy summer days are coming to an end and the leaves in Central Park are showing the first signs of Fall. This will mark a year since I first remembered Antonio.

Today starts normal. With my head hung low to avoid useless eye contact from strangers, I walk to *Shot of Joe*. My routine saves me from having to order, as the barista no longer asks. Some mornings when they are busy, my drink is ready for me and all I have to do is pay. I do not miss the call out of my latte on these days. I have not been joining in with the final shout either. I smirk as I pass the man with the rainbow wardrobe on my way out but he doesn't smile at me anymore. The door swings back hard and I thrust my coffee in front of me as I step back to escape the splash from soaking my dress. I shake it off my hand and keep walking. Two months ago, I would have cursed aloud to the guy - then again he would have noticed me.

I open the store and begin my inventory of merchandise to determine what I will shelve for next year, put on clearance, and donate. The change of seasons gives a slight variety to my routine that sparks a little excitement for something new, but it is short lived before it becomes tedious. Customers are scarce because of the heat, already scorching the pavement and causing the mirage of water to float above it. My sundress sticks to my legs as I work up a bit of a sweat rearranging shelves and pulling out merchandise from the back. I crank up the air conditioner, but give up on wiping the sweat from the bottom of my feet and opt on kicking my flip-flops off entirely.

The bell over the store front door rings. Quickly I push my feet into my flip-flops and come around a display cabinet of candles. I cannot see the customer near the front and walk toward the register thinking the person has already started browsing. Looking at my clipboard, I catch a glimpse of a man a foot taller than me out of the corner of my eye standing by the four-poster bed. With his back turned to me, he is tracing his hand over the sheets of the bed.

"Good Morning," I say, pushing fake cheerfulness into my voice. "Is there anything I can help you find? Those sheets are the softest -"

The man turns around and my clipboard drops to the floor as I grip my throat from a sudden loss of breath. My eyes grow wide and the tears flood to them and over my lower lashes.

"Excuse me," I manage to whisper and run to the storage room.

I lean against the wall right inside the door so that I am out of sight from the man.

Antonio! Impossible. My head is messing with me. Pull yourself together, Clarissa.

"Hello? Are you all right?" the man calls out from the storeroom floor. "I'm sorry if I startled you. Should I come back?"

"No! Ah … I'm fine. I'm sorry. Please give me a moment. I'll be right with you."

I wipe my tears and straighten my dress as much as I can. I know I look horrible with watery eyes, sundress sticking to my legs and now extremely pale from seeing a ghost. I push the hair off my face and twist it, pulling it forward. Throwing it back over my shoulder, I take a deep breath and walk out to the storeroom. The guy is at the register and has my clipboard in his hand.

He looks at me with the most caring, deep blue eyes. The jet-black hair against the dark olive skin only confirms my sudden realization. This man in front of me, if not Antonio, will be the closest anyone can ever come.

"I'm sorry for my reaction," I say. "You just look so very familiar to me. You did startle me." I hold the lump in my throat down, restraining myself from throwing my arms around his neck and pushing my lips against his.

"Your reaction suggests I may have frightened you," he says. A Spanish accent rolls the words off his tongue as Paulo's did when I first met him. "I was afraid you might come out of the back room with a gun. I hope my familiarity does not insight fear in you."

Forcing a smile, I take the clipboard he holds out to me. "Actually quite the opposite. How can I help you today?"

The guy's lips turn upward in a smile, his teeth bright white against his olive skin. "I'm not sure if I want to venture with my original purpose of coming into your boutique."

Determination to understand his original intent becomes so strong I grip the edge of the counter to keep from launching over it and into his arms. Surely, it is something very normal but every thought in my mind reassures me that the only reason to come into a boutique that sells bedding is to buy bedding. If this guy has any other reason looking so much like Antonio than it must be him! The emotion of my determination changes to agonizing hope and I fight a sudden rush of tears. I focus on the wood grain of the counter and blink the tears away, and then I look back at him. Memories of where I always found strength when in his presence leads me to his eyes and I immediately feel the comfort and peace.

"I'm sorry for my lack of composure," I say. I try to keep my voice steady. "It is highly unprofessional. How can I help you?"

The guy reveals a small piece of paper from inside his pocket.

"I am searching for a Clarissa Daniels," he says. His accent rolls my name off his tongue with such elegance.

"I'm Clarissa Daniels," I say.

He puts the paper back in his pocket and extends his hand. "Hello Clarissa, I am Antonio Santiago"

The blood retreats with force from the veins in my hands, rushing to my brain to keep me standing. My head whirls at the sound of his name. Despite the sudden clamminess of my hands, I extend one to shake his. As they touch, the surge of excitement shoots through my arm and gives a whirring sensation to my stomach. I inhale slowly filling my lungs in desperate need of air. Antonio's smile suddenly leaves his face, his eyes dart to mine, and I see in the deep blue of his eyes recognition. We connect - he sees my soul - he can end my search for him. My lips push high into my cheeks as my soul confirms that this is my Antonio.

Before he takes his hand back, he inhales a deep breath. He seems a bit flustered and turns his head away, glancing at the storeroom floor, before speaking.

"Perhaps this is not the place," he says. "The request I am about to make may sound very odd, and with your reaction it may be a bit dangerous for me. Will you join me for a drink after you close? Anywhere you -"

"Sure. There's one on 16th street, across from the park. I'll meet you there around seven thirty." I say.

Antonio smiles, his eyes light up, and his cheeks swell, hiding what I notice for the first time, dark circles under his eyes. I wonder if he has traveled far to find me or if he lives here in New York. A little part of me hopes that maybe he too, through some other means, remembers our time together.

In my last memory of him he did say he would find me should I ever be taken from him again. Today he found me but we are strangers. He does not appear, or at least let on, knowing who I am other than a name on a piece of paper. I am starting over. A feeling of dread settles in the pit of my stomach. My thoughts fade away with the gentle flow of Antonio's response.

"I'll be there ... thank you," he says.

Antonio walks toward the door but hesitates as his hand touches the knob. I watch him. He opens the door partially then pauses again. I hope he will run back to me and take me into his arms. He turns and looks at me with an intensity that I feel his eyes penetrate right through me into my thoughts. I hold my breath in anticipation.

"What is the name of the place?" he asks.

"Gustavo's."

"See you at seven-thirty," he says, "I will reserve a table."

Antonio walks out. I keep him in sight following him to the door then watch him stroll up the block from the window. Just before he disappears into a crowd of people, he looks back and smiles at me.

My hands begin to shake, the tears flood down my cheeks, and I grab onto the post of the bed to keep from collapsing on the floor. I stumbled over to the door and turn the sign to *closed* then run upstairs to my bedroom.

The armoire stares at me, closed and untouched. I grab both knobs in my hands, take in a deep breath, hold it, and then yank them open. They fling to the sides and almost slam shut again from the force. I stare into the armoire and gasp - it is full of clothing and accessories.

Every dress I had ever worn in my time with Antonio is included and several I had not seen before. I bend down and open the drawers. In the left drawer are gloves and in the right drawer is jewelry. I gently finger the pearl necklace Antonio gave me on that Victorian Christmas Day. Time seems to slow as I scan the contents; memories I did not know existed flow into my thoughts.

I remember the day he asked me to marry him in the Victorian era. It was a warm Fall afternoon by the pond. He stole his first kiss that day. I touch my cheek as the images change to a day he came upon me walking and dismounted his horse to walk with me. Faster the images come, becoming blurry at times and I catch his face looking at me from across the counter downstairs in my boutique. Too quick was the image to define time, but the blue of his eyes were alight with passion.

I close my eyes and all the memories fade. Opening them, I see the hand written note that had come taped to the front of the armoire. I laugh at my *grave consequences* that present themselves to me now. To remember and the possibility of Antonio being unaware of our past lives is not grave but instead a great blessing. I step back and allow my knees to buckle as I catch myself by falling onto the bed.

After several minutes, the tingling feeling in my legs causes me to stretch. Standing up, I pull from the armoire the hand written note. I refuse to reread it again or even look at it directly but I take a safety pin from my bedside table and pin the note to the green dress Lana bought me.

Feeling a sense of closure to the memories of the armoire, I am ready to begin a new relationship with Antonio. I reopen my boutique.

The day drags on with few customers until right before closing when an evening breeze picks up. It keeps me busy until six forty-five when the last customer leaves. I refuse to restock and close the register so I can take the time to shower before meeting Antonio

After my shower I debate an attempt of putting makeup on and pull out what little I have from years ago. Lana introduced me to the world of beauty and fashion but gave up on the makeup after a month or two because I had shown absolutely no signs of improvement. Looking at the many bottles, sticks, and compacts, I realize changing my normal appearance could have devastating effects. I close the drawer and continue primping in the areas of hair and clothes. I choose my usual style of jeans and a blouse but also put on a lace camisole underneath so I can leave the first three buttons respectfully open.

I am done with a good twenty minutes to spare before the time I agreed to meet Antonio. Outside my boutique, I hail a cab.

"Gustavo's," I say to the cab driver then lean back into the seat.

My mind plays through several conversations and ideas to hold Antonio's attention while leaving him with the desire to see me again. I reason to myself that whatever he came to talk to me about cannot be so devastating that it ends the connection between our souls entirely. After all, I have technically been engaged to him during two other lifetimes – that I remember.

Always a fiancée never a wife ... a grave consequence.

The cab pulls up to Gustavo's and I see Antonio waiting outside. When I open the door, he quickly walks over and holds out his hand for me. I take it and smile out of the excitement from his touch. His lips also form into a wide smile. He reaches into his pocket, pulls out his wallet, and leans into the cab.

"I already got it," I say.

Antonio straightens up, slips his wallet back into his pocket, and closes the door. "I will attend to the rest of the evening ... if you please," he says.

"Thank you."

The restaurant is not very busy, just as I had predicted. Antonio picks an out of the way table but not too reclusive. The bar and front door are visible but the table, slightly turned, makes our own nook in the corner, giving the sense of privacy.

The waiter is an old boyfriend. One of my one-week relationships before he told me he was not interested in dating just me. Feeling a little awkward as he approaches, I reach into my purse and pretend to turn my phone to vibrate.

"Hey, Clarissa," he says.

Antonio raises an eyebrow and I look sheepishly up from my purse.

"Hi Brian," I say.

Brian looks at Antonio then back at me with a smirk. I shake my head and try to laugh it off.

"This is Antonio, Brian."

Antonio extends his hand. "Nice to meet you," he says.

Brian keeps his digital order pad in hand and ignores Antonio's offer for a handshake. "So what'll it be?" he says.

Antonio places his hand back in his lap with a frown of disgust and shakes his head. He orders a beer, and I order a glass of Merlot. Before Brian leaves, Antonio calls his attention back and orders some appetizers. A grin of triumphant spreads across his face as Brian whips his body back around with an exasperated sigh. I raise my eyebrows.

A little passive aggressive.

My stomach growls with the smell of the food. The excitement of this meeting had kept me full all day so it was not until the scent of the restaurant that my stomach finally protests loudly for the taste. The music sounding through the speakers keeps my hunger a secret.

We sit in a bit of an uncomfortable silence. Briefly, Antonio interrupts it with a question about my day, which I answer with "fine," followed by a question about his day.

"I'll be getting to that in a moment," he says. He glances toward Brian approaching with the drinks.

When Brian leaves our table, Antonio takes a sip of his beer, places the mug down, and then leans in toward me. We make eye contact and again I feel our souls connect - I freeze with the wine glass at my lips. He breaks the gaze and looks down at the table. When he raises his toward me, I notice that he purposefully does not make direct eye contact.

"I thank you for meeting me like this," Antonio begins, "I know I am but a stranger to you."

I remain silent, giving him my full attention which fades the rest of the bar patrons into a low hum in the back of my mind.

"I hope - no - I ask for your honesty tonight," he says. "I know this is an absurd and rude request but it will help me explain things better."

I like the way this conversation is going. I want to jump in and shout 'it's me it's me,' but sanity keeps a safe hold on my tongue.

"I'll be as honest as I can," I say. "But I reserve the right not to answer a question."

He nods while rubbing his fingers against the condensation on his beer mug. The lines across his forehead contradict his nod.

"That is fair ... a question. I will make sure I ask them respectfully." He takes a sip of his beer. "First question ... I apologize ahead of time if you believe it to be intrusive. It is only to confirm I have the right Clarissa."

"Sure," I say.

"Are you seeing a man by the name of Paulo?"

Nearly choking on my sip of wine, I put down the glass a little hard and some splashes onto the table. Antonio hails Brian who is already on his way with some water, making my cheeks flush red from embarrassment and gasping for air. Antonio takes the water, hands it to me, and then asks Brian for a fresh glass of wine. Brian wipes the table then leaves without a word.

The water soothes the burn of my throat. All I need to hear now is that Paulo is his brother.

Brian returns with a new glass of wine and places it in front of me with a sideways glance. I frown at him as he walks back to the bar. Antonio watches him, raising his chin slightly and expanding his chest before exhaling and returning his attention to me.

"Are you okay?" Antonio asks.

"Yes," I lie hoping he does not hear the shortness of my breath from the rapid beating of my heart.

I concentrate on my heartbeat by placing a hand lightly against my chest. Alarm flashes in Antonio's eyes so I move my hand away nonchalantly and his eyes soften. Once my breathing steadies I think about his question, his direct tone sounds offensive as it replays in my head.

Was I seeing Paulo? Was he serious? After what the memories showed me about Paulo, there is no way I would 'see' him.

"No," I say.

The corner of his lip curves up in a half smile at my answer. "I am going to assume with your reaction to my question that although you are not currently seeing Paulo, you had at one time been intimate with him. Am I correct?"

"I went on a few dates with him," I say through gritted teeth, "I was not intimate with him."

Antonio raises his chin with a slight tilt. He looks at his fingertips as he rubs his thumb and pointer finger together. "I am sorry … this is very hard for me. I do not want to offend you," he makes eye contact again. "We are only strangers."

"You have not offended me," I whisper.

"That is good." He takes another sip of his beer.

Brian returns with a plate of sliced rustic bread toasted beneath sheets of bruschetta. On top of the bruschetta is a paste of minced basil, garlic, and Kalamata olives lightly drizzled with olive oil. The warmth of the bread only enhances the smell of the toppings more and makes my stomach growl loudly. Antonio orders another beer for him and another glass of wine for me as I reach for and eat half of my first slice before Brian turns away from the table.

"My original intent -" Antonio tries to hide a smile by rubbing his upper lip with his finger. "In searching for you, was to break you and Paulo apart." His smile fades and he stares at me as if he is waiting for a response.

"Why?"

"Paulo is my brother -"

The effect of a glass and a half of wine on an empty

stomach and only one slice of bread barely touching the lining of my stomach claims victory over my emotions. My breathing is too rapid for me to control and I feel the blood leave my face, my head starts spinning. I grab it with both hands but cannot seem to feel them. I hear Antonio's voice in the distance.

Not here. I think to myself.

Everything fades out of focus and turns black.

When I open my eyes, I am leaning against Antonio's chest, sitting sideways in a booth. He is holding a cold washcloth to my head. I close my eyes for a second and take in the feel of his heartbeat on my back. His smell is the same as I remember it. His touch is gentle but has the ability to be strong. I smile from the comfort I feel being in his arms.

"Clarissa? Are you okay?" he says. "I think she is fine now, please tell the bartender we do not need an ambulance."

A bright light hits my eyes and I automatically squint. I realize Antonio was talking to Brian who had been standing in front of the table, blocking the light above the booth. Sitting up I rub my eyes until the bar comes into focus.

"I'm sorry," I say. I turn to face Antonio. Our bodies are very close. His legs are facing forward under the table and his torso is facing me. He has one arm on the back of the booth, the other holding the washcloth.

"You have nothing to be sorry about," he says, "My approach was rash and intrusive. I am the one who should apologize."

"Please. It has nothing to do with your questions. I'm

coming down with the flu I think. I've been working very hard lately, neglecting my health - I have not been eating well."

Antonio hails Brian and asks for a menu. "Then you need food. I will pay, choose anything." He holds up his hand when I start to protest. "You may think you are fine, but if you faint in my presence again they may take me to jail on charges of tampering with your drink. Please ... eat ... if only for my own freedom."

"Well if you put it that way. I can't be the cause of an innocent man going to jail," I say.

He smiles with a slight hesitation and I think I see him lean toward me but then he straightens up, adjusting his legs beneath the table. I get out of the booth and sit on the other side so that I can see his eyes without making it obvious by turning around.

"You didn't answer my question," I say.

"Actually I did. My answer caused you to faint," he says. A worried look appears on his face.

"My not eating well and overworking caused me to faint, and maybe a bit of the wine. Your answer did not. Try me again."

He pulls up a corner of his mouth and raises his eyebrows. He looks me over seeming to assess if I am strong enough to hear the answer again. "Paulo is my brother -"

"Exactly as I thought. You didn't answer my question," I say. "I had asked why you would need to break Paulo and myself apart."

"Yes, well, if you had not fainted I would have been able to finish my answer."

"My sincere apologies please continue," I say with a tilt of my head.

Antonio's face suddenly contorts into a smug expression sending chills racing up my spine. It is the smile I had seen on Paulo.

"As I was saying, Paulo is my brother. He lives in Spain, as do I. He has the fortunate position of traveling the world for the family business ... selling wine. During these travels he tends to meet women and have intimate relationships with them."

Antonio takes a sip of his beer. Brian returns for my order. I order another plate of the same appetizers because I never looked at the menu and want Brian to leave right away.

Antonio raises a hand to Brian who stops mid-turn, "Are you sure you do not want an entree?" Antonio says.

"Yes," I say, turning toward Brian. He understands and leaves. I shift my attention back to Antonio. "I still do not understand what Paulo's worldly relationships have to do with me, and why you have traveled all this way to break it off." I say.

He pulls his lips into a tight line. "Paulo is married ... he has three children. He may have told you that he was offered a job and had a month to make the decision."

My eyes widen as my mouth drops slightly open.

"Yes. Well that is his favorite story," he says. "Paulo puts out the deadline for telling the company one month. He is very good at what he does. A month gives him ample time to gain the trust of the woman, have intimate relationships, and then tell her he must return to Spain. He will say that he has to tie up some loose ends before his first day of work."

Antonio suddenly feels like a stranger and worlds away from my initial impression of him. My protective instincts kick into full gear - from embarrassment. My hunger is gone and escape is the only thing on my mind but Antonio keeps a hold on my curiosity.

"I have seen that look," he says. "On many other women's faces. To my advantage, Paulo enjoys bragging to me about the women. He is under the belief that since I am not married I will approve and even admire his ... activities."

I take a few sips of wine and force some food into my stomach just to compose myself.

"How often does Paulo do this?" I ask.

"It has been going on for the last couple of years. There have been five so far. No one has fainted on me though. You're the first." He smiles and I sarcastically return it with a small laugh.

"You were also the first who had not been intimate with Paulo. He left one young woman pregnant. She had a baby boy two years ago and Paulo sends her money every month to keep her quiet about his identity as the father. The women in California are safe."

"Why do you search these women out and tell them about Paulo."

"I try to find them for my father ... it pains him. He is a strong man but he is old. I am to inherit the family business but Paulo's reputation can ruin it, leaving us bankrupt and disgraced. Who wants to buy from a company that has scandal within its own family? I am not alone ... my father and I make arrangements to clean up after him."

"So you pick up his messes like a toddler, but don't

give him any consequences ... sounds like your family business is babysitting." I cannot hold the bitterness in my voice, much of it due to my own shame.

Antonio's hand balls into a fist on the table. "Paulo has no regard for other's feelings or reputation. I cannot explain how it affects the family business," he says. "Aside from jail there is nothing that will stop him. All the women are willing and he is quite seductive when he wants to be." Antonio moves his hand under the table. "I do not normally go to this extent to tell a woman about Paulo. Usually I find them, tell them, and get on a plane back home, hoping they will have enough information to end it before they get pregnant. It has never taken me longer than two days, including the time to fly."

He brings his hand back up and turns his glass around in a circle between his fingertips. He looks down at the table appearing to be lost in thought - his eyebrows crease.

"There's something else," I say

"Yes," he raises his head. "You were different," he whispers, "Paulo boasted about you. I gather since you were not intimate he talked about your features more specifically. Aside from your hair being curly, Paulo gave me a perfect description of you. Right down to your mannerisms. I felt a - like I knew you. I became angry. I had a strong urge to protect you before ever meeting you. I demanded my father tell Paulo's wife about the baby in California hoping it will keep him home long enough for you to forget him. We had always kept her in the dark about his activities ... to protect her ... and the children. We were wrong to do so, as she informed us after our talk ... she is now living in the main house and we have not heard from Paulo since. I thought he would come back to you."

Neither of us says anything. Sitting across from a complete stranger that I feel I have known for centuries is the closest I have come to enduring eternity.

The desire to make him remember is too strong to cover any longer; I have to tell him something. If he handles it and stays, we will have a chance but if he leaves I deem this closure and finally move on.

"You are not the only one," I say.

Antonio looks up.

"I told you the reaction at my boutique was because you reminded me of someone," I say.

"Yes," he says.

"You did not remind me of anyone but yourself."

Antonio's lips part slightly.

"I have been having a recurring dream about you for the last year and a half. Not every night." The words fly out of me, relief to confront him about who we are to each other - half of one soul. "When I fainted it was in fact because of your answer - in each dream you had a brother named Paulo and he had the kind of character you just explained to me now."

The olive hue of Antonio's skin changes to a shade of white. I leave the words hanging in the air, bracing myself for him to run out of the restaurant. He stays.

"You could say I have had dreams of you also," he says.

He reaches over and touches the top of my hand.

"First sight," he says, then takes my hand in his. "You

are safe. Paulo will not harm you. I will not let him have your soul." He raises my hand to his lips and kisses it gently.

"Safe?" I ask.

"Paulo is not one to leave a ... how shall I put this ... conquest unconquered to be perfectly and crudely blunt. He was not satisfied with your response when he broke it off with you. He expected some begging. I came in search of you with the impression that he had returned to find you himself. Paulo is of such ill character that I would not be surprised if he were to use force in the event that you did not take him back."

My thoughts replay the memory of Paulo's attempted assault on me at the bank of the pond.

"And you don't know where he is?" I say.

"No." He releases my hand and leans back into his chair. He takes his last sip of beer.

"When did he last leave Spain?"

"Two weeks ago."

"When did he tell his wife about me?" I lean forward. Something does not add up.

"Paulo did very well at playing his role of a loving husband to his wife since his return from New York," Antonio says. "I told you that he has two children with her. She gave birth to a third three months ago. His wife had a difficult labor."

"He told me he returned to tie up loose ends because he was taking the job," I say.

Antonio adjusts in his seat. "Interesting. The one time he had a truthful family matter to return for, he still lied."

"Do you think he's in New York?"

"I do not know," he says. "I want to ask you a favor."

I raise my eyebrows.

He leans in and lowers his voice. "I assume you live alone. Do you have any place you can stay until I locate Paulo's whereabouts ... exactly?"

"No."

He looks down at his hands interlaced with each other. "Do you have a friend that can stay with you?"

"I have a very dear friend," I say. "And the last thing I would ask her to do is move in with me."

"Why?"

"Why? She has her own place and living together for an unknown period would probably demolish our friendship forever. I won't do that. I'm not going to be forced out my home and boutique for some guy who can't take no for an answer."

Antonio shakes his head, takes a deep breath, and lets it out. He looks directly into my eyes.

"Paulo is not just some guy," he says.

"I live in New York. I'm sure he is not the first guy who's wanted to assault me."

Antonio cringes and appears to shake thoughts from his head as he frowns. "You will not do this one favor, even if your life depended on it."

"It sounds like my life does depend on it in your view but there are many things that can kill me. I'm not going to live in fear."

He lets out another breath, leans back and puts one hand in his pants pocket, the other one stays on the table balled in a soft fist.

"Very well then," he says, "I have one demand since you insist on being so difficult in my attempt to keep you safe."

"Demand?" I say with a laugh. "You're hardly in the position to make a demand after only knowing me for one day."

Antonio smiles. "True. I will rephrase it. I have one pleading request from a stranger."

"Really. Only one?"

"I request that I may call on you daily, until Paulo is found."

I tilt my head. This is more than a request. This is a blessing to me. More time with him in the present. I sense no fear that he will dissipate into the wind after a kiss.

"You want to make sure on a daily basis I am not dead," I say.

Antonio tightens his brow. "I wish you would not put it that way - but yes, I need to see you are safe. There is an underlying reason to my request also ... like I said before there is something different about you and I want to explore more of that."

"In that case, you can see me daily. You know where my boutique is so you won't have any trouble finding me."

Antonio's forehead and hand relax. He calls Brian and pays for the drinks and food. I again try to protest and pay the tip but he will not have it. Mentally I make a checkmark in a column for him and vow to even it up in the near future.

"May I share a cab with you?" he asks.

"I'll make it home safe but I will be more than happy

to share a cab with you for the sake of having more of your company."

He offers me his hand and I slide across the booth, not so gracefully standing up. His hand, although offered as a mere gesture, becomes a bit of a crutch when I catch my hip on the table and nearly fall into him.

"Good catch … thanks," I say.

"Accepting my company more for safety now," he says.

I notice the smirk on his face. "It has possibilities," I say. "But I have managed quite a life time without your protection; it will be a tough sell to hand over my survival to you entirely."

Antonio interlaces his fingers through mine, as we walk out of Gustavo's. I give Brian a smug sideways glance as we pass him. He rolls his eyes but I see the smile creep along his mouth.

Antonio and I look up and down through the traffic. Cabs are scarce. A humid Wednesday night seems to be working against us, as people must be opting for the air conditioning instead of walking. We have to wait for a while until one drives by.

When a cab finally stops, Antonio opens the door and gestures for me to enter first. I give the driver the address to my boutique and sit back; Antonio's body is close to mine, but not quite touching it. We sit next to each other in the back seat of the cab making small talk.

"Have you always lived in New York," Antonio asks.

"No."

"Where did you grow up?" He smiles slightly and it

jolts me with the realization he caught me staring at him.

"I grew up on the West Coast. Brookings, Oregon."

"What brought you out to New York?"

I smile this time, my thoughts suddenly breaking into the memories of my solo trip across Canada.

"I came here for college. I was accepted into an interior design school."

"So you are a designer … who works in a boutique," he says.

Although he sounds sarcastic, even the bad light in the cab shows his face does not match the tone of his voice.

"I own the boutique and I didn't finish my interior design degree," I say. "I inherited a large sum of money from a great aunt. I started interior design school with a goal of owning a boutique but I was prepared to work in someone else's until I saved enough money. My Aunt's death allowed me to reach my goal sooner. I dropped out and with the help of my best friend, Lana, I opened my own boutique."

"And how did Lana help you," Antonio asks.

The cab slows and drives out of the flow of traffic to the edge of the sidewalk in front of my boutique.

"She helped me with the business plan," I say.

Antonio nods. He has his wallet out before I can even pull my purse onto my lap. He gives the cab driver some bills folded in half and says 'thank you,' then opens the door. The cab driver leans toward the rolled down passenger window thanking Antonio repeatedly in broken English. Antonio waves it off with a nod of his head and offers me his hand to get out of the cab.

When his hand touches mine the memory of him

REYES

reaching for my hand when I exit the carriage after the funeral in the Victorian era comes flooding back. I smile at him.

He places his palm on my lower back as we walk to the door, glancing up and down the street.

"It will be easy to notice people out of place," I say, "Foot traffic gets pretty slow here at night."

I can tell by the expression on his face he is not comfortable standing outside in the dark. Turning the key, I unconsciously make a frustrated groaning sound at having to twist extra hard until I hear the click of the bolt lock.

"I can fix that," Antonio says and holds the door open by placing his hand above my head and pushing me gently inside. Once we are in, he locks the door.

He takes a cursory glance around the boutique. "Where do you sleep? Do you have an apartment in the back?"

I laugh. "No. I have a loft apartment upstairs," I say.

Antonio looks at the stairs then takes another cursory glance ending at the storage room door.

"What is through that door," he asks. His accent enhances his commanding tone.

"That's my storage room," I say.

"Is there another door in there to the outside?"

"Yes."

"May I check it?" He walks toward the storage room.

I tilt my head and pull up a corner of my mouth. "Really?"

"Please … I know my brother all too well."

"If it makes you feel better," I say. I extend my hand

toward the door and give a slight bow.

He frowns at me and walks toward the storage room. I follow. At the archway he stops and turns around to face me.

"Stay here please," he says.

"Not a chance," I say, "Remember you are still a stranger. Small business owners can lose a third of their profits every year to theft if they are not careful."

He rolls his eyes then shakes his head as he rubs the back of his neck.

"You are determined to make this difficult for me," he says.

"I think your own perception of this whole thing makes it difficult for you. I'm enjoying the company, shall we?"

I step in front of him and start to walk into the storage room. He grabs me by the shoulders.

"Let me go first … a small request for your safety," he says.

"I got your back," I say putting up my fists.

He laughs and walks into the storage room.

I turn on the light and show him the back door. We browse between the shelves as I briefly tell him about my inventory.

"Is my storage room safe?" I ask as we leave.

"For now … I want to check out your loft."

I laugh. A shade of red appears quickly beneath the skin of his cheeks.

"Yes. That was a bit forward … my apologies," he says, "I am merely implying a desire to look at your loft for safety reasons only."

"This searching of my boutique is becoming quite an ordeal," I say. "I will let you check out my loft only if you stay for a cup of coffee."

Antonio smiles, and slips his hand into his front jean pocket.

"I would like that. Thank you," he says.

We proceeded up the stairs. I am allowed to go first to open the half wall sliders. As Antonio looks around the loft, I start up the coffee maker. After pressing the *on* button and hearing the usual gurgle sounds, I walk toward my bedroom a few steps behind Antonio. My heart leaps into my throat as I see him standing in front of the armoire.

"Don't!" I say.

I cannot see his arms. I do not want him touching it, opening it … something in my unconscious warns me it would not be good.

Antonio turns around slowly. His face seems to reflect my own absence of color.

"I wasn't going to open it," Antonio whispers. "Please tell me. Where did you get this armoire?"

"Is it familiar to you," I ask.

"Yes."

He begins to turn back to it, extending his hand out and reaches toward the top.

"Don't!" I say.

Antonio lets his hand drop but does not turn around.

"I'm sorry. It's just that -" he looks up at it again but keeps his arms at his sides. "Familiar, so familiar, it can't possibly be the same." He turns suddenly with a fierce gleam in his eyes. "I must know where you got this armoire."

I recognize his look. The same one he had when he told me to get on the horse and ride back to the house.

"What is it, Antonio?" I say. I take a step toward him, "What is so dangerous about it?"

Antonio's eyes widen. "How do you know of its dangers? How did you know what I was thinking?"

"I didn't. What do you know about the armoire?"

Antonio takes a deep breath. He grabs my forearm, a bit forcefully, and I hunch my shoulders at his grip. Ignoring my resistance, he takes me out to the kitchen and leads me to a chair. He nods toward it and I willingly sit down, anticipating his explanation. He sits in the chair across the table.

"The armoire is very familiar to me," he says, "I had been told as a young boy that it is one of a kind and passed down through my family for generations. I think it dates back to the Victorian era. My grandmother had it last and my mother was to inherit it but she passed before she could take possession of it." Antonio extends his arm out on the table making a fist and then leans back. He pulls his lips in tight and inhales a deep breath. "When my father and I cleaned her home to sell it, I noticed the armoire was missing. We asked all of our relatives but no one had any idea where it went, but I had my suspicions." He tightens his fist, the skin over his knuckles lighten. "I was told about it because my mother only gave birth to my brother and I."

"You don't have a sister named Selina?" I say.

"You met Selina?" he asks.

"Yes ... I think so. A woman came into the coffee

shop the first day I met Paulo. He left with her and later referred to her as his sister."

Antonio shakes his head and spreads out his fingers on the table palm down. "She is beautiful, but she is not his sister … she is his wife."

A flash of anger strikes through my emotions and I feel the shame of my previous desires for Paulo's attention. Yet it is not where I want to take the conversation so I dismiss the urge to talk more about Selina – force myself to accept the fact and move on.

"You said the armoire is one of a kind. Who made it?" I say.

"I don't know. The stories only talk about the first woman who owned it; a wedding gift from her husband - he was not kind, there is sadness about the life of the original owner."

"Tell me about her," I say.

"The original owner was forced into marriage, by her husband," he says. "He was a man of outrageous character. In the era this armoire was crafted, a woman very rarely entered into marriage out of love, but women were also respected and not touched until marriage."

I keep any hint of my first-hand knowledge from emerging.

"This man had taken liberties beyond what the era allowed … or approved. He essentially spoiled this woman by forcing her to have intimate relations with him. He then informed her father and her father was forced to accept this man to prevent public scandal upon the family's reputation. My mother told me the story as the oldest son, I do not know if Paulo is aware of this part of the history. My mother intended me to give the armoire to my wife, a tradition that has seemed to follow this armoire. I am very curious as to how it came into your possession, especially now with the knowledge that you were at one time dating my brother."

I look down at his relaxed hand on the table then to his eyes. His glare is one I feel compelled to obey. I have to tell the truth about the armoire, even if it means it will leave my possession. Strongly, it feels rightfully mine, but if it belongs to Antonio's family, I cannot keep it from him.

"It appeared at my back door. The same day I met Paulo."

Antonio nods his head.

"He couldn't have been the one," I say, "He was standing in front of me when the back door rang. He made no reaction to it and actually helped me bring it inside."

Antonio's eyes widen. "You lifted that thing?"

"Give me a little more credit - actually Paulo did most of the lifting."

Antonio nods his head again, "That only proves my suspicions. It is even more imperative I find Paulo. He would not leave this armoire here without the intent of returning to it or for you. I need to find another place to store it."

"Whoa! Wait a second. I understand you believe it is the same armoire, but until you have concrete proof - it stays."

Antonio scowls. "After the story I just told you, there is no way of me being able to prove my family is the rightful owner."

"Exactly! It stays put. I've already made it mine - my

favorite dress is hanging in it right now."

I quickly put my hand to my mouth. I did not intend that information to slip. Antonio looks directly at me.

"The coffee is ready. Do you want a cup?" I say. I get up from the table.

"Si ... Please." His answer sounds like he is far away. The words are full of his accent.

"Don't be disappointed. I said you can come by my boutique daily to make sure I am still alive ... you can add the armoire to your checklist." I Hand him a cup. "Sugar and cream?" I say.

"No thank you," he says. He takes the cup without moving his head.

"I'll be fine, Antonio," I say. "The armoire will be watched over. I've been okay long before you found me,"

I've been a wreck of emotions. I think to myself.

"You don't seem to understand, Clarissa."

Antonio puts down his cup. He makes eye contact and his lips slightly part as if to say something. It instantly puts me at ease. All of the independent fight dissolves and I feel myself wanting to go with whatever he says.

Yes, protect me. I'll be a damsel in distress for you.

"The armoire is not just an antique or a piece of furniture," he says. "The women who owned it were like guardians. I only know the story because my mother did not produce a female heir. There is something about that armoire, Clarissa. Something I cannot explain. Even I have never opened it. To hear you have opened it ... and placed a dress in there. I can only conclude this is why I feel such a connection to you."

I look down at my fingers as they trace the handle of my cup back and forth. The warmth of my coffee cup hides the increasing clamminess of my hands when I put both my palms against it. I close my eyes as my thoughts show me our time together beneath the willow trees. It may not be my boutique I must give up for him, but instead I am being asked to give up the thing that showed me we belong together.

"I do understand," I say. "More than you know and that I am willing to tell you right now." I look up at him. "I'll say this … there is something about the armoire that only the owners could have felt. It is the reason you feel connected to me - it goes both ways." I lean forward and rest my arms on the table as I stare into my cup. "I don't just agree to a complete stranger checking in on me daily to make sure I am alive. You must never open the armoire or suggest again taking it out of my possession."

Antonio drops his head in his familiar gentleman nod then reaches out his hand, palm up. I place mine into his without a thought given to his intent. He gives it the usual squeeze from lifetimes past sending the heat to my cheeks. I wonder if he knows the identity of my soul and the memories of the armoire.

"You are the current owner," he says. "I have no doubt in that and so I will give you that respect."

He raises my hand to his lips and gently kisses it. Keeping my hand in his, he then gets up from the table, walks in front of me, and lifts me with my help up from my chair. He takes my other hand into his.

"It has been a pleasure to finally meet you, Clarissa Daniels. I am thankful you have accepted my request to call upon you daily. If even for a few seconds, I will look forward to those seconds each day. I will see you tomorrow."

Antonio then lowers his head and kisses me once on both cheeks. He walks down the stairs and across the storeroom floor. I watch him from the top of the stairs. At the door, he pauses and I anticipate his turn. A smile spreads across my face. He does stop and turn around.

"Are you going to lock the door after I leave," he asks. One side of his mouth turns up.

An embarrassed laugh escapes my lips. I feel the blood rush to my face and know that even my neck is turning red now. I half run down the stairs, almost bumping into him. His reflexes are good and he catches me around the shoulders before I trip head-on into the front door.

"Saved you again," he says.

His accent slowly permits the words to fall off his tongue. My ear is so close to his mouth that I feel the heat of his breath but do not miss the slight tone of worry in his voice. Straightening up and standing firmly on my own two feet, I exaggerate the opening of the door and hold it for him to pass through.

"Goodnight," he whispers. His voice is deliberate, but the lines of his skin give way to his concern for me.

I shut the door and watch him blend into the shadows of the city lights up the street. I clap my hand to my head with the realization that I have no idea where he is staying. An entire night can give him a lot of clarity - he may never return.

He walks beneath the last street light I can see from the window and he turns around as though in answer to my fear. He smiles slightly with the wave of his hand, then steps into the darkness out of sight. I flop onto the four-poster bed; a sigh of contentment escapes my lips. I will see Antonio tomorrow and I have the chance to make new memories for my soul to remember. I can sleep tonight without tears.

THE TASTE OF LA RIOJA

The morning comes all too soon. Seeing Antonio and having some control over the situation allowed my mind to settle for a full night sleep. I cannot remember the last time I felt this rested – I want a couple more hours. When my alarm sounds off at six o'clock, I roll out of bed and into the shower.

My thoughts, happy with anticipation of Antonio's arrival, keep my mind occupied as I wash, replaying the moments of all our conversations. It does not take long, however, for frustration to creep into my blissfulness with the uncertainty of when I will see him. Our conversation last night had included so much about the armoire and me, but very little about him.

My morning routine is cursed by my internal battle of anxiety and excitement. Just as I am walking down from my loft to enjoy the enthusiastic atmosphere at *Shot of Joe* before opening, I see Antonio standing outside. He has a tray with two coffee cups in one hand and a white bag in the other. He holds them up grinning. I automatically smile back and do a small skip across the floor.

"Were you waiting long?" I ask when I open the door and take the tray of coffee cups.

"No. I just arrived. Good morning," he says then kisses both my cheeks. "Single shot green tea latte, with a dash of vanilla," he says.

"How did you know?"

"Paulo pays very good attention to details when he is pursuing a woman. He brags ... remember?"

"Paulo is feeling more like a stalker than an old boyfriend," I say.

Antonio's brow darts sharp toward the bridge of his nose. "That's good ... you are feeling his true character. He has great potential to be a stalker if he does not get his satisfaction from the relationship. Was he really a boyfriend to you? I thought you were only dating."

I slightly smile, "No. He never really reached the level of boyfriend, but it was easier to say that than the-guy-I-was-dating."

"Oh." Antonio rubs his hand along the side of his thigh. "Could you maybe not refer to him as an old boyfriend?" he says.

I let out a little laugh. "Sure. Are you jealous?"

I expect Antonio to brush off my question or side step it but instead he stands erect, puts his coffee down, and looks right into my eyes.

"Yes," he says.

I freeze, staring back at him. His eyes are clear, like the ocean on a sunny day but behind it is an intensity that captivates me. His lips slowly part and the corners move upward.

"I was sincere in my words last night," he says. "I feel a connection with you beyond strangers and it may at times spark jealousy, but I am up to the challenge. I will not interfere with your choices should your interests turn to someone else ... unless it is toward Paulo. Should your desires return to him I will not hesitate to intervene, for your own protection."

"You have my word that he won't spark my interests again," I say.

Antonio's lips part into a wide smile and he closes his eyes as he turns away toward the storeroom floor, breaking my trance. I shake off the haziness with a frown, grab the lighter from under the register, and light the candles. My rule about no food on the storeroom floor goes by the wayside, and after turning the sign to *open*, we talk over our pastries and coffee until the first customer arrives.

Antonio cleans up the cups and bag while I attend to the customer. I can feel him watching me as I walk around with the person, explaining the differences in the thread count of the sheets. After several minutes, I leave the customer at the back wall to pick some out for a guestroom, and saunter back to the register where Antonio stands.

"I know I have been quite cruel in the explanation of my brother," he says quietly. "However, I commend him on his account of the pleasure in watching you interact with your customers. I learned a little about sheets from his stories."

I smile, remembering the day Paulo had helped me in the boutique.

"Yes. You're explanation has been cruel and makes me feel extremely naïve," I say. "I was beginning to regret ever kissing him."

Antonio's forehead creases into several lines with his frown, his eyes narrow as he pulls in his lips – they lighten with the pressure he puts on them.

"Jealousy again?" I say.

Antonio relaxes his lips and tries to force them into a smile but it comes off comical with the creases in his forehead tightening. Laughing, I walk away into the storage room. He follows me and grabs my arm by the elbow. I turn in response, surprised to see a sad expression on his face.

"I am sorry," he says. "I only talked about my brother in that way to make you fearful of him. He can be very dangerous but you should never think of yourself as naïve for how you felt about him. He can be very charming when he wants to be."

"Okay ... but I don't agree with you about him being a danger other than hurting my feelings. You can stop wasting your time keeping me safe from that."

"My time is never wasted when I am with you and you're feelings are exactly what I am drawn to protect. As well as win over."

We both stand facing each other; close enough that I can feel the warmth of his breath. Neither of us leans into each other. Neither of us backs away. Only the ding of the bell on the counter frees us from our trance.

"Excuse me," I whisper. I squeeze past him and hear him suck the air into his lungs.

He stays in the storage room until I finish packing up the sheets for the customer. When she leaves, he comes out. "I must attend to some business. May I come back tonight and make you dinner?" he says.

"Sure." I say. "Um ... out of curiosity ... where are you staying?" I ask.

"The Essex."

"The Essex House? More than one night?"

"Yes."

How can he afford the Essex for more than one night?

My brow creases with my thoughts. That is one of the most luxurious hotels in New York, not to mention way out of my price range. Lana wouldn't even be able to afford that place more than a couple nights and she has stayed in some plush four-star hotels. My amazement scrambles my thoughts.

"You may use my kitchen anytime," I say.

He laughs then says, "Thank you."

He reaches out and puts his hand on my shoulder, leans in and gives me a kiss on my cheek. He pulls away with a seductive smile breaking the intensity of his narrowed eyes.

"I'll see you at six," he says.

Just outside the door, he glances back with a wave and the feeling of a static shock ripples in my stomach.

My day is typical for my boutique, a few waves of customers, but nothing that occupies my thoughts completely. My mind has many opportunities to analyze several things at once and takes full advantage to do so.

The memories the armoire showed me, and the many sides of Paulo, turn repeatedly within my thoughts. It causes a mental collision of the world I experienced in the armoire with my reality. I find myself reaching deep into my elementary school days of catholic education. Searching for a definition of souls, I strain to recall any teachings about them. The only thing I remember is that a soul lives on after we die.

My thoughts continue to flow like a river winding through small towns along its bank. I attempt to reason the memories with the definition of a soul. Antonio's soft expression stays in my vision as I replay the conversation under the willow trees. He felt at peace - that a search was over. I wonder if he feels at peace with me now - and why does he think Paulo is so dangerous.

A rush of customers interrupts my thoughts but slows after an hour allowing me an afternoon break to straighten up my loft. I keep my boutique open and attend to the straggling customers as they come in until closing time. Although it is less than a dozen, my clothes are clinging with sweat by the end of the day from their requests and my sprints up and down the stairs.

Antonio is on time and arrives just as I am turning the sign over to *close*. In his arms are two brown grocery bags. A wine bottle is sticking out of one and the plastic bags, which normally hold produce out of the other. I open the door.

"Come in. Can I help you?" I say.

"No. I'll be up in the kitchen," he says.

He walks right pass me up the stairs.

"You probably want to take a shower or something. You were just closing up right?" he says.

"Ah ... Yeah. A shower would be great," I say. I follow him up the stairs. Pausing at the top, I watch him unload the grocery bags. "You sure you don't need help?" I say.

"No. I think I can manage to find everything I need." A grin spreads apart his lips. "Please. Take your time in the shower. I won't start eating until you are done."

He turns back to the grocery bags on the counter and begins to empty them. I walk into my bedroom and shut the door. Nothing gives me a feeling that I should worry about him being alone in my kitchen, but I lock my bedroom door anyway.

The hot water washes away the sweat and seems to push me back into an evaluation of my soul. This time as my thoughts flow through the memories, I am more aware of Antonio's gestures. I see the smile where he only lifts one corner of his mouth and realize it strongly suggests he is holding back a thought. There is the rigid strength of his shoulders when he throws them back to confront Paulo and then the softness around his eyes as the shade of blue darkens with his passion. My mind is captured with this image and slowly the lines form at the corners of his eyes, as they get lost in the narrowing of his lids. I mentally draw back and see his entire posture hanging over his legs with his sweaty black strands of hair blocking his face. Chills run over my skin despite the hot water and I focus on the showerhead to pull my thoughts completely back to the present.

The cold water eventually pierces my skin. I fumble for the knob. Shivering, I tiptoe hastily across the bathroom floor for my towel. All thoughts are now in the present and I can hear the bangs of pots and pans – it sounds like a small restaurant.

Excited and hungry, I quickly dress and yank a brush through my hair several times, cursing at my forgetfulness to use conditioner. Accepting defeat, I clip my hair up. As I unlock my door, I hear Lana's voice echo in the back of my head. *Don't ruin this Clarissa, Play it slow.* I roll my eyes; she would say a lot more if she knew who was in my kitchen right now.

Antonio is at the oven leaning in and poking something with a fork. He closes the door and straightens up when I enter the kitchen.

"I hope you like chicken parmesan," he says.

"Yes. It smells really good." I walk over toward him, looking at the stove. My stomach, tightened with excitement, releases with the mixed aroma of tomatoes, basil, and chicken.

"No peeking," he says. He grabs his hands on my shoulders, turns me away toward the kitchen to the table, and then pours a glass of wine for me.

I see the name on the bottle covered only slightly by his fingers. "La Rioja Conte? I've never heard of that winery, where is it?"

Antonio says nothing but raises one eyebrow then walks back to the stove.

Picking up the bottle, I turn it around in my hands looking for some note about the winery. The label, a plain cream color with black framing, is empty aside from the name. I look over at him putting the food on the plates. He glances at me and pulls up one corner of his mouth in a half smile. I place the bottle back onto the table and lift my glass. I slightly swish the red wine around inside. It holds to the edges more than my own favorite brand of Merlot. I sip it slowly and it flows down the back of my throat smooth, no after burn, coating it in a soft blanket of taste.

I have found a new wine.

"Where can I buy this wine, it's the best I've ever tasted," I say.

He walks toward me with two plates in hand and a

smirk on his face.

"It is the best," he says.

He lays a plate in front of me and sits down with his, then pours us both more wine. He raises his glass. I raise mine.

"To my great grandmother, Señora Conte," he says. "Who gave my great grandfather, Roberto Conte, the inspiration for the taste of this wine?"

I stop breathing and it feels like all the blood rushes out of my face. My heart seems to crash into my rib with one hard final beat. Forcing the glass to my lips, I lean it to my mouth in an attempt to cover my shock and tip the glass. Unfortunately, this is the same time my body shifts into survival mode and inhales a deep breath. The wine flows straight into my windpipe and sends me into a coughing fit.

It takes about two glasses of water for me to regain control of my breathing.

"I'm sorry," I say.

"Are you okay?" His hand is still on my back.

I nod, wiping the tears from my eyes.

He sits down in his chair but keeps his attention on me as if I might start coughing again. "I thought it was my toast," he says. "I could not help notice that immediately after I mentioned my great grandfather your face lost all color."

"I was a bit surprised by the mention of your great grandmother being the inspiration. Is this your families' winery?"

"Yes," he says. The worry lines in his forehead recede. "This is why Paulo travels so much. I thought I had mentioned this before."

"You probably did, I must have missed it."

"That's understandable," he says. "I have given you a lot of information about Paulo that cannot be easily swallowed. I also believe my feeling of connection towards you has not provided a socially acceptable distance for allowing you to trust me. I am sorry, please tell me if I am being to forward. I do not want to scare you."

"I'm not scared ... of you or Paulo."

Picking up my fork, I smile with confidence at him and take a bite of my chicken parmesan. To my disappointment, he dodges my poke at his intention to make me believe Paulo is dangerous and also takes a bite.

We eat our dinner in silence aside from minimal talk about our day. Antonio clears our plates from the table when we are both done, and then walks over to me and extends his hand. I take it and grab my wine glass with the other as I see him flash a glance toward the couch.

He places the wine bottle on the coffee table and takes my glass from my hand putting it down. His movements are slow but determined and I get the sense he is preparing to tell me something. The sweat pushes at the pores in my palms, increasing with the fear he will feel them as he takes my other hand in his. He gently tugs at me to sit next to him on the couch then faces me, looking directly at my eyes. An immediate calm fills me and the sweat retracts from the edge of my pores.

"Clarissa," he says. "I want to ask you something."

His voice beckons me farther into the gaze of his eyes and I notice the thin darker shade of blue lines streaming out from his pupil toward the outer circle of his iris. He looks away from me over the couch toward the kitchen, then back to me.

"Tell me about the armoire," he says. "I feel there is more to it, things you have not felt comfortable to share with me. Please, I beg you."

I pull my hands from his and my attention is suddenly free from his gaze.

"I can't."

"I need to know how you use it."

"Antonio, the connection between us is real. Please do not ask me to define it further. I can't tell you where it came from because it just showed up at my back door. If it is the armoire that belonged to your family you should be telling me how to use it."

Antonio's eyes widen. "You admit you have used it … for something other than hanging clothing," he says.

I take in a short, quick breath. "I …"

The risk of losing him is too obvious. There is no way to explain how the armoire made the memories visible to me without sounding crazy. Even if I try, it is too early to come back from such a judgment or venture into a discussion of souls to see if he has similar memories.

Antonio's expression changes and he looks toward my bedroom. He pulls in his lips, as his face appears to fall in sadness. I want to reach out to him, pull him into my arms.

"I do not seek to take the armoire from your possession," he says. He looks into my eyes. "I only seek to understand the nature of it. I believe I owe credit to the person who left it at your back door, even if that person is my

SEE MY SOUL ~ END MY SEARCH

brother. He brought you into my life.

"Your brother deserves some of the credit. Isn't he the reason you came to New York?"

"True." Antonio says. A corner of his mouth pulls up slightly. "I have another question for you." He adjusts his body, pulling his knees closer to mine and taking my hands into his again.

"Another?" I say.

He pauses, taking in a deep breath and slowly lets it out. "May I kiss you?"

My heart beats quickly and I cannot control the sudden smile that spreads across my face. Antonio leans in as a response to my smile but appears to wait for an answer.

"Yes," I say.

He puts one hand behind my neck and gently pulls me toward him. He pauses right before our lips touch and I can feel the warmth of his breath just as I did in the memory of Christmas day. My eyes close automatically.

"Thank you," he says. Then he touches his lips to mine so soft that I feel the full tingle of the first touch all the way down my throat.

He reaches his other hand around my lower back and I wrap my arms around him. He pushes his lips harder against mine and I feel the air rush by my cheek as he inhales deeply through his nose. He leans back, pulling me on top of him while slightly breaking the kiss. It is only long enough to take another breath and tilt his head to the other side. I let go of some inhibitions as I remember every touch, kiss, and emotion ever felt with him. I want to be closer to him. The physical nature of our skin does not allow the closeness my soul demands.

Antonio seems to feel the same as he takes my head now in both of his hands and pushes his lips harder against mine. I feel his teeth behind his lips and grab unconsciously at his wrists. Antonio peels his lips from mine but keeps my face in his hands. His gaze is intense, and his eyes move rapidly as if searching for something in mine.

"Clarissa," he says. His accent is deep and rolls the 'r' in my name. "Tell me the passion I feel raging in my soul is also within you."

A smile spreads across my face. I can do or say nothing else.

"I feel as though I have ended a lifelong search," he whispers. "The satisfaction in my finding you is such that I never want to be parted from you."

Antonio takes his hands from my face and traps both of my hands in his. "I do not want to scare you," he says. "I beg your forgiveness if my manners are too forward but I have never had to restrain myself so much before. You challenge my character and all my morals. I feel that although I only met you recently, I have known you for a lifetime."

The tears fall down my face uncontrollably. My body feels weak and I want to curl up in his embrace as an assurance that he remembers me ... the identity of my soul.

"Oh, I am sorry. I have scared you." He drops my hands and swiftly stands up.

"No ... Please ... Stay." I say through my tears, grabbing for his hand. "It's not fear I'm feeling ... it's relief."

Antonio sits back down, but keeps an arms length between us.

"Relief?" he asks.

I nod and smear my tears across my face with the back of my hand in an attempt to wipe them.

"I just wonder if you remember me," I say.

Antonio moves closer and wipes a tear from my cheek. "Remember you?" he asks.

"Do you believe in two souls being meant for each other?" I ask.

A silence falls between us and as the seconds pass, I prepare myself for him to jump back up and walk out the front door. He inhales a deep breath then slides his tongue across his lips.

"Regardless of what I believed in yesterday, today I believe my soul belongs to you."

He leans in and gently kisses me. When his lips release mine, he brings me into an embrace and places a hand on my head.

"We will take this slow," he says. "I will earn your trust and prove to you my belief that this connection between us is more than first sight. I have but another question for you … if you will allow me to ask it."

I sit up, aware he notices my forehead creased with lines of confusion.

Antonio lowers his voice to a mere whisper. "I cannot know your feelings until you tell me. I can assure you that I have never felt anything as this for another woman. I also know my feelings will only grow for you, and so I beg of you … should you feel different about this connection … about me, at any time, that you take pity on me and release me. If it should come to that, I will leave you and not torment you with my agony."

"Okay," I say.

Within my thoughts, I scream at him for dodging the confirmation that he remembers me from the armoire. I know this is Antonio - I see the true identity of his soul - why can't he see mine. Doesn't he understand the reason he feels this connection is because we have found each other in every life we have lived on earth. I seethe with anger and my muscles tighten with an attempt to hide it from him.

I let out a sigh as he pulls me down onto the couch next to him. He strokes my hair and gently kisses my neck - it softens my anger. We lay in silence and I am able to hear his heart with my ear pressed against the inside of his forearm. His heartbeat pushes my thoughts into the memories of him with each beat. Again the images of us together move through my mind, but this time it is to the rhythm of his heart. I feel myself drift off to sleep.

A CASE OF DEHYDRATED NOODLES

The sound of dishes brings me back to consciousness. The daylight from my bedroom window glows from under the crack in my curtains. I know the feel of my bed underneath me and sigh with content. Antonio is in my kitchen – but I am in my bed. My state of content is pushed aside by a growing confusion. I lift the covers up and notice I am fully dressed. The armoire stands against the wall, emitting peace within the room. A feeling of being safe flows through me. For the first time in my life, there is a sense of purpose for myself - other than a childhood dream of being a bride. I sigh and listen to the hum of the traffic outside until my body catches up to the wakefulness of my mind.

Rolling out of bed, I groan as I run my hand through my hair. It is full of snarls. After a good three minutes of brushing it, I am able to get it through with minimal pain.

Antonio is looking into my bedroom when I walk out of the bathroom. A smile spreads gently across his face when he sees me.

"There's coffee and eggs in the kitchen," he says.

He opens the bedroom door wider for me to pass. I walk toward him; the smile on my face refuses to be anything but a full one. He puts his hand under my chin as I pass, causing me to willingly stop and face him. He raises my head to his, tilting his own head down, and gently kisses me.

"Good morning, Clarissa."

The sound of my name as he says it never fails to arouse the passion inside me.

"Good morning," I say.

He steps to the side and extends his hand, gesturing toward the table. He follows and pulls out my chair.

"Thank you," I say and sit down to a hot cup of coffee and breakfast. The warm scent of scrambled eggs with parmesan cheese sprinkled on top combines with the smell of the melted butter on sourdough toast as it filters through my nose. "How did you -"

"I heard you shut the bathroom door."

He pours himself a cup of coffee and sits down with me at the table.

"Are you eating?" I ask.

"I already ate. I didn't want to wake you."

I glance over to the clock on the stove.

"It is nine o'clock," he says.

I swallow hard, take a sip of coffee and start to get up. "I have to open the boutique," I say.

He grabs my wrist. "Your sign says you open at ten on Friday and Saturday."

"Oh right … lost track of time." I Sit back down and I notice a smug expression spread across Antonio's face.

"What's that look for?" I ask. I look back toward the bedroom then down at my clothing.

"No. That did not happen," he says. "My morals are much stronger than my desires. I slept on the couch after I carried you to your bed."

I devour gracefully my breakfast then excuse myself to take a shower.

The kitchen is spotless when I come out dressed and ready for the day. The shutters on the half wall are shut and Antonio is downstairs lighting the candles. The scent of lavender and vanilla are already beginning to permeate my loft.

Antonio sees me walking down the stairs and meets me at the bottom. He grabs me around the waist into a big hug and kisses me as he turns, putting me down on the floor in front of him.

"I have to go back to the hotel for a bit. Can I bring you lunch?"

Antonio's kindness is greatly appreciated and something I could get used to but my independent nature will not allow him to buy or fix another meal. It was rightfully my turn.

"May I treat you to lunch?" I ask.

Antonio laughs. "Paulo spoke about your choice in restaurants also. If you do not mind I would like to keep the selection of meals under my control."

I push my bottom lip out in a false pout. "I'm not that bad," I say.

Antonio looks down at me with his eyebrows raised. "The case of dehydrated noodles in your cupboard speaks otherwise."

He's right. I can't cook and therefore depend largely on the greater New York area to provide me with meals on the nights Lana does not show up with Italian take out and wine. A sheepish grin covering the red hue to my skin confirms for Antonio his observation, but my stubbornness will not allow the admittance of defeat.

"Good. That is settled. You will not go hungry, I promise," he says.

Antonio kisses me on the forehead then leaves. As he walks out the door, he turns the sign to *open* and looks back with a wave.

I stand at the boutique window for several minutes before snapping out of my blissfulness and into work mode. I begin the day with a rag and glass cleaner, dusting the many trinkets and shelves. Customers come in the usual waves and although I keep busy, time seems to taunt me by moving slowly toward lunch.

Fifteen minutes before lunch I decide to remake the four-poster bed in the window. Not because it needs to be done, but to pass time and strategically place myself so I can watch the sidewalk for Antonio. I jump at least a foot when someone knocks loudly on the window right in front of me. Lana is laughing at my startled reaction and walking toward the door.

"Brought lunch! Sorry it's been a few days," Lana says. She walks pass me straight upstairs with a cursory glance at my figure. "Doesn't look like you've suffered much fending for yourself. Come and get it."

I look out the window up the street then I follow her upstairs.

"Ah, Lana," I say halfway up the stairs.

"What?" She moves quickly pulling out plates and setting up sandwiches and chips on each. She takes down some glasses from the cupboard and pours the sodas into it.

"Sit down. I've got to vent," she says.

I glance toward the stairs before I take a seat.

"Um, Lana. I ... well, I have ... um ... I'm not available right now."

Lana stops halfway through her bite of sandwich. She looks up at me.

"Oh! No way! Are you serious! Who?" she says.

"Antonio."

"Who? When?"

I glance again toward the stairs shoving my hands deep into my jean pockets. "'Bout five minutes."

"Oh Shit ... sorry. Help me clean up. You can put it in the fridge. We'll eat it for dinner tonight."

She scoops up the food haphazardly and puts it back into the wrappers. She throws it into the fridge as I pour out the soda in the sink.

"I owe you one," I say.

"Yeah you do ... I'm cashing in tonight. No canceling." Her eyebrows almost touch in her frown of warning to me.

"No canceling," I say and follow her down the stairs.

Lana half runs toward the door, which makes me run to keep up with her long legs. She comes to an abrupt stop just a few feet from the front door.

"Caught," she says.

Standing at the door is Antonio. He has a take-out bag in one hand and a tray with two soda cups in the other. Lana looks back at me with a sly expression.

"Cute. I get full details tonight," she says. She looks back toward the door, stepping aside for me to pass her and open it. She then steps in front of me and with much more exaggeration than necessary squeezes pass Antonio.

"Hi, just leaving," she says to him. "Tonight, Clarissa. Closing time," she says loud enough for Antonio to squint at her voice. She turns back to him and with a glance from head to toe then says, "Bye."

Lana gives me thumbs up behind his back as she leaves.

A smug expression spreads rapidly across his face, I roll my eyes and he parts his lips into a large smile.

"Upstairs?" he asks, holding up the bag of food.

"Please."

I follow him up the stairs and when we reach the top, he puts the bag on the table and hesitates. He squints his nose.

"You already ate," he says.

"No. Why?"

"Smells like a deli up here." He glances toward the kitchen.

"Oh … Lana brought some food over, but I told her I already had plans," I say. "We're going to eat it tonight."

"That explains her quick exit and thumbs up," he says. "I'll have to coordinate your meals with her."

My hands push immediately into my hips, "I'm not three. I appreciate the kindness but I won't for a minute rely on you both for my meals." I say.

Antonio bursts into a deep throaty laugh. "You already do," he says. "I only meant it as a favor to her so she could save some money. What did she bring? My choice might be better to save for tonight."

He ignores my creased brow and clenched jaw as he scans the kitchen then tosses a glance back at me. I fold my arms across my chest. He smiles then opens the refrigerator. He pulls out the bag, looks inside it, and takes a breath.

"Sandwiches. Yep, we should eat this now," he says. "I brought Chinese. Does Lana like beef and broccoli?"

"She likes sandwiches," I say.

He laughs again, and then seductively allows his face to soften as he looks in my direction. He gently closes the refrigerator door, puts the bag on the counter, and saunters over to me. As he walks closer his eyes focus directly on mine destroying the anger I try to maintain. He places his hand lightly under my chin and lifts it.

"May I please treat you and Lana to a Chinese dinner tonight," he says. His voice is deep with his Spanish accent and quite seductive.

"Yes," I say in defeat. From now on, I will have to keep my eyes away from his if I ever want a chance at winning an argument.

Antonio smiles triumphantly and gives me a quick kiss on the lips.

"Thank you," he says. "Now sit down and I will get the plates you both just put in the sink. Which sandwich is yours?"

"The roast beef," I say. I sit down hard on the chair and fold my arms back across my chest with a fake pout on my face.

Antonio laughs shaking his head. He puts the plate in front of me and I take a bite of Lana's sandwich. He unknowingly is eating my turkey sandwich, which I let myself take pride in this silent victory. I have no doubt that if I had demanded to have my turkey sandwich he would have graciously taken Lana's and eaten it - bite taken out of it and all.

Half way through our meal, I hear the bell over the front door ring. I look over my shoulder and downstairs but I am unable to see anyone.

"I'll be right down," I shout.

Mouthing a thank you to Antonio I get up, wipe my mouth and head down stairs. At the bottom of the stairs, I look around but still cannot see anyone and conclude that the person has left and somehow managed to keep the bell silent - it has happened before. Turning around to head back upstairs, I catch a shadow out of the corner of my eye standing in the storage room doorway.

"Can I help you," I ask. I turn toward the shadow, ready to reprimand the customer for entering an obvious off limits area.

Time seems to slow allowing every single strand of hair on my body to lengthen sharply to its longest length. As the person in the doorway turns around, I stop breathing. All the blood rushes away from my face and my muscles tense.

"Good afternoon, Clarissa. It looks like I startled you again," says Paulo. He moves toward me.

The sound of a chair pushed away from the table and thrown to the ground reverberates in the rafters from the loft. Antonio is halfway down the stairs before I regain my breath.

"Antonio!" Paulo says. He takes a step back from me. "I am not surprised," he says. "It was only a matter of time before you seduced yet another of my girlfriends for a sole purpose of destroying my character." He whips his head abruptly back toward me. "What did he tell you that I do? Did he tell you I was married? Had kids?" His head cocks to one side and his eyes are wide and bloodshot.

Antonio side steps in front of me with one long stride. He closes my view from him with his widened stance. I take a step out from behind him to keep Paulo in my line of sight. Antonio shoots me a pleading glance. I crease my eyebrows.

"I only told her the truth, Paulo," Antonio says. "Just as I told all the other women you deluded into believing you are a man of moral character."

Paulo bellows out a laugh, throwing back his head. "Moral character," he says. "You speak as though you have some. Is it not you who got on a plane the day after our conversation about Clarissa? I said I did nothing with her and left her alone. Antonio, have you not come to conquer her heart because I believe she is my other half?"

Antonio responds to Paulo in Spanish. I cannot understand but the tone is harsh and stern. He takes my hand in his and brings it behind his back, stepping in front of me. Before Paulo is out of my view, I see his eyes widen then narrow with his laughter.

"You have conquered her heart," Paulo says. "My dear Clarissa, have you found love in my dear brother? This is too ironic. I felt such a kind of love for you that I could not lead you on when I knew you did not know your true identity. I could not fuse our souls forever under those circumstances." He extends his hands palms up and shrugs. "I am married in the image society paints but it is without love. I do not desire that for you, yet here you stand, with my brother. If it were not for my moral character we would be together ... you must admit this is ironic. Are you certain you have the correct soul?"

I take another step to the side. Antonio looks down at me again with a pleading glance and pushes my hand behind him. I do not obey and stand my ground remaining only halfway behind him.

Antonio again speaks in Spanish to Paulo. Paulo looks up toward my loft then back at me. A hard frown appears on his face. Paulo's eyes become fierce as Antonio continues in Spanish, the words flying out of his mouth. Antonio's grip on my hand tightens and I see his shoulders tense. Paulo's hands ball into a fist and he leans forward. Pulling my hand abruptly out of Antonio's grip, I push myself between them.

"I don't understand what you're saying but it looks like you guys need to take it outside," I say.

Antonio grabs my wrist. I yank it from him and step into a squared stance in front of him. He moves forward and I feel his body against my back.

"You are not welcome here," Antonio says through a clenched jaw. "There is nothing here for you anymore. Go back to your wife - be a father."

"I have not heard Clarissa ask me to leave. This is her boutique, is it not?" Paulo says.

They stand in silence staring at each other. I push back my shoulders.

"You left me, Paulo." I say. "You wrote me a letter without the slightest hint of love in it. Then you broke up with me so I could find love. I offered you to stay until I did and you chose not to. I do not date married men and I have found love. I want you to go."

Antonio puts his hand on my upper arm and squeezes it slightly. I glance up at him over my shoulder. I think I catch the beginning of a smile on his face before it returns to a fine line.

Paulo walks toward me ignoring the tension building in Antonio with each step. Paulo leans down until his mouth is next to my ear. Chills race up my spine and send the hairs that just began to relax on my neck back up. Antonio holds my arm tight as his other hand grabs Paulo's shoulder.

"Very well then, Clarissa," Paulo whispers. "I mean you no harm ... but for the sake of your soul I must tell you ... it is not societal marriage that will bring you peace."

Paulo straightens up; his eyes are a deep shade of green filled with malice. They seem to hold the same evil I saw in his eyes at the pond. His words feel as though they have a double meaning.

Paulo turns to Antonio, giving him a private vengeful glance, and then glares at Antonio's hand on his shoulder. Antonio lets go and Paulo walks out the door, not looking back.

I follow Paulo as far as the door, locking it, and immediately flip over the sign to *close*. Saying nothing, I walk pass Antonio and upstairs. He follows me, but I ignore him. I vividly remember Antonio's look when he returned from his encounter with Paulo at the pond. This need to protect me from Paulo makes it certain he will go after him, ignoring the change in times.

Paulo is an asshole ... I can see this on my own. I

think to myself.

My fists ball up with the building frustration at loosing Antonio to a stupid sibling fight over me or because I had just publicly declared, I have found love. My own patterns of relationships dictate that this is now the beginning of the end.

"Clarissa?" Antonio whispers. He sits next to me on the couch.

My eyes search his for the intensity I had seen in them after the encounter with Paulo that left him physically wounded. His eyes are calm. He places his palms on my cheeks.

"Clarissa, I'm here. He will not hurt you … he will not try anything now that he knows I have found you. I will hunt him down to avenge any harm done to you."

"That's exactly what I am afraid of. You will do something stupid out of protection for me or my heart and end up in jail. I don't date felons either."

The tears fall down my cheeks onto his hands. He does not attempt to wipe them or take his hands from my face.

"I don't plan on going to jail, Clarissa."

"You will," I say.

"I don't understand." Antonio's brow furrows.

"It has happened before. I cannot explain how I know but you fought Paulo in a past era. You were not armed and Paulo had a sword. You were injured and made the choice to protect my reputation … leaving me. This is modern times. If you fight like that with him again, you will be arrested and I am sure he will have you charged and deported … not allowing you to return."

Antonio slides his hands from my face they slap down on his thighs. He leans back into the couch. I turn to face him and put a hand on the back of the couch, I lean toward him.

"You don't need to fight for me," I say. "This is New York, I'm an adult, I can get a restraining order, just stop trying to protect me and see me for this connection we feel."

He closes his eyes.

I throw myself back into the couch, slapping my hands over my face, and let out an exasperated groan. "Stop trying to protect my reputation and see my soul for who I am," I say behind my palms.

Antonio does not move. I let my hands slide off my face. I allow my head to drop under the immense weight of the physical exhaustion of my emotions.

"Who am I kidding," I say. "You will always be the gallant do-gooder … maybe another lifetime." I throw my head onto the back of the couch. "Go get Paulo," I say.

"How could you know?" he asks. "How could you possibly know about the details in my dreams that I have never spoken to anyone about."

"What?"

He looks at me. "What you just described was a vivid dream of mine almost a year ago. I was protecting a woman Paulo was just about to assault. It was during the Victorian age I think, or so my clothing suggested. It was a short dream, hazy, and when I woke up I was unable to remember what the woman looked like but I felt a pulling desire to protect her. I had feelings for this woman of an intensity that

I have never felt for any woman before … until I met you."

I sit up quickly. "Please … tell me more about it … what were you wearing?" I ask.

"I believe you already know."

"Please."

Antonio inhales a large breath and lets it out slow. He bends over his knees and runs his fingers through his hair. Unconsciously, I move from the couch and bend down on my knees in front of him. I grab his wrist and look up into his eyes from underneath and he takes my face between his hands.

"Yes. You know my dream," he says. "I have at this moment the chance to repair the damage I had done to you in the past."

Antonio closes his eyes and kisses me. I put my arms around his neck and he pulls me up into him. Standing up he squeezes my body to his as he grabs a large chunk of my hair behind my neck. His other hand finds the middle of my back and pushes me into him. I force my inhibitions to crumble, allowing myself to enjoy the love I feel for him. The passion between us grows and the tears of relief flooding down my cheeks add a salted flavor to my lips.

Antonio places his hands on either side of my face, barley cupping my ears and looks into my eyes.

"I was not able to kiss you like that in my dream. It was not allowed during that time and I felt great torment at being close to you but not able to hold you or put my lips upon yours."

His lips spread apart slightly in the beginnings of a smile, then fade to a serious line.

"I love you, Clarissa. I told you my soul was yours. You told Paulo you have found love. I believe you may be my other half."

Antonio wraps his arms around me and I rest my head against his chest, breathing in his scent. The slight odor from perspiration filters through my nose with the air and I smile slightly with a tinge of perfumed musk I remember from the Victorian Era. I conclude this must be a natural smell and take a slightly deeper breath. He strokes my hair then lets out a sigh.

"I do have to look for Paulo," he says.

I push away from him abruptly. "You can't. Let it go, don't repeat history." My eyebrows crease with the clenching of my jaw. "Promise me ... please."

He shushes without a finger to his lips as he brushes the hair away from my face. I am amazed at how quickly it calms me and I have to concentrate to keep an angered look.

"It will not be through a battle like the dream. I will not confront him physically. I just need to find him. I have to know his whereabouts, especially now that he is in New York. I will be safe - I need you to be safe."

I do not let the anger subside. Antonio sighs again. He kisses me gently on my lips, my cheeks, and then my forehead.

"He is dangerous, Clarissa. He can do more damage to you without any physical means. You do not know my brother as I do ... his belief ..." He pulls his lips inward and looks over my head. He inhales a deep breath. "I need your trust, and your promise that you will not allow him to have any of your time or attention."

"You are prohibiting me from talking to him?"

"I am asking that you not give him the opportunity to assault you physically or destroy your soul."

"Destroy my soul? What are you -"

"It is too complicated to get into right now. I have to use this time to locate Paulo."

I allow myself to relax. His hint at sharing the information that he hides behind his pulled lips and one-corner smile is worth the wait.

"When?" I ask.

He lets out a long breath. "When I think you will understand."

My jaw drops open.

"Clarissa, there is not a simple explanation to all this and your inhibitions to following your feelings are so thick I do not know if you will believe a word I tell you. I love you … with my soul … but until I am sure you are my other half, I will not …" He shakes his head. "I need your trust. Things like this cannot be forced."

I visually follow the green line in the design of my rug. Antonio is silent. I turn back to him and he raises his eyebrows.

"You will give me this," he says.

I stare into his eyes.

"I will tell you, Clarissa … everything I remember. We will remember together, I promise."

"Don't make it to long … and if you get bored with me, tell me before you break up."

Antonio laughs then kisses me hard on the lips as he picks my feet off the ground. I let myself enjoy the moment and fall more in love with him, knowing it will only hurt more in the end – this is too perfect.

"I will stay here until your friend Lana arrives. Then I will return to my hotel. Can you have Lana take a cab with you to the Essex after your time together?"

I look up at him. "It will be late," I say.

"Time doesn't matter," he says. He squints away a thought that must have caused him discomfort. "I need to see you. I don't want you sleeping here tonight. If it were not for Lana coming, I would take you over to the Essex right now. Could you go to her place tonight?"

"I'm not going to let Paulo run me out of my boutique. Besides there's Chinese food in the 'frige that some guy left and it would be rude not to eat it."

I put my hands on my hips and clench my jaw. Antonio laughs, probably at my attempt to look stern, but my bloodshot eyes from crying contradicts my efforts.

"Okay. I see no victory for me in this discussion," he says. "Promise me you will come to the Essex when she leaves … I want to see you."

"For that reason only, I promise. What room number?"

"The Penthouse. Top Floor," he says.

I gasp. Antonio reaches into his pocket and pulls out a small gold key.

"You'll need this. Take the elevator that is marked penthouse. Put the key into the keyhole before you press the call button. It will take you right up to my front door."

He places the key into the palm of my hand, closing my fingers over it. Then he pushes my bottom jaw shut with his fingertips.

"I'll be waiting for you. Don't lose it please," he says.

Antonio stays until Lana comes. He makes his exit much like Lana had earlier in the day. He gives thumbs up when he is out the door, making me laugh. Just before he is out of sight, he turns and blows me a kiss. I catch it and put it to my heart. Lana rolls her eyes and walks toward the stairs.

"Start spilling it," she says. "I want all the details, no skimping."

I jog up the stairs after her. "What did you bring? We have food already, remember lunch?" I ask.

"Sandwiches don't taste good after sitting in the refrigerator all day, besides wine doesn't go well with roast beef." Lana holds up a bottle of wine in her hand.

"Antonio didn't think so either. We ate the sandwiches and there's Chinese food in the 'fridge." I say. I grab two wine glasses out of the cupboard.

"This is warm," she says. "No reheat required. Sit down and save the Chinese food for your dinner tomorrow. We have more important things to talk about - spill it."

I tell her about Antonio walking into my boutique and the immediate connection we both felt. I leave out the discussion about the armoire between Antonio and myself, and the altercation with Paulo earlier in the day. I just fill in the blanks with basic happen stance ways of two people meeting and feeling an instant connection, all the while alluding to Antonio's need to save women from Paulo's character of being a jerk and cheating on his wife.

Still unsure about what the warning of the armoire's grave consequences might turn out to be I keep Lana in the dark as much as I can. She has endured enough consequences from my failed relationships, and most recently my near emotional death, to last her a lifetime.

We finish eating our take-out from *Antipasti* and settle into analyzing my newfound relationship. Lana is her usual cautious reminder of reality for me; I am the lawyer arguing my case for another chance at love.

"So let me get this straight," she says. Her *are you crazy* look surfaces across her face. "You met him three days ago, or maybe less ... he came out to save you from Paulo's manipulation of women when there was no saving to be done. He professed a connection with you he has never felt before, and today told you that he loves you?"

"Correct," I say.

"Correct! Clarissa, are you so hopelessly a romantic that you can't see the scheme right in front of you? How do you know you aren't falling for a con artist, or two ... they could be working together, have you thought about that?"

"I just know, Lana. Don't be mad, here me out."

She rolls her eyes and leans back against the couch.

"Hear you out? You mean talk yourself out of logic," she says.

"Okay. Okay. I see your logic, but there is something I didn't tell you yet."

Lana raises her eyebrows and waits. Her expression gives me all the indication that nothing I say will show her anything romantic about the situation. I have to try. I must release some of the secrecy about the armoire to bring it all together for her. With the minimal information I gave her, even I can see the utter ridiculousness of the relationship.

"Do you remember when I didn't call you for a few days and you came looking for me?"

Lana straightens up and a look of curiousness falls over her face.

"Yeah," she says.

"Well, remember the dreams I told you about?"

"Yes." She lets the sound of her 's' hang in midair.

"I don't have them anymore," I say.

Lana throws her head back and her hands into the air. "Of course not, Clarissa, you're in love now! Nothing like the lust of a new relationship to cover a broken heart for a while."

"It's not like that, Lana. I don't have the dreams anymore because Antonio is the guy in that dream."

"What?"

I lean forward. "Antonio is the guy in the dream, right down to the color of his eyes, his demeanor, his voice, and his smell - everything Lana. That's why I believe in the connection. I feel it too."

Lana's mouth hangs open. She closes her eyes and shakes her head. "Only you. Only you, the hopeless romantic, would have the ability to create the man of your dreams into reality. I can see I have no hope in showing you logic. I will be here when he breaks your heart. That is all I seem able to convince you of right now, you are my best friend."

"And you will be there for my wedding if he doesn't?"

"What! Don't tell me you're getting married to someone you've only known for three days!" she says.

I laugh. "Of course not," I say. "I have actually known him for about a year now. Remember he is the man of my dreams."

Lana laughs. "Yes I will be there for the wedding. Please just be careful. It still looks like a scheme to me."

"I will."

We sit in silence for a while, and then make a bit of small talk. Lana starts complaining about work and I am able to be the friend and show her reasons to give people benefit of the doubt. We're a good pair. I hold the hope and dreams. She holds the logic.

As Lana talks, I keep up my part as listener but my thoughts take me to another place. Paulo's statement of societal marriage not making me happy and Antonio's refusal to explain what he meant about the other half of his soul, begins to morph in doubt about his love for me. The memories of the armoire have to be of my past life … my soul living on after the end of each human life. Yet, I cannot figure how I would be unable to remember this stuff on my own. Possibly this is all one big déjà vu. Lana's voice floats in and out of my thoughts as I think about them from every perspective.

"Clarissa!"

"Huh?"

"Thinking about Antonio?"

The blood rushes to my cheeks. "Sorry."

Lana waves her hand in front of her and throws back the remaining sip of her wine then pours herself another glass.

"Lana, do you believe in souls?" I ask.

Lana creases her eyebrows. "Souls? Like religion souls?"

Laughing slightly at her obvious undertone of entering a religious discussion, I say. "Yes. Souls ... as in those talked about in church."

"Oh come on now, Clarissa. We've only had one bottle of wine. Are we really going to talk about religion? You know I believe in some sort of higher being but I really am trying to get away from my catholic school brainwashing. Provable fact is the only religion that works for me ... and you know that."

"It has nothing to do with the alcohol ... or proving facts ... just something that I was thinking about the other day and I want to run by you." I say.

"The other day when you met Antonio?" she says.

"No after that."

Lana rolls her eyes and groans.

"Okay, for the sake of discussion," she says. "How are we defining souls?"

I ponder her question. It is good, not having much of a grip on my own belief in souls; but I feel an understanding growing along with the love toward Antonio.

"For the sake of discussion ..." I say "Would you find it logical that a soul is the core existent of our being and that our human body is but only a vice to which it enters the earth?"

Lana inhales deeply. The hypothetical discussion is drawing her in, I can tell. It is only a matter of seconds before her business tone seethes through her words and she assesses this discussion from all angles. I love her for this - when I need to work something out that my own head cannot seem to grasp.

"A soul would be who we are," she says, looking away toward the wall. "Our emotions, desires, everything that is not human flesh or bone. Correct?" She turns back to me.

"Correct."

She puts her hand to her chin and closes her eyes slightly. "The soul lives, so to speak, in a human body while on earth," she says.

"Yes."

"What happens when the human body dies?"

"The soul returns to heaven," I say. "I would guess to God, but it will return to earth if it has not found its connection, its soul mate."

"What?"

"Say a soul is forever in search of a match, or its other half." I say. The thoughts seem to string together as I talk aloud. "A soul that another soul is drawn toward since the moment it is created. Imagine the human body is a mere tool for it to survive on earth while searching for other souls. To find the one soul it will forever be connected too."

"What happens when it finds the other soul," she says.

"They are then fused together. That's when people will describe finding their soul mate, one true love, etc. and the souls are then free from the search. When the human body dies they return to heaven as one."

She takes a deep breath. "So we are just hosts and the soul is a parasite," she says.

"Wow, you just took the romance right out of it," I say.

She smiles.

"Think about it, Lana. There has to be a reason why people feel such a strong connection to one person, someone they want to spend their life with and not go after every other good-looking guy on the street. What makes someone stop after almost a lifetime of looking? Then there is déjà vu. Maybe these are memories contained in the soul from lifetimes past, repeating some of the same searching in a new time period."

Lana looks at me with one eyebrow raised. "Hosts, parasites, and now time travel. Clarissa, you have just defined your search for that one true love in four words. Maybe this is why you are so unlucky ... how can I bring you back into a reality that is sure to never give you happiness?"

I turn away from her. Without being able to tell her the full experience I had with the armoire, she will never understand.

"Okay. I know I won't convince you or even be able to put it across to you so that you can see it my way," I say. "You do remember my wish. I don't want to be a vegetable and you have to pull the plug, right?"

"Clarissa! You're freaking me out here. Talking about souls; a real intense three-day relationship with a guy you dreamt about; and now death? Have you joined a cult?"

"No. no cult. Just hypothetical. Just promise me again you won't let me become a vegetable. I don't want my soul to be forever trapped. I do believe it has found its match in Antonio."

Lana forces a loud sigh out and shakes her head. "I promise," she says. "Now you promise me at the first sign of the hairs on the back of your neck raising you will end this relationship with Antonio."

I cannot promise that. The thought alone of ending the relationship with Antonio is torment. I scratch at a stain on the knee of my jeans.

"Okay," she says. "At least promise me you will let me know so I can help you get out of it."

She keeps her sobered gaze locked on me.

"I promise," I say.

She smiles and pours wine in each of our glass until it barley reaches the rim.

The conversation about souls seems to have sobered us both up. I am feeling emotionally exhausted after this afternoon preceding our conversation about souls. I slowly lean forward and slurp some of the wine out of my glass so I can take a real sip. It makes Lana laugh and she attempts to pick up her glass. She manages to bring it to her lips but the remaining minutes she had to sobriety causes her hand to shake dripping the wine down her shirt and onto her lap.

"Ah shit," she says. Then she chucks the rest of the wine down her throat and puts the glass rather hard onto the coffee table. "That's better," she says as the wine dribbles down the corners of her mouth. She wipes it roughly with the back of her hand.

I laugh as she falls back onto the couch in the enjoyment of her sobriety fading away.

"There's one more thing," I say. I look down to my

glass feeling her eyes on the back of my neck.

"I'm listening," she says.

"I will be spending the night at the Essex."

She lunges forward, picking up her feet from the floor to keep from falling back into the couch. She rests her arms on her thighs and looks up at me from beneath her hair hanging forward, with her jaw dropped and eyes wide. I cannot help but laugh.

"Lana … don't."

She straightens up raising her palms. "Nope. No judgment here," she says. "Luckily you're not famous … it would suck to be your body guard."

"I don't need protection!"

"You do when you take chances like this."

I get up from the couch but Lana grabs my hand. "I'm taking the cab with you … pack a lot of condoms."

I yank my hand out of her wrist and walk to the bedroom. Her forced laughter fades slowly into periodic 'ha' sounds.

In the cab, I tell Lana that Antonio wanted her to take the cab with me. I hope for some reprieve from her concern but she just raises one eyebrow. We arrive at the Essex and I slide out of the cab after giving the driver my half of the fare. Lana grabs my hand just before I clear the door, causing me to hit my head.

"I'm on your speed dial, right?" she asks.

"You're number one," I say and then look at my hand.

She reluctantly lets go and I feel her watching me until I am inside. I pull out the little gold key from a pocket on my overnight bag and push it in the keyhole below the call button. My throat feels like it is swelling, causing me to take a large breath.

Lana's accusations of Antonio and Paulo working together as con artist flash in and out of my thoughts as I wait for the elevator. My memories of Antonio keep the hairs on the back of my neck from rising so I ignore her warning. My palms sweat and my own warnings flow into my thoughts. Tonight I have control of the situation – no fading away. Lana's voice shouts in the back of my head 'take chances like this' and I almost turn away from the elevator door but it opens as if in answer to my inhibition to take a risk.

I step inside. There is a button with the letters PH on it. I press it and the doors shut. The elevator races up then comes to a gentle halt. The steel doors open to two white doors with a single gold plate that says *Penthouse*. There is enough space to step out with a luggage cart and turn it sideways. I knock on the door using the gold brass knocker under the nameplate. One of the doors quickly opens and Antonio takes me into his arms and lifts me off the floor with his face buried into my neck, and backs into the room. He shuts the door with his foot then puts me on the ground. His lips part into a wide smile then he kisses me. His muscles seem tense with his restrained excitement to make the kiss soft.

"I can now relax," he says, looking deep into my eyes.

The skin beneath his eyes have grown dark since I saw him last. The deep shade of his blue eyes seems to enhance his look of exhaustion in the dull light of the entryway. He takes the bag off my shoulder and leads me by the hand farther into the penthouse.

Just beyond the hallway, where I entered, is the main sitting area with two couches, a full writing desk, and a TV armoire. Off to the right is a full kitchen with a black granite wine bar. A dining table stands in front of the bar, large enough to seat twelve, and behind the table is a bedroom – the double doors open wide. An identical bedroom is off to the left. Antonio guides me into the one on the left and puts my bag on a chair next to the king size bed. A full bath is adjacent to the room with a claw foot tub barely visible from where I stand.

"This is your room … yours anytime you want to use it. There is no one else who occupies this penthouse. I would greatly enjoy your company," he says.

I hesitantly smile, looking over his shoulder into the other room. He follows my glance.

"I sleep in the other bedroom across the sitting room," he says. "Please settle yourself, take a shower if you choose. Are you hungry?"

"No. Thank you. Lana and I ate. I am more tired than anything," I say.

"Oh but of course. It is late. I will leave you now so you can sleep. Goodnight."

Antonio leans down and kisses me then leaves the room closing the doors behind him. I sit on the edge of the bed. My inhibitions burst up like a steel wall around my heart. Lana's voice screams in my head *what are you doing?*

She is right. I think to myself. *I am jumping into this too fast. I will have to talk to Antonio tomorrow … after a good night of sleep.*

I flop back onto the bed and a drowsy haze sweeps through my thoughts. I imagine it flowing up and over my steel wall of inhibitions where it forms a bed of clouds beneath me. I let out a quiet sigh and feel my body sink into the bed as my legs dangle over the edge.

A FAMILIAR FAMILY TREE

Again, I wake up fully clothed under the sheets. This bed is considerably larger than my full size bed and much more elegant with the all-white sheets in gold trim. It matches the cream and off white colors of the room. I take a moment to look around. The darkening shades still hang in a bunch to the side of the window allowing the sunlight to dance across the floor onto the foot of the bed. Despite the uncomfortable feeling of my jeans, I push my head into the seven pillows, extend my arms over my head and stretch my body as far as I can under the covers. My feet are bare, by Antonio removing my shoes I guess, but nothing else. A smile spreads my lips creating a thin line as I realize where I am. I sense his presence in the other room.

It takes me a few more minutes to force myself out of bed. Grabbing my overnight bag from the chair, I walk into the bathroom. It alone is the size of my loft bedroom and bath combined.

Shower or bath? I sigh.

The shower lasts for a good half hour and I do not lose any hot water. I dress quickly and tie back my hair still damp after a quick towel dry.

Opening the double doors of the room, my eyes immediately begin to search for Antonio. Classic guitar music is playing in his bedroom. His doors are open. The moment I step out of my room, his voice gives him away.

"Good morning, Clarissa."

He stands up from his chair, newspaper in hand, and walks toward me placing the newspaper down on the coffee table in front of the couch. He takes my shoulders with his hands and kisses both my checks. Unconsciously my body tenses, thinking of my conversation with Lana the night before.

"Good morning," I say.

"Are you hungry? I took the liberty of ordering breakfast since you open your boutique soon."

"What time is it?" I ask as I look around the room for a clock.

"Only seven o'clock. You don't open until ten o'clock today, correct?"

"I'm sorry," I say. I place a hand to my head. "A lot has happened in the past week. Is it Saturday?"

Antonio laughs. "Yes. It is Saturday," he says.

"Ten. Yes ... I'll have breakfast, thanks. Have you eaten?"

"I have. I am not one to sleep in. I have been up since five thirty."

"Oh."

I sit down at the table in front of a plate with a silver lid. Again, Antonio sits with his coffee watching me eat. I shift in my seat a couple times then finally give up on trying to find a comfortable position under his curious stare.

"Thank you. This is very good," I say.

"You are welcome. I will be sure to tell the chef," he says. "Did you sleep well?"

I swallow the food a little forcefully to answer and

have to take a sip of the orange juice to help it down as I nod.

"Yes. Thanks again for putting me to bed. I don't normally sleep in my clothes."

"I am not so sure about that, but maybe someday I will have your trust to be able to take them off and put your pajamas on. You did not look too comfortable when I put the covers over you ... and I did not want to wake you."

The blood rushes to my face and I feel the blush warm my cheeks.

"What is the music that's playing?" I ask.

"Oh, classic guitar. Just some of my favorite pieces," he says.

"Who is the guitarist?"

"I am," he says.

"That's you playing?"

For the first time his gaze strays away from me to the bedroom. I notice a bit of flushed cheeks on him.

"Well myself and my father. We play together in the evenings when I am home. It is something we have done since I was a little boy."

"Will you play for me sometime?"

"Yes. I would like that. Maybe you will join me in a trip home to Spain and my father and I can play for you."

I almost choke on my food. "I would like that," I say and take a sip of my coffee.

There is a moment of silence as I eat and Antonio is back to watching me as he slowly sips his coffee. The music playing in the background, lulls me back into the emotions aroused within during the intimacy beneath the willow trees; yet it does not break down my inhibitions.

"Antonio."

He raises an eyebrow and I get lost for a moment in his eyes as ours meet.

"Yes, Clarissa."

"Tell me about your family."

Antonio sighs. "What do you want to know?"

"Anything you are willing to share."

He lets out a quiet laugh. "I am willing to share everything about my family with you. I only ask because my family has a long history. How far back would you like me to go?"

"As far as you can."

I search within his eyes for the Antonio of centuries past. His cheeks push up, creasing the skin beneath his eyes triggering the blue of his iris to burst. The Antonio I remember is there, deep within, but not so far, I fear, that he has forgotten me. I have hope in being able to help him see my soul as the Clarissa from his dream.

"For the sake of time I ask that I be able to give you the abridged version," he says. "Let us sit on the couch where it is more comfortable."

Antonio gets up grabbing his coffee and refreshing it before walking to the couch. I do the same and walk over to sit next to him. Placing my mug on the coffee table and resting my back against the arm so I can face him; I pull one foot underneath me. Once I sit next to him, Antonio places his mug on the coffee table, turns to me, and takes my hands into his.

"There is great history in my family that makes me proud but there is also sadness and shame. As far as I can remember is only my own life, but I will share with you the family stories."

I wait for him to continue. His Spanish accent alone has lulled me into a calm stillness, waiting for the characters of the stories to come alive in my imagination.

"As you know now, La Rioja Conte is my family's wine. It is from my mother's side when they owned Conte Vineyards and contains the richest history. My father was not close to his family and a bit of an orphan. My mother's stories go back to the Victorian era in England with a man by the name of Alejandro Bellesara."

My breath escapes me in a gasp and the beads of sweat form suddenly in my palms. I take my hands out of his and grab my coffee. I hold it in both hands resting it close to my legs in case it slips from my growing perspiration. I inhale a deep breath and let it out discretely.

"You see now ... my family's stories are old and many. What time is it?" He looks at his watch. "Eight o'clock. Okay very abridged version so there is time for questions."

"Please don't limit your stories for sake of time," I say. "I'd rather have them to be continued."

"Okay. Somewhat abridged so we can at least get to my father's time," he says.

"Deal."

I lean back against the couch and he does the same.

"So as I said, my family stories begin in the Victorian era with Alejandro Bellesara. Born and raised in the northeastern part of Spain, Alejandro married an English woman named Emily. The marriage was out of love, which was very rare during that time. Alejandro moved to England so his wife would not have to be far from her family and she gave birth to two sons. The eldest son was Antonio, whom my mother named me after … but I will get more to that in a moment. The second son was Paulo. He is not the Paulo my brother is named after, but as you will hear soon, should have been because their character is much the same."

The tingling feeling in my feet begs me to adjust but I ignore it. He has no need to describe to me why his brother matches Paulo Bellesara's character; it is one of the same soul - as I hope Antonio will soon confirm he is the soul of Antonio Bellesara.

He takes a sip of his coffee. "Emily died after the birth of Paulo and Alejandro was left to raise the two boys alone. He befriended another man who had a son and two daughters. Alejandro died when Antonio was about twenty-two years or so, leaving him in charge of his brother and the estate."

My heart beats faster and the sweat in my palms makes it hard to hold my coffee. I bite my bottom lip to keep the words inside my mouth.

"The oldest son of the family Alejandro befriended, Robert I think his name was, became a good friend to Antonio and Paulo. Robert's father also assisted Antonio and Paulo with the settling of the estate when Alejandro passed. Antonio ended up falling in love with Robert's youngest sister. Her name was Clarissa."

He pauses and the smile creeps across his face. I try to mimic the surprise but it comes out in a half smile with creased eyebrows. He laughs and glances at his watch.

"A possibility for our connection," he says.

I nod, unable to find a voice adequate to sound anywhere near sane.

"My family seems to like the names Antonio and Paulo, maybe this love story has cursed us to always be in search of a Clarissa."

"Curse," I say.

He swallows forcefully the sip of coffee he just took.

"Not in a negative manner … I will continue and you will understand."

I take a sip of my coffee and let the silence between us be my consent.

"Clarissa's father died before the marriage," he says. "Her mother had passed already, and her older sister was married, living in a town about two days distance in a carriage ride. Clarissa's older brother lived with his wife in France. Their engagement was now troubled with where Clarissa would live. I must also add that during this time, Paulo had entered the militia. Antonio, being the oldest, had inherited the family home, which left Paulo, the younger brother, having to work. His inheritance was not enough to carry the lifestyle he was used to, much less a decent income. This made Paulo bitter and he became a soldier who … took liberties that were not socially acceptable during this time upon women … and at times extremely damaging to a woman's reputation."

His face contorts into a squint and he pulls his lips inward as though he is remembering the actual events.

"Your dream?" I ask.

His head jerks up and his eyes are wide. Then as

though recognition suddenly brings into focus the time he told me about the dream, his face softens and he nods.

"Yes ... the same time as my dream ... but I never thought of the two together."

Antonio glances again at his watch and frowning he says, "For the sake of time I must give you the abridged version. The wedding never happened. Paulo tried to assault Clarissa and although Antonio was able to stop him, they fought."

He pauses and looks at me, his features soft and the sunlight seems to find the small pores and light them with a morning glow. He seems to play the story in his head, trimming the details to give a brief synopsis. I am about to plead with him to explain every detail he knows when his brow becomes wrinkled as he again pulls his lips inward.

"For the sake of Clarissa's reputation," he says. He looks down into his cup. "He went against his heart and broke off the engagement. Clarissa went to live with her sister and Antonio never married."

I watch Antonio, waiting for him to raise his head but he does not move. Hearing him talk about himself in third person feels odd, I want to reach out to him and tell him he is Antonio Bellesara but something tells me he must discover this himself. The tears well in my eyes and begin to cusp the edge of my lower lids. He never came for me - he left me. My failed relationships may be described easiest as a curse stemming from this one life when I gave my love unconditionally to him ... let go of all inhibitions ... and was left always waiting for him to come.

Antonio reaches out and wipes a tear from my cheek

with his finger. They do not seem to alarm him.

"Shall I go on," he asks.

"Yes," I whisper.

"I believe you are right about the dream."

"How so?"

"I believe I was given the chance to be my namesake and although I understand his decision … and might even choose the same path … it hurts to think I harmed you in that way. My feelings for you now are strong and if Antonio Bellesara had the slightest emotion toward his Clarissa I cannot but determine he was a man of extremely high moral character. The other family stories prove this I believe."

He runs his fingers through his hair and rests his elbow on the back of the couch. He looks away toward the kitchen behind me.

"Deep within me there has always been a keen familiarity toward this Antonio," he says. "Maybe because I know this is my namesake, but there always seems to be something else lurking - unexplainable. Then I met you and before seeing you in person, I could not picture Clarissa. When I heard Paulo describe you, the Clarissa in my dreams became real, I was able to give her a face although still a bit hazy. In your loft when you looked up at me from the floor, the hazy picture became clear and I saw you as the Clarissa in my dream."

My hands hold tight to the coffee mug that is now empty. It is all I can do to keep from throwing my arms around him and telling him that he is Antonio Bellesara. He takes the coffee mug out of my hands and puts it on the table then takes both my hands in his. His breath falters at the feel of my sweaty palms. He looks into my eyes and I see a growing intensity within his as they slightly narrow from our touch.

"You feel the connection also," he says.

I nod. "Tell me more."

He smiles wide and lifts my hands to his lips.

"I believe you know the stories, maybe more than I know them myself if you were -"

He shakes his head and laughs more forcefully. I frown at his reaction. Is his laugh a refusal to ask me if I was there, living the dream with him?

"I will continue," he says. He lets my hands drop to my legs, shifts his body, and leans against the arm of the couch.

"Wait!" I say.

My sudden burst seems to catch him by surprise. He smiles but also frowns giving him a dumbfounded look of confusion.

"You were going to tell me something about souls … tell me now," I say.

He sighs and looks over my head. "I cannot."

"Why?"

"Clarissa, there is a connection and maybe deeper than humanly possible, but I am not ready to share my belief about my soul … it is not a topic to be rushed. Do you want to hear more about my family?"

I lay my head into my hand and rest it on the back of the couch. "Okay," I say.

"Very well then," he says. "Paulo did end up marrying. As disrespectful as his character was, our family does give credit to him for carrying on the lineage. I would not be here if he didn't. He found a woman who was the single heir of a large dowry and used his charm and militia status to get her alone. He had his way with her and then blackmailed her father with the threat of damaging her reputation by making what he did to her public. The woman's father could do nothing but accept the marriage of his daughter to Paulo. He kept her pregnant most of the time and did not stop his relations with other women.

You see now why I say my brother resembles this ancestor. My mother did not remember this story when she named him. She only remembered the Paulo who was a son to this woman and Paulo Bellesara. Now the Paulo for whom my brother is named, watched his father's public demise and the immoral activities result in a drop of societal status. He broke off from the family entirely and made his own way in life. He was a man of good character and made a good fortune. The lineage and the stories continue with him as we do not have any information of what became of the others, Paulo Bellesara II edited them I believe, as well as the stories of his own children."

Antonio gets up and pours himself more coffee, offering me some. I wave it away.

"The Paulo who spoiled the woman and forced her to marry him," I say. "Is he also the Paulo who brought the armoire into the family?"

"Yes."

We both sit in silence avoiding eye contact; maintaining a respect for this connection we feel but will not confirm. As much as my mind craves to hear more of his family's history, hoping internally it will include the story of Christmas day or the willow trees, I cannot risk the damage to this connection from the growing desire to make him accept the past memories I saw.

"What time is it," I ask.

"To be continued," he says.

He stands as I get up and walk into the bedroom. He does not follow but waits by the entryway for me to get my things. I walk into his arms all too naturally when I meet him in the hall. He too seems to need the physical touch and we kiss passionately for several seconds. When he releases me enough to see him, he looks right into my eyes.

"Will you come back tonight … Please."

I sigh. Against my better judgment, I say yes, justifying to myself that it is to continue the story of his family history.

"I close at five. I can be here by six," I say.

"Can you plan on spending the night? You're boutique is closed tomorrow."

I hesitate. It is unclear if he is asking me to spend the night with him or in the other room to assure himself of my safety from Paulo.

"I aim to earn your trust, Clarissa. My invitation is to occupy your bedroom here. I am selfish in that I would like you to be here in the morning again."

"Yes. I will spend the night."

"May I ask one more thing," he says.

I tilt my head and raise an eyebrow, unsure what he might possibly want to ask.

"May I spend the day with you tomorrow? There is a

place I want to take you."

Silently I contemplate ideas as to where he would want to take me in New York that I may not already know about.

"You have peaked my curiosity. My day is yours tomorrow. See you at six," I say.

Antonio kisses me on each cheek, my forehead, then my lips, lingering longer here with this kiss.

"See you at six," he says with his lips just barely touching mine.

He presses the call button and occupies my lips until the elevator doors open and are about to shut - twice. I finally break away from his embrace and step inside. Once downstairs, I run out to the street and hail a cab. I look up to the penthouse window as the cab pulls away and think I see through the glare of the sun his silhouette standing between the open curtains.

When I get back to my boutique, I toss my shoulder bag into my bedroom and waste no time in closing up the loft and lighting the candles. The flow of customers is busier than usual but I welcome the passing of time instead of questioning the reason for it.

Lana calls several times during the day and stops in briefly during lunch to catch up on how the night went. Although she makes a pouty, 'I'm so sorry' look when I tell her there was no sex, she quickly changes it to a stern 'good for you' look and reminds me to keep my phone handy. I do not share the story of Antonio's family but instead I describe in detail the penthouse and the breakfast he ordered. I do tell her about the guitar music, which scores Antonio a few romantic points even in her book.

Lana agrees that being able to stay in the Essex penthouse is reason enough to venture a little further into the relationship with Antonio. Yet her encouragement comes with several repetitive reminders from her to be careful.

Thanks to the steady flow of customers, closing time arrives just as I am getting excited to see Antonio again. Lana's minimal support also releases some of the inhibitions formed out of our conversation about Antonio and Paulo being con artists. I blow out the candles, close up, and repack my overnight bag. I choose two outfits for the following day and throw in one additional shirt that can go with my skirt or jeans depending on where he is taking me.

Bag in hand, I grab my purse from under the register and head toward the front door. Waiting outside in his brushed jeans, burgundy t-shirt, and a black leather coat thrown over his arm is Antonio. He smiles when he sees me and I fumble with the lock on the door. He reaches for my bag and holds it while I lock it. When I turn around I am in his arms, his lips quickly find mine.

"I missed you," he says.

"I missed you too."

"I thought we might have dinner out."

Antonio takes my bag and laces his fingers through mine.

"Technically we eat out every night," I say. I reach for my bag. "Please let me take that."

"I've got it," he says and squeezes my hand.

He leads me over to one of the horse and carriages that stand outside Central Park for tourists. He raises my hand and nudges me into one with a hand to my lower back then follows sitting down next to me. He places my bag on the floor by his feet then nods at the driver. We take off with a slight jerk of the carriage.

"Where are we going?" I say.

"We are eating out," he says. He taps a large picnic basket on the floor with his foot.

I smile and lean my head against his shoulder.

I am not going to analyze anything tonight, I think to myself. *I am going to allow emotion and my gut to guide me.*

Antonio kisses the top of my head and we both sit silently as the horse trots alongside traffic, pulling our carriage behind.

I close my eyes and breath in deep coughing slightly from the combination of car exhaust and horse hair. I feel Antonio's chest vibrate with what I guess to be laughter, but I keep my eyes closed. He strokes the hair off my cheek and lifts my chin for another kiss then puts his arm around my shoulders. I adjust to lean my body against him and look around at the park. It is familiar to me yet all seems new in his arms.

The summer heat appears to bring an abundance of couples out and the sidewalks are growing more crowded as the traffic in the street takes on the relaxation of leaving the daily routines behind. I watch the couples walking and holding hands with a fleeting sense of superiority at now being one of them. Antonio again puts his hand under my chin and gives me a long gentle kiss. The carriage slows and when the upstart jerks us apart, we both let out a slight laugh. I lean my head against his shoulder again.

We slow to a stop in a line of carriages on the opposite side of the park. Sporadic escalations in laughter and voices blend into the rumble of the passing cars and horse snorts. Antonio gets out first and reaches for my hand. He pays the driver and grabs my bag and the basket from the carriage. I insist on carrying my bag and he does not object. The bulge in his arm that his muscle makes when he lifts out the picnic basket suggests it is probably heavy.

We meander in and out of handholding couples until we find an empty tree to sit under. Other couples speckle the open grass and play small games of Frisbee or fetch with a dog. The sun continues to heat the air as it nears the horizon and gives off a surreal feeling to the people around us. They almost seem to fade in the glare as the shade of our tree encloses us into our own private world.

Antonio pulls out a thin blanket from the basket and unfolds it onto the ground. We both sit down and he then proceeds to take out one thing after another from the basket. La Rioja wine, basil and pepper crackers, thin slices of roast beef, havarti and brie cheese, a jar of three different kinds of olives in virgin oil with herbs, rustic bread, and tiramisu get their respective spots between us. My mouth begins to water. I notice a thermos left inside the basket before he closes the lid.

"What's in that?" I ask.

"Coffee," he says. He puts the basket aside. He also places the tiramisu back into the basket. "Dinner first," he says. He opens the containers of goodies and gestures me to begin.

"This is wonderful, Antonio. Thank you."

He pauses in opening the containers and turns his attention to me. "You are welcome, Clarissa. I thank you for allowing me to again enjoy your company."

His Spanish accent is strong and his voice is low. I inhale with the ripples it sends underneath my skin. A smug expression appears on his face at my breath. We comment on the weather and he asks about my day to which I say 'fine' between bites of food.

He swallows a sip of wine. "Why did you select bedding ... why not sell clothes?" he asks.

I laugh. "I think my choice of clothing speaks for itself," I say. "Lana can tell you about that in detail, she has frustration with my style to a point of causing herself stress. I don't think I would be successful if I sold clothes."

"So why bedding?" he asks.

I look away, scanning the other couples dotting the grassy field. The sun is setting and many of those with dogs are leaving. A chill blows across my arms in my silence cooling the humid air around us.

"My boutique is in a way everything that comforts me," I say.

Antonio sits up from his lying down position and leans on his arm, turning sideways, as he looks up at me.

"Explain that to me," he says.

I sigh. "That could be hard."

"Please try. I am intrigued to know more about what comforts you."

Antonio seems to push his accent with his words purposefully.

"There are two favorite times of day for me," I say.

~ 290 ~

"One is evening just before the sun sets … like it is now. I consider sleep as a time when my mind can take me places I have never been. My dreams can introduce me to people I have never met, or work out my frustrations and give me answers. I enjoy soaking in a warm bath during the fall and winter months in the evening. I will light a candle in the bathroom and soak until the sunlight disappears and only the candle disturbs the darkness of the night. It is an end without the sadness of a good-bye; content closure."

I pause and watch the last remaining dogs chase each other in a group as they take turns at being leader. The evening sun casts shadows across the couples having their own private moments.

"What is your other favorite time of day?" Antonio asks in almost a whisper.

"When my eyes first open and I'm lying in my bed. I take my first conscious breath of the day stretching as far as I can and pushing myself into my bed. I replay any dream I remember from the night before. It's a beginning and I like the possibility in that."

"And so your boutique sells things to give everyone those special moments," Antonio says. He sits up to be eye level with me.

"I never thought of it that way, but yes. That would explain it. It is also a way to keep my two favorite times with me throughout the day."

"An ending without a good-bye," he says.

Antonio's lips are so close to mine when he says the words that I tense to keep myself from moving. My eyes close and I feel his breath heat my lips. His hand gently touches underneath my chin and he whispers, "Closure without good-bye." Then he presses his lips hard against mine.

His teeth push against my lips as the passion increases sometimes catching them in small bites. He opens my mouth with his and his breath rushes into my throat. My own passion escalates making my head feel light. Despite the intensity, he is able to lay me down onto the blanket gently and the weight of his body settles on top of me. We continue to kiss, wrapped in each other's embrace. Antonio swiftly rolls over and lifts me onto him. His hand brushes my hip then traces my spine up to my neck. He grabs my hair in his hand as he makes a pleasurable groan and my body immediately tightens. I yank myself away from the kiss and sit up. Antonio sits up but keeps some distance between us. His mouth slowly closes as he stares at me. He runs his hands through his hair and takes a breath. He reaches out to me but I shy away from it still held captive by the image of me lying on the hard floor by the four-poster bed.

"I am very sorry, Clarissa," he says. "I allowed my passion to overcome me. I apologize."

I turn to him; his eyes appear to be underneath a thin sheet of water.

"No. It's not necessary to apologize," I say. "It was nice … maybe too nice. I just -"

I hesitate. There is no way to put into words the fear I am feeling; a fear that he or I will suddenly disappear. The memory suggests to me now a possible sign or warning. If we never married in the Victorian era … and possibly not in the era of the memory under the willow trees … then my consequence may be a curse of never being able to be his wife.

"Tell me more about your family history," I say.

"What?" He straightens up and clears his throat.

"I want to hear more stories about your family. They fascinate me and your voice is comforting."

"Okay," he says. He pauses as though he is giving me a minute to change my mind. "May I ask you a question first?"

"Only if I have the option not to answer," I say. I force a smile to give him a sense that everything is all right.

"Was I to forward just now? Did I scare you?"

"That's two questions," I say.

"True. Pick one to answer."

Leaning over, I kiss him on the cheek then whisper in his ear. "I will answer both. No."

"No? Then why -"

I put my finger to his lips and he stops talking. I look down and play with a thread of the blanket.

"I can't help my own inhibitions so I have to trust my instincts," I say. "I want you more than anything, but not like this. The connection I feel to you is strong but I need to know you feel the same before we go any further … I don't want to lose you."

Antonio places his hand on the side of my face and runs it lightly down my neck. He traces my collarbone then puts his hand under my chin and raises it up until our eyes meet.

"You will never loose me. You can only send me away and I hope I will never have to feel that pain. I will take it as slow as you desire because I have no intentions to take it further in a physical way … I am a bit ingrained in my traditional culture … I will only make love to my wife."

He smiles seductively. I falter in my own breathing at his innuendo that he might be a virgin and hinting at a proposal with his expression. Unable to speak I manage a tiny smile.

"I hope, Clarissa, that my wife will someday be you."

He does not move his intense gaze upon me. I stop breathing for a second and have to inhale deeply before answering.

"Is that a proposal?" I ask.

"Not at this time," he says. "You are not ready and I cannot ask you until I believe I will receive a yes that is absent any inhibitions."

I am speechless. My eyes lock on his and the sound of his breathing is deep and steady holding me captive in all my attention. He slowly opens his mouth as he smiles. At this moment, he will receive a yes as my answer. I force my eyes closed with a squint and try to turn my head down. His hand will not let me turn away and instead with it he brings my lips toward him and kisses me.

"My family," he says. "I believe I left off at the part of Paulo's son, also named Paulo, leaving the family and making a name for himself."

Opening my eyes, I lay down on my side, propping myself up on one arm. Antonio settles in taking up the same position facing me and continues where we had left off in the story of his family.

"Well. We don't know much about the family after

that, aside from Paulo," he says. "Paulo Bellesara II, produced two females. He was able to provide a large dowry for his daughters, despite severing his family ties, and marry them off well. Our stories are then lost again with the two daughters but oddly they pick up again with my great grandmother, named Rosario."

Antonio laughs to himself and fiddles with a blade of grass he picked.

"It is as though there is a secret in our past and a black screen has fallen over part of my ancestry. I have been unable to get the stories from anyone ... I am only told they have been forgotten. My great grandmother became Rosario Conte when she married Roberto Conte, a son of a vineyard owner. The owner is my great-great grandfather, Sebastian Conte. Rosario and Roberto produced two daughters and two sons. They were ... here are the names again ... Antonio, Paulo, Maria, and Sofia."

"Do you feel any familiarity to this Antonio?" I ask.

He pulls his lips inward and this time I am certain he is trying to hide information. He fiddles absently with the blade of grass for a while until I put my hand on his and he looks up. I raise my eyebrows taunting him to release what he is thinking. He sighs.

"I had a dream about him," he says. He looks back down to the blade of grass.

"About him ... or were you -"

He slides his hand out from underneath mine and rolls over to his back placing his palms behind his head.

"I'm not sure. There are pictures of those ancestors so it is hard to determine if it was from a recollection of the pictures while I was asleep or a dream like Antonio Bellesara."

He rolls back toward me. "The ownership of the armoire is explained more with that family and I believe it was in the background of one of the pictures."

"I thought you didn't have proof," I say.

"The picture is fuzzy. My mother told me about the need to protect the armoire and give it to my wife some day."

Antonio raises his eyebrows as if to return the taunt to divulge more of my own knowledge of the armoire.

"Is that right," I say.

He laughs and rolls onto his back again. "Okay. Some other time," he says and continues with his family lineage. "My grandmother, Sofia Conte, had my mother, Maria, her only child. Sofia married Andre Moreno. To keep the vineyards within the family, my great-grandfather, Roberto Conte, provided jobs and homes for his children and their spouses. When my father, Carlos Santiago married my mother, he came to work at the vineyard. My mother was the last to survive from her siblings and when she passed, the vineyard became my father's property. Maria and Carlos Santiago, had myself and Paulo. Selina, my nephews and niece, and my father all live at the vineyard now."

"And Paulo," I say.

Antonio squints and clenches his jaw at the sound of Paulo's name. "He stops in from time to time," he says. "When it conveniences him, or my father and I demand him to return. You see my father and I care for Selina and her children. I shouldn't use the word care, because she also manages the vineyard."

"What happened to Antonio Conte?" I ask.

Antonio sighs and looks up into the canopy of the trees. "I do not know. That is part of the dark secret but they did allude to Paulo Conte's character being identical to Paulo Bellesara's. As I think of it … I remember my grandmother would say Antonio Conte's name with sadness. The same sadness one would use when you remember a person who suffered during their life."

"How do you mean suffer … physically?" I ask.

"I don't think so. It was more … sorry for my reference, but … women talk … more filled with worries over a suffering of the heart."

"Oh. Your mother didn't elaborate on any details of this suffering?"

Antonio laughs. "No. I do not remember, it is not a topic you would elaborate to a ten-year-old boy. That is how old I was when she began to share the stories in detail … I think she knew she was dying."

"You don't remember any stories about Antonio Conte or his horse?"

"His horse?" Antonio asks. "No. I do not recall any story about a horse."

"Do you recall a dream where you might have owned a horse named 'Shoes'?"

Antonio bellows out a loud 'ha', throwing himself back a little as a few birds fly out of a nearby tree.

"A horse named shoes," he says. A corner of his mouth turns upward. "That sounds like a name I might give a horse but no, not that I can remember."

"What is the Spanish word for shoes?" I ask.

"Zapatos." Antonio rolls back onto his arm and stares at me.

I look away, disappointed he does not seem to have had a dream about the willow trees.

"Should I know a horse named Zapatos," Antonio whispers.

"I don't know. Maybe it's just a feeling - something about the connection."

Tears push against my eyelids. I press my hands against my eyes but the attempt does nothing except help them fall onto my cheeks.

"Are you crying?" Antonio asks. He leans toward me.

The darkness hides my face but the dim light of the park lanterns on the path behind us casts its yellow hue across my shoulder.

"No," I say.

"You are crying. Why do my family stories make you so sad?" he asks.

"It's not the stories, it's frustration of trying to understand this connection between us," I say.

"Why try to understand it? It might be something we are not meant to understand but to allow to happen - beyond our control."

"Something within our souls," I say. My voice cracks from my tears.

"I do not know how to define it, but I do believe it is a blessing from God and nothing to fear. You have my soul, Clarissa ... I only hope it is enough to earn your trust. I am only waiting for you to be with me in this connection ... without inhibitions."

"I am waiting for you to see me, Antonio. I need you to love me before I can give you my soul. You say you have given me your soul, but I don't understand how in a week."

"It has been the most wonderful week of my life," he says. "It has brought clarity and comfort to things I cannot explain with my limitation of your language. I see your soul … you … right before my eyes, but do you believe in what you want me to see?"

"I have reason to believe it," I say.

Antonio pulls me toward him and I feel his warmth penetrate through my skin. In his arms, I am content. I let out a sigh. I then feel Antonio's chest rise and fall in his own sigh.

"When you believe in your soul you will have no desire to define it. It will make sense to you in a way no one else will understand unless they believe in their own soul," he says. "Give yourself time." He pushes me slightly away and with a large smile. "Let us return home for our coffee and tiramisu," he says.

I purse my lips in defeat and help him pack up the basket, concentrating on his slip of tongue in the reference to the penthouse as being 'home'.

We walk hand-in-hand out of the park. The city lights are considerably bright when we emerge from the park and I blink in an effort to adjust my eyes. Antonio hails a cab. He tells the driver to take us to the Essex, then leans back and brings me close to lay my head on his chest. He strokes my hair as he hums one of the guitar songs I heard this morning.

Once we enter the penthouse still wrapped within each other's arms, Antonio lights some candles instead of turning on the lights. I bring out the coffee and tiramisu from the picnic basket but it sits untouched as we discuss mundane topics such as our favorite movies and books. We both seem emotionally drained from our conversation in the park.

It is comforting being in his arms and hearing his voice but after a couple hours, my eyelids feel heavy and I slowly fall in and out of sleep as I listen to him. Determined not to sleep in my clothes tonight, I excuse myself to change, leaving Antonio on the couch in midsentence.

"Can you manage?" he asks.

I grunt and shut the bedroom door to his quiet laughter.

I do 'manage' as he put it, to wash my face, brush my teeth, and change into my shorts and t-shirt. When I return the CD of Antonio's guitar music is playing low from his bedroom and he is sound asleep on the couch. I pull a blanket from the armchair and lay it on top of him, and then I sit on my knees with my face in front of his. I feel his breath on my cheek, bend down, and kiss him gently on the lips.

"Goodnight, Antonio," I say. He smiles ever so slight.

I sway as I walk back to my bedroom and keep the doors open so that I can listen to his music. I fall asleep to Antonio's guitar and the low rumbling sound of his snoring from the couch.

WILLOW DOCK

One of the double doors to the bedroom is slightly ajar and Antonio's guitar music is playing in the other room. It's the song I remember hearing as I drifted off to sleep. The notes are clear, strong, and then flow swiftly into each other as I imagine weaving in and out of the grapevines of a vineyard. I close my eyes allowing the music to fill my thoughts and then stretch as far as I can reach, pushing my body into the softness of the bed.

The music stops mid song, restarts, and then takes off to a completely new melody. The notes clash into a fierce plucking of several individual sounds. The change forces the music deep beneath my skin and I want to get out of bed and move with the beat. As abruptly as the new melody began, it changes back to a soft flow of notes. I relish in my private serenade.

After several more minutes, the sound of the guitar fades and I hear a rustling of movement in the other room. I jump out of bed a little too fast, catching myself on the edge, and limp out of the bedroom. Antonio is walking toward his room with a guitar in his hand.

"Please … don't stop!" I say.

He turns around. The smile on his face lights up as he steps into the morning rays of sun seeping in through the windows. He slowly walks to the armchair and sits down. I sit down on the couch and pull my legs underneath me. He hands me the blanket I had put on him the night before then takes the guitar and places in on his lap. He gives me a soft look as he mouths the words 'good morning.'

He plucks at the strings on the guitar slowly. They gently take my thoughts back to the grapevines. As he strums the cords and plucks the strings, he releases a seductive melody of worlds past. My thoughts run away to our private spot of grass under the willow trees as I watch him.

Periodically he looks up from the strands of hair hanging against his temples, and then back at the guitar. The morning scruff of his unshaven face moves with his jaw as he pulls his lips inward or lets them open slightly as he changes between the chords and individual notes. His hands are skillful; gracefully creating melodies I have never heard before. I watch, as his palms appear frozen at times while his fingers speed over the strings. They are strong, extending into proportionately shaped fingers that show fading signs of hard work.

The room seems to disappear from around us and the willow trees become brighter and more real within my thoughts; changing with the music to replay all of my memories from the armoire.

This moment with him, engulfed in his music, pulls my soul closer to his and begs for freedom from the skin that holds them apart.

Antonio strums the last chord and lets the sound fade away into the silence. He looks up at me. His expression is soft and endearing - my Antonio. He puts the guitar gently on the ground and takes my hand into his. Slowly he pulls me up from the couch and wraps his arms around me; my head comes to a rest on his chest. His heartbeat is strong and I feel mine fall into sync with his. With a deep breath, he pushes me away from his chest just enough to see my face, lifts my chin with his hand, and sets his gaze upon me.

"You feel it too," he says. "I will say it again in this perfect moment to make it official for you … I love you, Clarissa Daniels."

He kisses me gentle at first, and then increases with passion as I too respond with my lips.

He pulls away with a slight laughter. "You do not have to tell me you love me in words. I believe I know how you feel. That was a very nice kiss, it told me a lot."

Antonio embraces me in a hug and caresses my back. I sit down on the couch and he walks away to the kitchen.

"I had some bagels delivered; may I prepare you my favorite," he says.

"Sure," I say. "Thank you for playing your guitar."

"You are welcome."

Antonio walks over with a bagel and coffee, setting it on the table in front of me. His look is smug and I cannot prevent the smile on my face from turning into laughter.

Cream cheese, chunks of avocado, and tomatoes, flow over the edges of the toasted bagel. He sits down next to me and watches with a cup of coffee between his hands. The steam rises from the mug to his lips. I raise my eyebrows to him and slowly pick one of the halves. He smiles and nods for me to take a bite. I try at first to be graceful but as the half reaches my lips I realize it will end up all over my face if I do not open wider. I open my mouth as wide as I can and bite down through the tomato, avocado, and just as my teeth push through the cream cheese, the tomatoes touch my nose and slip off the backside. I lunge forward just in time for it all to splatter on the plate and grab the napkin Antonio seemed to have pulled from midair. Extremely embarrassed at my disastrous attempt to be civil I taste the combination of toppings in my mouth and groan my satisfaction. My eyes widen as the taste flows down my throat.

"So. How much time do I have with you today," Antonio says. He leans back on the couch.

"Wow! This is good ... What do you mean?" I say.

"Do you want to be back at any certain time, or do I get to have your company until tomorrow. Your boutique is closed tomorrow, correct?"

"Yes," I say. "Where would you take me for two days? I'd need to stop by my boutique to pack for tonight."

"We will be back here tonight ... possibly," he says. "I want to be sure that if we decide to stay over, the choice is available to us."

A sly smile parts his lips.

"I have nothing planned," I say. "You can have me all day, but there's a catch."

He raises an eyebrow. "A catch?" he asks.

"Yes. I must know where we're going."

"Deal," he says. "However, that is not much of a catch because I was going to tell you anyway."

He gets up and walks over to the kitchen then returns holding a single picture in his hand. He gives it to me.

"I want to take you there today and have the option of spending the night," he says.

The picture is of a house overlooking a lake. The surrounding trees are green and the sky a perfect blue absent a single cloud. What catches my eye immediately in the picture, sending a tingling sensation underneath the surface of my skin are two Willow trees at the edge of the water. They are identical to those Antonio and I sat underneath at the vineyard. I look up at Antonio, my mouth slightly open. He sits down next to me.

"What is this place?" I ask.

"It is the original Conte Vineyards. The house stands on the property that was once a small villa. A devastating fire took the vineyards. Before the fire, the grapevines covered two full hillsides. There was a main house with two guest quarters adjacent to it. According to the old photographs, it was a beautiful villa."

My breath becomes a bit unsteady causing a sigh to come out in place of my voice. I inhale to steady it and calm myself from the abrupt confirmation of my memory with Antonio when he was Antonio Conte.

"It was," I whisper.

"What?"

"It must have been," I say. "Is there anything left of the villa?"

He takes back the picture and sighs looking down at it. "Nothing," he says. "The fire burned it to the ground. The family held it off at the water's edge but the two Willow trees were all that survived. They did not have the money to replant the grapes so they sold most of the land to build this house giving the family a place to live. Without land or money to plant enough vines to make a living, they moved

Conte Vineyards to Spain. Roberto Conte had family in
Madrid and so he took his wife and children to live there.
With the remaining money and a few years of working odd
jobs in the city, Roberto replanted Conte Vineyards in
northeast Spain. This house remains in the family, a piece of
our history."

"I would love to go out there," I say. "The option to
stay until tomorrow night is available, I would like you to
show me where the vineyards once stood."

Antonio shakes his head. "The land has been
developed. The picture shows all that is left of the vineyards.
It has become a bit of a resort area for New Yorkers."

"I still want to go … when do we leave?"

"When you are ready," he says. "Take your time. I
have some paperwork I must attend."

Antonio gets up from the couch appearing to be lost
in thought. He gives me an absentminded peck on the
forehead, and walks over to the desk by the window
immersed in the picture. I watch him as he puts it away in the
desk drawer, takes out a portfolio with La Rioja Conte
written on the front, and then picks up his cell phone. I walk
into the bedroom shutting the doors behind me.

I soak in the bathtub, and allow my emotions to run
away with the images of Antonio dancing in my head.
Seconds later, an image of Lana screaming, 'He's a con
artist!' penetrates my thoughts. I submerge myself physically
covering my ears to erase the sound of her voice from my
mind. The submerging works. The warm water and bubbles
take my thoughts back to an internal admiration of Antonio.

When I emerge from the bedroom with my bag

packed I notice Antonio hunched over the desk with his cell phone to his ear. He is rapidly talking in Spanish, his tone of voice increasing with what seems angry passion then it changes to a burst of laughter.

He sees me after I sit down in the armchair and winks at me. Seconds later, he hangs up his phone and closes the portfolio.

"Un momento," he says.

"Huh?"

"Oh sorry … give me one minute."

He walks into the bedroom and I see him bend over a few square boxes stacked on the floor. I walk over to the doorway.

"What are those?" I ask.

"Hm," he says as he straightens and looks back at me frowning.

He appears distracted and I guess possibly the phone call.

"The boxes," I say pointing to a stack of four.

"Oh … it is my family's wine. The one you tasted the other night."

Antonio opens a box and pulls out a bottle identical to the one we drank in my loft.

"Rioja," he says. "When my family was able to plant the vineyards in Spain they chose the northeastern region … La Rioja. There is a specific wine made from grapes grown on freestanding vines and pressed by foot in stone troughs. It is a tradition that has remained for nearly 2000 years."

I take the bottle from his hand and roll it around to view the label. Antonio smiles wide.

"We have recently earned the rank amongst the few Rioja vintage families who produce this wine," he says. "The blend is unique to the grapes allowed and the way it is pressed and aged - only seven specific grape varieties are permitted in Rioja wines. They are all from the Rioja sub regions. My family grows two types of grapes and we have to purchase the other five from nearby vineyards. My father and I are working on acquiring more land to grow all seven varieties of grapes."

"Is Rioja the only wine your family produces?" I ask handing the bottle back to him.

"The only one we distribute to the public. My father and I have experimented with single grape wines on our own but the Rioja process is time consuming so we have not put forth much effort in anything else. Our goal to acquire more land has taken the remainder of our free time."

Antonio puts the bottle back into the box and then folds the flaps into each other. He then picks up the box and puts it next to my bag out by the couch.

"This case will be yours … you can share it with Lana," he says.

He kisses me when I try to protest.

"I want you to have it," he says. "I'm going to bathe and shave, and then I will be ready to go. We will drop the Rioja at your place on the way to Willow Dock."

He closes the bedroom doors behind him, leaving one slightly ajar. I flop onto the couch with a hotel magazine. The guitar music begins to flow from his room and I smile at his gesture as I lean back into the couch and wait for him.

Amazingly, it takes him less than half an hour to

shower, shave, and pack a bag for our trip. He slings his bag over his shoulder and picks up the case of wine as if it weighs nothing. I shoulder my own bag and hold the door open for him as we step out onto the landing in front of the elevator.

The entire ride down Antonio's face holds a smirk and he does not release any hint of his thoughts. When the doors open, I head out of the elevator toward the street but Antonio grabs my waist as he shifts the case of wine over to his hip. Laughing, he jerks his head toward a door with a gold plated sign marked *parking*.

We walk into the underground garage for the Essex and stroll past many high-end cars. I feel like I'm on a tour in an auto show. There are Mercedes Benz, Porsche, Bentleys, and BMWs. Antonio shuffles in his hand a set of keys against my side and I hear a beep come from a car in front of us. He slides his hand away from my waist and walks to the passenger side of a black BMW with lightly tinted windows. He opens the door and gestures for me to get in. As I squeeze past him and slide into the car, he bends his head down and kisses me.

He gets in on the driver's side and starts up the engine. The gentle roar vibrates under my seat and it seems to scream a desire for speed. I see Antonio's smile flash across his face at the sound of the engine. The black leather seats are soft and slick, the control panel glows an electric blue, and orange suggesting this machine has the ability to break sound barriers. We roll out of the garage into the flow of traffic and I notice the black paint taking on a blue color under the sunlight.

Antonio turns the car toward the highway. His cheeks rise with his smile the closer we get and when it is time to merge, he pushes down on the accelerator forcing my body back into my seat. The smile on his face is now full as the roar of the engine shouts in delight at its freedom. I laugh aloud. This is Antonio's comfort. His release after a hard day's work, he and the car unleash as we head toward open road.

The drive is definitely better than the last time I took it. A BMW is by far much more comfortable than the car of the 1920s that Paulo drove. It also takes a considerable less amount of time and I am a bit disappointed when we reach our destination.

Developed as much as property lines would allow, the hillsides are unrecognizable. We come to a stop in front of a black rod iron gate that opens with the press of a button under the stereo of the car. Antonio parks just inside the gate. He tells me to wait a moment. I watch him disappear behind the car and then reappear next to me as he opens my door. He offers me his hand.

I let out a gasp as I take in the full view directly off to the side of the house. Down the hillside next to the lake are the two Willow trees several generations larger. The house is a modest size for the estate homes that surround it and the large wooden front door reflects the one that adorned the original villa. Through the slim floor to ceiling windows on each side of the entrance, I can see through to the other end of the house a wall of windows.

Antonio puts his arm around my waist, bends down, and whispers in my ear, "Do you like it?"

"I love it. It's beautiful," I say.

The sense of returning home causes goose bumps to rise on the surface of my skin.

"Let me show you the inside," he says.

He laces his fingers into mine and leads me through the front door. He does not stop until we reach the opposite wall of windows. Outside the windows is a level area of pea gravel and orange slab stone. Aside from the smaller size, it is a very close replica of the courtyard from Conte Vineyards. Looking onto the small patio, I feel a sense of sadness for the loss of the villa that once covered the ground beneath my feet.

"After you," Antonio says, opening one of the doors to the patio.

A cool breeze rising up from the lake as I walk to the end of the patio brushes against my bare arms. The hillside gradually declines to the shore of the lake about ten feet below. The wind blows the hair off my shoulders and away from my face wrapping the skirt I chose to wear between my legs. Unconsciously, I put my hands at my side to hold the skirt from flying up - It curls around my wrists. I close my eyes, feeling the warmth of the sun on my face.

Antonio places his hands on my shoulders and I feel his lips press soft against my neck.

"I always imagined taking a picture of my wife standing here in her wedding dress," he whispers in my ear.

Without thinking, my emotions and instincts take over and I turn around into his arms just as I did at Conte Vineyards.

He pulls me tightly into them and our desire equally

intensifies as we kiss near the patio's edge. The wind blows against my back as though it knows our souls' desire to be closer than the barrier of our bodies will allow. Antonio peals his lips slowly away. His breathing is short – rapid; his eyes seem to search my face as they had done decades ago. He moves his lips apart as if about to say something but I put my finger to them. I know this déjà vu.

"Yes," I say. "Yes, I am the woman who will one day be your wife."

His eyes still search mine within his stare as what appears to be currents of confusion washing over his thoughts with the creasing and relaxing of his brow. I see the struggle in his eyes that I have been fighting since the day we met. He takes my face in both his hands.

"You are already my wife ... in my soul ... my heart, but I cannot ask you what I must for you to become my wife in this lifetime."

I retract my chin in confusion and frown as I wait for him to explain. When the silence between us is not immediately broken by his voice a fear of rejection rises in me.

"I don't understand," I say.

Antonio holds both my hands in his, my hair now blowing in front of me over both shoulders in the breeze. He leans his head onto mine, our foreheads touching, and looks down into my eyes.

"To ask you to be my wife would be asking you to give up all that is comforting," he says. "I would make all attempts to replace it in Spain but at this point in our relationship I do not believe you love me enough to part from your boutique."

Of course. I inhale a quiet deep breath of the fresh air.

"It is possible to take on a partner," I say. "I am willing to live in Spain ... I understand your tie to the winery."

Antonio smiles but shakes it away with a frown. "You are very smart ... I do not doubt your business capabilities but I need your love to be unconditional. I do not feel your inhibitions are allowing you to give me that. If you left New York now ... sold or tried to manage your boutique from Spain -" he glances over my head toward the lake.

"Antonio," I say.

He lowers his head; his eyes narrow with the forming of the lines on his forehead.

"I love you. I will trust you," I say.

Antonio brushes his hand down the side of my face.

"I know," he says. "I can feel it."

He kisses my head then puts his arm around my waist and nudges me back through the door.

"I will get our bags," he says. "Please look around and choose your bedroom. I will only be a second."

Antonio gives me a quick kiss on my lips and walks out the front door. Just after he passes the threshold, he looks back and winks at me.

I stroll through the house and glance in all the rooms. There appears to be five bedrooms and I choose the room that overlooks the lake. It has a four-poster bed adorned in bright white sheets and a white down comforter folded at the foot. Soft sheers hang across the bars connecting the four posts at the head and drape down to the floor. I open the window to let some of the breeze in, and air out the musty smell.

It cuts through the window frame with a whooshing sound and sends the thin layer of dust on the dresser into the air. Each particle catches the light and rides the wind current as it sways the sheers hanging from the bed. This room reminds me of the one I saw through the upstairs balcony of the Conte Villa.

Antonio walks in as I am running my fingers along the sheets. They are sateen. He sets my bag on the chest at the foot of the bed.

"I should have known you would pick the master," he says. He turns up one corner of his mouth.

Creasing my eyes with my smile I say, "Wouldn't you have insisted anyway?"

"True," he says. "Did you bring a sweater?" He looks out to the lake through the window.

"Yes."

"Grab it. I want to take you down to Willow Dock."

I find the sweater in the bottom of my bag and tie it around my waist. He throws his arm around my shoulders and guides me out of the room. We leave the house through a single glass door off the kitchen. It leads out to a small balcony facing the lake and we walk down three flights of stairs. I stare at the willow trees as we pass causing me to slip when the path underneath turns to wood.

"Saved you again," Antonio says. He catches me around the waist.

"I can still protect myself," I say.

"I'm sure you can but I will always be here for you."

He turns to face the water and extends his arm. "Welcome to Willow Dock," he says.

The dock on which we stand extends out into a calm blue lake for about twenty feet and at the end of the wooden planks are two white Adirondack chairs. Antonio interlaces his fingers through mine and leads me over to them. He gestures to the chair on the right and I sit down. He sits and places his hand palm up on the armrest of his chair nearest me, I put my hand in his, and he laces his fingers again through mine.

"This is my boutique," he says. He stares out to the lake, his eyes squinting with the glare of the sun reflecting off the water. "This is where I feel the closest to my family. All my family's stories seem to come together here."

I gaze out onto the lake. The breeze coming off the water is cool and it feels nice against the warmth of the sun shining down on me.

"This is your comfort," I say.

"Yes. This is where my life has clarity."

The calm he mentions is apparent in the deep tone of his accent as the English words roll of his tongue. His accent seems to be the strongest when he speaks without much thought - from his heart. I find myself trusting his words more when they are heavy with his Spanish voice. My name always comes out with deep undertones of his accent.

"Antonio."

"Yes?" He turns to me and I see in his eyes a calm I have not noticed before. The blue is a light shade and appears to reflect the sky within. My breathing falls into a steady rhythm with his gaze.

"Thank you for sharing this place with me," I say.

"You are welcome."

He glances out to the lake then back at me and squeezes my hand. He leans toward me and whispers, "I feel you belong here."

"I feel at home - at home with you," I say.

Antonio nods with his lips pulled inward then they spread into a smile. We both sit back in the chairs, holding hands, and allow the breeze to wash over us. I feel myself drift off to sleep under the warmth of the sun. Antonio's breathing is steady and matches the slight gusts of breezes. With my hand still laced in his, I fall deeper into my thoughts until they become dreams.

I drift into the stage of sleep when I know I'm dreaming but can't wake myself up; aware of my surroundings and the dreams playing without control. It is difficult to determine the real thoughts from the dream.

The sound of footsteps grow louder behind us, but physically I still feel the breeze against my face and the hard wood of the chair beneath me. I refuse to open my eyes; content in this peace.

"Someone is coming," I say.

Antonio does not answer and I figure he too has fallen asleep. Keeping my hand in his, I turn around to look behind me. My breath suddenly stops and I clasp a hand to my neck with a sense of tightening in my throat. I cannot make a sound. Walking up the dock is Paulo. He puts two fingers against his mouth in the signal to keep quiet.

He steps cautiously around to my right side and kneels down next to me.

~ 316 ~

"Don't get up," he says.

I look over at Antonio. Paulo brings my attention back with a hand to the side of my face.

"He is a sound sleeper," Paulo says, "He won't hear us if we whisper. I did not come to harm you. I told you I would never hurt you."

Paulo's eyes are a dark green but do not seem to possess the evil I saw in my boutique.

"What do you want," I whisper through my clenched jaw.

"You must know by now what I want. I told you I did not marry for love. Must I live in constant torment now that I have found you ... my other half?"

I search his eyes for some inclination of his lie. Paulo closes them and squints tighter then looks back to me.

"I love you, Clarissa. Even you must have realized when my brother told you about the other women that I was always searching for you. I could not make love to you because I was in love with you. Just being with you was enough for me."

My heart speeds up, pounding through my chest. Everything I know about Paulo in reality and from the memories is clashing. There are so many contradicting emotions in me and in his mannerisms. I cannot tell the truth from his cons.

"I don't love you, Paulo."

He shakes his head. I frown with frustration.

"You left me. What is the real reason you're here?" I ask.

"I have been searching for you," he says. "I have

learned - seen our memories without a vice. I see your soul - the identity of your soul and it is my other half. You belong to me and I belong to you. I am your other half, Clarissa, we cannot exist without each other."

"You are married!" I say.

"My soul is not married. Clarissa, my brother cannot fully give his soul to you. He is too attached to the family heritage. He will ask you to give up everything and be a part of his life. You do not deserve this. Love me Clarissa. I will become a part of your life."

My frustration reaches its boiling point. Paulo's words have to be untruthful and the simple fact of his wife and children living without him burns a sour hole in my heart.

"No!" I say.

Antonio jumps up from his chair and sits in front of me so quickly that it startles me. Confused at his sudden appearance I turn to where Paulo was kneeling but he is gone. It was only a dream.

Antonio grabs my shoulders. His eyes are wide. "Clarissa, are you okay … you were dreaming."

I blink and look around. The sun is lower in the sky suggesting early afternoon. I look behind the chair up the path - it is empty. There are no footprints or shadows. I listen for the sound of a distant car engine but only hear Antonio's breathing, as he seems to wait for reassurance from me. I shake my head and turn back to him.

"I'm fine," I say.

"What was it you dreamt about that made you shout?" he asks.

~ 318 ~

I can't tell him. He will worry about my safety or use it to explain why I'm not yet ready to be his wife.

"I don't remember," I say. "I'm okay. How long was I asleep?"

"Only a couple hours. You sure you don't want to talk about it?"

He straightens up and lets his hands slid down my shoulders to my hands. He holds them lightly.

"No. I do want some lunch though," I say and sit up in the chair pulling my hands out of his.

Antonio stands up, his one-corner smile suggesting he is storing away my refusal to talk about my dream in his 'not ready to be my wife' box. He pulls me up by my hands and gives me a soft kiss on the lips. I can sense the reservation in his touch.

"Good idea. Let's go back to the house," he says.

Antonio prepares some sandwiches from cold cuts he brought from the penthouse and pours us both some lemonade. We eat our lunch on the patio overlooking the lake. He does not ask any more about my dream and I force myself not to let it resurface in my thoughts. Our conversation consists of superficial topics.

Our afternoon passes as we sit on Willow Dock. We stay there well into the evening and watch the sunset, while Antonio plays impromptu chords and notes on a guitar he pulled from the entryway closet. I allow my emotions to command my words and mannerisms trying to prevent critical thinking from seeping into them. Internally I assure myself it is okay to submit to the connection that brought us together, but despite all this a sense of fear brews quickly inside me. The day is becoming too perfect.

Antonio seems to sense my restraint of emotion as he kisses me on our walk up to the house under the bright reflection of the moon.

"Where are you, Clarissa," he asks. "Is it the dream you had?"

"I'm here. I am always here when I am with you," I say.

"Physically … but I feel the inhibitions in your kiss."

I look directly into his eyes and as always, they calm me.

"Everything is perfect when I am with you," I say.

"Maybe too perfect," Antonio says raising his eyebrows.

I can only slightly smile. He hugs me and lingers with his arms around me after an initial squeeze.

"I will not leave you," he says. "I am here and will wait for you to meet me. You have as long as you need or desire."

I inhale his smell and give myself over to the assurance of his real presence in the firmness of his chest and his arms around me.

"Thank you," I say.

We walk the rest of the way in silence. When we reach the house, Antonio puts his guitar down on the floor next to the couch and takes a small matchbox from a glass bowl on a desk next to the windows. He lights the candles on the dining table and coffee table. They fill the room nicely without taking away the view of the stars through the wall of windows. He sits down next to me on the couch; a mischievous smile spreads across his face.

"What are you up to," I say.

"Ask me anything. Anything you would want to know about someone you have just met."

"Hm," I say.

"General topics only," he says.

"Like?"

"Like what is my favorite music, color, or book."

I pull my lips in as I think. He has a good idea. I don't know a lot about his basic interests.

"I know you like your coffee black," I say.

Antonio nods.

"What is your favorite wine," I ask.

"La Rioja Conte," he says.

"That's logical," I say. "What is your favorite drink?"

"A cold beer. No real preference, but I tend to prefer the taste of those from small American Breweries."

He sits back into the couch.

"What is your favorite color?" I ask.

"Green with a hint of gold streaks … like the color of your eyes."

I feel the heat of the blush on my cheeks.

"Thank you," I say.

I think of how to stay general but find out a bit more of what his life was like before I met him.

"Tell me about your first love," I say.

"I cannot," he says. A smug expression spreads across his face hinting his expectation for a protest to his answer.

"Why? That's a general question, even for friends," I say.

"I did not say I would not answer, I said I cannot answer. I do not feel it is my place to tell you about someone you know all too well yourself. You should tell me about my first love because I know how I feel about her, but I do not know your favorite color."

My cheeks burn again with my blushing. "My favorite color is purple," I say. "Tell me about the first girl you kissed and it can't be me."

Antonio laughs. "No. You were not the first girl I kissed. That was when I was fourteen and she hit me."

Now I laugh. "Did you forget to ask," I say. I remember how he made it a point to wait for my answer before he kissed me the first time.

"Yes, and since that day I have never made that mistake again," he says.

"Did she ever forgive you?"

"Under the circumstances … she had too. She married Paulo."

The smile suddenly fades from my face.

"Paulo's wife, Selina," I say.

"Yes, the very one. She was not attracted to me, she preferred Paulo. When she told him I kissed her, he challenged me. He quite enjoyed the attention from the other girls when they heard how he fought for her."

"How did she become his wife?"

Antonio sighs. "I am two years older than Paulo and was just turning fourteen when I kissed her," he says. "I thought being older, she would be flattered by my affection. I was definitely wrong. Paulo was her age and they became good friends after she hit me, and Paulo won the fight. As they grew up their friendship became more intimate. I believe she was Paulo's first love but he was not ready to stop searching after he learned the feelings of intimacy. He started traveling as the distributer for the winery and not only took great pleasure in meeting women on his trips but also in the attention Selina gave him when he returned home. On one such return, she informed him that she was pregnant. Our father forced him to marry her or be disowned by the family."

"He didn't marry for love," I say.

"No, and he has held bitterness toward our father ever since."

"Is that why you find the women and tell them he's married … to protect the reputation of the family?"

"The reputation of his wife and children -" he says. He steals a glance out the window.

I see his reflection in the windows from the candlelight. His eyes suggest he is far away in thought and the creases in his forehead tighten. He looks off to the floor away from me and pulls his lips inward. With a deep breath, he inhales and turns back toward me.

I told you my family has recently acquired the status amongst the vintage Rioja family names," he says.

I nod.

"This honor is not without strict adherence in the method the wine is produced but also in the morals of the family and associations. Conducting business with the wrong vineyard can strip us of this position and ruin the winery. Likewise, proper conduct can strengthen our position amongst these families and bring great profit in business and

connections. Paulo's wife and children hold the Santiago
name and in the La Rioja region of Spain, the Santiago
family is the owner of La Rioja Conte wine. His children's
future can be extremely difficult, or have great opportunities
solely dependent on the reputation of the family. For that
alone, my father and I cannot have Paulo disgrace the family
throughout the world."

"Why not give him a position in the business that will
keep him in Spain?" I ask.

Antonio frowns and I see his jaw clench. His face
shows signs that I have approached a question that he does
not want to answer. I anticipate his lips to recede inward but
he looks away.

"If we prevent him from traveling he will only do
more damage," he says. "We came very close to that once."
He turns back to me with a stern glare and hard lines defining
his features. "That is all I will say on the matter. It is
imperative that I find him."

I suck in a quiet breath between my teeth. "Do you
know where he is now?"

"My father has noticed transactions on the family
account in Texas. We believe him to be there."

"So that means I can return to my loft."

Antonio takes in a deep breath. He squints and
tightens his lips into a thin line.

"We have learned not to depend solely on
transactions from the family account to tell us where he is. I
still do not want you to be alone," he says.

He softens his expression and strokes the side of my
face as he brushes away a strand of my hair. A sudden

frustration of having my freedom regulated bursts inside me.

"I can't move into the penthouse," I say. "And there is not enough room for you to move into my loft. Aside from the lack of space, I won't live with someone without a ring. You will need to find a way to assure yourself that I can be alone."

Antonio looks down at his hands balling into fists on his lap.

"You will not allow me to protect you from my own brother," he says.

"I will not allow you to imprison me with your company. I want to be with you but I can take care of myself."

"What would have happened if I was not having lunch with you when Paulo came back," he says. "Did you not see the rage in his eyes?"

"The rage was for you. He will not hurt me," I say.

Antonio seizes my hands tight and squeezes them in his large palms. It gives me an odd sense of comfort, as his hold is strong but not painful.

"He has the potential to hurt you. I cannot take that chance. I cannot lose you."

"You will not lose me," I say. I try to pull my hands out of his purposefully testing his grip. He tightens it slightly and I give up.

"Tomorrow night I stay at my loft," I say.

He inhales deep and pulls his lips together. "There is no way I can convince you to stay with me again?"

"None."

"May I stay with you?" he asks.

"No. You will not sleep well on the couch and I also want some space of my own."

He nods and lightens his grip. I yank my hands free and rub them slowly around each other.

"You're right," he says. "I have taken much of your own time and your time with Lana. Have her stay with you."

"Antonio! No. I am staying in my loft, by myself, just as I did for months before I met you and many years before I met Paulo."

The frustration makes the words come out more forcefully than I intend. Instead of fueling the disagreement, Antonio bursts into laughter.

"Yes. Maam! End of discussion."

He gathers me swiftly into a hug on his lap and kisses me forcefully with passion. He peels his lips from mine with a popping sound and stares directly into my eyes; his cheeks swell with his smile.

"So there!" He says.

"So ... there," I say.

GIRLS NIGHT IN

The drive home from Willow Dock is uneventful but twenty miles out from the city, my phone goes crazy with text messages. Scrolling through them, I realize there must have been no service at the house. There are messages from Lana starting the morning we left and every few hours throughout our stay. I quickly text her back saying I am okay and spent my weekend with Antonio just outside New York City. She responds with a demand that I put aside the coming Friday for girls night and be prepared to fill her in on all the details. I agree.

The week passes steadily. Antonio pleads to be able to cook and eat dinners with me each night since I demand to stay alone at my loft. I have no problem relinquishing my control over cooking dinner however; his culinary skills are excellent and save me from a week of noodles. During one such dinner, I insisted on being given a copy of the compact disc with his guitar music and he of course obliged without argument. The next night when he showed up to dinner, he attempted to take it back because I was using it as background music in my boutique. He lost that argument also; oddly, a little less gracefully than my freedom to stay at my loft ... I had to agree to spend tonight at the Essex after Lana left.

In my mind, the defeat is minimal. I still have the CD

and the freedom to play it whenever I want. His guitar music helps me get through the days until he arrives for dinner. My love for him is growing more each day and saying goodnight to him is getting harder. Last night I think he noticed because in teasing with an over confident manner he reminded me of my sleepover at the Essex tonight.

Lana shows up fifteen minutes before closing and I catch her glance just as she comes through the door - I gesture toward the last customer. She nods her head and a mischievous look appears on her face. I try to stop her but she ignores me.

She saunters to the back of the store where the customer is looking at the wall of sheets. Pretending to look also, she strikes up a conversation with the customer in a loud, obnoxious tone, and doesn't let up. As Lana had probably planned, the customer becomes annoyed and leaves my boutique despite my attempts to attend to her on the way out. Lana flips the sign on the door to *close* and turns around with a triumphant look on her face.

"You just forced a couple hundred dollars out of my store. Pay up," I say. I reach out my hand.

"Not a chance," she says. "She was only browsing."

Lana runs around the storeroom floor blowing out all the candles. I close out the cash register and put the money in the storage room safe. She comes around a display case, grabs me by the hand, and yanks me up the stairs.

"Pull out the wine ... the good stuff if you have it. I'll order the take out. Italian?" she says.

Lana is already dialing before I answer.

"Of course," I say just for the sake of acknowledging

her.

I open the flaps to the case of La Rioja Conte. Lana notices the bottle and raises an eyebrow as I pour two glasses.

"New?" she asks. She takes the glass I hand to her.

"Antonio's," I say. I hold the glass up for our toast. "To happiness … a best friend … and a new boyfriend … I couldn't be happier."

Lana raises her eyebrows. She takes her first sip then holds the glass away from her. Her eyes widen.

"How much does this wine cost?" she asks.

"I don't know. I never bought a bottle … but isn't it good?"

"Good is an understatement," she says. "This is the kind of wine restaurants charge hundreds of dollars for a bottle. We drink this slowly tonight."

"Deal," I say. "So where do you want me to start?"

Lana puts her hand to her chin and closes her eyes as if she is deep in thought.

"Start with how you ended up taking a spontaneous trip with him and forgot to tell me," she says. "I want to hear everything, leave nothing out."

She sits down and exaggerates making herself comfortable. I laugh and sit on the couch next to her. I tell her about the house at Willow Dock, concentrating on the physical details of the house and that it has been in his family for years. Then I weave in the information about La Rioja Conte. This opens the subject of Paulo and I divulge his visit to my boutique and his character that Antonio shared.

She agrees with Antonio about Paulo's behavior and

humorously gives her permission to refer to Antonio as my boyfriend. However, she stresses the minimal length of time I have known him and the irony that they came into my life within such a short period. Apprehensively she asks me to consider Antonio's offer to stay at the loft or for her to sleep over a few nights.

Our conversation wanes into the night, only interrupted when the food comes. We finish off a full bottle of wine.

Lana stops at the counter as I am walking her out. She quickly turns around to face me.

"You will lock the door after me and promise to go to The Essex tonight," she says.

I roll my eyes.

"Yes, mother," I say.

Lana's expression softens, contrary to her normal reaction of sarcastically responding back or laughing.

"You love him, don't you?" Lana says.

My mouth opens slightly in surprise. I have not told her I love Antonio. She laughs.

"I know you, Clarissa, probably better than yourself. I can also tell you it's different this time."

"How so?" I say.

"I think you know. You haven't slept with him, you get excited to see him, and you light up when you talk about him. I've seen you in what you call love, but you have never had this glow … It's not your normal. I think this is the love you've been looking for."

I hug Lana and feel the tears welling in my eyes from her recognition of my feelings and underlying hint of acceptance.

"I do love him, Lana ... and he loves me. I'm so afraid of losing him."

Lana pushes away from the hug and looks at me. The lines of her face are firm.

"This is exactly the relationship you don't want to hold back in," she says. "You've got to be honest about how you feel. If everything you've told me is true then he's the kind of guy a girl like you can marry. Already he cares about your safety, makes sure you eat well, and can't relax unless you are with him. Unless he turns out to be a stalker ... I think he's your prince."

I let a small laugh go. "You mean you don't think I'm being conned," I say. I raise an eyebrow.

"If everything you told me is true, he sounds like the real thing. I think you have to trust him on Paulo though - he's bad news. Do you want me to wait until you get your bag together?"

"No," I say. "I'll be fine. Good night."

Lana waits until I lock the door to walk up the street.

Putting my bag together doesn't take me long. I had released my excitement building throughout the week by packing and unpacking each night as my mind changed with what I would bring. All I had to add now was my toothbrush and paste.

Tonight I'm soaking in the tub and Antonio will play his guitar for me in the other room. I think to myself.

I put my shampoo back in the shower. The armoire appears to shine with my own happiness and I have no urge to open it. I loose myself in thought as I stare at it and wonder what memory I might have now that Antonio found me. A small inclination to open the doors out of curiosity stirs in me but I zip up the bag in an effort to ignore it. The bell over the boutique door rings.

Having locked the door behind Lana I figure she used her key to return because she is worried about me being alone now also.

I shout out of the bedroom. "I'm fine, Lana, I'm leaving right now."

She does not respond. When I pick up my bag and turn to walk out the bedroom, Paulo is standing in the doorway. I drop the bag as my breath escapes me and it lands hard on my toe. I squint in pain.

"Now why would you leave when I just got here," Paulo says. He leans against the doorway and glances at the bag I dropped. "I am just in time. Unless you know why I am here and you are ready to run away with me," he says.

I spread my feet apart and settle into a protective stance, bracing my lower body. "Move out of the way Paulo, I'm leaving and so are you," I say.

I pick up my bag from the floor without taking my eyes off Paulo.

"I am leaving? Where am I going," he says. He straightens up and takes a step toward me.

"Don't come any closer. Turn around and leave my boutique or I'm going to call the police," I say.

Paulo scans the room and an evil smile spreads across his face.

"How do you plan on doing that without a phone - shouting? Let us not damage our eardrums. I have only come to save you from my dear brother."

"I don't need saving!" I say. I take a couple large steps, and push with all my weight to force myself past him.

I'm not strong enough and Paulo captures me in his arms. He presses his lips hard against mine. His teeth scrape my lips and I clamp my mouth shut as he tries to force it open with his. The alcohol on his breath is strong but he doesn't seem so drunk that his balance or strength suffers. He slams me up against the door jam and places his hand on my neck.

"He does not deserve you, Clarissa."

His hand tightens around my neck as he talks and I reflexively grab at his wrist. This makes him smile slightly.

"He will make you give things up. He made me give up on love. I will not let him imprison you. I love you."

Paulo spits as he forces the words out, his grip on my neck tightens more. Panic begins to cloud my thoughts and I feel my conscious slipping; I am unable to breath in enough air to remain calm.

The conversation with Paulo from my dream on Willow Dock races through my thoughts then flashes to the banks of the pond. I jab my knee with all the force I can manage into his groin.

Paulo releases my neck and bends over facing the bedroom. I hit him on the back of the head with my bag and run toward the stairs. Just as I reach the top step, Paulo grabs my hair and yanks me back, catching me in his arms. He jerks me around then grabs the back of my neck. Again, he forcefully kisses me; his other arm is tight around my waist. He bends me backward off balance and I see the store front door as I hang over the stairs upside down. I push at his chest with my hands. I try to scream but can't get much out as I hold my mouth shut, fighting against his kiss. He peels away from my lips and inhales through clenched teeth. As he bears down to kiss me again, I see the dark shade of green in his eyes - the same in his last assault. I shout at him to stop but he only laughs blowing the stench of warm alcohol from his mouth.

"You will love me one day. My brother has kept you like a glass vase, not wanting to break you. I can live with you, Clarissa. We can make life messy. Have fun - adventure."

"No," I say. I push harder against his chest.

I twist my body with all my strength and the adrenaline pumping through my veins. Falling down the stairs to my death is my goal – the only escape from Paulo's intentions.

My struggling throws him off balance and we both hit the iron platform at the top of the stairs. His hand, trapped under my body, pins me under his weight, as I hang half way off the top step. He wrenches out his hand and puts both arms on either side of my face.

"We are meant to be together, Clarissa. I found you first."

I seize the moment and thrust with force my legs upward. We somersault down the steps. The pain riddles through my body as I slam onto the hardwood floor of the storeroom, but I push myself to my feet and run toward the door. I fumble with the doorknob; in the reflection of the door, I see Paulo pushing himself off the floor and I scream.

I pull on the door repeatedly but it doesn't budge. Fumbling for the lock, I see in the reflection of the glass Paulo steady himself on his feet. I turn around ready to brace myself against the door but just as my elbow touches the glass, I'm thrown down, the bell crashes at my feet. I roll over to get up again and a blur flies pass me.

"Paulo!" Antonio says.

"Antonio … No!" I reach out in a feeble attempt to grab Antonio's leg.

Déjà vu rips through my panic. I have to stop Antonio from doing something that will tear us apart.

They both throw punches and slam each other to the floor in rapid sequence. My boutique crumbles under their blows, deafening the sound of the breaking glass with their shouting in Spanish.

"Antonio … Stop!" I say.

Antonio turns and Paulo grasps the moment to hit him across the jaw. Antonio falls to the floor and Paulo stumbles, regaining his balance.

He stares at me from under his bloody brow, the evil in his eyes. His hair is full with sweat and clings to the sides of his face as his leather jacket hangs off one shoulder, exposing his torn shirt. I cautiously push myself to my feet securing my balance after each shift of my weight. Paulo smiles showing his teeth smeared with blood. The hairs on the back of my neck stand on edge. Antonio lays motionless on the floor.

Paulo looks from him to me, smiling wider with each glance.

Whatever I decide to do must be done within a split

second. Paulo and I are both standing. He wants me and he wants to be rid of Antonio. I want to be wherever Antonio is. If he dies, I will welcome death. If he has a chance to live, I will survive at all cost.

My gut instincts act without my brain. Everything seems to happen in slow motion as though I am watching myself do it rather than being within my own body. I throw myself toward the register landing hard across the counter and hit the alarm button underneath at the same time Paulo yanks my feet. My head hits something hard and I feel myself drift off into darkness.

"Clarissa?"

My name sounds distant. I turn my head toward it and a sharp pain strikes my temple.

"Clarissa? Are you all right?"

I recognize Antonio's voice and force my eyes open. Blinking to adjust my eyes in the brightness of flashing lights, I search for his face. He is kneeling beside me with my hand to his lips. A smile spreads across his face when I find his eyes bruised and red. He brushes my hair off my forehead and I wince at the pain.

"I'm sorry," he says. "I am so sorry I did not get here sooner."

I try to tell him it's not his fault but the words don't leave my throat. My body aches. I welcome the pain because it means I am alive and he is real. I take in a breath and slightly jerk from a sting to my lips. I touch it with my tongue and taste the blood.

"You hit your head pretty hard," he says. "The

ambulance is here, they will attend to you, and then I will take you home."

He calls over to the paramedic and steps away to make room for them. He kisses my hand before letting go and then walks over to a police officer. The paramedic asks me an assortment of questions to which I am able to answer in only a whisper at first. As I talk, my voice becomes stronger. After determining I am not at risk for paralysis, they help me sit up more and give me an ice pack for my head. The verdict of my wounds is a concussion and minor fat lip. The paramedic tells me I hit the side of the counter when Paulo pulled me by the legs and knocked myself out when I hit the floor. Amazingly, I have no broken bones from the fall down the stairs. The paramedic jokes that Paulo softened the first and hardest blow by being underneath me as we tumbled down.

I see Antonio shake the officer's hand and then he walks back over to me. The paramedic gives him a reassuring nod, gathers up the medical equipment, and moves aside for him.

"Can you stand?" Antonio asks.

I nod and he pulls me up slow and gentle by grabbing me around my waist. He continues to hold me with an arm around my back and puts his lips soft against my forehead.

"Let's get you home," he whispers.

"My boutique," I say.

All around me is broken glass, overturned shelves, and sheets on the floor.

"I will help you clean," he says. "Right now I want to get you safe and comfortable. Please, let me do that for you."

I shake my head. "I don't want to clean it. I need to lock it up," I say.

The lights from the cop car reflect of the pieces of glass on the floor. Carpeting the wood in what looks like large drops of blood. I am willing to leave, but not at the risk of more damage from looters.

"The officers need to look around a little more," he says. "I did not damage the door when - they will lock it. Please Clarissa I need to take you back to the Essex."

I lean into him as he guides me around the shattered glass on the floor and out onto the sidewalk. Parked across the street is his car and I wonder how much he saw before he ran in. He helps me into the passenger seat, hesitating each time I wince at the tightening muscles in my lower back and thighs. He shuts the door slow then runs awkwardly around to the driver's door. He waves to an officer before getting in.

Antonio puts the key in the ignition and revs up the engine with a few pumps to the gas pedal. He punches the accelerator, pushing into traffic, and we speed pass the police cars. I quickly count four as we drive by them. At the last one, I catch a quick glance of Paulo bent over the hood in handcuffs. His head is turned toward the flow of traffic and I see an evil smile spread across his face as we pass. I gasp and quickly face forward. Antonio grabs my hand into his and brushes his thumb in circles over my knuckles.

He doesn't say anything in the car over to the Essex or in the elevator. I prepare myself for some form of reprimand to my stubbornness and refusal to believe the severity of Antonio's concern for my safety. I avoid eye contact and consciously focus on the pain in my muscles and head.

Antonio holds me by the waist all the way into the bathroom. He turns on the water of the claw foot tub and pours in some bubble bath. He leaves the room for only a second before returning with two candles. I remain in my slumped standing position as he places them on a table next to the claw foot tub.

"Do you need help undressing?" he says.

The tears rise quickly to the cusps of my lower lids and down my cheeks at the sound of his voice. They burn the cut on my lip from my refusal to raise a hand to wipe them or move in anyway at all.

"No," I whisper. "I think I can do it."

I feel the rush of emotion from Paulo's attack set in. I crave the hot water in the bath but don't want to be alone. I know it is only a matter of seconds before my knees give away under the shock of what happened spreading throughout my body. A sense of exhaustion from the absence of my adrenaline gives me no desire to care for myself even when I know everything will be okay.

Antonio starts to walk toward the door.

"Antonio," I whisper after him.

He turns around. His expression is soft, far from the anger I expect to see in the lines of his brow.

"Stay ... please ... play your guitar."

Antonio walks toward me and lifts my face toward him between his palms.

"I will never leave you, Clarissa. I am here. Paulo will never harm you again."

He kisses me on my forehead, then he slides my shirt

up from my waist. I raise my arms over my head and squint at the ache in my back rippling through the muscles. He drops my shirt on the floor then reaches behind me and unhooks my bra. Closing his eyes, he inhales a deep breath then he unbuttons my pants and slowly pulls down the zipper.

"You are so beautiful," he says and presses his lips against my collarbone. "Can you manage from here? I would never forgive myself if I lost control of my passion while you are in so much pain."

"Yes," I whisper. "Thank you."

He smiles and leaves the bathroom.

I almost call after him to finish undressing me and take me into his arms. I crave the softness of the bed under his naked body and want him to lose control of his passion but my soul begs me to stay quiet. I know he is not the kind of man who will accept my offer and to ask him would be offensive to the brink of disrespect. He has alluded already our first time will be as husband and wife and after tonight I cannot take that away from him.

I pull off my bra and jeans. The water is just hot enough to ease the sore muscles. I slump down into the tub and brush the bubbles over my chest. Antonio returns with his guitar in one hand and a dining chair in the other. He sets the chair down next to the foot of the bath and turns off the water.

Sitting down, he picks up his guitar and starts to pluck individual strings in a relaxing melody. He adds a few chords but maintains the soft flow of notes. I close my eyes and allow the music and hot water to wash away the emotional affects of the assault. A smile stretches my lips as I begin to believe I am going to be okay.

Antonio pauses in his playing and I feel his warm lips on mine.

"I love you, Clarissa."

His face is less than an inch from mine when I open my eyes and an immediate calm spreads over me.

"I love you too," I say.

Antonio starts playing again.

"Antonio," I whisper.

He stops playing.

"What will happen to Paulo?" I ask.

He sighs and puts down his guitar, then picks up a washcloth, and kneels down beside the bathtub. Gently he turns me slightly away from him with his hands on my shoulders and dips the washcloth in the water, then starts washing my back and shoulders. I lean forward and put my head on my knees.

"He was arrested," Antonio says. His voice hints at a reservation in talking about Paulo to me so soon. "He won't be out for a while because we put a stop on his funds. He will not be able to post bail."

"What did they arrest him for?"

"Breaking and entering, vandalism, and attempted -" He closes his eyes and bends his head low. He takes in a deep breath.

"I will have to testify," I say.

"You may ... If any charges are filed on him. I will be in the court room if your appearance is required." His voice is soft and his accent is deep and soothing.

"I know you will," I say. "I can do it … but … is there any other way? Any other way he might be able to change and be a father?"

Antonio stops washing my back and lets his hands hang over the edge of the tub into the water. I turn in search of his expression to guess at what he is thinking.

"It is over Clarissa."

Antonio's voice seems to flood with sadness – defeat.

"My father and I have to stop cleaning up after him before it kills us both. We have tried many things but we are out of options; Paulo is who he is. Maybe in another life he will make better decisions."

"Do you really think people get another chance like that," I say.

"People don't, but I believe souls do. Maybe his experiences will help his soul find a connection. Fill him with love."

"Do you believe that our souls are in a second chance?" I ask.

"I don't know. I told you before, my soul has been in a lifelong search for the connection I have with you. I am only waiting for you to feel it as strongly as I do."

I let go of my legs and face Antonio. He brushes the wet hair from my face and smiles softly. Looking into his eyes, my soul seems to tear out of my body and grasp him in a sphere of light. Every reason that fuels my inhibitions is silenced as I stare into his eyes. I feel a trust in him for my life and my soul.

"I do feel it as strong as you, Antonio. The connection and the fear - if there is any hint of being broken apart. I will stay every night here if you'll have me. I'm sorry for being so stubborn when you only wanted to protect me. I'll sell my boutique and move to Spain with you."

My words fly out of my mouth with the realization of my feelings and desperate need to have Antonio understand I am his, in every way possible.

He puts his fingers on my lips. "Do not allow your fears of Paulo's actions push you toward something you do not want. I know you love me. You also love your boutique. It is your comfort … your connection to your great aunt."

"No, Antonio!"

His refusal to accept my commitment on my terms scares me, I need him to commit, and I want to move forward with him as his fiancé. I am desperate for his proposal.

"You are my comfort," I say. "Paulo's actions only proved to me what my heart … my soul … truly wants. When I saw you lying on the floor I almost gave in to death just to be with you but then something inside me told me you would survive, so I chose to fight for life. I had to be with you at all costs. The sore muscles and pain in my head is nothing to the heartbreak I would've had to endure if Paulo killed you." I pull my knees underneath me and sit on them. "Do you hear me? I love you. I want you. I can't be apart from you. Take me to Spain, take me back to my boutique, take me wherever you want, just please make this connection between us permanent before either of us thinks of a stupid reason to make it fit social norms."

"I am not going to leave you," he says.

"Someday you will have to go back to Spain," I say. My voice quivers with the falling tears of my desperation.

"You will have to return to La Rioja. What then? Do I to stay and wait, miserable without you, unable to follow because of my boutique? Antonio … please … see the identity of my soul … it has always been yours."

Antonio takes both my hands in his. He looks deep into my eyes, searching for something. I replay all the memories I experienced from the dresses of the armoire. Repeatedly I see them in my mind as he looks into my eyes. Then I see it. His eyes lighten to the blue I saw on Christmas day. All my memories of Antonio are now one, sitting here beside me, while I sit naked in a bath, suffering from physical and emotional pain, but feeling nothing but love for him. He leans in slightly closer. I feel his breath sting the cut on my lip.

"Clarissa Daniels," he whispers. "Will you be my wife?"

Emotional angst releases in tears, my smile splits open my lip more but I feel no pain.

"Yes." I say, half laughing, half crying.

Antonio kisses me, ignoring the bit of blood seeping from my lip.

We're engaged. He is my fiancé. I cannot be happier than I am right now.

My happiness unfortunately does not last but thirty seconds before fear of the consequences to my actions burst into flames inside me. *The consequences will be grave* rings in my head. A feeling of remorse and a sudden understanding of my decision in accepting his proposal to be his wife - it is the beginning of the end. All of the memories suggested I was his fiancé but none of them showed me becoming his wife. I prepare myself for heartbreak and build back a small wall of my defenses around the fear.

I consciously bring myself back to this happiness, determined not to let any consequence of my decision to be his wife squelch the romance of this moment.

"Antonio," I say quietly so I don't spoil the mood.

"Yes my dear Clarissa?"

"The water is cold. May I have a towel Please?"

Antonio laughs and walks to a small cabinet where he pulls out a towel. He holds it up for me and I turn around as I stand so he can wrap me in it. I step out of the bath and into his arms, my wet hair soaking his shirt. At this moment, I realize I have nothing to change into.

"Ah … I don't have anything to wear," I say.

He smiles down at me and walks out of the room. When he returns he has my bag. He helps me get dressed then takes his guitar out to the bedroom where he starts playing.

After brushing my teeth and tying my hair up in a loose bun, I walk out to the bedroom. Antonio is sitting on the edge of the bed. The sheets are turned down and he pats the bed for me to sit next to him.

"Come to bed," he says. "It is late and you need rest. I will play until you fall asleep."

I shuffle over and slide under the covers. He brushes some strands of hair off my face with his fingertips and looks at me softly. As he plays, I let the melody lull me to sleep.

A RUBY AND TWO DIAMONDS

The morning comes with the smell of fresh coffee and bacon. Again, Antonio spoils me with a delicious meal. I push my body into the bed and stretch as far as I can. My muscles are tight and the ache throughout my body shortens my stretch substantially in comparison to my usual. I squint at the pain and get out of bed slowly.

The warm water of the shower makes movement easier. Antonio has a hot cup of coffee in his hands for me as I emerge from the bedroom and I notice the black and purple hue around his eye. I frown at what appears to be painful. He smiles back as he puts his arm around my waist, holding the cup out for me.

Leaning in he whispers in my ear, "Good morning, did you sleep well?"

Then he kisses my neck, each cheek, my forehead, and then gently presses his lips against mine.

"You made me the happiest man on earth last night," he says.

"You've made me the happiest woman on earth."

Antonio helps me to the dining table and pulls out the chair at the head where I willingly sit down. He places in front of me scrambled eggs, bacon, and buttered toast on a plate. He sits down in the chair on my left amidst the newspaper scattered across to the other end of the table. He pushes it aside then leans back into his chair and slowly sips his coffee.

He watches me eat stirring an uncomfortable consciousness within. I sense that he wants me to assure him I'm okay, but doesn't want to approach the topic directly.

I eat slowly beneath his worried stare. My mind churns ideas of how to approach the subject of setting a date for our wedding.

"I want you to meet my father," Antonio says.

I swallow hard. "Sure. When?"

I take another bite.

"How about this afternoon?"

His face is motionless. I nearly choke on the food in my mouth and sip my coffee to force it down.

"This afternoon? He's here?" I ask.

"He's flying in today to deal with family matters."

"Paulo?" I ask.

Antonio nods with his lips in a thin hard line.

"Is this a good time?" I ask.

"This is as good a time as any. He knows about you."

"He knows about me? How?"

"My father and I are very close."

"Will he like me?"

The nervousness brews inside me and I can feel my appetite diminishing.

"He will love you, Clarissa. You are the first and only woman I have asked to marry. He is already impressed. My father had become settled on the fact that no woman would be able to capture my heart."

My cheeks flush with color. Antonio smiles. I seize

the opening to approach the subject of a date for the wedding.

"When will we be telling him we're getting married," I say.

"That is entirely up to you. You have already told me yes. The party is for you."

"You don't think your father would want a wedding for you?"

Antonio laughs slightly. "My father knows my beliefs. He knows that when the time came for me to ask a woman to be my wife and she said yes, at that moment she becomes my wife. The paper is for legal and tax purposes, the wedding is a party to celebrate with friends and family, and the church is to fulfill publicly with God the binding contract. My soul, which is the other half of yours, only needed to hear a yes to the question to make the marriage real between us and in the eyes of God."

A sense of warmth spreads throughout my body.

"In your eyes, I am your wife," I say.

"Am I not your husband in your eyes," he says. He takes my hand into his. "You have only provided me with one social tradition that you cannot live without for us to make our marriage official." Antonio reaches into his pocket and pulls out a ring.

It is a delicate design containing three small stones - a single ruby, held securely between two diamonds. The shimmering silver band has a slight blue tint to it when it catches the light. He slides the ring onto my finger then places his hand on top of mine.

"Now you have a ring," he says.

Antonio stands up and lifts me by the waist. He leans

down until his lips are close to mine but he does not immediately kiss me - he pauses. My breath becomes unsteady with his hesitation.

"Good morning, my dear wife," he says, and then pushes his lips against mine.

I throw my arms around his neck. In our souls, we are husband and wife. The party, church, and paper are only for the public eye … they can wait.

I pull away from the kiss and bring my hand in close to see the ring. It fits perfectly.

"It's beautiful, Antonio."

I sit down and turn my hand so the stones catch the light.

"It belonged to Antonio Bellesara and has been in the family for centuries. It came into my possession when my mother died. She hoped for me to find a love that stole my heart the way Clarissa captured Antonio Bellesara's. She would be happy to know we found each other - Antonio and Clarissa."

My heart speeds up.

"You found me," I say.

Antonio kisses me and we build in passion until a small screech escapes my lips from the soreness. He quickly releases his embrace and apologizes.

"Lana has been texting you all morning," he says nudging me back into my seat. "I took her number from your phone and told her about last night. I said you would call after you woke up and had something to eat."

"You told her about Paulo?"

"Yes."

"Antonio, she must be freaking out right now. She's probably had a heart attack. When did you talk to her last?"

"I hung up the phone just before I heard you turn on the shower. She sounded okay on the phone but did demand I have you call her."

"I'll call her right now," I say and walk into the bedroom.

Antonio calls after me and picks up my phone from the coffee table. I scroll through the text messages. It appears one was sent after Antonio talked to her.

UR N trouble. Call me now!

I laugh knowing she is fuming but I would have felt the same about her.

I dial her number and begin calming her down by refreshing the details of the night before. When I can no longer emotionally take it, I switch the subject.

"Lana, I have something to tell you," I say. "It's good so don't freak out on me."

She doesn't say anything.

"Lana?"

"I'm here," she says. I hear the suspicion in her voice.

"I'm married," I say

"What!"

She unleashes into a verbal outrage of the psychological factors of the events the night before and how they can cloud judgment then ends with an extreme reprimand to me about not having her at the wedding. Her voice softens slightly but still not enough that I can put the phone to my ear.

"When did you get married?" she says. "I saw you

last night and you weren't married."

"There hasn't been a wedding," I say.

"What? Then how can you be married?"

"I would rather talk to you about this in person. Can we have lunch tomorrow?"

"You're going to make me wait until tomorrow," she says.

"Under any other circumstances I wouldn't but Antonio's father flies in today and I'm going to meet him for the first time."

"Okay. I'll wait." She pauses, makes a big sigh, and then says, "I'm happy for you Clarissa. Congratulations. Do you have a ring?"

"Yes," I say.

We set a time for lunch then say goodbye. With my boutique in shambles, I have a bit of an extended vacation. Emotionally I am in no rush to clean up. I lie back on the bed and sigh a breath of relief.

Antonio comes in and lies down next to me. He caresses the side of my face with his fingers.

"Did it go okay?" he asks.

"She'll be fine, but I have plans for lunch tomorrow."

Antonio smiles. "That works out well. My father and I have some business to attend to and it may take the full afternoon into evening. I don't want to burden you with it, do you think you could stay at Lana's place and I will pick you up when we are done?"

"How late will you be working?" I ask.

"I do not know but you may want to prepare to spend the night. We have worked well into the late hours in the past and this current situation calls for some immediate action."

"Do you want to share?" I say.

Antonio sighs as he closes his eyes.

"You've been through enough," he says. "You had to relive it when you spoke to Lana, and I could sense the anguish in your voice. We will be discussing the matter in great detail."

"You don't need my perspective?"

"I need your comfort and safety more at this point."

"Okay." I say. "I will give in for the sake of giving you assurance. It's the least I can do for my husband."

A wide grin appears on his face. He grabs me around my waist and pulls me on top of him. We kiss passionately until my lip causes me to lighten the tension. He seems to understand and responds by lightening his own pressure on my lips, but his arms around me tighten.

"You make it very hard to keep my mind on the tasks I need to accomplish today," he says.

Antonio groans seductively as he kisses me again.

"We don't have to attend to any responsibilities today. Let's stay here all day and attend to the pleasures of a husband and wife," I say.

He groans again. This time it does sound like a groan of pleasure but with playful frustration.

"I would love to enjoy the pleasures of husband and wife, but I do not believe my father would think it an acceptable excuse for making him wait at the airport."

He rolls off the bed and brings me up to him for a quick kiss. He tells me to take the time I need to get ready so he can gather some paperwork.

I'm ready to go before him and watch as he hurriedly straightens up the penthouse. He puts most of his cleaning attention to his room, leaving the kitchen with a sink full of dishes. I walk over to the sink and begin washing them.

"Do not worry about those," Antonio says. "The maid service will get them. I am just making room for my father."

"Oh," I say.

Antonio emerges from his room with a small bag and puts it by the couch.

"Please tell me you won't be sleeping on the couch tonight," I say as Antonio walks toward me where I wait in the entryway.

A seductive look spreads across his face.

"No," he says. "I am not planning to sleep on the couch. I am actually planning to spend the night with the only woman who owns my heart, my soul, my ring, and the title of my wife."

He picks me up into his arms - my feet are barely touching the floor, and he looks deep into my eyes. His lower body pushes against mine closer than we have been before. I have to arch my back to see him and it only makes me push against him more.

"The only thing I have left to give you is my body, if you will have it," he says.

I smile. "I'm selfish and will feel cheated in this marriage if I can't have you," I say. "Have you so close that I feel you in my heart, soul, and inside my body, all at the same time?"

He embraces me in a kiss with the strongest passion I have ever felt release from him. He pushes me against him with one of his hands between my shoulder blades and the other on my lower back, his fingers press into the crease of my jeans. I hang by my arms wrapped around his neck as he turns in a circle before letting me slide down his body until my feet rest flat on the floor. Pulling his lips from mine, he again groans.

"Not selfish at all my dear Clarissa, but we need to go now or I do not think I will ever be able to leave. Your clothes are beginning to look very bothersome to me and I feel a strong desire to tear them off you."

Antonio does not wait for a response but instead takes my hand and pulls me out the door.

The airport is crowded with business travelers and vacationers combined. Between the screaming children, frustrated parents, and miserable businessmen, my mind quickly snaps out of the sexual fantasies I've had since the Essex. Antonio and I exchange glances as we wait for his father at customs.

After thirty minutes of waiting, a flood of travelers begins to move through. Antonio stands behind me and bends down to rest his head on my shoulder with his mouth next to my ear. I feel his breath inhale and exhale, which does not help me keep control of my own desires. Antonio wraps his arms around my waist and kisses me on the neck letting out a slight groan. I grab his hands laced in front of me.

"I know. I know," he says. "You just smell so good and you have made me so happy. If my father does not arrive soon I may call him a limo and escape with you back to the Essex."

I turn to look at Antonio and he abruptly straightens up. His face quickly changes into hard lines across his cheekbones and brow, and his shoulders push back. I recognize his stance immediately and turn around searching for the Roberto Conte I had met at the vineyard during my last memory the armoire gave me.

Unintentionally I gasp at an older man emerging from the crowd. His features are an aged version of Antonio and other than the absence of Rosario walking by his side and a pipe shifted to the side of his mouth, the man is Roberto Conte.

As he nears, the hard lines of his face mimic Antonio's, distinguishing a slight difference between this man and Roberto. Within several steps his large round eyes beneath the aged wrinkles and narrow nose separates him more from Roberto in likeness. I wonder to myself what Antonio's mother must have looked like as it now appears he took more physical features from her and I created a likeness from desperation to have more proof that my new husband is of the same soul as Antonio from the armoire memories.

Antonio steps to my side, keeping his arm around my waist. My palms become moist and I discretely rub them slow against my skirt hoping they won't end up damping it.

"Father, this is my wife Clarissa," Antonio says looking down at me.

A lump of air stops halfway down my throat and I swallow hard. I did not expect him to introduce me to his father as his wife. I grab a clump of my skirt to dry my hand as I anticipate a handshake. I notice a quiver with the corner of Antonio's mouth before he turns back to his father. He pries my hand from my skirt and laces his fingers through it.

"Clarissa, this is my father, Carlos Santiago, Owner of La Rioja Conte."

Antonio's father puts his duffle bag down by his feet and extends both his hands. I hesitantly place mine in his search for any facial expression that might hint at his disgust to my sweaty palms. Carlos leans in and kisses me once on each cheek. He keeps a closer distance than I expect from a stranger, all the while keeping my hands in his.

"Clarissa. Welcome to my family," Carlos says. "I only wish we could have met under better circumstances."

He releases my hands and stretches a hand out to Antonio. They both pulled each other into a hug and give a few hard pats on each other's back.

"Congratulations," Carlos says. "I hope you and I can resolve the family matters quickly so that we may have a wonderful party to show off your new wife. She will make a beautiful bride." He bends over and picks up his duffle bag. "First I must eat, they do not feed you on the airplane like they used too," he says.

Antonio laughs and it softens his face releasing the tension in his shoulders. He takes his father's duffle bag from him and swings it over his shoulder. On the drive back to the Essex I sit in the back seat listening to both of them speaking rapidly in Spanish back and forth. My two years of the language in high school makes little difference in understanding them. The strong tone of voice and periodic glances from Antonio in the rearview mirror hints that the topic includes the events from the night before. I hear Paulo's name followed by a pause. Antonio shrugs his shoulders and his father continues in a calm direct tone. I slouch down into the seat and let my head fall back. I focus on the passing scenery until my eyelids become heavy from the deep soothing voices of the men. The Spanish lulls me to sleep rather than intrigue my curiosity.

My afternoon is much of the same when we return to the Essex. They acknowledge me periodically out of respect but not as part of the conversation. Antonio sets out some cold cuts and sodas for lunch. I step in to help and become the sole sandwich maker with only periodic acknowledgements. When I begin to clean up the kitchen, Antonio reminds me that it is the job of the housekeeping staff.

He and his father continue in Spanish, shuffling through papers, scrolling through their phones, and making calls. I retire unnoticed to my bedroom and flip through the channels on the television.

The desire to begin the cleanup at my boutique develops inside me and builds a growing strength to face the emotional angst I am sure to endure when I first see it. Watching Antonio now as he interacts with his father, I realize he is still very much a stranger. His business mannerisms are foreign to me, as I was not in a position to witness them in the eras of the past memories.

I turn the ring around my finger as I think; noticing the shimmer in the stones and the single ruby. The ring had belonged to Antonio Bellesara and if I had only walked back to the house instead of to the pond, I may have worn it then. It is ironic how it's a perfect fit. Antonio has only known me for a few weeks, I can't imagine in that time he would be able size a family heirloom to fit me and the fit is too good for coincidence.

Looking at him leaning over the table now with one hand on his hip and the other pointing to the papers in front of his father, he seems so similar to Antonio Bellesara. At one point in some odd twist of history, he was once making plans about me in that manner but now it is about Paulo's wife and children. A sense of safety and admiration challenges my independence. Antonio appears refined and calm in his mannerisms and they seem so ingrained in tradition. It moves me emotionally toward him and I understand as I watch him now that I find safety in this kind of strength. The consistency of tradition will give me something to hold onto that predicts the way he will respond to situations.

The majority of my past relationships with spontaneity led to abrupt ends - always illogical in my own understanding. One such relationship with a guy named Alex had me trying one new thing after another but we never just hung out at home and watched a movie. As adrenaline rushing the relationship became so did the end when he ditched me on a bungee jump trip for the guide. I don't know if I was more pissed that I had to catch a ride with an old woman checking off her bucket list or finding out my boyfriend also dated guys. I don't think Antonio's tradition and rigid attention to societal perceptions would leave room for this possibility and his adrenaline rush appears to come in the form of his car. I feel Antonio can be my strength because I can count on him.

My thoughts take me far away, several hours pass,

and I don't notice Antonio walking toward me until he is only a couple steps away.

"I am sorry my dear Clarissa. You must be extremely bored," he says, sitting down on the bed next to me.

Shaking my head to regain focus, I look into his eyes. They appear tired.

"No. I'm fine. How's everything going?"

Antonio closes his eyes, puts his head in his hands, and laces them through the black waves. He seems to force a smile that comes out more like a grimace.

"Things are being addressed," he says. "My father has been informed about all the events that occurred before and after I found you. He is angry and it is hard for him to focus … I need to ask you something."

"Sure."

"You must promise me that you will be selfish in your answer and not think of me," he says.

I lean my head to the side and crease my eyebrows. Antonio takes my hand in his.

"I want to give my father the liberty of the penthouse tonight," he says. "May we stay at your boutique?"

"Of course." The words leave my mouth quicker than I intend from the sudden understanding of his question. Antonio stares into my eyes. I lean toward him making my eyes purposefully wider. "I will be okay with you there," I say. "The door is not damaged and it will give me a head start on the cleaning tomorrow morning before I have lunch with Lana."

"Are you sure?" Antonio asks, still staring at me. "I can rent a modest room a couple floors down for us if you are not comfortable."

"I'll be comfortable in my own bed, and I'll feel safe knowing you are with me. I believe my thoughts will be somewhere that Paulo's attack will be unable to penetrate them."

My eyebrow rises in search of his confirmation to my statement.

"I believe it is in my power to make you feel safe … and most definitely distract you." Antonio smiles and kisses me gently on the lips. "I will give you a moment to pack, let me know when you are ready."

Antonio gets up from the bed and leaves the room. I see him talk calmly to Carlos in Spanish. Carlos glances past him toward me then suddenly begins speaking rapidly in an authoritative tone. Antonio returns the tone, with a smirk on his face, and then Carlos throws up his arms and walks into Antonio's bedroom. Antonio looks back at me with a large smile across his face. I laugh and walk into the bathroom to pack my toothbrush.

SHATTERED GLASS BENEATH SPLINTERED SHELVES

Antonio and I arrive at my boutique in the late evening and are lucky enough to get a parking spot two doors away. Despite my reassurance to him that I will be fine, my palms began to sweat as I unlock the door. I don't realize my hands are also shaking until Antonio puts his on top of mine and turns the key. I push the door open but he holds the knob, blocking my entrance with his arm. He tilts his head to look at me. I avoid his gaze.

"Are you sure about this? We don't have to stay here," he says.

"The time will eventually come when I have to clean this mess up and re-open my boutique," I say slowly in an attempt to hide my quivering voice.

"It doesn't have to be today."

"This is actually the best time," I say. "Paulo is in jail; there is no chance of him coming back tonight."

Antonio grimaces at the sound of Paulo's name.

"I'm right here. You don't have to be tough," he says.

I look directly into his eyes and instead of making me cry his eyes immediately calm me as they have always done. "I'm not being tough. I brought you," I say. I push on the door.

Antonio's hand slides of the doorknob and he gently places it against my lower back.

I gasp with the first sight of the storeroom. Shattered glass twinkles from beneath the splintered wooden frames. I stare at the back wall and take in the piles of sheets on the floor.

"That's going to hurt," I say.

Antonio moves his hand to my waist and flattens his palm against my hip. I turn my head side to side with my eyes closed.

"It is a substantial loss of inventory," I say. "Because I can no longer sell the bedding that is anywhere near the shattered glass ... which is pretty much all of it."

Antonio doesn't say anything. Tears well up in my eyes as I think about the amount of work and the time that it will take to reorder what I cannot sell. I sigh and feel Antonio kiss the top of my head. The physical damage in front of me begins to wane from my initial shock into a stabbing feeling of intrusion that I sense deep in my stomach. *The Boutique* is the constant in my life and I cannot separate in my thoughts the merchandise from the sentimental connection I have with it. It is as though Paulo was successful in assaulting me.

The lingering reminder the damage shows feels worse than if he had killed me. Despite my new life with Antonio, the option of taking on a partner does not seem to exist anymore. Yet I cannot just walk away from my boutique because it has to be in good condition to sell. The tears fall steadily down my cheeks now. Antonio turns me around and brings my head to his chest.

"I will pay for the damage," he says. "It is after all my fighting with Paulo that caused this."

There is no way I can explain to him that the money means nothing. The merchandise itself should mean nothing. It is the assault on me, because my boutique is so much of me. My thoughts change to the armoire and the note attached to it passes through them … *The consequences would be grave*.

Antonio pushes me carefully away from his hug. He grabs my hand in his and the tears increase with the feeling of his large palm engulfing mine. The security I feel in just that simple touch makes me want to curl up within his full embrace. We walk up the stairs.

"In the morning with the daylight shining through the windows," he says. "It will be easier to take it all in."

I put my bag down and remake the bed, grasping at a mundane action to keep my thoughts from causing too much emotional torment. Also, I am not going to have Antonio share my bed without clean sheets. I choose my highest thread count that I used for the one time my parents visited and I slept on the couch. They are a bit too fine for everyday use but with Antonio living out of the Essex, at least the sheets can make my measly full-sized bed more elegant.

He calls for take-out from *Antipasti* and meets the delivery boy at the door. I set up the table and open a bottle of La Rioja.

I pour us both a glass, while Antonio puts the food onto plates. We sit down and he raises his glass. I do the same but my hand feels numb and unattached from my body.

"Tonight we only talk about us," he says. "About

what makes us happy … to my lovely wife, Clarissa."

The glint in his eyes calms me immediately and I feel the blood slowly flow back into my hand. I can feel myself holding the wine glass now as much as I see it.

"To my husband … Antonio," I whisper.

We sip our wine at the same time.

Antonio brings up the topic of a wedding but since we agree we are already husband and wife, we discuss party plans.

We remain at the table finishing the bottle of wine after we are finished eating. Our conversation stalls as we pour the last of it into our glasses. I take my last sip and quietly place my glass on the table. Antonio stands up, takes my hands into his and pulls me from the chair. He walks backward into my bedroom guiding me gently. When he reaches the bed, he slowly brings me toward him until our lips barely touch.

"Now to distract you," he whispers.

I close my eyes. He lays my hands on top of his shoulders and I interlace my fingers as I inhale a deep breath. His cologne fills my lungs as the softness of his lips touch my neck.

He continues to give small kisses traveling up to my chin then presses his lips hard against mine and the desires he ensues inside me mask any pain from the cut re-opening. Our mouths explore together; every touch seems in perfect synchronization. He pulls my shirt up and over my shoulders only breaking away from my lips to allow the shirt to slip over my head. I catch a glimpse at the deep blue shade of his eyes. His eyebrows crease.

SEE MY SOUL ~ END MY SEARCH

Remembering this is his first time I wrench myself in close and raise the passion with force, moving my arms underneath his and pressing my fingers deep into his back. I almost laugh as he throws himself back onto the bed, pulling me on top of him. We yank the clothes off our bodies vigorously as our hands fumble to touch every inch of each other's skin. Antonio thrusts himself into me.

"Me e perdido todo esto," he says at the peak of his rhythm. He collapses onto me with his head in the crook of my neck.

His heartbeat pounds against my chest and his breath burns my neck. He grabs my face between his hands and kisses me several times. "May God hear me when I say to my wife, I love you Clarissa Santiago."

I lose my breath for a second at hearing him put my name before his, then the elation of the moment takes over and I smile widely. I grab his head and kiss him.

"I love you," I say.

Antonio rolls off me and lies on his back with his arm hanging over the edge of the bed. He gives a loud sigh.

"What did you say?" I ask.

"Hm?"

"You said something in Spanish right before -"

"Oh." He laughs. "It is not something I should repeat," he says.

"Translate it. That's our new rule - if you say it and I hear it, you have to translate it for me."

He turns to me and smiles his one corner smile.

"You can learn to speak Spanish," he says.

I frown. "Translate," I say.

He laughs again and adjusts so that he is lying on his side. He circles my breast with his finger and slides it down beneath the sheets to just above the hair between my legs. He intertwines the soft mass in his fingers.

"I said ..." He looks up from underneath the black strands of hair hanging in front of his eyes. "I have been missing all of this."

I feel the blood heat my cheeks with intensity and he laughs muffling it between my breasts. He then pulls himself on top of me, holding his weight with his forearms on either side of my shoulders and shakes his hair so that it all falls forward. His smile fades and his face becomes serious with the hard cut lines I saw in the airport.

"I am now aware of what I missed," he says. "It is a wonderful feeling ... something that I now see should only be shared between a man and his wife."

He looks off to the side and retracts his lips into a thin line. He breathes in deep then looks back at me.

"It makes the disgust toward my brother boil to rage ... he is fortunate I did not know this feeling before he tried to hurt you."

I reach my hand to his face and softly trace the hard lines of his brow and cheekbones. They soften under my touch and he lets his head fall to my chest. I wrap my arms around him. Only a couple seconds pass until I feel his lips moving against my skin. He pushes into the bed with his hands raising his body slightly off me and continues to kiss me all over until he reaches my thighs.

He slides his body against mine quickly and when his face is above mine looking down he says, "I am going to make love to my wife again." He pushes my legs apart with his knee.

The morning sunlight coming through the open window wakes me. Without opening my eyes, I reach across the mattress. It is empty. I open my eyes and look around. On the pillow next to me is a piece of paper. He went to get coffee.

I stretch, pushing myself into the bed. It is not nearly as comfortable as the one at the Essex and my body still aches from falling down the stairs. The passion Antonio and I released the night before adds new aches so I have no problem adhering to his request in the letter to stay in bed.

My eyes wander around my room. It seems worn down and dirty compared to the Essex. It won't be long before I put it on the market. I should ask Lana today if she wants to switch careers and buy it from me. She might welcome the opportunity, even though it means taking a considerable pay cut.

My gaze stops at the armoire. I notice the right door is slightly ajar. Too quickly, I sit up and swing my legs over the side of the bed, my body shouts back at me in pain.

I sit on the edge with the sheets wrapped around me and my jaw dropped. I stare at the armoire. Immediately accusing Antonio in my thoughts the anger grows inside me and hatred at myself for trusting him.

My love for Antonio pushes sense back into me and I give him the benefit of the doubt. I have to check - make sure everything is still there. Most specifically the pearl necklace Antonio Bellesara gave me. I cautiously reach out and put both my hands on the rose knobs. I pull the doors slowly open. The armoire is empty.

I throw the doors the rest of the way open and see only the green dress Lana bought me with the note pinned to the hanger. All the other dresses are gone. I wrench open the drawers at the bottom, they are empty. The shoes, gloves, purses, and Antonio's necklace are gone. Nothing but my green dress hangs in the armoire.

"No!"

I throw the doors shut.

I hear Antonio shout my name and his footsteps running up the stairs. I turn around to see him in the doorway holding a tray with two paper cups in one hand and a white bag in the other. He stares at me then glances at the armoire. His eyes are wide.

"Everything is gone," I say. I sit onto the bed facing the armoire.

Antonio puts the bag and coffee on my dresser and sits next to me.

"What do you mean everything?" he asks.

"None of the dresses are there," I say.

I feel Antonio look toward the armoire but he doesn't say anything.

"That dress," I say pointing. "Is the one I put in it. There were four dresses when it first came to me. They gave me memories."

"I don't understand," he says.

Looking straight ahead, I let the words flow.

"I never needed any proof that the armoire belonged to your family," I say. "I had already met them."

Antonio inhales a short breath through his teeth but I ignore it.

"The first time I opened the armoire there were the four dresses, all reflective of different eras. I chose the black dress first and when I put it on, I was standing at the funeral of Clarissa's father. Antonio Bellesara was behind me. I met you for the first time."

I pull the sheet up against my stomach. "It happened again, each time I opened the armoire and put on a dress, I was with you. Antonio Bellesara gave me a pearl necklace for Christmas. It's gone now. Paulo attacked me before but Antonio, actually you, caught him before he could hurt me, just like you did the other night. I didn't open the armoire for a long time after that. I couldn't bear to fade away from you again. When the temptation grabbed me again I put on the white dress and a man that had the eyes of Paulo came to my boutique and drove me to Conte Vineyards. The villa that used to be at Willow Dock.

This is the reason for my reaction when you walked into my boutique for the first time. I knew your name, I knew who you were - the hardest part was you didn't seem to know who I was. I believe you are the soul of Antonio Bellesara and I am the soul of Clarissa Lanton."

Antonio grabs me into his arms. He kisses me passionately. I push away in surprise.

"You don't think I'm crazy," I say.

"Clarissa, you are anything but crazy. My dreams all make sense to me now."

"You knew about the armoire?"

"I had no idea about the armoire, but the names you

speak of, the details, how could I not believe that you were there. Your mannerisms have always reminded me of the girl I dreamt about but could never see. You have just put words to my most perplexing memories. Clarissa, my dear, you have given me clarity where I had none."

Antonio kisses me again and holds me close to his chest. He leans back and looks down at me.

"You must have understood why I felt such a peace when I found you ... such a feeling of a lifelong search at its end." he says.

I put my hand on his face and brush my finger over his eyebrows.

"I could not put into words our connection until now. You have always been my Antonio. But I am so afraid that something will break us apart and our souls will again be searching for each other."

"I will always find you, Clarissa. My soul will always search to be close to yours, but I believe we have broken the cycle."

Antonio raises his eyebrows and pulls up a corner of his mouth.

"How?" I ask.

"We are married."

"Not in the way of society," I say. "You asked me before and I said yes, that's why we were always engaged."

Antonio sighs. "I told you that I strongly believe a marriage occurs when a man asks a woman and she says yes."

"Yeah." I say.

"In my belief, God is witness to that moment and so it

is a marriage of our souls in his eyes," he says. "You have always believed that a ring was the binding agreement to marriage in addition to saying yes. Did you have a ring in any of the memories?"

I close my eyes and try to remember. It was something I hadn't noticed.

"I never had a ring from you," I say.

"Now you do," he says. "My belief and your belief of when a marriage is bound have been satisfied. We are married, regardless of any social tradition or legal paper. To us, with our souls, in our hearts, we are married ... in the eyes of God. I might conclude the armoire is empty of all clothes but yours because this is truly your wardrobe now - a wedding gift from Antonio to Clarissa."

"But the armoire was given to Paulo's wife," I say.

"Maybe because Antonio was never married, but remember I chose your reputation over my love for you and broke your heart as consequence. My family has never known the original owner of the armoire or the identity of Paulo's first wife."

Antonio turns my face towards him by placing his fingers under my chin. "I told you Paulo said many things about you -"

"Yes," I say.

"What I did not tell you is I overheard him explaining to Selina that the armoire was your vice and he could tell you had used it. That is also the reason he returned home."

"I'm not following. What do you mean my vice and why would Paulo leave if I used it?"

Antonio runs his fingers through his hair.

"Selina has a very strong belief in the meaning of souls," he says. "To explain it briefly, one half of the soul has a vice which helps them remember their past lives and the other half of that soul dreams simultaneously when the vice is being used."

"You mean you could feel me too," I say.

"Feel you? No. It was a dream - what do you mean feel?"

Antonio grabs my face between his hands.

"Clarissa, were you able to feel me like you do now in those dreams?"

"They were memories for me and yes, I was physically there."

Antonio wraps me in a tight embrace. He pushes me away then brings me close and presses his lips hard against mine. He breaks the kiss with a wide smile.

"You mentioned the necklace you had received from me, Antonio Bellesara. Like your ring, it has been passed down through the generations. I have it in a safe at home in Spain. I will have my father send it here to New York when he returns. It is rightfully yours and I will guess it is the very necklace that is missing from the armoire."

He shuts the armoire doors and kisses me gently on the forehead.

"I have some coffee and pastries, take your time getting dressed," he says.

I get up, grab a pair of jeans from my dresser, and slip into a t-shirt. When I walk into the kitchen, Antonio has the coffee and pastries sitting out on the table – he has waited for me.

While eating, we talk about how we will go about cleaning the storeroom floor. Antonio insists on doing the heavy cleaning and wants me to take it slow and just get an inventory of merchandise. He tells me he will pay for any re-ordering despite and gives me a hard look when I try to protest. He is adamant that if it becomes too emotional to clean we will leave and try again another day.

I internally shove any feelings from the night of the attack far behind the mental wall I have built in my mind. As long as Antonio is with me, I will be able to keep it hidden. I walk downstairs, he is close behind, and I know he will assess every action and expression of mine during the clean-up.

My stomach churns with the emotional battle inside me as I tally the inventory and watch Antonio sweep up glass. By lunchtime, my stomach aches so much that sharp pains stab at me from within. I am ready to leave and have lunch with Lana. Antonio insists on driving me adding a reminder that I will spend the rest of the afternoon with Lana. He says he will pick me up at her place.

"Paulo is in jail," I say. "I can take a cab and meet you at the Essex."

Antonio wraps me in his arms and presses his lips forcefully against mine.

"This time it has nothing to do with Paulo," he says. "I am dreading the rest of the day because I will be apart from my wife. I want to pick you up immediately after I take care of the family business with my father, rather than call you and have to wait for you to arrive."

I release a small laugh with a click of my tongue. "So

you are making me wait ... and you have the control of time," I say.

"Yes." He smirks and pulls me tighter around the lower back.

"If I leave the control in your hands I may not see you until tomorrow morning," he says. "You and Lana have a lot to talk about and may gossip well into the morning hours. I am being selfish. I want to have you again tonight."

He kisses me again. The passion increasing as I reciprocated the kiss.

"You're right," I mumble between a kiss.

"I know," he says.

He nudges me upstairs telling me to pack a bag for the night.

As I am packing, Antonio comes into the room. He walks over to the armoire and runs his fingers along the edges, tracing the wooden rose vines in the panels.

"Clarissa. Pack for a few days. I want to go out to Willow Dock and sit under the trees. I think the air will do you good."

"Okay," I say.

He turns toward me and I notice his eyes are soft and seem to suggest his thoughts are far away.

"Is that something you would want to do?" he asks.

I step closer to him and put my arms around his neck. He looks down and I see him come back from his far away thoughts.

"Yes. I want to go," I say. "I have a memory of us under the trees that ended to soon. I will need to take some work though so I can place some orders."

Antonio frowns. "If you must," he says.

"I must," I say. "If I'm going to shape up this boutique to sell it, I can't have it full of empty shelves."

Antonio's eyes widen and he picks me up into a big hug and spinning me around. "You will not be looking for a partner?" he asks.

I smile. "I can't run a boutique from Spain," I say. "Well I can, but the time I would have to be away from you to attend to this small boutique in New York would be too much to ask you to bear. Didn't you just say you could not be apart from me for an afternoon?" I raise my eyebrows and push up the corner of my lip into a smug expression.

"Yes. I would not be able to bear it. We will find you a nice boutique in Spain or you can set up the wine tasting room we are planning to build."

"Deal," I say.

Antonio walks out of the bedroom. I listen to the strong echo of his steps on the stairs before returning to my packing.

I pause halfway in zipping up my small duffle bag. Lifting my hand, I stare at the ring on my finger. Antonio's rapid Spanish echoes downstairs as he talks to his father on his cell phone. His tone suggests he might be talking about Paulo or my decision to sell my boutique. Both topics can be the reason for his escalation in volume and occasional spurts of laughter. I turn the ring around my finger and the excitement of being alone with him for a few days makes my stomach tickle. If this ring signifies our marriage then this trip is our honeymoon.

All I need is some sexy lingerie.

I smile at the thought. Lana would love to go shopping after lunch … especially to buy me sexy lingerie.

Antonio drops me off at Lana's apartment complex and watches me as I walk into the building. I glance back to see him merge into traffic and speed off, the smooth roar of the engine lingers in my ear. I smile, remembering the thrill he gets from punching the accelerator.

Lana is waiting for me and says we are dining out as she pulls her apartment door shut. She leads the way to a wine bar with sidewalk seating. *An Aged Grape* is scripted in purple lettering on a green canopy over the entrance of the restaurant. Lana nods to the host and walks straight over to an empty table.

The sweat smell of the flowers wafts up behind me from a large planter box behind my chair.

"Consider this your bridal luncheon," Lana says as we are sitting down. "Bring us two glasses of your most expensive red," she says to the host. The host nods and walks into the restaurant.

Lana leans forward and reaches toward my hand.

"Let's see it," she says.

I slide my hand out from under the table and place it in hers. Her mouth drops open and I notice a glint in her eyes as though a thin layer of tear water is washing over them. She blinks then looks up at me.

"It's amazing, Clarissa. Such an old world, classic feel."

I smile. "It's Antonio," I say.

"It's you, Clarissa. If I tried to make a piece of

jewelry to reflect you, I wouldn't come close to this - this ring is you."

I had not noticed before, but looking down I see what she might be implying. It does have the classic feel of a hopeless romantic like me. It is petite and dainty but also strong. The blue shade of Antonio's eyes is reflected in the blue tint of the band while the red ruby represents his heart. What makes me fall in love with the ring is the two diamonds that represents our souls.

Lana breaks into my thoughts. "I am curious though. How is it that you guys are married? You said there was no wedding and I left you the same night he asked you."

"You will laugh."

"I won't. Tell me how it's possible," she says.

"It's a matter of our definitions of marriage," I say.

"So you're not married."

I laugh. "Not in the legal sense," I say. "Or in the walk down the aisle sense but in our definitions of marriage we are husband and wife."

"Explain," Lana says. She sits back and folds her arms across her chest.

"Well, Antonio believes a marriage is between a man and a woman when a connection of the souls is felt and the man asks the woman to be his wife. The woman says yes and at that moment, since God is witness to everything, the couple is married. The wedding is a social tradition made for people to celebrate with friends and family but it doesn't marry two people per say. I agree with him but I need a ring to signify that binding contract. So … I said yes to Antonio when he asked and he gave me a ring. Both of our definitions were met and we are now husband and wife."

Lana stares straight ahead. Her eyes gloss over. "I'm not laughing," she says. She wipes away a tear that is just about to fall. "I have always teased you about being a hopeless romantic but here you sit in front of me, the pinnacle of what all little girls want their love story to be. Saved the other night by the man of your dreams … literally, he then asks you to marry him. You are living a real life fairytale."

"So you'll help me pick out some sexy lingerie for my honeymoon?" I ask. "We are heading out to Willow Dock tomorrow."

"Of course! Where's our food? I have just the place, you'll love it!" she says.

She looks around for the waiter. Despite her attempts to hail him down, our food comes several minutes later. Lana asks for the check to be brought with another two glasses of wine.

Halfway through her salad she looks at me with a tilt of her head. "There's something you haven't told me," she says.

A sheepish grin penetrates my expression. "You read me too well," I say.

"Tell me, Clarissa - straight up."

"Do you want to buy *The Boutique*?" I ask.

She slowly shakes her head. "I support you in all this," she says. "I just - it seems a little too good to be true. Are you sure you want to sell your boutique?"

"I need to sell my boutique and I want you to be the first to have the option of buying it."

"Why?" Lana leans forward.

"I can't manage it from Spain," I say.

I wait for her to put the two together.

"Spain," she says. "Of course. That's his home ... his family business ... why would you live in New York? Clarissa -"

"Lana -"

She puts up her hand.

"I'm worried. My best friend will be in another country with a man she has known for a month."

I open my mouth to say something and she shakes her head with her eyes closed.

"I told you I support you. Even with this - I can see you're happy and I will miss you to death but I'll never give you any guilt. Please just promise me I will be the one you'll call if this all falls through. I will pay for your plane ticket home."

"That won't happen," I say.

"If it does -"

"Okay," I say. "My boutique."

"I can't buy your boutique," she says.

"Why not? You hate your job."

She smiles and looks out to a couple passing by. "Sometimes I do," she says. "But I can't leave my job now. I will have to travel to Spain just to see you. My job takes me to Europe several times a year - that's several times I don't have to pay for the flight. I can use vacation hours in between and stay with you in Spain. If I plan it right I could be out of the states for a month or so and have two full weeks with you."

"You would do that for me?" I ask.

Lana throws her head back and laughs.

"No way, I'm doing that so you can find me a Spanish prince!"

I laugh with her.

When the waiter comes to take the plates, Lana hands him the check with her credit card. I protest but she puts her hand out.

"I said this is officially your bridal luncheon," she leans forward. "Seriously though, Clarissa. I will help you sell your boutique. The market is bad right now and you should not delay your life with Antonio for a brick building."

"Thank you," I say.

Lana takes me to several specialty shops for lingerie. I have to rein her in on some things or I will be too self-conscious about letting Antonio see me in them.

"Modest and romantic," I remind her in one store. "As little color as possible."

My phone rings with a text from Antonio as we are leaving one of the shops. It says that he is done and he wants to come pick me up. Lana hails a cab and tells the driver he will get a huge tip if he gets us to her apartment complex quick.

It's late in the afternoon and a warm breeze is picking up. I look up to the sky as I get out of the cab and see dark clouds creeping over the tops of the high-rises. The smell of the rain hitting the warm pavement rides on the tail of the wind. We make it inside just as the large drops of rain begin to fall.

Only about fifteen minutes later Antonio arrives at

Lana's apartment and she congratulate us both. As the elevator door shuts on her floor, Antonio pulls me into him for a kiss. We abruptly break apart when we hear the ding of the door opening. Our breathing is shallow and unsteady as a man hobbles in leaning on a cane. Antonio and I step to the back exchanging glances at each other; he tries to steal a peek inside my shopping bags. When the elevator reaches the ground floor, Antonio grabs my bags with one hand then laces his finger through mine with the other.

His car is almost a block from Lana's apartment complex and we jog toward it.

We get in the car quickly. For the first time, Antonio leaves me to close my own door as he runs to get in on his side. He merges quickly into the flow of traffic. I catch a glance at the storm clouds between two high-rises.

"It's going to be a bad one," I say.

"Possibly," he says. He looks up from under the windshield. "A lot of rain but we should be at Willow Dock before the wind gets too strong."

"We're heading out there now?" I ask.

"Did you forget something?"

"No. I just thought we would go back to the Essex tonight and then leave tomorrow. Isn't your father leaving tomorrow? I'd like to see him before he goes."

"My father will be staying until Wednesday. Paulo will be released then and my father wants to take him home immediately."

"Doesn't he have to stay in the U.S. until his trial is over?"

Antonio sighs. "That is the business I have been

attending to. The District Attorney didn't charge him with any felonies so Paulo's lawyer made a deal that if the charges were dropped, Paulo would return immediately to Spain. My father wants to take him back to his wife and away from me until arrangements can be made that will keep you safe."

"And so you don't kill him," I say.

Deep inside I know Antonio will not be able to see his brother without initiating some argument or fight. If they fight this time, I don't think he would stop until he is killed or he kills Paulo.

Antonio tightens his grip on the steering wheel.

"There is some truth to that," he says. "My father believes that Paulo should be far away from me, preferably at home, when he learns of my marriage to you and I want to explore other living arrangements so you do not have to live under the same roof."

Antonio looks over at me. I nod. We don't have to exchange words. The history of Paulo's soul dictates that the future is unpredictable as is Paulo's reaction to me now being Antonio's wife.

My thoughts wonder to the armoire and the memories of Antonio. An intense desire to destroy the armoire grows inside me. I can't put words to it but I know with Paulo out of jail, I don't want him to have any chance of taking it and giving it to someone else. If it is my vice and some grave consequence has yet to happen then I must destroy it. My thoughts cannot leave this idea. I create many ideas to destroy the armoire but each time I see Paulo saving it and giving it to someone else. If I destroy it, Antonio will have to help me by guarding against Paulo or anyone else from stopping me.

"Antonio," I say.

"What is it? I noticed you were far away in your thoughts."

He looks over to me with soft eyes and a worried brow.

"The armoire needs to be destroyed," I say.

"What?"

"The armoire - it can no longer exist."

"Clarissa, you have no idea what you are saying. That armoire has been in my family for years. It introduced you to me. We even agreed this morning it was probably the wedding gift from Bellesara to Clarissa as it is from me to you."

"Paulo stole it then and he will steal it again. It can't be in his possession. I must destroy my vice." The fear of the armoire falling into Paulo's hands comes through my tone, raising with each word.

"I won't let you destroy it," Antonio says.

His grip on the steering wheel tightens and I hear the revving of the engine. Although it is getting dark, I can see the creases in his forehead. We are having our first fight where neither of us are willing to give.

"Please Antonio, you have to listen to me. Trust me. The armoire can no longer exist."

"Clarissa, you are being unreasonable."

"I am being a protector of the armoire … and our souls," I say.

Antonio does not respond. His silence makes my fingers tingle with fear that he may physically try to prevent me from destroying it by taking it away. I want to reach out and soften his tense body, but I refuse to give in. Every thought in my mind commands that I destroy the armoire; I cannot rest with it in one piece and Paulo free. The landscape speeds by outside the window and I watch it - listening to the engine. Antonio's silence becomes physically painful. I turn to look at his face.

"Antonio!"

It is quick, but for me it happens in slow motion. The shrieking of the breaks pierces through Antonio's warning to hold on, the edge of the road disappears beneath the hood, and my body seems to float off the seat. I have full awareness that I have forgotten to buckle my seat belt.

WE ALWAYS HAVE A CHOICE

The force of the crash causes my body to land on top of Antonio. There is no response from him. Although his lips are on my neck, I can't feel his breath. I can't feel my legs. My own weight is crushing what I love most and I can't move.

The rain falls outside, echoing off the tree trunks surrounding us. I strain to listen for the sound of a car coming down the country road. The crash had thrown Antonio's car far enough that we may not be visible to any traffic. I had hoped for the headlights or taillights to be on but the blackness around me says otherwise.

"Antonio," I whisper.

My breath is barely able to leave my lips. My head lies against his and I can feel his mouth on my neck. It feels moist. I close my eyes tight to hold back the tears. I have to be able to see. My mouth touches just below his left temple. I pucker and stretch my lips to his skin. He is still warm.

"Antonio?" I try to make my voice louder.

Still there is no answer.

I blink purposefully to stay awake. I know this is the time to pray - be strong for both of us. The rain falls harder and I hear the wind pick up. It makes the tears come faster - time is important. What we need and don't have. My eyes feel heavy. They are closing.

"Stay awake," I say. "Stay awake."

The rain settles and the air around me feels warm. I open my eyes and see the lake at the end of Willow Dock. I walk out toward the wood planks. I feel sluggish as though I have just woken up from a nap, the crash only a nightmare. I can see Antonio's silhouette sitting on one of the Adirondack chairs and walk toward him, the sun feels warm against my arms.

Antonio does not turn around at the sound of my footsteps creaking the wood beneath my feet. I walk up to the chair next to him. He is dressed in khakis and white a button down shirt. His skin is dark olive as though he has been sitting out here all day. I must have fallen asleep when we first got here and slept through the night into the next day. The week has been emotional and my body must have slept off the trauma.

"Hello," I say.

Antonio does not answer.

"Looks like it's going to be a great sunset tonight," I say.

There is still no answer from him. He must still be angry. I sit down in the chair next to him.

Together we are motionless in the warm sun and gaze onto the lake. Something comes over me and tears flow down my cheeks. Without looking at him, I say, "I love you."

He does not answer. His eyes still fixed on the lake in front of us. His sits with his elbows on the armrest of the chair and his body lazily laid out, as his feet hang close to the edge of the dock.

I close my eyes to catch the tears. I feel the sun

setting and the cool breeze blow up from the lake. The cold engulfs me and my chest feels heavy. The weight grows heavier with each breath. I gasp for air and my eyes shoot open. I inhale a shallow breath and the smell of mud, rain, and blood brings my thoughts back to the car. My head is still against Antonio's. I must have fallen asleep and so I scold myself internally then in silence curse the sky.

I call for help. It is a feeble attempt to keep hope. The rain stops but the cold is sharp. Paralyzed on top of Antonio's body is the only thing that keeps me warm. I try to wiggle my toes, but feel nothing. I try to wiggle my finger and a sharp pain races up my arm. I mentally grasp at this pain to keep me awake.

I softly blow on Antonio's neck. I whisper to him, anything I think will give him good dreams. I purse my lips to feel his skin. It is still warm. I allow myself to drift. My body must be keeping him warm enough to stay alive.

I concentrate on my heartbeat, calming it so his will follow if we are in harmony. With my eyes closed, I concentrate on my heart, my breath, and lay absolutely still. I want to feel his heart against my body, no matter how faint.

It is not long before my mind takes me back to Willow Dock. It is early in the night and the stars are just starting to fill the sky. He is in the same position beside me. I turn to look at him. He makes no response.

"I'm here," I say, "I won't leave you."

He makes no movement – only stares out toward the lake as if waiting for something. I reach out for his hand, but pull back just before my fingers touch his. He is too deep in his thoughts. A private moment and even as his wife I feel like an intruder. I look out toward the lake.

"I'm glad you brought me here. I needed to feel the air of the lake again," I whisper.

His continued lack of response makes the tears flow again. They gush from my lids down my cheeks, tickling the hairs on my face. I reach a hand up to wipe them and the pain shoots through my arm. I quickly retract my hand to its original position.

I don't need to open my eyes. I know where I am and that my mind has taken me to the lake but my body is still in the car hidden in the ditch. I can smell the mud. Fortunately, the rain has stopped and I can hear the cars on the road ... but they are passing. None of them makes a sound that gives me hope they are slowing down. The night will hide our skid marks and any signs of damage to the surrounding trees. I resolve that it will be dawn before anyone finds us. I concentrate on my breathing again. Slowing my heart rate to conserve myself I commit to surviving. I purse my lips again and hold them against Antonio's neck. I wait to release my breath to be sure the warmth I feel is his. He feels warm. I focus on the spot where his lips touch my skin. I feel something moist and concentrate harder. There is warmth. It is very slight, but compared to the cold damp air around us, there is warmth on my skin that is not my own. I smile and feel my bottom lip tare and taste the fresh blood as I slide my tongue over it.

I listen strenuously again to the sound of the road. The intervals between cars are longer. The night is becoming more still and the world is falling asleep.

I imagine the bed at the lake house, waking in the

morning to the warmth coming through the wall of windows. I allow my thoughts to again, take me to the warmth. I sit in the chair next to Antonio. He of course has not moved.

"This is getting a little old," I say.

"Yes ... it is," he whispers.

I turn toward him. He does not move but I see the breath from his mouth in the air.

"Can we go inside where it is warm," I say.

"I am warm."

He does not take his attention off the lake.

"Antonio ... I can see your breath. I am cold. Can we go inside?"

"I am happy here, Clarissa. My heart does not ache. My mind does not worry. I am at peace here."

I glance at the lake. The full moon has raised high into the sky and the white paint of the chairs glow under its reflection. I try again to reach out and feel his hand. I do not believe he is warm. I again pull back just before touching the small finger of his hand.

I look over to his face. Something makes me question his intent to remain. I had told him the truth of the armoire and how I now want it destroyed. Maybe he feels connected to me because of the armoire and my intent to destroy it has come across as intent to destroy our marriage. It is just the opposite but my inhibitions will not allow me to clarify. I am too exhausted from the events of the week and the argument.

"Do you want me to go?" I ask.

He does not answer. I let the question hang in the air and do not take my eyes off him.

"You told me you are here," he says. "Are you asking

me permission to leave?"

"No. I'm here. I'll stay with you until you're ready to go inside … may I hold your hand?"

Without turning or moving any other part of his body, he turns his hand face up. I place mine gently on top of his. Our fingertips and the edges of our palms touch. He feels warm but the cool air flowing between our hands does not help to determine if it is his body heat or mine. I put my head back and close my eyes.

I know how this all works now. I feel the cold rush back into my blood, the smell of mud and rain is again inhaled with each breath, and the only warmth is between my chest and his.

This time though I sense something different. My fingers are touching something cold. It's not metal, but something soft, like skin. I move my pointer finger and feel the tip of his. I gasp. My hand is in his, just as I placed it in his by the lake.

"Antonio. I'm with you. I'm here. I'm going nowhere without you. Stay with me."

I wait for a response but there is nothing. His condition has not changed. I cannot shake the cold to return to the lake. The periodic rain and physical pain keeps captive my awareness. The night slowly moves forward. The break in rain is the only thing I have to gage the passing of time. I sing to Antonio, in what short breath whispers I can. I tell him every story I can think of that might bring him happiness. I replay verbally the first time we met. Tell him in detail about the feeling when we first kissed, then I hum quietly against his skin the song he played for me on his guitar the first morning I woke up at the Essex. This song takes me through two breaks in the rain, repeating it over and over. My body feels warm when I am humming so I don't stop.

The warmth builds and I know I am returning to the lake. I keep humming the song to Antonio at the lakeshore.

"That song was inspired by you," he says.

"It's my favorite of all the ones you have played for me." I say.

I interlace my fingers in his. He turns and looks into my eyes. I take in a deep breath, and he smiles at me.

"I hear someone coming," he says. "We will not be alone much longer ... I love you Clarissa."

I am just about to tell him I love him too when he leans forward to look behind us, taking his fingers out from mine.

"No," I whisper.

Something jerks in me and the pain returns suddenly - more severe. I try to open my eyes but can't focus. I hear many voices. The mud, blood, and rain are all swimming intensely in the air of every breath.

"No." I try to say louder, but can hear nothing from my own voice.

I try to open my eyes again. The smell of burnt rubber, hard musty smells, and the sound of breathing behind a mask, becomes louder with each of my own shallow breaths. I feel the cold rush toward my chest and a sharp pain shoots up my back.

"Argh!"

My scream escapes me without warning. I focus and

see the firemen pulling me from the car. Tears flow furiously down my face. I attempt to talk but the questions from the surrounding paramedics, the look from the fireman behind his mask, and the noise of the Jaws of Life ripping into the car drowns out my own thoughts.

Another shock travels up my spine when they put me onto the gurney. I hear the collapse of the legs and sense the motion of them pushing me into the ambulance. With the light blaring in my face, I close my eyes to escape this reality.

Go back. Go back. I have to find him.

Nothing. The noise of the siren is too loud to release my mind. I feel a needle poking several times into my arm. Doctors always have a hard time finding a vein to draw my blood. The pokes grow in intensity and nothing like I remembered. Usually it hurts. I will have to tell them to try the other arm. The poking decreases to the feeling of a small pin prick, so miniscule in comparison to the pain in my body; and nothing to the pain in my heart with the separation from Antonio - this time possibly forever.

My physical pain begins to lighten. It all makes sense now. They have found the vein and the painkiller is flowing through quickly. I welcomed the drug to release my mind. I picture the lake in my head.

I'm coming, Antonio. Don't move, I'm coming back.

Silence - the sound of the wind - my breathing - it is smooth - strong.

I am here. I brought myself back to Willow Dock but I am several yards on the path behind him. I can feel the warmth of the sun rising on my back. I focus on the two chairs at the end of the dock. He is leaning forward. His hands on the arms as if he is pushing himself up.

"Antonio!"

I commanded my legs to run and they responded.

"Antonio!"

He is standing, but he did not turn around at the sound of my voice.

I hit the dock with uncontrollable speed that I stumble and have to use the chair to stop myself. It slides forward across the dock and catches Antonio in the back of his shins. He turns with a half-smile toward me hanging over the chair totally off balance.

"Saved you again," he says. He looks down at the back of his shins.

I straighten myself up and walk to him and look into his eyes.

"I don't know how much time I have," I say. "Listen to me, please."

I don't wait for him to focus on me or give me permission to continue.

"I love you," I say. "I have always loved you, even when I was ripped out of the memory and forced to survive, not knowing when I would see you next. Antonio, I will never leave you, and I need you to stay with me. I can't live in my world without you, now that I have found you. We're meant to survive. We're meant to be together forever, 'til death do us part ... Antonio look at me!"

He does not move from his gaze over me toward the lake. I grab his head in my hands and pull him to face me. He is too calm. His features are soft, his eyes a light shade of blue, and his breathing steady and slow. He is too peaceful to fight - he is giving up. I know he wants death - the next life - the hereafter, or whatever it is. My heart races, as I know he is resolved in staying here on the dock. He will not come back even if the doctors hook him up to a machine. If I return without him, will he lie there forever in a hospital bed, waiting for me to be at the point of death again, here on this dock with him?

Antonio jolts me out of the horrid image of sitting by his bedside for the rest of my human life, when he gently places one hand on my heart. My heart responds to his touch beating even harder than I think possible. I look deep into his eyes; they are still too calm for fighting. We have so much more to learn about each other. The tears flood my eyes and I realize I have to fight for both of us, make him understand we could not leave our human self now because this is not our time. I grab his hand against my chest pushing it further toward my heart.

"This is not death, Antonio. This is life. Can't you feel that pain running through you? Can't you hear the voices? You said we wouldn't be alone. They came for us Antonio! Help them! Give them your heartbeat! Give me your heartbeat!"

My tears make speech almost impossible. The calm of his eyes do not change and his face is so serene I have to fight against its soothing effect upon my heart. As I battle to get his attention and make him fight for his human life, time and breath are slipping out of my control and my heart begins to calm.

"I will not leave you … don't leave me," I whisper. I

ignore the tears wetting my mouth.

The ache of losing him again bears down on my soul, my heart feels heavy and sluggish. He has to give in to the pain, walk away from the warmth and the fresh air. I put my forehead to his lips.

"Kiss me," I say. "Kiss me before I return."

He keeps his hand on my heart but reaches to the small of my back with his other hand and pushes against my body with both. The air rushes to my throat and comes out in a gasp causing me to look up into his eyes. He is smiling slightly causing his eyes to glimmer as though the sun is shining from underneath the surface.

He leans down keeping his eyes on mine. They cast an extraordinary calm over me as a slight breeze blows against the back of my neck. I ready myself to take in every feeling, sense, smell, and taste of what will be our last kiss but his lips do not meet mine. He pauses, his eyes so close to mine, strangely growing brighter. I feel his breath against my lips. It is warm and a smell of blood gives me hope that he is somehow bringing us back together.

"Where would I go that I would not be with you," he says.

His lips turn up slightly in a smile, hinting that he knows or senses something I do not.

I close my eyes and put my lips to his. He is warm. He takes his hand out from under mine and wraps both arms around my back pulling me into him with strength unknown to me. Our lips stay pressed against each other and the smell of blood fades. A new smell of fresh air blowing against us from the lake fills my lungs without any form of satisfaction.

REYES

I pull slowly from the kiss and place my head against his chest. His heartbeat is strong – even. I concentrate on my own and soon our hearts are beating together. Our bodies press against each other with my arms around his neck and his around my back. The sun cloaks us in a blanket of morning light. Even as I mechanically take air in, it doesn't seem to make a physical difference, as though my body might be able to thrive without it.

I listen to Antonio's heart. It slows with every beat - mine does the same. Slower and slower our hearts beat, I stop taking in air altogether. Both of our hearts beat once more, the faintest sound I have ever heard, and then I feel a sudden silence of movement inside my chest.

All my pain is gone. I open my eyes and look up at him. A glow of the purest sun is emanating from underneath his skin. My own body fills with warmth to the point of melting my existence and my soul no longer feels trapped inside the flesh and bone of my body. Moments from lives past that I never knew before play through my thoughts, my walls crash around my mind and understanding comes so clearly I am almost ashamed at having clouded these memories.

The light emanating from underneath Antonio's skin wraps around us both, he is beautiful, each line of his features flawless and soft. He smiles at me and I feel my soul grab his, freeing itself from the confines of my human shell. There are no more boundaries between us. We are free in the most pure sense of the word.

"Until Death do us part?" he asks.

"Never," I say. "Never shall we part."

He squeezes me harder and puts his lips to mine.

"I've missed you," he says. He leads me off the dock.

"I'm here now, every part of me," I say. "I will never leave you."

"I know. Our souls are free, Clarissa, we will never need to return to human form. The search is over."

Antonio guides me with his arm around my shoulders. His words make perfect sense now, but memories of what I was leaving behind penetrate this euphoria.

"What about Lana? She will be lost without me, and your father? What about him?"

Antonio laughs slightly.

"My father is strong, he will welcome death when it comes and maybe return another day to find the one he is to love. Lana? She must learn to accept love before she can even begin her search. She too is strong. I am sure she is happy in that you died with me. Imagine what you would have done to her if you returned without me?"

I let a small laugh escape me. He is right, the torment Lana would have seen in me if I returned without Antonio would surely drive her insane but I am still restless because there is unfinished business.

"Paulo," I say.

Even in this freedom of our souls and transparent human shells, Paulo's name causes Antonio to tense.

"He will be even more jealous of us now that we have freed ourselves from the demand to return. Maybe now he will realize that you were never his and search for the love that is meant for him."

"His?"

Antonio stops walking at the willow trees and turns toward me. His eyes changing to the dark blue I saw the day he sat with his head between his hands in Robert Lanton's library, refusing to look at me.

"He always thought you his, Clarissa. He found a way to make his soul remember through his different lives."

"He remembered me? You? Before we met? How?"

Antonio closes his eyes and shakes his head. He brings me into his chest and puts his hand behind my head.

"I do not know," he says. "We never have to go through that again. We don't have to return."

I step away causing Antonio's eyes to open and search mine for the reason.

"We have a choice? To go back?"

"There is always a choice, Clarissa."

"How?"

"Are you planning to leave me?"

Antonio raises his eyebrows in jest, but I can see the concern in his eyes.

"No," I whisper

"Not yet," he says.

"I feel a strong desire to protect Lana … from something or someone … I -"

The words are stuck in my throat. I don't know if I can say them just now, tell him I fear Paulo will try to harm Lana as revenge toward us. My words will hurt Antonio if I say them. The pain will most certainly cast me back into human form without him.

Antonio pulls my head up with his hand under my chin. His eyes search for the rest of my sentence but he finishes it for me.

"Lana is strong and very smart," he says. "She will survive and make choices that are good for her."

His eyes move side to side, looking in mine and seem to wait for reassurance that I am going to stay.

"You're right," I say. "There is too much unknown for me right now to make a good decision."

"You protected your soul well this past life," he says. "Almost too well."

An edge of pain escapes through his words, suddenly I feel the desire to protect only his soul – the soul that kept mine alive, keep it attached to mine. An immense feeling of love rushes through me, the sense of butterflies from my human life give flight and escapes through the transparent layer of skin still holding my human form around my soul. I smile back at him.

"I love you," I say.

Antonio kisses me gently. It feels as though he is touching my soul. He parts away the branches of the Willow trees with one hand and softly pushes me toward the opening, whispering in my ear as he does.

"After you … my dear Clarissa."

I walk over to the base of the willow tree and sit down. He sits next to me and lays me on the ground then pulls me on top of him. We pick up just where we had left, but I know this time I will not be left with a handful of buttons. I unleash my full passion for him. He laughs between our locked lips, which turns into a deep moan as he rolls over holding his weight slightly above me. I grab him around his back and try to pull him down but he resists. I open my eyes and he is smiling at me.

"You are remembering," he says.

"I am creating new memories," I say.

Antonio pushes his lips against mine amidst a low deep groan causing my one remaining wall of inhibitions to crumble under it.

About the Author

Staci Reyes has used the craft of writing to momentarily step away from her daily routine throughout her life. She has decided to share these stories with others through self-publishing. May they take you, the reader, to a new corner of your imagination.

Acknowledgements

Thanks begins with Kim who was first to read my manuscript when it was titled *Clarissa's Antonio*. Her encouragement and critique allowed me to share it with others. Laurel's enthusiasm and suggestions continued this development of the trilogy (this being the first book). Stormy's excitement over Paulo's character gave him the Ducati Monster in Book Three (to be published in the future). To the supportive team at *Write to Sell Your Book*, Diane O'Connell who gave professional guidance and support; and my editor Matt Marinovich, the first guy to read the manuscript – the blue spandex can be found in the electric blue chiffon dress. My husband; he is a constant support and the encouragement behind my decision to share this story with a growing collection of readers. He is a wonderful father to our children and the other half to my soul. My parents; for being always supportive of my goals. To all whom I had talked about the plot – thank you for listening. Finally, to an unnamed person in particular who started the spark of an idea to publish with a simple phrase - "I'd read that." Here it is for you.

18015113R00236

Made in the USA
Lexington, KY
10 October 2012